MIND GAMES

BOOKS BY WILLIAM DEVERELL

FICTION
Needles
High Crimes
Mecca
The Dance of Shiva
Platinum Blues
Mindfield
Kill All the Lawyers
Street Legal: The Betrayal
Trial of Passion
Slander
The Laughing Falcon
Mind Games

NON-FICTION
A Life on Trial

MIND GAMES

WILLIAM DEVERELL

M&S

National Library of Canada Cataloguing in Publication

Deverell, William, 1937–
Mind games / William Deverell.

ISBN 0-7710-2678-1

I. Title.

PS8557.E8775M46 2003   C813'.54   C2003-902377-X
PR9199.3.D474M46 2003

We acknowledge the financial support of the Government of Canada
through the Book Publishing Industry Development Program and that of
the Government of Ontario through the Ontario Media Development
Corporation's Ontario Book Initiative. We further acknowledge the
support of the Canada Council for the Arts and the Ontario Arts Council
for our publishing program.

Typeset in Bembo by M&S, Toronto
Printed and bound in Canada

This book is printed on acid-free paper that is 100% recycled, ancient-forest
friendly (40% post-consumer recycled).

McClelland & Stewart Ltd.
The Canadian Publishers
481 University Avenue
Toronto, Ontario
M5G 2E9
www.mcclelland.com

1 2 3 4 5   07 06 05 04 03

To the British Columbia Civil Liberties Association

"This life's dim windows of the soul
Distorts the heavens from pole to pole
And leads you to believe a lie
When you see with, not through, the eye."

– William Blake

CHAPTER ONE

Dr. Allison Epstein
Psychiatrist

Clinical Notes

Date of Interview: Monday, July 21, 2003.
Subject: Timothy Jason Dare. Age 35; date of birth June 7, 1968;
height 6'1"; weight 171 lb.

The patient is physically healthy, athletic in fact – he arrived on a bicycle and climbed five flights of stairs. He presented as rumpled in appearance but reasonably clean-shaven; unruly auburn hair falling below his shoulders; straight, attenuated nose; penetrating, deep-set green eyes, and a generally gaunt and haggard expression.

At the beginning he was pleasant, even engaging, though some-what combative.[1] But as the session progressed he grew increasingly anxious, reciting several troubling stressors, the combined impact of which led him to my door. Later, I observed that occasionally instead of responding to a question, he wandered off into a world of his own.

Central to the patient's emotional deterioration is the recent failure of a relationship with Sally Pascoe, 34, a visual artist. The

---

[1] There was, perhaps to be expected, some preliminary jousting – he had difficulty reconciling himself to his unaccustomed role as patient.

patient grew up with her in the same Vancouver neighbourhood, and they've lived together for the last twelve years. Other major stressors include "stalking" by an alleged psychopathic murderer and "getting kicked in the scrotum" by the professional association of which we are both members, the psychiatric division of the College of Physicians.

He is clearly suffering a stress disorder. This condition has been exacerbated by the sporadic occurrence of claustrophobic dread, an episode of which I witnessed as I accompanied him to the elevator. He hesitated there, then took the stairs.

Selections from the transcript follow, with my notations.

I'm told you're a good old-fashioned Freudian.

Does that seem *démodé*, Dr. Dare? I try to use an array of tools.

He did some spectacular work with wealthy Viennese women suffering hysterical – or perhaps I should use the current newspeak, histrionic personality disorders, but . . . Never mind. Evelyn Mendel says you have an exceptional talent. McGill?

Yes, I just left a practice in Montreal.

What brought you to Vancouver?

My husband was offered a position.

You don't wear a ring.

That's right.

You kept your name?

So did he. Richard Spencer.

Assertive, independent, yet prepared to accommodate the aspirations of her goal-oriented partner.

I was warned about this.

Yes, that's fairly put, I suppose . . . what do you prefer . . . Timothy? Tim?

What do *you* prefer?

Whatever you're comfortable with.

How about you? Allison? Allie?

I'm Allis to my friends. Which is what I hope we'll be after we stop sparring like newly met children in a schoolyard.

He took that the right way – he is capable of laughter.

I'm Tim to *my* friends. You'll like Vancouver when it stops raining. Do you have kids?

I'm afraid not.

You're working at it.

Very quick to pick up nuances. His reputation in that regard was well demonstrated here.

What does he do? Your husband.

Richard is a partner in a media consulting firm, Spencer, Lang, and Associates. They do some polling, public relations. But let me ask – why me? I know Dr. Mendel gave you my name, but what kind of therapist were you looking for?

She said you did dreams. Mine are trying to tell me something. She also said you were smart and attractive.

Attractive?

I'm just repeating. Does that make me sexist?

Probably.

He laughed once more, genuinely. In his favour he doesn't seem one to put on a false face.

I've been in the business only four years . . .

That's good. Fresh approach. I've been seeking someone who doesn't know me. Someone new in town. Not set in her ways.

Or maybe someone who doesn't feel offended by your published critiques of what you call the psychiatry industry?

That was unprofessional of me, but I had allowed him to get under my skin.

I'm impressed – you've done some homework. You a strong feminist?

3

Tim, might I be allowed to ask some of the questions? We only have an hour today . . .

I was just wondering about your Freudianness. Don't get me wrong, I don't support the industry that specializes in debunking him, he remains the master, but those Viennese women were victims of an age when gender oppression was the norm. He failed to factor that in . . . Sorry, I suppose I'm procrastinating.

His cross-examination of me, and his brief rambles, seemed an indicator not merely of discomfort but of a slightly manic state. He finally took to the couch, though I continued to sense resistance as he kept his arms folded.

I've always thought this configuration too distancing. I prefer to see my patients. You read as much by watching as listening, even if it's only the play of silence on a face. I grant that your methodology is more orthodox – the mere presence of the therapist distracts the patient from the free flow of imagery.

You through?

Sorry.

After he finally allowed me to take some of his history, another tussle followed when I attempted to explore the nature of his current concerns.

Jesus, this is hard. Okay, crisis number one: my partner for life – or so I assumed – broke up with me ten days ago. I'm having a hell of a problem coping.

What's number two?

A psychopathic killer is stalking me.

Uh . . . Well, that's a big item.

Yeah, and another secretary quit on me, and my office is chaos, and I've been threatened with being purged from the medical ranks. But the biggest item is getting kicked out of Sally's life like a bad habit.

Okay, sure, but . . . sometimes dramatic but less relevant

material clogs the circuits. I'd like to assess the seriousness of this stalking threat.

I sense incredulity.

Not at all. Tell me about it.

Okay, well, this goes back to the murder of Dr. Barbara Loews Wiseman. You remember that, six years ago? Maybe you were still at McGill.

Yes, but . . . Remind me.

Okay, Barbara was a brilliant therapist, a friend, more than that, a spiritual guide during my internship. Feminist, lesbian. She specialized in anger management. Robert Grundison II, a kid who's hog rich, stabbed her to death because he decided she was Satan incarnate.

I remember the news stories . . . He was hallucinating

So he claimed, so did the army of shrinks who testified – I was the main witness against him, the *only* expert witness who disbelieved him. And of course the jury found him not guilty by reason of insanity. Sent off to a mental hospital to *rehabilitate*! Can you imagine? Sick, evil . . .

Slow and easy.

෧෩෩෧

Ah, Allis, what a piece of work you have before you. As you led me from your consulting room to confront the dreaded elevator, I saw you woefully shake your head. How, you were wondering, can you expect to repair this tattered psyche in the weekly hour allotted to me?

I'm sorry that we ran out of time today, your patient having wasted much of it with his fiddling and farting. I should have known better than to try to grasp the reins of therapy. I felt you were less interested in an everyday bargain-basement marriage breakdown than by the grim portents of murder, and I needed desperately to talk about Sally, my grief, my suppressed anger, I wanted pity and solace.

This evening, even as my mind replays today's awkward session, do you sit with Richard at the dinner table, entertaining him with my persecutory delusions? "He claims someone wants to *kill* him?" "Yes, dear, and I can understand why."

When you asked me to take the lead, to waltz you down the byways of memory, I was briefly lost. Where to begin? Was I to pick up the thread a year ago, when disintegration began? A decade ago, when there were youth and hope? A lifetime ago, before the patterning of childhood warped the bell curve of normality into the shape of a burned-out light bulb? How to begin my unburdening, how to describe the clutter of neurotransmitters and synapses, hormones and hemostats, that comprise Timothy Jason Dare?

Sorry I emoted so much. I've cooled off. A couple of beers, some soothing jazz . . . (Picture this skinny geek in his undershorts aboard his old sailboat tooting mournfully on a clarinet. Dispossessed of home, that's where I live now, my classic wooden cutter, the *Altered Ego*.)

Anyway, having botched today's first session, let me whip my thoughts into line, reassemble them in more coherent fashion, to prepare for our next session. (By the way, Friday afternoons are fine, I'm rarely in court then, and I'll be able to use weekends to recover from whatever catharses come my way.)

To put my fears in perspective and to set the stage for what follows, let's go back six years ago to a scene so graphic that my mother, if she cared to lift it for one of her books, might be forced to tone it down. (We haven't got around to Victoria Dare, who, having published a horror novel, has been sued for libel by an overly sensitive small-town politician who saw himself portrayed as the killer. The trial is only a couple of weeks away. An added stressor.)

We are in Dr. Barbara Loews Wiseman's consulting room. She is staring at a raised dagger, desperately pleading, trying to persuade Bob Grundison that God has not ordered him to kill her, that she isn't Satan in the guise of a psychiatrist. Imagine the dagger descending, thrusting . . .

The image is fixed? Now let's fast-forward to a couple of weeks ago – this was just before Sally cut me adrift – to a hearing to determine whether this killer might be released by Order-in-Council onto the already treacherous streets of Vancouver.

The inquiry was at the provincial mental hospital, Riverview. Usually I enjoy my trips there, my ambles about the grounds with patients. But this promised to be a strenuous day of listening to the Grundison family's hired psychiatrists, psychologists, and social workers: I was on a panel struck by the provincial cabinet – they were tossing us the buck; if Grundison were to celebrate his freedom with a psychotic rampage, they would blame the experts.

I arrived slightly frazzled from the long traffic-jammed taxi ride to Riverview, and before we convened I apologized to all – though I was only fifteen minutes late. The panel consisted of me, Dr. Irwin Connelly, and Dr. Harriet Loussier, the hospital's chief psychologist. A pair of lawyers for the Grundison family was present, along with several medical experts (one of them my nemesis, Dr. Herman Schulter) and a clutch of supporters and relatives there to bear witness to their love of Bob Grundison. He'd been excused from the room – we wanted to speak frankly about him.

Also present were his parents. Robert Grundison Sr. is a staunch pillar of capitalism, owns several tall buildings, shopping centres, a hockey team. But he's highly regarded: a philanthropist who gives handsomely to Christian charities. His confident body language, even as he sat, expressed power and control. In contrast, his pink-complexioned wife, Thelma, exuded an odd serenity – though with the glassy-eyed aspect of a lush. Sitting next to them was the

Honourable Ephriam Wright, an Alberta cabinet minister and evangelical pastor with the unusual reputation, given those careers, of brightness.

The day dragged on. The experts (three of whom, including Schulter, had testified at his trial) concurred: as an adolescent, Grundison had suffered occasional delusions (talking to God, chiefly, though the evidence was vague and came mainly from members of his church), then was revisited by his disease six years ago, when he was twenty-one. Now, Grundison was not only stabilized but cured.

Much was made by Herman Schulter (the clubby, deferential chair of my discipline committee – would he yank my practising certificate if I denied freedom to a killer?) of Grundison having resolved "aggressive behaviour patterns" by channelling his energy into sports. Grundy, as he's often called, had formed a couple of leagues while at Riverview, basketball and softball. Schulter's view was that this showed enterprise, leadership.

I listened to such confident prognoses with growing discomfort. I was on this panel because I had a history with Grundison. Six years ago, new in practice, puffed with arrogance (behold the youngest winner of the B.F. Skinner Prize at Stanford), I was the only witness the Crown could find who dared to claim Grundy was faking schizophrenia.

Grundison was arrested several minutes after leaving Barbara Wiseman's office, wandering around Broadway and Cambie, ostensibly in a daze. Schulter, who was rushed to the cells to interview him, testified that his affect was flat and shallow, a vacant stare, face muscles flaccid, eyes lifeless, toneless, his memory train not intact.

I interviewed Grundy at length, gave him tests. Not psychotic but psychopathic, I concluded, a cold-hearted killer.

So now I was in a conundrum. I've never believed (nor, I suspect, did Barbara Loews Wiseman) that Bob Grundison was delusional, but the rest of the world seemed to believe that – who was some long-haired, wild-eyed forensic psychiatrist to disagree? And how could I argue he was insane now, and required continued treatment? However psychopathic, he was mentally competent by the definition of the law. He cannot be tried again for murder, yet he's a murderer.

Ephriam Williams stirred the room to wakefulness with a fervent speech in praise of the killer: athlete, Boy Scout, never in trouble, gosh darn it, he'd known the lad since he was old enough to throw a snowball. A stirring, rodomontade sermon, urging us, as doctors of the mind, to believe in the healing powers of our own great science, to pronounce this fine young man fit to return to the bosom of his loving parents, of whom young Bob was the only issue.

As he was reminding us of Jesus' mandate to forgive, I remarked to myself that the late Dr. Wiseman didn't seem to be represented here, or much remembered. She'd only seen Bob four times before dying at his hand.

Though her file on Grundy indicated she'd made little progress in bringing him to terms with a seething, barely suppressed anger, one of her entries has always intrigued me: *I see no sign of a breakthrough. I sense a terror lurking within him, but its source and character are not clear.*

Over lunch, Connelly, Loussier, and I engaged in heated debate. The conversation went like this, give or take a phrase:

I said, "We have to find some way to keep this misfit inside."

"But he's not psychotic, Tim," Connelly said. "That's a dilemma for you, isn't it? You never thought he was legally insane in the first place."

"It's a different kind of insanity – moral insanity."

"There's no question that he has a severe antisocial personality disorder." This was Dr. Loussier. In her sixties, a formal woman, and wise, she's been chief psychologist here for five of Grundison's six years.

"Statistically, there have to be seventy thousand APDs walking the streets of Vancouver." Irwin is in love with his statistics. He is a kindly old fellow, mentored me through some difficult times. "They've set up a massive system of home support. He'll be watched at all times. What can happen if we let him go?"

"A repeat. Maybe it'll be you next time, Irwin. He's a dangerous psychopath."

"Once capable, always capable," said Loussier. "Five episodes of violent behaviour within the facility. Those are the ones reported. No one injured, thank God."

"Because they were all attacks on inanimate objects," Irwin said. "I've been known to kick a chair myself. I agree with Schulter. He has learned to take out his anger in essentially harmless ways."

"Like ripping apart a mattress," I said. "Smashing a radio."

"Both those events were early on. He's been off inhibitors for three years. Damn it, Tim, it'll look bad if we don't let him go – it's as if we're protecting our own."

"Maybe we *should* protect our own."

The image thing, though mentioned only once, had a subliminal effect upon the remainder of our discussions. Would we be seen as biased against one who offed a shrink? If Grundison had killed a lawyer, might we send him home with a wave and a smile?

I could not come up with a justification for keeping Grundison in the system. I'd sworn on oath to a Canadian jury that by the McNaughten rules the man wasn't insane. But the eminent Dr. Schulter and three other psychiatrists had testified to reverse effect and been believed, and Grundison had been found not guilty. Now these same psychiatrists were of the opinion he was of sound mind. Who was I to try to undo all of that?

So I caved in. "May the Lord have mercy on our souls."

"Let's see some rigid terms of release," Loussier said. "Abstention from alcohol, for one." When arrested, Grundison had a medium-level reading of .05. "We'll want reports on how his counselling program is going."

"From those hacks his family hired? Let's get someone independent, who can't be bought. I want to have a few words with him before we let him go."

Having prejudged the issue, we returned to the hearing room and hurried along the remaining witnesses. Thelma Grundison, in a somewhat wheezy voice, went on about how much she doted on her son. She would be providing stern but loving care at The Tides, their manse in Ladner, by the moiling waters of the Fraser's South Arm. Her husband, I gathered (he didn't testify), would try to be there when he wasn't away on business – most of his companies are in Calgary. I had the sense of a long-continuing pretence of marriage, a de facto but not acknowledged separation.

Other witnesses included a mental health social worker who had set up the home-care program, and an anger counsellor who would work with him this summer.

Last of all, we heard from Grundy himself. He'd been on the grounds, playing softball, the Aggressives, perhaps, against the Incoherents. Freshly showered, he made his way to a chair at the front: he's light-footed, despite his muscular build. I remember having noted six years ago an athletic grace to his movements. His coiffed, blow-dried hair added to the power image he sought to portray.

He is of medium height, has his mother's red complexion, and his features are marred only by an indentation on the chin, where a puck had struck him. Otherwise, he's quite handsome. Many young women had been attracted to him – to their misfortune. He'd been seeing Dr. Wiseman for his inability to stop bashing them when undergoing his aggressive behaviour patterns.

Grundy worked the room, pausing to squeeze arms and shake hands. He kissed his mother delicately on the cheek. His gesture of affection to his father was interesting, a light-fisted blow to the shoulder, a jock-jocular gesture. Ephriam Williams squeezed Grundy's elbow, ruffled his hair. I found all these physical dynamics irksome. It was as if pressing the flesh was making do for true feeling, an easy substitute.

Irwin asked him to sit, and introduced himself. "You know Dr. Loussier, of course, and you've met Dr. Dare. He wants to ask you a few questions."

Grundison's look held mine longer than cordiality required, suggesting he was overplaying advice not to drop, shift, or bat his eyes. In particular (Schulter doubtless advised), always look directly at Dr. Timothy Dare, the charlatan who has achieved a much-inflated reputation for his accurate reading of flared nostrils, twitches, and general body discomfort.

"How are you doing, Mr. Grundison?" I asked.

"Nervous, I guess. Not bad. That sounds formal, everyone calls me Bob. Or Grundy." A slight smile. Still no loss of eye contact.

"How did the softball game go?"

"Fourteen to eight." He laughed. "Over five innings."

"That must have helped your batting average."

"I hit a few." He broke contact and focused his eyes on neutral space behind me. Avoid aggressive phrases, he'd been told. "I dropped a couple of easy flies too." Be prepared to admit to your faults and weaknesses.

"But that's not your best sport, is it?"

"No. It's hockey, Dr. Dare."

Grundy had made it to Junior A, an unrefined player, an enforcer. Following that, he'd gone to college for two years, the last semester aborted by his arrest for murder. "So you're going back to university."

"Yes, to continue my psychology studies at SFU."

"Why psychology?"

"I want to help people. I think I owe it."

I wasn't believing a word. Would Simon Fraser University even have him? Wouldn't they be concerned he'd mistake a social sciences professor for the Antichrist?

"You still have only a vague memory of killing Dr. Wiseman?"

A hesitation, then he blurted, "That wasn't me. That was someone else."

He reacted as if he'd said the wrong thing; his medical witnesses, too, stirred uncomfortably at this hint of the divided self.

"If not you, who was it?"

"No, I didn't mean it that way. It was me, but . . . I was ill. I had a psychotic episode."

"You're sure it wasn't someone else, Bob?"

"No, not at all, and I know what you're getting at. Multiple personality – I think it's called dissociative identity disorder."

He'd learned such phrases in college. But I'd implied before, to no effect, that he knew how to fake a delusional episode.

"Dr. Dare, I know that you have your doubts about me, but I'm willing to prove myself to you. I'm going to continue the anger management. I'm not denying that I have a problem with my temper, even though I don't know where it comes from. I intend to keep looking for answers to it, for answers to myself."

Well rehearsed, well spoken – with the convincing earnestness of the true sociopath. He'd scored high on the Hare checklist, on both the antisocial and emotional detachment scales. But at that first interview I had picked up elusive nuances and shades, undertones pointing to his guilt. How to express that convincingly to a jury?

"Okay, let's see you prove yourself. We're going to recommend your release, Bob, but if you ever as much as threaten anyone, raise your fist, if you're caught with a weapon – you'll be back here in a wink." That seemed, under the circumstances, the most useful therapy I could give him.

Here, Irwin unexpectedly broke in. "And, Bob, you're going to be required to report regularly to Dr. Dare, so he can monitor your progress."

I thought Irwin had attempted a tasteless jest. But he carried on, serious and stern, listing conditions of curfew, substance intake, a regime of therapy, "and absolute, unfettered cooperation with Dr. Dare." I tapped Irwin on the shoulder, interrupting him, inviting him to join me in a whispered tête-à-tête.

"Did I agree to this?"

"Isn't that what you suggested?"

"I didn't offer *myself*." I hesitated to tell Irwin he might be getting on in years, his hearing failing.

"For God's sake, Tim, don't embarrass me." That was said too loud; ears were straining to hear. Irwin lowered his voice. "Who could be a better warden than you? Take him up on his challenge to prove himself. You can be well guarded during the interviews. Let me handle this."

Irwin turned away, left me hanging. "I should mention that the Ministry of Health will have to charge for Dr. Dare's services . . ."

"Just send me the bills," said Grundy's father – amiably, but he'd been watch-checking, toe-tapping: he had business elsewhere. Thelma Grundison remained immobile but for the occasional suck of a breath mint.

After we wrapped up, I glumly watched another exhibition of nudging and elbow-gripping. Grundy, not quite hidden by his well-wishers, pumped his fist.

Irwin insisted he'd done me a favour. "Damn it, Tim, you don't even bill half your patients. You're always complaining that you're living on credit cards. Sock it to them, old boy." I surrendered.

Irwin had thought this out wisely, knew I would relent. He knows I'm fascinated by the criminal mind, by psychopathy. Indeed, I *am* curious to learn more about Grundy's emotional mechanics.

However, most of his therapeutic time, at least during the summer, will be spent with Dr. Martha Wade, who has bravely volunteered to hold anger management sessions on weekends at The Tides. She's primarily a juvenile psychologist – she's worked with gangs – so she's a good choice, considering her patient's emotional age.

Martha has already met several times with Grundy and his family, and insists she has no concerns for her safety. She will stay overnight in a guest cottage, will have the run of the estate: the riding trails, the heated pool, the nine-hole pitch-and-putt. I've never been at The Tides but am curious to visit, to observe the pampered subject in his lair.

Grundy was released a few days later, in time to enrol in a summer-school course. My first post-release interview with him was looming, and I was disturbed occasionally by images of Barbara Wiseman's last moments.

In the meantime, my relationship with Sally had just blown apart, so I was in separation shock when Grundy came to my office to set up a schedule of appointments. Accompanying him – because I insisted I would not see him alone – was a young man who handled Grundison Incorporated office security, whose func-tion now was babysitting his boss's son. He was introduced as Lyall DeWitt. Tall, lithe, lighter than Grundy, his hair cropped short. I noted a judo-club emblem on his jacket.

I'd hired a temp to reorganize my files, but she was having difficulty, and the office seemed in more than its usual disarray. I ushered them to my less cluttered consulting room, a stuffy Edwardian space with subdued lighting and walls lined with books, curtained windows overlooking Fourth Avenue.

I asked Grundy how he was adjusting, and he said, "Great" and thanked me for having "faith" in him. His eyes were darting about, taking in the room, noting the back door, an exit to the fire escape and the alley.

After a brief comparing of calendars, it was agreed we would see each other alternate Thursday afternoons. I would continue to insist that Grundy be accompanied.

"I drive for Bob," Lyall said. "I'll be around."

"You known each other long?"

"Ever since college."

"How are you getting on with him?"

"Swimmingly."

I couldn't read Lyall: the sardonic lift of eyebrow might have expressed contempt for Grundy, for me, for the whole process. But it also might have been a confident message: I have matters well in hand. I hoped he was a black belt.

Before dismissing them, I had Grundy step outside the room so I could talk in confidence with DeWitt. "Do I understand you were college buddies?"

"Yeah, but it was kind of a locker-room thing. I was in phys. ed., he was a jock-of-all-trades. No big deal. He was rich, he had contacts."

"And he connected you with Grundison Inc."

"Sure, I got a good job out of it."

A relationship more mercenary than intimate. "Tell me your honest feelings about him."

"He's a lamb."

"Has he been making any threatening noises to anyone?"

"Don't worry – I can handle him."

I wanted to pursue this, but Grundy was waiting, maybe worrying that we were in deep conspiracy. Before seeing them off, I threw Grundy a question prompted by Barbara Wiseman's notes — he'd accused her of prying into his mind, and I asked him why.

"That's what psychiatrists do, isn't it? I was just kidding, Dr. Dare." (Translated: I wasn't kidding.)

Barbara certainly hadn't bought that: *His words were curt, but a moment later he covered up with a laugh, saying, "But I guess that's your job."*

"Did she say something to prompt that response?"

"It was a long time ago, sir." He shrugged. I didn't pursue the matter, and he walked down the stairs with DeWitt.

Had Barbara been digging for something close to the gut? Sadly, she hadn't transcribed her questions, and, like me, she wasn't a believer in that intrusive device, the tape recorder (though I appreciate that yours is hidden, Allis). There had been other brusque reactions, particularly when the subject of the female gender was raised. *Unrepentant misogynist?* she wrote.

He wasn't a willing patient; he'd been sent to Barbara by his family. Over the first three sessions, all her efforts to chip away at his barriers were futile.

She hadn't got around to transcribing her notes for the fourth session — the day before she was murdered — and her notepad was never found. I suspect Grundy stole it, trashed it after he ran past a desk under which the terrified receptionist was hiding, and escaped onto the street.

Now, observed from my second-floor window, he was striding with confidence, joking with his chauffeur as they jaywalked to a late-model minivan: black, with Playboy mud flaps. As Grundy opened the passenger door, he looked up at my window. I thought I saw a grin, but from the distance wasn't sure.

The next night, returning from a training run to Point Grey, I saw a similar van — black, darkened windows — parked on

Creekside Drive, near the homeport of the *Altered Ego*. I slept fitfully, my brain cells tuned to be aware of any lurching of the boat, a heavy footfall.

Intuition serves us like a blind man's dog, and I've since had a prickly sense Grundy was near, once in the shadows of night, then once during the day – I didn't get a clean look; a man ducked into a shop doorway when I turned quickly.

I won't be surprised, Allis, if you chalk these alleged sightings up to incipient Paranoid Personality Disorder. I'm slowly coming to the conviction that, yes, there is a plot to get me, and unseen hands are directing it. There exists a presumption against coincidence, so why would all my calamities be happening at the same time unless I've become the plaything of a jesting god who wants to drive Timothy Jason Dare insane?

How am I going to get through the next week? I have two court appearances. My mother's libel trial begins, as well, and I should be there to help her face the wrath of Clinton W. Huff, the oversensitive mayor of Jackson Cove. Sally leaves for Europe on Tuesday.

Maybe I should take a Prozac. But I fear drugs, the curse of habit, of addiction.

CHAPTER TWO

Date of Interview: Friday, July 25, 2003.

Generally, Tim presented as less anxious and combative than earlier this week, and less frantic, but still garrulous. He was again unable to cope with the elevator, despite my advice that he undergo a deconditioning program.

I've suggested other tools, particularly self-hypnosis. Tim is adept at hypnosis, and has employed it with his patients, but for some reason he is disinclined to go that route, and one wonders how committed he is to search within himself.

"Look for the father" is often a reliable rule of therapy, but for some reason he shies from speaking of the man he calls Peter, a former medical student – whereabouts unknown. Tim is close to his mother, though, and fond of her.

Despite all, it appears he is maintaining a busy practice – he's much in demand by the courts. He agrees this is a healthy way to sublimate his many concerns. He hasn't had more sightings of anyone "following" him, and one hopes he has put such fears behind him.

We devoted most of our time to seeking the factors underlying Ms. Pascoe's decision to separate from him. Some of those quickly became apparent, as in the following extract.

What kind of artist is she?

Brilliant. She's just finished a series of portraits of people at their day-to-day tasks – quite revelatory. She does landscapes that Tom Thomson would have held in awe. Her perception intrigues me, I've never been able to comprehend the artistic gift. But mostly she earns her living as a children's book illustrator. She does the Miriam series, *Miriam's Funny Picnic, Miriam Goes to France*, ages five to eight. You can't go into a bookstore without . . . well, maybe you don't frequent the children's section. There's a therapeutic coincidence at work here, by the way – she wants children too. I'm afraid I'll bequeath some of my neurotic tendencies, so that's one of the hot-button topics. But the thing is, I've known her since early childhood, losing her is like a limb being chopped off, an appendage.

A limb . . . ?

"I need to break out," she said. "I need room to grow." I moved out of our house, a bungalow in Kitsilano – you know that district? Anyway, now she has room to grow and I'm living on a boat at Fishermen's Wharf. Foundering. I don't know if she's having an affair, and I can't bear the thought.

You're speeding, Tim. I'm trying to catch up.

Excuse me.

You used the word *appendage*. Does that say anything to you?

That I . . .

A long pause here. Possessive of Ms. Pascoe, stifling her creativity?

All right, I threw that out loosely, but I get your point – I was taking her for granted. Doing so blithely, thoughtlessly.

Why do you think she spoke of needing room to grow?

Familiarity was a prison. We'd known each other since Grade *One*, for Christ's sake. There's more to it than that – *I* was a prison to her. She illustrated *Miriam Goes to France* without ever having been there. I'm phobic about flying. She wanted to travel; I kept her grounded . . .

⟨∞⟩

"Maybe you have it backwards," you said. "Maybe she kept *you* grounded." Touché, Allis, you threw a perfect dart. Your point is proved. After Sally kicked me out of the nest, I flew wobbily out of control, and seem to have landed on my head. She insists the signs had been there for a year, a gradual deterioration, more frequent lapses, missed dates, forgotten episodes.

My speech patterns may have been a little disordered again today (I don't think I'm better with you yet), so as I sit watching the gulls drift by outside the *Altered Ego*, feeling more relaxed after our bout of therapy, let me put events in order. Go back with me a couple of weeks ago to the Pondicherry Restaurant . . .

As was customary, the chef, Nataraja, greeted my arrival with one of his Buddhist aphorisms: "Accept totally, acceptance is the path of understanding," and with that, he levitated me to my regular table by the window. The Pondicherry is my favourite lair, where the spiritually correct chef (also owner and maître d' of this six-table hole in the wall) guarantees his curry is organic, his cumin and cardamom ungenetically modified. I'm likely the most faithful of its meagre New Age clientele, and feel in a large way responsible for its survival among the trendier eateries of Fourth Avenue.

For perhaps the first time in recorded history, it was Sally, not I, who was late. She received my kiss with an oddly cautious reserve. Normally, she exudes the kind of perky energy one often finds in

—
21

bantamweights. (Visualize a five-foot, mop-haired, thin-hipped Goldilocks whose sky-blue eyes seem in a constant state of astonishment. Thirty-four but you could mistake her for twenty-four.) Clearly, she hadn't recovered from our spat the previous night, and her strained smile and the leeward tilt of her head, as when she is stressed and about to unburden herself, set me worrying. (At this point, I was still labouring under the smug belief that I knew this woman as a Tennessee preacher knows his Bible. I'd been analyzing her for two decades.)

Nataraja settled her in her chair, purring, "Surrender is the ultimate leap. Happiness comes when we dare to soar."

The message didn't seem lost on Sally, who used it as a homily for an oft-repeated sermon: We Never Go Anywhere. Chained to ill-travelled Timothy Dare, she feels stuck, trapped, immobile. She's never been to a tropical beach or soaked in the glamour of Paris or Rome, and – here's the rub – now we had a chance to fly to Europe: her publisher was proposing to send her to the Children's Book Fair in Bologna and she could bring a companion for half-fare.

My response was too quick. "That person, regrettably, will not be me."

"I'm flying to Munich, then meandering down to Italy. I'm booking two weeks off. I am not about to miss out on a free European holiday." *Miriam Goes to Munich.* There was rigidity in her pose, a stubborn set to her features.

"They'll make an unscheduled landing in Greenland and march me off in a straightjacket."

"*Damn* it, this isn't a relationship, it's an exercise in futility." I sensed a scene looming. I'm not good at scenes. (This dismal conversation, and all others included within quotation marks, are as best remembered but subject to small inaccuracies. My intent is to offer a vivid, animated record, however pathetic.)

Sally proceeded to recite a catalogue of my recent transgressions, the most grievous being my failure to show up, last week, for dinner at her publisher's home. My defence (an emergency: a delusional patient off her meds, a self-inflicted knife wound, I was up till midnight with her) bore little weight, since in truth I'd forgotten the function – or blocked it. Sally had been (her word) "mortified." The host had invited an editor, two writers, a marketing director; my chair had sat yawningly empty, like a thoughtless snub.

"And yesterday – you expect me to believe you simply forgot I was making dinner?" The previous evening's quarrel, revisited.

"Sally, I was up to my ears, I had a fitness hearing this morning..."

"*You* should have a fitness hearing. Ever heard of the telephone? It was invented about a century and a half ago. I read somewhere that women should go on alert when their partners constantly make up lame excuses for not being home. Especially if their love life hasn't been up to snuff."

This innuendo added fuel to my anxiety. What prompted her to imply faithlessness – was it a form of projection, a seeking to lay blame for some guilty liaison of her own?

"Sally, my secretary quit on me." (Claiming she couldn't abide the chaos of my practice.) "My professional association is bringing me up on charges of careless practice." (And I'd just helped loose a monster on the streets, the psychopath Robert Grundison II.) "I'm distracted. I'm sorry if I haven't been a firecracker in bed. I am not seeing another woman."

"I shouldn't have suggested that . . . anyway, it isn't the point."

Then what *was* the point? Her frown and a slight pursing of the lips hinted of a struggle for the best way to put this.

We paused to give our dinner orders, both of us choosing the shrimp curry (I'm semi-vegetarian, no fundamentalist). My appetite vanished, however, as with trembling voice she began to work her way slowly, inexorably, to the point.

"Tim, I love you, but it's like living with a mad scientist. I think I'm even catching your neuroses – example, that paranoid suspicion about your late nights. I'm sorry, I'm not . . . it's not that."

"Say what you're about to say."

"I think we should separate for a while."

I froze while she fought tears and poured words. She needed room to grow. She needed room to breathe. She needed to explore. (Explore!) She was thirty-four; life was passing her by. (The subtext: she plans to cast about for a more adventurous companion, centred, unphobic, possessed of emotionally stable sperm.) We'll still be friends. We'll always be friends. Let's do this for a while, okay? See where it takes us . . .

Out of nowhere, out of the vastness of nowhere: a declaration of independence, of emancipation, a severing of a union that, though not sanctioned by licence and ceremony, I had always pre- sumed was a bond for life. I was stung, hurt beyond measure. I am not, regrettably, much skilled in relationship therapy (but even experts in that field have been known to botch their own mar- riages), and in any event was too numb to call upon my own meagre expertise.

So I begged. This was too bizarre, too quick, too off the cuff, naturally she was upset, there had definitely been a lack of atten- tion, of consideration, so please, I urged, let's hold off any sudden moves, let's give it a few days, let's talk about it, I'll take therapy for my fear of flying, I'll change my ways. I stooped to a guilt-maker: I couldn't go on without her; I couldn't *live* without her.

That may well be true, Allis. I've been in love with Sally as long as I can remember. I've loved no one else barring my mother – an affection satisfactorily resolved at the appropriate stage of childhood.

My self-debasing pleas only had the effect of vexing her. "This isn't something off the cuff!" When she began to weep, I suddenly felt – as Nataraja might say – that I'd been led to the path of understanding. This wasn't a heated reaction of the moment but a decision she'd struggled with for some time. She'd put me to the final test of Europe and I'd failed. She'd anticipated that, anticipated my whining plea of contrition, steeled herself for this moment. She was in vast pain with remorse, failure, guilt. But I also sensed relief – she had said it, the worst was over.

"You can have the house," I said. "I'll live on the *Altered Ego*."

She cried harder, and didn't resist my moving closer to her or taking one of her hands. With the other, she dabbed her eyes.

"I guess you intended to have this conversation last night," I said. Over a dinner painstakingly prepared.

Quickly, she leaned over and kissed me on the cheek. "Thank you," she said. The several customers of the restaurant had gone silent, caught up in the drama of others' lives. From the back, I heard someone sniffle.

I found myself functioning at an almost autonomous level, calmly parcelling out the family treasures, working with Sally on how to tell friends and parents (I have only a mother, she only a father), and reassuring her that she must keep the house with its skylit studio and that I wouldn't feel cramped in the thirty-foot cutter that, for the last three years, has kept me in a state of penury. A fear of watery depths is one ailment the god Phobus didn't deign to assign me.

"You could move into your mother's house for a while. Victoria has lots of room."

"I will not be running home to Mother." Victoria Dare is a fifty-two-year-old entrepreneur, voracious reader, rejection-slip collector, and (finally) author of a novel, *When Comes the Darkness*, a horror thriller that your squeamish patient set down after Chapter Two and hasn't found the courage to reopen. I read enough to know that the central character, a serial killer, is so sexually blocked that he achieves orgasm only through the murder of young women.

Anyway, Allis, you won't have to dig deep to learn that Victoria (never *Mom*, a word her progressive child-rearing manual warned was lazy exercise for the learning child) made me what I am today.

Let me catch myself – that isn't entirely correct, I mustn't resist the deeper truth. I have always struggled more with the father I never knew.

I heard your silence when I told you about my misbegotten beginnings. (But I'll bet your lips puckered into a round smooch of curiosity, one of your telltale looks.) Yes, I am of unknown authorship, conceived in a tent during a romantic moonlit night on the shores of Kootenay Lake. His name was Peter, a medical student, that's about all we know.

Eventually, Allis, we'll work through this source of psychological warp, but I'm not ready.

So let us return to the Pondicherry Restaurant, to Tim and Sally – there they are, twenty-nine years from the day they met on a playground, carving up the carcass of their life together, divvying up stereos and coffee grinders. (Who cared!) I believe I slipped into a Category 300.6 disorder: derealization, existence is unreal, the surrounding world a sham.

(This isn't the first episode in which I've suffered estrangement from the self – add that to your ever-growing list.)

As if to confirm this diagnosis, there occurred a surreal event as we were debating custody of the hand-blown wine goblets. Outside, a tall, stilettoed, miniskirted woman emerged from a Cadillac convertible, high-stepped onto the sidewalk, and stared directly at me through the glass. Let me introduce to you the dark-haired, pouty-mouthed, bold-breasted Vivian Lalonde, graduate student, twenty-three, who has been in therapy with me for the last month.

In a thrice she was standing at our table, hovering over me. "Dr. Dare, I'm sorry, I have to talk to you."

"Vivian, this is not the best time." This Amazon, six feet tall in heels, is a histrionic attention-demander with a history of unhappy male relationships – intelligent but obsessively flirtatious. I'd probably erred in telling her the Pondicherry was my favourite restaurant.

"I've left him."

"Let's make a very early appointment. I'll see you at eight tomorrow, how's that?"

"I have nowhere to go. I walked out with what I have on me." A dress of pricey design, the top unbuttoned to reveal the barest glimpse of braless breasts. She was staring at me intensely, ignoring Sally, who shifted uncomfortably. Introductions didn't seem warranted.

"I just feel so lost and alone, Doctor."

I thought of telling her, to use the cloying argot of the pseudo-therapist, that I shared her pain – her plight eerily echoed mine, though this was her second failure at marriage, one that hadn't lasted half a year.

I rose and ushered her toward the kitchen doorway, out of the hearing of all but Nataraja, who was sorting through his spice jars.

"You have your parents' home to go to."

"I can't face them."

"That's the first thing you should do."

"He'll think it's my fault."

Note the reference not to mother but to father, an overbearing surgeon who was footing my bills and who'd been no less opposed to this marriage than the first. He wanted his daughter to be happy – that, he insisted, was all that counted. Vivian's mother, an ineffectual self-doubter, offered little support.

I explained she'd interrupted a deeply personal discussion. Her eyes finally went to Sally.

"That's your wife." She had no trouble deducing that, as she'd seen Sally's self-portrait on the wall of my office.

"Please, Vivian, do as I suggest."

She finally agreed, reluctantly, to go to her parents' home. As she left, Nataraja drew me aside solicitously. He'd observed Sally's tears, my gloom, but mistook their source. "Stick with Sally. That other one may be built like a B-52 bomber, but she doesn't have all her buttons done up." Nataraja will often show me another face. He'd lived well and decadently as a spiritual leader until convicted of tax evasion. He is a handsome man of forty, dark, with soulful eyes.

I slumped back into my chair. Sally was unreadable, a look she often takes on in defence against my alleged ability to read her thoughts (if I try to do so, it's without mischievous motive).

"She's a patient," I explained.

"Obviously."

"Smart. She's studying for her masters."

"In what — reproductive biology?"

"Design arts."

Sally repeated, with exaggerated mimicry, "'I walked out with what I have *on* me. I have nowhere to *go*.'"

"What would you have me do? Offer to put her up on the *Altered Ego*?"

"What is she, some spoiled brat? She couldn't take her eyes off you."

Under the circumstances, I thought it self-indulgent of Sally to be jealous as she was casting me from her life. On occasion, I've shared the secrets of the couch with her, but now the relationship had changed: I ought not to give insider information to a stranger. However, Sally read something unintended in my silence.

"Timothy, you haven't . . . *done* anything with her?"

"How absurd."

Again, I wondered if she was projecting. I have not, either despite or because of my long relationship with Sally, become inured to the attractions of a well-formed female. I've looked, considered, had fantasies. (Yes, even with patients, even – let me hold nothing back – with Vivian Lalonde.) Yes, I engage in flights of fancy. But does Sally do more than that? And if so, with whom? With whom had she shared that table at her publisher's home? I have been conjuring dismal scenes: the evening a disaster, Sally gulping her wine, unburdening herself to the marketing director of Chipmunk Press. She finds it helpful to talk to him. He enjoys her straightforwardness. Don't phone me, I'll phone you.

Also at that dinner was Ellery Cousineau, the earringed name-dropping senior editor of the Miriam books – but surely Sally sees through his empty, practised charm. Someone unknown? A ripple-muscled surrealist from the Vancouver Artists' Coalition?

This is something new, distrust. It has simply never come up in the course of my life. Now I find Jealousy sitting around a table with my old friend Paranoia, laughing and scheming. I acknowledge jealousy, I know I must manage it – it is an axiom of our profession that disowned emotions backfire on the disowner.

Business taken care of, Sally and I carried on like characters in an Albee play, avoiding, talking yet not connecting – I promising to take therapy for aircraft avoidance, she touring Europe, dipping through Bavaria, to Switzerland, to Venice and Bologna. I following up by relating, with false exuberance, my tactical plan to win my two-day bicycle rally this fall, *le prix de Okanagan*.

Nataraja bowed as he presented the bill. "When you open the door to surrender, you find enlightenment within." And upon receipt of that last Buddhist fortune cookie, we walked home through misty streets to the pimple of a peninsula by Kitsilano Beach, where for more than a decade we've shared a home. We spoke no words. All had been said, all decided. The shrink and the artist were a divided primary family unit. The next day, I would move my essentials to the *Altered Ego*.

I didn't attempt to go to bed with Sally. In fact, I didn't sleep. I sat up all night. I ate breakfast at five a.m. in an all-night diner, then dragged myself to the two-storey stand-alone building on Fourth Avenue where I share the upper floor with three accountants. (Our hold on it is precarious. The landlord wants to buy out our leases, the computer graphics firm on the ground floor wants to expand upstairs. Another item for the worry pile.)

I was hunched over my desk asleep at eight a.m. when Vivian Lalonde knocked on the door. Rumpled, unshaven, my hair falling over my eyes, I listened groggily to an account of the calumnies of an uncultured sportsman who talked only about golf and fishing, and who yesterday had dared call her a spinny bitch.

"Did you stay at your parents'?"

"Yes." She finally seemed to notice the state I was in. "Have you been drinking or something? You look a mess."

"I'm . . . never mind. So how did everything work out at home?"

"I didn't think Father would be that supportive. He's hiring a van to get my things."

Eventually the truth would have to come from her: she'd set up her marriage to fail in order to please her father, as she had her first relationship. But I felt annoyed at her, at her hunger for trauma, at her trivial dramas. Get an education, get a job, get a life, I wanted to shout.

I found myself staring blankly at Sally's self-portrait, her gift to me on my thirtieth birthday. And suddenly I unravelled. I lost all professionalism, found myself challenging her grief against mine. I told her I hadn't slept, that she'd stumbled last night into a domestic funeral, that I'd lost the only woman I had ever loved.

What a fool I was to have unburdened myself. But I had to release, to vent, and if it hadn't been Vivian Lalonde it would have been hypersomniac Katerina Welch or Larry Jankes with his body dysmorphic disorder.

Ironically, my anguish acted upon Vivian as therapy.

"Oh, Timothy, that's terrible. I didn't realize . . . I'll come back another time."

She calmed completely, her own marital plight a dim concern against mine. As she was about to leave, she turned to me and, before I could shy away, kissed me on the lips. An impetuous act of compassion? Let us hope.

I struggled through the next twenty-four hours, rescheduled patients, escaped to the sea aboard my cutter. But I could not escape Sally. I remembered how she used to sketch as she squatted on the bow, her T-shirt powdered with artists' chalk, blonde curls ruffling in the wind.

She'll summon me back within days, I assured myself. A week, perhaps, to save face. I will return non-gloatingly to her bosom. I'll mend my ways. I'll carry a Daytimer. I'll buy a pager, a cellphone.

To allay her worries, I called her several times during the week to assure her I was coping. She was solicitous, then launched into rundowns of her day from which I picked up a lilting tone of freedom. I came by the house one evening to fetch my clarinet, but she was out – where, at half-past ten? I still had my key, and I prowled like a ghost through the darkened rooms. I felt smothered by all the loss and loneliness, by the smell of her in our former bedroom, and I grabbed my clarinet and ran.

I had a dream that night that seemed almost facile, too obvious. I was playing my clarinet before the gates of a fortress with many windows. You may deduce that I was trying to entice Sally to one of them, but more likely to enter the fortress of her life, proving my talent, proving I was worthy, if even only as a musician. But now I was being drowned out by sounds from within, an oom-pahpah band, a lusty Liederkranz, "Valderee, valdera." The fortress, I realized, was actually a Munich beer hall. Sally was nowhere to be found. She'd taken a hike . . .

Now I spend my dream-filled nights bobbing on the waters of False Creek, in the shadows of the great bridges that connect to the heart of the city, amid the throng of seiners and pleasurecraft tied up at Fisherman's Wharf. For one so scattered as I am, it is good discipline to be confined aboard a boat, where tidiness rules, where everything must have its place. I've undertaken a spate of sanding and varnishing, trying to achieve the mindlessness Nataraja counsels.

I tell myself that I'm lucky to have the *Altered Ego* to escape to. The true claustrophobic revels in the freedom of the sea. Upon her, I've spent many pleasant days and nights, often weeks at a time, drifting about mystical Desolation Sound, the Charlottes, the Broken Islands. She's a graceful lady in her polished dress of teak and mahogany. Everything I need is here. There is a small shower in the head. There's standing room in the main cabin, barely. I have my books. I have my clarinet, my jazz collection, Grappelli, Parker, Peterson. I have loyal Vesuvio, my Italian aluminum racing bicycle.

Yes, Sally will quickly realize she's made a tragic blunder in sending me away. Life will be a bore without Timothy Jason Dare.

But just yesterday, I'm sorry to say, she buttressed her will. When I called to suggest lunch, she gently put me off. She *did* want to see me, she felt "tenderly" toward me, thought the idea of dating was fun, but she was worried about her resolve weakening, worried that she'd never achieve the strength to break free, to test herself as an independent person for the first and maybe only time in her life. I listened bleakly, uttering vacuities like "I understand" or "You're to be admired, darling." Then she said she thought it in our best interests "not to actually *meet*" for several more days. It's like kicking smoking, she said.

Why had I never – in my cruellest nightmares – imagined that the former first mate of the *Ego* would suddenly mutineer and cast this solitary sailor afloat? I thought I'd known Sally's every caprice. How had I missed the signs? I, of all people.

I have been butted from Sally's life like a cigarette, dismissed as a bad habit. That's what has finally driven me to the couch: the casualness of it all, the flip finality. I'm comforted only by the thought that worse could happen. I could be slashed to death by Bob Grundison. Wouldn't Sally Pascoe be sorry then?

CHAPTER THREE

Date of Interview, Thursday, July 31, 2003.

Timothy arrived ten minutes early, but on the wrong day, thinking it was Friday. He was even more excited and disturbed than on our first session, so I was obliged to ask another patient to wait, promising Tim twenty minutes.

Yesterday, he received an anonymous note in the mail, *You are next.* The writer had sketched a heart shape below the words, pierced with what could be a sword or an arrow. Tim has taken it as a death threat, though I urged him not to jump to conclusions. I reminded him it isn't uncommon for therapists to receive bizarre notes from former patients.

I fear a paranoid disorder is at play. Not for the first time, he ascribed his burdens to "mysterious powers," mystic or divine conspiracies "to fuck up my head."[1] The note, he says, has been

---

[1] I have determined that Tim is not religious, and he disdains psychic phenomena as "irrational folk legends." So his talk about being subjected to the whim of divine spirits seems a form of avoidance.

"working like a worm into my brain." He claims that "Grundy is watching me again." He is vague about why he is so certain of this. "I can sense him, smell him almost." Yet he never sees the man he presumes to be Bob Grundison.

He became more settled after we talked it through. I assured him we would do more work on it tomorrow, on his regular day.

Slow down and relax, okay? Let's allow things to settle for a bit.

I'm sorry, I'm a little shattered, I haven't received a good death threat in years. Red-ink lettering. A dagger through the heart.

It looks more like a sword. Or an arrow. What do the words mean to you, *You are next?*

This is from Barbara Loews Wiseman's killer. I am next.

Have you called the police?

Of course not, I'm not going to have them rooting through my patient files.

Then what have you done about it?

Gave it to Dotty Chung, a friend, a private eye. She knows Grundy. She used to be with the city, lead officer on Dr. Wiseman's murder.

It seems like a feminine hand to me somehow. Cupid's arrow . . .

Bob Grundison is not Cupid.

Date of Interview: Friday, August 1, 2003.

Because of difficult personal circumstances, I cancelled all patients today except for Timothy Dare, who arrived breathless, excusing himself for being late. He'd been stopped en route by a police-woman for bicycling without a helmet. He explained to her he'd lost it somewhere. Subsequently, we found the helmet in my waiting-room closet, where he'd left it yesterday.

This is another graphic instance of his absent-mindedness, which is apparently not simply a consequence of his stressed state. He feels it is part of his "characteristic behaviour pattern." He also forgets appointments with his patients. Twice last winter he had to buy replacement raincoats. He is able to laugh at this. In fact, during his recounting we both laughed, a welcome tension release for me.

He rode up in the elevator today, which I took as an encouraging sign that he's trying to come to grips with at least one of his phobic responses. He was much more relaxed than yesterday, and revealed a side that is both compassionate and entertaining.

However, Tim appears no closer to reconciling himself to the loss of his partner – his self-esteem has been damaged by this – and I fear he's regressed to the point of pursuing Ms. Pascoe surreptitiously.[1] The possibility must be explored that he is projecting onto Grundison his own regrettable behaviour with regard to Sally. He has had odd and frightening dreams relating to her imminent departure for Munich.

Aside from several minutes of tape, these clinical notes are transcribed from memory, though I jotted a few reminders while we sat on a park bench. I wasn't functioning in top form, for reasons the excerpt below will make clear.

I'm sorry, Allis, about yesterday, barging in.

That's fine. If you like, we can take a little extra time today, I had a hole open up. That's a terrible way to put it. My next appointment had to be cancelled . . .

You aren't looking well. What happened? Did you lose a patient?

---

[1] I would not call this activity, which continued until she left the country, stalking.

I'm afraid so.

Oh, my God, I'm sorry. Suicide?

His faculties of observation are so well tuned that he seemed able to read this from my distracted manner and slumped posture.

Carbon monoxide, he locked himself in his car. He couldn't live with awakened memories. Parental sexual abuse.

That's terrible.

He was coming along, his energy level had improved, he was no longer talking about the worthlessness of life. Though that should have put me on alert, that's when one suddenly has the energy to implement a suicide plan.

Whatever you do, don't take on the responsibility.

I know I shouldn't. It's hard to put that aside, though.

Look, maybe you need to take the rest of the day off. I'll come back next week.

No. I can use some company.

It feels ominous that I'm filling the space of a dead man. Let's not waste a summer day – how about a walk in Stanley Park?

⁂

As we strolled from your Denman Street office to the mowed margins of Vancouver's great park, we traded roles; I listened and counselled. I hope I was of some help to you in this, a therapist's worst horror: the catharsis with morbid consequences. Just remember: Things happen. Don't listen to the whispered seductions of Self-reproach and her evil sister, Guilt. Confront them, unmask them, send them fleeing.

But yes, be sad, don't be afraid of that. It's to your credit that you cared so much for this religious, trustful, and troubled young man – too young to have been toughened in the trenches of life. One can't be a therapist without empathy. One can't be empathic and not be hurt. Is there another profession so emotionally exhausting?

And doesn't that speak to the fact that the suicide toll is so high among our own colleagues?

When you said it felt good to be able to talk to someone, I wondered about your husband, the media consultant – isn't he someone? I suspect Richard is a busy man with all his public relating.

I could see your shoulders lift, your tension ease as I launched into stories from the Kafkaesque world of Timothy Dare. I was pleased, finally, as we picked our way among the goose droppings by Lost Lagoon, to make you laugh. I play the sad clown well with my tales of seeding the town with coats, caps, and scarves. Not to mention the occasional file. It is as a result of one such lapse, and its awkward consequences, that I'm up on charges. They're seeking a scapegoat over a boondoggle caused by my losing a patient's file – but we'll get to that.

As for Grundy Grundison, maybe I am inventing a spectre. Dotty Chung had a casual chat with the babysitter, Lyall DeWitt, who said Grundy was home on the evenings I thought I spotted him. He told my sleuth Grundy faithfully attends classes at SFU and rarely makes trips into the city, and never alone. Dotty suggested I take a little holiday.

I've decided I'm making too much of that note, *You are next.* You're right: what therapist has not, now and then, received garbled, menacing letters? I've persuaded the courts to sentence many wrongdoers to penal or mental institutions. Any one of them could be my correspondent.

So am I not showing progress? Note that I took the elevator down as well as up, and didn't implode in panic. Note that I am now cognitively aware of former irrational thinking.

If only the dreams would go away. They seem to foretell doom . . .

This one, for instance, Saturday night, after too much wine and loneliness. Aware, even in sleep, that Sally would not be there to greet my awakening, I went deeper, into a Stage I-REM dream featuring (yes, it's back) an oompahpah band in lederhosen serenading Sally as she signed copies of her latest, *Miriam Runs Away from Home*. I was struggling toward her table. I was late. So far, this dream is as obvious as a fart at a funeral.

But it becomes tangled. My progress is halted by a banjo player, who says, "He's vaiting for you." *Who's* vaiting for me? Sally disappears without as much as a curtain call, and I'm in a panic, lost in a crush of people propelling me to a car. Then I'm in the front passenger seat, Alpine vistas below, brakes screeching as we fishtail around a bend, and I can't escape – the door handle is missing.

I look at the driver, and an even greater fear grips me. He is in a robe, wearing a false beard, and as he removes it, I see Bob Grundison – he is the spectre of death . . .

Whereupon I bolted upright in my cot in the bow of the *Altered Ego* and banged my head on a beam. I was in a sweat, tangled in my sheet like a mummy.

He's vaiting for you. Help me with this one, Allis. Why was a banjo player even *in* a brass band? Why was he serving as the messenger of Death?

As I wandered about the *Ego*, numbly brewing tea, I was returned to the real world by the discovery of a hair clip among my socks. I'm continually finding scatterings of Sally from our sails together. A sketch pad, vistas of Desolation Sound cross-hatched in soft pencil lead. Her spare toothbrush, a tampon.

I sat down to camomile tea and dry rye toast and ascorbic acid tablets and garlic pills – a breakfast routine so ritualized that Sally (in a bad mood) claimed it drove her around the bend. A shiver wriggles up my spine as I consider that bend, and now we see how free association helps unravel the metaphors of dreams: her brakes are screeching, my door handle is missing, we go off the road.

I am no aficionado of cars, though I occasionally ride in a taxi or with Sally in her Saab. One can at least escape from a car (given door handles); elevators and airplanes make for a far grimmer test of courage. My preferred conveyance is Vesuvio. Astride it, I can whisper through the streets at night, unseen. I can wheel silently past the bungalow on Creelman Street to ensure that Sally is safely at home, her car in the driveway. Occasionally, when I cruise the alley, I see her silhouetted behind the wide windows of her studio.

So far, I've not seen any man being entertained, though on one occasion, at dusk, I saw her entering a Kitsilano pub with the queen of punk, Celestine Post, who collects men as some do buttons and pendants, who knows the singles bars. From a vantage point outside the open door, I watched them spread maps and books on their table. Michelin maps? *Frommer's Guide to the Single Men of Italy*?

The next morning, I called Sally on my newly purchased cellphone, and claimed false surprise and falser delight when she told me Celestine has snapped up the cheap ticket to Europe offered by Chipmunk Press; they're leaving in a few days. I take relief only in the fact her tripmate isn't, for instance, Ellery Cousineau. (A frequent flier who owns a Cessna and has told Sally he'd like to "take her up.")

Sally has promised to meet me on her return. She's promised we will talk . . .

Enough of that. I haven't told Sally about the strange note. Let her have her carefree holiday, unaware that someone is *vaiting* for me.

Or is that someone you? You're waiting, silently demanding: Open up, tell me about your father, stop blocking. I will, I will . . .

At Beaver Lake, in the silence of Stanley Park, you sat on a bench to make notes while I watched dragonflies dart among the floating lilies and listened to the shouts of red-winged blackbirds.

As we walked along the seawall promenade, I must have sounded as effusive as a tour guide. Was I being tiresome? You didn't need the local booster to point out the convoy of sailboats bobbing in the wake of a grunting tug, the North Shore mountains gazing disdainfully at us.

Welcome to my world, Allis. I've studied by San Francisco Bay, visited Boston and New York, travelled Canada by train. But where else would any person of average sanity prefer to live but here in Vancouver, my enclosed, familiar, coherent world? I'm a product as well of its West Coast eccentricity, its manic depressiveness – morose and soporific in the winter rains, kinetic, vital when the sun crawls from hibernation.

We must have looked like an odd couple in that park. Dishevelled me, in my old khaki shorts; graceful, ever-fashionable you, in your long, belted skirt. Do you remember, on the seawall, how I pulled you from the path of three careless line skaters, and almost tripped over my own feet as you and I made contact? And do you remember how I averted my eyes when we came upon a hand-holding couple too obviously in love? What did you surmise? That I was unable to bear their happiness?

(The book fair in Bologna will be a long series of cocktail parties. People engage in aberrant behaviour at conventions. Celestine Post will set no good example. I must confront these concerns. It's no vast calamity if Sally has a fling. She has to get it out of her system. She'll love me the more when it's over.) And I realized: I was being selfish – I'd merely lost a companion; you were grieving a loss of life.

A thoughtful stillness came over you, and I let you stay there a while, only too aware of how my distress pales in the face of your young man's death. In a perverse way, that realization has begun to work as therapy for me. I must not take matters so much to heart. Things happen.

I was glad I was able to divert you from your thoughts with my account of the bizarre trial of Huff versus Victoria Dare. An arcane message to me from Clinton Huff bears deep analysis, so let me replay the scene.

First, as a preface, late Sunday dinner at my mother's house – an unpretentious frame structure in working-class Grandview, just off Commercial Drive. I'd stopped off at the Kowloon Moon for takeout (I've never mastered the kitchen; without Sally, my life has become a restaurant), and as I toted in the steaming cartons Victoria was at her computer dashing off one of her eighty-dollar-a-pop obituaries.

This is her latest business venture, writing death notices and seeing to their publication in newspapers, where her own ad also appears in the classified columns. (*Unable to find words for your loss? Literary Consolation Services will be pleased to help.*) Composing euphemism-laden obits nets her a better income than did her last job, managing a used-book store, but she finds the work boring.

Maybe, as well, it influenced her choice of genre for her novel, though deeper factors were at play: her father was a mortician, and both he and her mother drowned in a float-plane accident when I was seven. (Birth of a neurosis. You were expecting something more tangled and obscure?)

Victoria greeted me with a hug. At fifty-two, she seems even more striking than in her youth: tall, slender, black hair streaked with white falling to her waist. Expressive eyes that don't always let strangers know she's teasing. She still smokes, against my advice.

She printed out her latest obit and asked me to critique it. *Until his brief ailment brought his heart to its final pause, Pops, as he was fondly called by relatives and friends, remained an avid gardener, whose roses were the envy of his neighbourhood.* I told her I was reminded of Emily Dickinson.

Sitting beside her printer was a pile of manuscript. Victoria is hoping this new novel will sell more than the thousand hardcovers of her first effort. *When Comes the Darkness* didn't make it into paperback.

Over corn soup and garlic prawns we talked about Sally, whom Victoria has known for nearly three decades, having replaced, in part, the mother Sally lost in childhood. They remain pals and share secrets. Sally had come by the day before, Victoria said, but they didn't talk much about our separation.

"I didn't press her, we hardly raised it. My attitude was: If she wants to vent, I'm all ears and sympathy. But we talked about Europe and about my inexpressibly revolting trial."

"Yes, and did she mention any male friends she might be seeing?"

"I don't think she's ready for that."

"It might take a little time – is that what you're saying?"

"Honey, this is just a hiccup. She needs a break from you – she's an artist, it's hard to be creative when someone is pinging off the walls. You're too wrapped up in the drama of all your incessant emotional crises. It would help if you somehow restructured your life a bit, got your act together." Victoria is an expressive talker, her hands active, emphasizing points with chopsticks.

"I *am* getting my act together. I'm seeing a shrink. Allison Epstein, who wants to dig into my childhood. That involves you."

"It's always the mother, isn't it? There's a whole industry out there blaming mothers. I've no doubt she's a part of it."

I was perplexed that she was so defensive. Was she afraid of stirring up the working-mother guilt that has always oppressed her? I was a latch-key kid, and somehow she blames herself for all the time we couldn't spend together.

Victoria abruptly changed the subject: she had her own crisis, her libel trial. She was set upon my coming to court, to meet with her lawyer, to help him get a handle on Mr. Huff.

The lawyer, John Brovak, is from the bull-in-a-china-shop school of litigation. Notorious for his lack of subtlety, he's reputed to have once mooned a judge in open court. I'd recommended against hiring him, insisting she didn't need a lawyer – her publishers are represented by a respected Queen's Counsel. Her response: "I want a good old-fashioned brawler in my corner. I want someone with oversized testicles to take on the evil dwarf."

She was needled at the Q.C. for having proposed a nuisance settlement of thirty thousand dollars – ten times the advance she got for the book. She wants vindication. It is only a coincidence that the fictitious Clint Huff has a living counterpart who also happens to be mayor of a small town. She'd picked the name at whim – it had a rural, good-old-boy flavour.

In the novel, Mayor Huff commits ritualized, sadistic murders, and the real Huff has been on television, taking such vigorous umbrage that one might conclude he's revelling over his time in the spotlight. He is quite eccentric, though not without intelligence – apparently he is a capable English teacher. Adding to the weight of his claim is that he physically resembles the short, stocky, bespectacled killer in the book.

The non-jury trial, at the New Westminster courthouse, has been assigned to Judge Betty Lafferty, who, when in practice, had a history of defending the downtrodden. It is feared that she might favour the mayor of Jackson Cove over the well-heeled defendant publisher. Clinton Huff has no Q.C. in his corner; he is, in fact, representing himself, and not well. His try for an injunction against distribution of *When Comes the Darkness* has been thrown out; the book is still in the stores.

When I arrived by taxi, early, I found John Brovak outside the courts by the stern-faced sculpture of Sir Matthew Baillie Begbie, an infamous nineteenth-century hanging judge. (He is recorded as once having told a jury *they* should be hanged for bringing in a wrong verdict.) Begbie was clutching a pipe, Brovak a cigar. He is in his late forties, tall and burly, with a nose that has seen repair work, unkempt even in his black barrister's robe, looking as if he'd hurriedly dressed for Halloween.

"Huff's a fruitcake, Tim, active in the Libertarian Party, which attracts oddballs like flies to shit. His hobby is suing the government." He showed me a file. "Look at this, the guy refused to fill in a census form, and he took it to the appeal court."

There were other legal challenges in the file: to the firearm registry law, to various acts and bylaws. Judges had rejected his suits in peremptory fashion, often with one-paragraph decisions. There seemed sufficient evidence for a preliminary diagnosis of compulsive litigious disorder.

"You'll thank me for bringing you here, pal, you'll have a couch doctor's field day. He's got his own Web site. You want more information about how to challenge the government, log on to FreedomFirstForever.net."

"I don't want him to know I'm on a watching brief. Don't announce me."

Brovak told me that Huff was in the second-floor corridor, could be easily identified by the leather elbow patches. "He looks friendless – I don't think there was a big turnout from Jackson Cove. Can you imagine those fucking suits – offering him thirty grand."

I left Brovak to his cigar and made my way upstairs. Milling about near the courtroom were a small assemblage of the curious and a few reporters. The man I took to be Clinton Huff was wearing a checked sports jacket of a cut popular in the 1970s and was gazing solemnly at a larger-than-life print of a bejewelled Queen Elizabeth II and her consort. Huff is about fifty, balding, no moustache to compensate – instead, a flared structure of trimmed beard on chin and jowls. It makes him look leprechaunish.

As I walked past him, he turned my way and for some reason began to gape at me with a puzzled intensity, as if I were the last person on earth he expected to see on the second floor of the New Westminster Courthouse. I've had no previous connection with this man, so assumed he'd mistaken me for someone else. I was dressed too casually for him to think I was but an interested spectator.

Finally, he approached. "Excuse me, would you happen to be consanguine with anyone in Jackson Cove?" A precise, formal manner of speaking.

"Consanguine?" His use of the word startled me.

"It means related to."

"I don't believe so."

"Forgive my presumption."

I would have pursued the matter but court was assembling, and this odd conversation was aborted.

In the spacious oak-panelled room, I found a seat on the front row with a view in profile, at the far side of the counsel table, of Sanford Whitaker, Q.C., grey-templed and lean, an affected expression of boredom – letting us know this case is almost beneath his dignity. Victoria was behind him, as were two representatives of her publishing house, New Millennium Press.

Clinton Huff sat not far from me, at the near end of the counsel table, a determined set to his face as he neatly arranged a formidable array of legal texts.

Judge Betty Lafferty, a pleasant, unaffected woman in her mid-forties, caught my eye as she surveyed the room and smiled. That caused Huff to turn in my direction, with a look of curiosity if not suspicion.

Brovak was the last major actor to arrive, striding down the aisle with his briefcase, swinging it up on the table directly beside the mayor, crowding him. This brought about the first tussle of the day, as Huff asked, "Is this not the plaintiff's side of the table?" Brovak merely responded with a grunt as he sat and brought out his files. The strategy was to be close and intimidating.

Huff rose to complain that this invasion of his territory was unfair. Lafferty listened politely, then just as politely urged Brovak to offer Huff more elbow room. "I think you should extend the courtesy, Mr. Brovak. It's a small request, and he's not represented."

Brovak moved his kit a few feet, positioning himself almost in front of me. "Okay, but fair warning – just because he hasn't got a lawyer, I'm not going to treat him with kid gloves."

"I would never expect that of you, Mr. Brovak. However, I intend this to be a fair hearing."

"Well, that's good, if I take it you're inferring that the court won't be bending over backwards for any individual here."

Huff wasn't cowed. "I think *implying* is the verb the learned counsel was seeking. My Lady, I'm well able to represent myself. I not only teach English, I can read English – as well as any lawyer, and perhaps better than many. The sum and substance of this trial is what is in a book."

"Let us hope it will be as simple as that," said Judge Lafferty. "Do you have an opening statement?"

"Yes, it is my position that the defendants were at worst malignantly purposeful and at best criminally negligent in incorporating me into a horror novel. I have several authorities here that speak of a duty of care in defamation cases."

Lafferty's eyes widened, perhaps in alarm, as he opened one of his texts. "This isn't the time to make argument, Mr. Huff. We have to hear the evidence first."

Brovak twisted toward me and said in a stage whisper, "This is right out of *Alice in Wonderland*." Huff turned and caught Brovak, still facing me, point a finger to his head and twirl it.

"My Lady, before I continue, as a point of procedure, can I have the man identified with whom my learned friend was sharing a jest?"

Lafferty puzzled over the request for a moment. "That gentleman is Dr. Timothy Dare."

"And what, pray, does he do?"

"He is a psychiatrist. I believe he's also the son of the defendant, Victoria Dare."

I presume Huff's researches had told him something about me, though obviously he hadn't seen my photograph. He seemed startled.

"A psychiatrist . . . yes. I note he isn't sitting with his mother, and I would appreciate knowing if he's here for any other purpose."

"Mr. Huff, I think you should get on with your case."

"The Rules of the Supreme Court state that I've a right to know who the opposite party's witnesses are." Clearly, he had primed himself in the law.

Lafferty's politeness toward the plaintiff may have provoked this bluntness from Brovak: "Well, if you want to know, Mr. Huff, he's here to analyze you from a mental point of view."

Sanford Whitaker, Q.C., grimaced. Clinton Huff seemed indignant.

"I haven't decided yet whether to call him as a witness," Brovak said. "Right now, he's just here to watch you."

Victoria smiled at me and gave a triumphant nod.

Again, Huff was prompted to call his evidence. He glanced at me, then passed to the clerk a hardbound copy of *When Comes the Darkness*. "This is Exhibit One, and an audited statement from New Millennium for their last financial year will be Exhibit Two." The combination of Brovak's effrontery and my mere presence was having an effect: Huff's voice was strained, his facial musculature tight. "I call as my first witness: me, Clinton W. Huff."

He was facing me as he took the oath but avoided my eyes. "May I commence by pointing out I've been a secondary-school teacher for twenty years and have been twice elected mayor of Jackson Cove. In both capacities, and particularly among a number of students, I have been the subject of ridicule since this book was published. I will now read some of the iniquitous passages. May I see Exhibit One?"

He turned to a bookmarked page and cleared his throat. "'Clint liked what he saw beaming back at him from the mirror. Yes, he was a jolly, suspender-slapping, beer-swigging, clap-on-the-shoulder kind of guy, well liked by the folks of Bogg Inlet' – note the use of the proper noun, as in Jackson Cove, as well as the maritime connotation – 'five years an alderman' – in my case it was also five – 'and now, after four failed elections, mayor.' I won on my third try and have been re-elected."

He saw me jotting notes on the back of an envelope and went into a throat-clearing stall. "Fourth try, if one were to count the federal election in which I ran. Excuse me, my Lady, but must Dr. Dare stare at me so rudely?"

"Try to ignore him, Mr. Huff."

"Yes. Page twenty-seven. 'Clint had a special date tonight' – and by the way I, too, am a bachelor – 'so he figured he'd put on one of his good suits, the one with the bold check' – I happen to own such a suit. And farther down, 'He always liked to smell good on his dates, so he slavered his face' – I suspect *slather* is the correct word, even for this colloquial manner of composition – 'with his favourite cologne, Chanel pour l'Homme, before going downstairs. When he put his ear to the trapdoor he could hear the woman wailing. "Don't worry, my dear," he called. "I'm coming."'" I have a trapdoor in my house that leads to a root cellar."

Huff carried on gamely, with frequent stops for water, reading these passages to a courtroom silent but for the soft thump of keys on the court reporter's steno machine. From time to time, he'd flick a look my way. At one point, Brovak, sensing the curious energy flow between me and the plaintiff, pretended to confer with me, causing Huff to lose his place in the text. When he ran out of coincidences, he recited a bloodcurdling scene, a rape victim choked to death with a wire cord. He finally stalled when a spectator made a noisy exit from the gallery.

"You don't need to read the whole book, Mr. Huff," said Lafferty.

"This material goes to the issue of punitive damages. The Clint Huff pictured here isn't merely a disreputable character, he is a sadistic monster. He obtains sexual release through murdering innocent women. Even the school principal asked me – thinking it was quite a joke – if I would be playing the part in the movie."

"Well, that's just it," said Brovak, rising. "People who know you think it's all a joke. No one takes it as intentional. No one sees you as a sadistic monster."

"I was subjected to malicious gossip and humiliation. For Christmas my class gave me a bottle of Chanel pour l'Homme."

Brovak boldly carried on, though he hadn't been called upon to do so. "Where is Jackson Cove, Mr. Huff?"

"Do you want to answer counsel's questions now?" the judge asked.

"Yes. I've nothing to hide. Jackson Cove is in the West Kootenays, on the shore of Arrow Lake."

"How many people live there?" Brovak asked.

"Three thousand, four hundred and fifteen."

"And do any of these good folk think you're a serial killer?"

"I would submit that the test is whether one is held out to opprobrium and ridicule."

"Yeah, there was so much ridicule you were re-elected mayor two Novembers ago – *after* the book came out."

"Yes, but in the meantime, someone went around stencilling *Wanted* on my posters. It was ignominious."

"I'll give you another big word, Mr. Huff." Brovak emphasized each syllable: "Coincidence."

"Of course the defendants will fall back on that, but they were, at the very least, grossly negligent in not doing a name search."

"They're supposed to call every town in North America to see if there's a Clinton Huff in it?"

"I am not unknown. I ran as an independent in a federal election. My name was in the newspapers, on television – not often, but a few times during the campaign. My photograph was shown on the CTV network, and the *Nelson News* did a feature article on me."

Here was a man who'd never achieved the level of importance he felt was his due. But I felt something deeper was at work – his anxiety about psychiatrists argued that he kept secrets he didn't want revealed. I noted how orderly were his files and binders and papers, two pens and three sharpened pencils lined in a perfect row. The language of tongue and body, as well, was marked by the rigidity of the obsessive-compulsive personality. I wrote on my envelope: *Neurotic camouflage? Fetish? Hiding shameful ritual?* I wasn't expecting the effect this had on Huff.

"My Lady, may I be permitted to see what Dr. Dare is writing?"

"No, Mr. Huff." Lafferty's patience was finally waning.

"The *Supreme Court Rules* state that I have a right of discovery of all written material."

By this time I was feeling sorry for Huff, but paramount was my concern for my mother. If there was merit in the negligence argument, was she at risk? As a layperson, I wasn't sure. So while the judge was explaining the law of discovery to Huff, I conferred with Brovak, suggesting a line of attack.

Thus armed, he began softly. "Mr. Huff, have you ever met Victoria Dare?"

"No."

"Are you aware of any reason – like maybe she never studied every loser's name in the election results – that she might know your name?"

"I'm not privy to what she knows."

"Well, Mr. Huff, Victoria Dare never heard of you. And you know what, *I* never heard of you. Nobody in this courtroom ever heard of you. In fact, I don't think anyone outside Jackson Cove has heard of you."

Huff's voice broke. "Who do you think you are, impugning my name? I am a respectable person. I demand a little consideration!"

He might have been admonishing some miscreant in class. He was close to unravelling, and Lafferty must have seen this too, for she ordered the mid-morning break. Huff almost stumbled from the witness box.

The gallery slowly cleared, and Victoria signalled me to join her outside, pantomiming puffing a cigarette. I was about to join her but had a premonition Huff was standing nearby – perhaps it was his body heat, the smell of anxiety. I turned to find him staring at the note I had jotted: *Neurotic camouflage? Fetish? Hiding shameful ritual?*

His expression can be best described as a soup of helplessness and fury. He was unable to look at me or speak. He retreated to his table, picked up his briefcase, and walked unsteadily from the courtroom.

Outside, I watched him move slowly down Carnarvon Street, his head bowed. Victoria demanded to know my thoughts about him, so I told her about the note, his reaction, and my hypothesis: Huff held some shameful secret that had little to do with being defamed in her book.

When he turned the corner, we presumed he was walking around the block, clearing his head, but that was the last we saw of Clinton W. Huff. He didn't reappear after the recess, and a search party couldn't find him. When court finally resumed, Judge Lafferty, despite urgings, declined to dismiss the action, and adjourned the trial *sine die* "or at least until the plaintiff can give some explanation for his sudden absence."

The few reporters went off to write their stories. Brovak, mounting his Harley-Davidson, said, "Well, they've heard of him now."

Likely, Allis, my guess that you had lost a patient through suicide stems from the fear that tormented me after Huff disappeared: I worried I'd driven him to take his life. But he's surfaced in the Jackson Cove Hospital, where he's being treated for stress problems. In the meantime, the publishers have withdrawn their offer of thirty thousand dollars. (I tried in vain to persuade Sanford Whitaker, Q.C., to pay it, to salvage some of the man's pride.)

But I doubt that this chapter is closed. Clinton Huff took umbrage at the firearm registration law, so it is likely he's among our armed citizenry. Have I made another mortal enemy? And there's the consanguinity factor. Who is my Jackson Cove look-alike?

I passed through the place once, with Sally, on a camping trip in the Interior. A tourist town, a minor ski hill, a warm springs (so tepid that the local Chamber of Commerce can't make false claims), and the funky old Jackson Cove Warm Springs Hotel. I read somewhere they've converted the main street to resemble a Swiss village: false-fronted shops, ornamented balconies. (A motif of my recent dreams: a coincidence?) The town is perched on the western bank of Arrow Lake – about a hundred kilometres from Nelson, where Victoria begot me.

Do I dare go to Jackson Cove to probe the rumours of consanguinity? What confounding truths might be revealed?

CHAPTER FOUR

Date of Interview: Friday, August 8, 2003.

I had telephoned Tim on the weekend to tell him, in the event he needed to reach me, that I was taking a few days' holiday but would be back in time to see him today. He acknowledged my need for a break, wished me a relaxing time, and suggested we cancel for this week. But I found him in my waiting room at about three p.m., looking forlorn. I had other patients, and I wasn't able to see him until five o'clock. Afterwards, since I was free for the evening, I joined him for dinner.

I can't say he's suffered a severe relapse, but some of his earlier distracted thinking and erratic behaviour patterns have re-emerged. There have been several significant stressors: another hand-printed note with a threatening connotation, an extremely odd "therapeutic" session with his patient Vivian Lalonde, a difficult encounter with the professional discipline committee, and, just yesterday, his regular appointment with Bob Grundison.

Outweighing all this, however, is the absence of Sally Pascoe, who left a week ago for Munich. He has received what he calls a "profound message" in a greeting card she e-mailed him from an Internet café in Switzerland. He continues to have problems coping with being alone, and – a step forward, finally – has realized how much she kept his home and social life organized. He is now paying more than lip service to his admission that he took her for granted. Indeed, he seems almost lost without her. She aided him in a cluster of small ways, in grooming and appearance, going shopping with him for clothes, reminding him to wear a tie for court, ensuring his socks matched.

The challenge I've set for myself isn't an easy one: I may be able to help him understand his possessiveness, the pressures he places on Sally, but does he have the will to change?

I'm sorry to do this to you, Allis. I've done a backslide. I'm fine, actually, it was a little blip. How was your holiday? A ranch in the Cariboo, wasn't it? Riding trails, that sort of thing? Your husband go with you?

He paced, seemed disinclined to sit.

No, I went with Dr. Evelyn Mendel. Please sit down, Tim.

And how was it?

Relaxing. There was a lovely swimming lake. Let's find out what's bothering you.

First of all, this.

He handed me an unsigned note: I know where you live.

My gracious.

Grundison won't admit he sent it. I've moved my boat to a more secure location.

Tim, surely this is a police matter.

Dotty Chung is on the case, she's armed, she . . . Never mind, I got this weird postcard by e-mail, it's almost diabolic.

He showed me a colour printout. Against an Alpine background, a herdsman was blowing into an elk horn, presumably summoning his flock.

Sally chose it for its banality, that's what I first thought. And what's he wearing?

Leather shorts.

Lederhosen! And who does he look like?

No one I know . . . Who drew the glasses on him?

I did. Now he looks like Clinton Huff – who, incidentally, came to me in a dream the other night: Huff, in leather shorts, with a German accent!

What do you read into that?

There's some synchrony going on that I don't understand.

Okay, a while ago you had a dream involving a musician in lederhosen, prompted by Sally's planned flight to Munich. You told her about this dream before she left?

Yes, she thought it was uproarious.

And she sent you this card as a joke. And it prompted another dream. End of analysis.

Yes, but look at her note.

Above the illustration, a paragraph about beer halls and alpine meadows and rain, and it ended: Hurrying off for dinner. Love you (I do). Sally.

What do you find odd about her message?

Dinner with whom? Hans, the polka player?

Tim, tell me, what best describes your feelings about Sally right now?

Okay, I'll say it. Resentment. I'll acknowledge that. I'm going through hell while she's traipsing through the Alps. I know that's unworthy, I just . . . I *want* her to be happy, I just want a little piece of the action.

How do you deal with her when she's distressed?

Try to pin down the cause.

A typical male reaction. Men fix, women listen. Instead of looking for a quick solution, you may find that allowing Sally to unburden herself helps the worries come tumbling out. Ever buy her flowers?

What?

Buy her flowers, chocolates.

On special occasions . . .

And if there were no occasion?

I guess . . . not often.

What would you say to her if she were here right now?

He stalled, and a sadness came over him.

I love you.

What else?

Don't get tangled up with someone who will hurt you.

That seems less self-referential.

This second brief excerpt relates to Sally's oft-expressed concern that, according to Tim, she believes he tries to read her thoughts.

It was just a game.

A game that you constantly practised on her?

Well, yes . . .

How do you think she felt?

Invaded?

She might not have had much of a sense of privacy, Tim.

༺༻

I was Rasputin, the mad monk, in control of her every mood and whim. She had no place to hide, no secret door to a cozy, private place away from the needy, grasping neurotic. Had I been possessive to the point of obsession?

So all right, Sally, flutter away on your flight of freedom, enjoy your dinner with Hans, have your little affair, take two of them, buy a supply of condoms. I'll take my punishment like a man. I should have more incisively interpreted the e-mailed picture: after all, what does the horn symbolize? And this one seemed ten feet long.

She'd accused me of being, to use a polite word, inattentive in bed. Yet lately she'd shown little fervour herself. So maybe our love life had become platitudinous, a routine. Maybe *I* should have an affair. (And how close I've come to having one foisted on me.)

In my dream, however, Huff was hornless. He came in the form of a census taker. He didn't want to count me, and I felt forced to explain my existence. He didn't believe me, wanted proof. Was my father alive? I wasn't sure. Where does he live? I don't know. Somehow, I found myself in an Alpine village, where that same ridiculous band was playing. The banjo player looked like me, except older and scraggy.

Why this recurrent musical motif? Was I attacked by a banjo while an infant? I have some musical ability, but I play a respectable instrument, the clarinet. I hear you speculate – "He has suppressed fears he'll learn his father is a wastrel or a scoundrel – the banjo, an instrument he abhors, represents that fear."

I had another nightmare: I was in a courtroom. Herman Schulter was sentencing me to a hundred lashes. Wait – that wasn't a dream. That was Monday. Let me unscramble my thoughts, as I try to do each evening after my fevered rambles in your consulting room. I'll start with blue Monday.

I was late arriving at the hearing, which was being held in the Broadway Medical Building, a location obscure enough not to excite the curiosity of the media.

The room was closed to all but the three members of the panel and one witness, Dr. Irwin Connelly, my mentor, who has volunteered to scrutinize the state of my practice. This was the third in a series of time-squandering sessions – presumably an exercise in reforming me, so to speak, but the panel has the power to recommend my suspension, and if Dr. Schulter gets his way, it will. The other pair, Dr. Werner Mundt and Dr. Fred Rawlings, may lack the backbone to defy him. Rawlings is a retired lightweight, Mundt made so many errors in private practice that he was forced to take up teaching and is now an assistant dean at the University of British Columbia.

Schulter greeted me amiably, not at all perturbed that I was ten minutes late. He is a round-backed shuffling bear who hides his lack of empathy behind the false front of cordiality, and has managed to disguise his inferiority complex with a brilliant feat of over-compensation. Neither of us dares mention the word *rivalry* (or, horrors, *envy*): he was everyone's favourite forensic sharpshooter until – forgive the self-congratulation – Tim Dare rode into town.

(I wonder, also, if a remark I made in passing last year at a cocktail party – I was tipsy, others in the trade were present – reached his ears: something to the effect of him being an egregious poseur.)

A book I wrote about the profession, *Shrinking Expectations: Analyzing the Analysts*, was well received by reviewers but hasn't made me popular with certain colleagues, and both Schulter and Mundt are reputed to have taken umbrage. The latter is a known pill-pusher, and in one chapter I excoriate colleagues who play lickspittle to the drug conglomerates.

But Schulter was wearing his usual happy face today. "The good Dr. Dare finally graces us with his presence."

Though I'd vowed to be pleasant, my goal was to cut this nonsense short. "Before we get underway, I'd like to offer a few words of caution."

"Indeed you may."

"I'll try to put this as politely as I can. There's nothing to hear at this hearing. Since we last met, Dr. Connelly has been in my office, helping me sort out the shambles my last secretary left in her wake. He can tell you I'm trying to engage a replacement, and am seeing two applicants this afternoon."

"You promised a *few* words." Schulter prompted a chortle from the others.

"I'll keep it short for you then. This hearing is a waste of time."

Schulter, Mundt, and Rawlings all looked blankly at me. Irwin Connelly, sitting next to me, was tugging my sleeve, urging me – I supposed – to be more subtle, indirect.

"Because if there is any disciplinary action, I'll appeal. And I'll continue to appeal, and it will get into the courts, and the press will be alive to the entire scandal. And then the boom will come down."

The matter was of such delicate nature that the discipline committee had forgone the use of a lawyer to lead the case against me; it was thought sufficient that Dr. Schulter had a degree in law – though he'd never practised. Nor was there clerk or notetaker.

I lost a file a few months ago at the Pondicherry, the very restaurant I took you to, Allis, after having forced you to listen to an hour of my lamentations. I think I left it on the very chair you sat on. Not long after the file disappeared, a tidbit found its way into a column in that pugnacious magazine *Frank*. I think the line went like this: *What high-ranking member of the B.C. cabinet is so addicted to having a spanking good time that he is now seeing a shrink?*

Other media treated the matter as too hot a potato – *Frank* has been sued many times for libel – but the upshot was that I lost the Member for Shuswap South as a client. A byzantine political conspiracy followed, and a message was filtered through to the executive director of the College that Dr. Timothy Jason Dare should have his ears boxed.

I'd thrown down the gauntlet, but the panel was staring at me in an odd way. Schulter began to smile. "Would you be more comfortable without the helmet, Tim?" A graphic instance of a brain overburdened. I removed the helmet, saying lamely I thought I might need it for protection, and won a brief laugh.

Professor Mundt assured me that I'd nothing to fear from them – their only intention was to help me. I was so offended by this patronizing that I snapped something to the effect that I didn't need a unit from the medical Gestapo breathing down my neck.

Irwin felt it necessary to reprimand me. "Now, now, Tim, accommodate these people, they're doing a thankless job."

I decided to sit back and let them do their shtick, but just as Irwin was being called upon to describe his archaeological dig through my office, my cellphone rang. When I took the call, Schulter allowed himself a frown of impatience.

On the other end of the line was Melissa Leung, a legal aid lawyer. She urgently required my services in Provincial Court to prevent a gross miscarriage of justice. A seemingly sane man was about to be thrown into a mental institution by an alcoholic judge.

"Give me fifteen minutes." I rose. "Gentlemen, I'm sorry, I have an emergency. Please carry on without me."

I remembered to grab my helmet as I left. I heard no protests, though in the sullen faces of the panel I could read the suspicion that I'd prearranged my emergency. I learned later that Schulter recessed the hearing for several weeks – he is a patient hunter, and will stay in the chase.

The Provincial Courts were about two klicks away, on seedy lower Main. The quick route to the Downtown East Side is over the Cambie Bridge, swooping around the behemoth that is B.C. Place Stadium, gliding downhill past Pigeon Park, where the homeless huddle on benches, then quickly to Cordova and Main, skid row, to the fortresslike bunker that houses our criminal courts.

The miscarriage of justice was in recess as I entered the court. Melissa Leung, a short-haired waif not turned thirty, was at a table struggling through a ten-pound medical text.

"I'm lost somewhere between catatonic immobility and inappropriate affect."

Those terms had been used in evidence by Dr. Endicott Sloan, a trencherman to the Crown who bills for three or four opinions a day. He was in the gallery, looking uncomfortable at my unexpected presence, as he awaited cross-examination.

Melissa's client, a street person in his fifties, was charged with assault, though witnesses said he was defending himself from bullies. Sloan had typed him as schizophrenic, therefore unfit to stand trial. Were his opinion to hold, the accused, despite a compelling defence, could find himself lost forever in the bowels of Riverview, his trial held in abeyance until, if ever, he's pronounced cured.

Melissa looked weary. "I just walked in on this today. They wouldn't give him legal aid and I felt sorry for him. We can't pay you anything, he's just a drifter."

"No problem."

"He can't seem to respond to anyone. I had fifteen minutes with him, and he refused to say a word. Maybe he's not too aware of what's going on around him, and maybe he's slow – but I don't think he's crazy."

Harvey Bigelow, a pink-nosed judge whose career has stopped giving meaning, is never one to doubt the word of Crown experts, and was reluctant to let me see the alleged offender. "I'm anxious to get on with this." Meting out justice was interfering with his more liquid activities.

But I was permitted a few minutes with the accused, in the courtroom. This gentle giant, as he shambled in, seemed about as catatonic as Dr. Sloan. He was confused, though, and it took me a few minutes to determine his real difficulty – he was both hearing and speech disabled, and when presented with a writing pad could only crookedly write his name. But he responded eagerly to my hand signals, knew some rudimentary sign language, and showed no signs of illness beyond a below-median intelligence – and given that he'd survived so long on the street I wasn't sure of that.

Sloan, watching, must have realized his error. He is one of those doctors who lard their scripts with jargon: any inappropriate ornate phrase will do. But I avoided embarrassing him, and after a quiet tête-à-tête with the prosecutor, the charge was withdrawn and the accused released to the street. Sloan could not look at me.

I've gone on at length about this episode because it's an example of the kind of shoddy forensic practice that *should* draw the attention of a medical inquisition. Dr. Sloan didn't innocently mislay the file of a person of reputation. He talked to a penniless vagrant for about ten minutes, found him unresponsive, certified him insane, and practically sentenced him to life in the Coquitlam River gulag. (A full critique of slipshod forensic work is, by the way, to be found in Chapter Five of *Shrinking Expectations*.)

The scene is also useful in sketching a typical picture of your patient on the job. I work both sides of the street, selling my services to the Crown for the occasional felony, more often going to bat for some outcast on legal aid. In this line of work I make less than the average chicken farmer in Jackson Cove – bills for taxis, restaurants, and severance to departing secretaries add up – so I supplement with a private clientele.

But bravo! I succeeded in hiring a secretary that afternoon. For some reason I've attracted a series of fingernail-polishing misfits, three of whom quit on me, two were let gently go.

I hired James Lombardi, a former patient, a manic-depressive (a term I prefer to the politically correct Bipolar I Disorder), who saw my classified in the *Sun*. James had just been fired as private secretary to a local tycoon after an unauthorized spending spree (I assume he was off his lithium). He is a business-school graduate, a fifty-one-year-old workaholic, dapper and balding. He is dying to work with me. "I worship at your altar."

I'm the saviour who originally diagnosed his condition, who grabbed him by the lapels when the news sank him lower, who told him a mood disorder was a sign of artistic temperament: look at Van Gogh, Tchaikovsky, Shelley. Now he draws with a rough talent and composes saccharine poetry. Otherwise, he lives a normal life: a West End apartment, a gay francophone partner who is teaching him French, breakfast at the Bagel Bar every Sunday morning.

His disorder is mild, but a careful monitoring of his intake of lithium carbonate might keep him marginally manic as he whirls through the tasks of bringing order from chaos (just joking). I gave him a tour of the office, and he managed not to grimace too much, though he said my billings were a shambles and the computer, a relic, would have to go.

The first test of his lasting powers came on Tuesday, his first day of work, as he was opening my mail. I'd already told James about Grundy Grundison, warning him to beware of letter bombs, but the note, *I know where you live*, still jarred him.

"Oh, my. This is *very* Vincent Price."

I picked up the envelope by the corner. It was postmarked Vancouver, had been mailed Friday. Again: no return address, mine written in the kind of block capital letters a young child might print, as was the note. I was undecided whether to confront Bob Grundison or to play a more slippery game. He was to make his first regular visit to my office on Thursday.

"Surely I'm not about to meet this ogre?"

I told him Dotty Chung would be here too, hidden.

As I phoned her, James went back to his tasks, humming the theme from *Jaws*. My initial rush of fear was now tempered by the chilling reassurance that my suspicion, with its slight, worrisome air of paranoia, had grounds: someone *was* stalking me.

Dotty and I met for lunch at the Granville Island Market and took our sandwiches to the pier. This former industrial area, a bridged wedge of land in the heart of the city, has been custom-gentrified: corrugated metal is the motif of many of the smart shops and cafés. It was a fine day, a few clouds clinging to the mountains, tourists in abundance, the little tub of a passenger ferry disembarking a convoy of Nikon-toting Japanese, but I was morose, lacked appetite. Dotty listened silently as I threw fish-burger crumbs to the gulls, then said, "First thing we're going to do, buddy, is move you."

A note about Dotty Chung. She's a bristle-haired compact tank, in her late thirties, single, blunt, and streetwise, the best cop the city ever lost. I met her after she finally graduated to detective – sex crimes, then homicide – but after a dozen years on the force, she found herself still unable to adapt to its air of patriarchy, and resigned. She runs her private investigation business not far from where we were lunching, in the Pier 32 office complex, and lives a stone's throw away in Sea Village, in a two-storey houseboat.

And now she's my good neighbour. Her proposal was startling in its simplicity. I'd move the *Altered Ego* to Granville Island, tie up at her houseboat. She'd be my first line of defence.

She waved away my protests. "I need the company. My casa is your casa. I'm hooked up to city water." I'm not sure if she was intimating my deodorant had worn off, but the thought of a real shower was tempting. We were a stroll away from Fishermen's Wharf, so we walked over and soon were aboard the *Ego*, motor-ing back to Granville Island.

Dotty sat with me at the stern, studying the note. "You sure he doesn't mean your house in Kitsilano?"

"In the course of his prowls, he must have discovered that I'm no longer there. Note the sense of triumph, of discovery. '*I* know where you live.'" Sally will have to be alerted. But how do I reach her?

Dotty had pulled together some information on Lyall DeWitt. College swim team, soccer, karate club. He is the only male among four siblings, his mother a homemaker, stern but not uncaring, his father a plant foreman, a former steamfitter, up from the ranks. Lyall graduated from the Vancouver police academy after his B.A., but instead of joining the force accepted a job with Grundison Inc., where he was put in charge of its Calgary security office. The only blemish on his record: an assault charge for bashing an intruder against a concrete pillar at the Grundison Tower, for which he was given a discharge.

I may have no alternative but to waylay Sally at the airport – it would be unwise for her to stay alone at home. I've thought of moving back there until her return, but I couldn't abide the ghosts and memories. Could she be persuaded to move into the *Ego* with me, forgive, start afresh?

We pulled into Sea Village, a gated community of houseboats, where we moored behind Dotty's twenty-horse runabout. I just had time to use her upstairs shower, a luxury after the dribbling hose in the *Altered Ego*'s head, before retrieving Vesuvio and returning to the office for my afternoon clients.

Until I walked in, I'd forgotten that one of them was Vivian Lalonde. She was wearing a revealing short, fluted skirt, a halter top. More conservatively dressed, she'd still be stunning, but she has a need to advertise herself, to set her snares for the men she feels compelled to play with and discard. I hadn't seen her for a few weeks – she'd cancelled once, perhaps feeling awkward at having kissed her broken-hearted therapist, but I preferred to ascribe that to empathy or pity. And then her father had rewarded her, for the latest failed marriage, with a Mediterranean cruise.

She seemed in well-enough spirits, chatting to James as he set up my new computer and colour copier.

"And here he is now," he said. "In a little less of a frazzle, we hope."

The threatening note was still on my mind as I led Vivian into the consulting room, so I was ill-prepared for what happened. The session began routinely enough.

"How's the summer shaping up?"

"I'm taking a course at Emily Carr."

"Good. How was the cruise?"

"I was surrounded by old fogies. I spent a lot of time thinking."

"About what?"

"You, Timothy."

"In what sense?" A tickle of concern here.

"I'm not sure . . . about what you're going through, I suppose. You were so sad that morning."

"Thank you, but I'm fine."

"Really? You seem on edge. Are you and your wife still . . . ?"

"Apart, yes." I found myself being peremptory, businesslike. "All right, Vivian, we have an hour, make yourself comfortable."

She sat on the overstuffed armchair that some patients prefer to my couch – they can stretch their legs out on the equally over-stuffed footstool. She was looking brightly at me, sitting up, chest thrust out, legs crossed. "Forgive me for thinking about you."

Her tone was teasing, but I didn't bite. "Still at your parents'?"

"I rented a bachelorette in the West End, thirty-sixth floor. Incredible view, all ocean and mountains. I like to study on the balcony. You should come up and see a sunset, it's dizzying."

I shivered. "How did your parents feel about this move?"

"Oh, I fought with Dad, he wanted me to stay. I told him I have a life, and I'm going to live it."

"You seem in better spirits."

"Yes, I think I've really got hold of myself. It's like . . . I know where I'm going, I feel I have . . . a target in life?" She kicked off a shoe and stretched a leg across the footstool, then tucked in her top, bringing her breasts into sharper relief.

"What sort of target?"

"Goals. Not just about my career — life goals. I'm going to get somewhere. I had another bad marriage, so okay, forget it. Life is what you make of it, some things you have to put behind you. You've taught me that. I'm young, healthy, independent, not bad to look at, and I'm not dumb. I actually have this sense that . . . if there's something out there I want, I can get it."

I heard an echo from an earlier session: she'd recalled, as a child, her lavishly generous father telling her she could have anything she wanted. Certain suggestions become imprinted.

"I'm too comfortable to get up. Would you mind?" A seductive pout as she pointed to the water cooler.

She couldn't take her eyes off you, Sally had said. True, but Vivian was a relentlessly flirtatious young woman. Sadly, one too often sees this trait after a history of sexual abuse by the male parent. I say no more, Allis — I shouldn't have said that. But a transference seemed now to be occurring — not the positive transference of psychiatrist as surrogate daddy but as prey. She was displaying, signalling: I am free, I'm available. Was I her target in life?

I fetched her the water, wondering how to divert her from a mistaken course. "Vivian, I want you to tell me what's going on in your head right now."

She drew her leg from the footstool, curled it under her. "About what, Timothy?"

"What do you think you're really saying to me?"

A shrug. "What are you reading?"

I didn't hand her the glass but placed it on the table beside her. I caught a scent of her: clean, lightly perfumed. I confess I felt unbidden stirrings. Instead of reaching for the glass, she grasped my hand. I resisted the urge to jerk it free.

"You're nervous about something, Timothy, and I think I know what it is. Don't think your own messages haven't been received.

You're not so hard to read yourself. Do you remember when you put me under?"

The euphemism, I presumed, was in reference to my having hypnotized her during our third session. That is a tool I use only on rare occasions, when there seems no other way to remove a block. She had seemed unusually keen on trying it, but instead of recognizing, for instance, a reciprocated childhood passion for Daddy, she produced blander, though not insignificant, memories – her favourite pre-adolescent game was pretending to be a princess.

"I was under your control. You could have done anything you wanted, and I'd wake up and wouldn't remember it. Anything you wanted."

I tried gently to pull away, but she came with me, like a hitched caboose, rising from her chair, tightening her grip on my hand.

"I could sense you wanting to touch me, I was waiting for that. But you were too shy. For a while afterwards, I wasn't sure what was happening between us . . . until you let your hair down. Remember? You poured your heart out to me, you shared so intimately. And there was such a deep connection."

Suddenly she pulled my hand to her breast; for a moment, I couldn't move – my hand felt impaled there, a burning erotic wound. I finally staggered back, but again Vivian moved with me, and in a scene from a French burlesque, we fell in tandem over the footstool onto my Oriental rug.

Alerted by the thump of falling bodies, James entered, then hesitated, as if unsure if he'd stumbled into an unusual form of bodywork therapy. I pried Vivian's fingers loose from my hand and bolted to safety.

"Oh, *excusé moi.*"

"It's all right, James, a little accident."

He managed to blank his face of all curiosity – an exceptional feat, I thought – and stepped out and closed the door.

"Vivian, I'm going to have to recommend another psychiatrist." She remained seated on the floor, looking wounded.

As I was explaining to her that she shouldn't feel embarrassed, that this was hardly a historical first in therapy, she looked woeful and begged forgiveness. She'd misread me, she'd comport herself more appropriately, she felt secure with me, I'd helped her so much already.

I heard an inner whispering: end this doctor-patient relationship. Beware, Nataraja had warned: she doesn't have all her buttons done up. But wasn't that the point of my working with her? I earn my livelihood from the unbuttoned, and, given the precarious state of that livelihood, doesn't she have the right to the therapist of her choice?

I told Vivian to forget any romantic expectations: she was in therapy, I was merely her guide. She was free to come back in a week's time to tell me if she accepts those terms.

She was limp and resigned as I ushered her out, and I worried that she might become deeply depressed – she is subject to severe mood swings. But she politely took my hand, murmured more apologies, and slipped out.

This seemed a textbook case of the sort of attachment that can be inflicted upon those in the business of dispensing empathy – patients will often misread therapeutic closeness. I'd shown myself to her in a moment of vulnerability, and a defenceless man presents an adorably pitiful picture: the heart goes out, and as a by-product, the woman feels empowered.

James urged caution. "May I suggest that you not see this femme fatale again in the absence of witnesses." He was right: this is a dangerous age. Guardians of correctness prowl the land, and I am at risk if I continue to treat this histrionic woman, with her shallow emotions, her constant demands for approval, praise, her need for excitement. I resolved to ask her permission to explain the matter to her father, advise him that I am bowing out.

I managed to survive two more patients that day before wobbling home astride Vesuvio to spend the evening pacing on board the *Ego* and playing Cole Porter tunes on my clarinet before a night of sleepless tossing in my bunk.

The next morning James handed me a computer printout – the card from Sally – and you know how unsettling I found it.

By mid-week I'd started to flail, and was poorly armed, therapeutically speaking, for Grundy Grundison's first appointment with me, on Thursday.

Despite the repulsion I felt at his savage execution of Barbara Wiseman, I'd made up my mind to do justice to my task as watchdog. I can't deny being lured by the handsome fees, but a more compelling inducement is my interest in the criminal mind. This is yet another aspect of your patient that bears examining – his fascination with evildoers. Bring them all to me, your mass murderers and serial killers, send me all you've got.

Why am I so gripped by the act of murder? I suppose we are all curious about the unpredictable, about whether we are capable of such a deed. It also struck me that an equally powerful explanation is at play: I've been seeking a reason to send Grundy back to Riverview. A minor slip – drinking, breaking curfew – might not banish him there, but any violence would. Even a mailed threat.

Dotty Chung was with me at the front window overlooking Fourth Avenue, aiming a camera, as Lyall DeWitt parked the black minivan and he and Grundy stepped out. While making their way to the building, Bob nudged Lyall, directing his attention to an attractive woman waiting for a bus. I couldn't hear Grundy's remark to her, but she ignored him.

"Couple of pigs," said Dotty. She is an unapologetic feminist, once divorced, and holds most men in little favour. "I'm taking cover." She retreated behind the back staircase door, which I usually keep slightly open for ventilation.

When James came in to announce that they had arrived, I observed them in the doorway behind him, whispering. I read Grundy's lips: a decorative phrase, then a syllable that begins as the upper teeth stroke the lower lip. Possibly V, more likely F. As in fag.

I invited them to sit. Lyall took a chair against the library wall and Grundy stretched out in the armchair. I asked a few neutral questions: summer school ("Haven't missed a day"), his daily regimen ("Classes, library, maybe a game of touch football or baseball, then I usually head off to bed"), relations with mother ("Fine, just great"), father ("All those business trips, I think he's too wrapped up in money").

I asked him to expand and was rewarded with sanctimony: we are put on earth to help others and not just ourselves, it's the Christian way, do unto others. Clearly, behind Grundy's outward show, lay enmity for the distant, uncaring father.

"Do you go out at all?"

A pause. "We went to a bar once."

"Where?"

"I don't know. Out in Whalley. Hector's or something. They had a great country band."

"He didn't have a drink." This from Lyall, who was looking about the room with a bored expression, scrutinizing the book spines, the degrees on the wall, Sally's canvas.

"Dr. Dare knows that," Grundy said. "It's a given."

"Then why did you to go to a bar?"

"Good music. Thought we'd do some talent-spotting, look over the girls."

"Did you meet any?"

"Exchanged a couple of phone numbers. Is that sort of thing off limits – making new friends?" A grin to disguise the slightly acerbic tone.

"And are you making any?"

"Not really. No enemies, either, thank the good Lord."

He smiled boyishly, patted down a tuft of hair. The charm he occasionally practises is typical of the sociopathic personality: the lips smile, but the eyes lie.

"How about old friends. Still see any of them?"

"No, I'm pretty well out of touch with them."

"Old college buddies?"

"Well, there's Lyall here, of course."

I let a few moments pass, locked onto Grundy, waiting.

"I don't think you could call me unpopular. I had lots of friends until this . . . until my difficulty."

"Tell me about some of these friends."

"Ben Thomas, my neighbour for years . . ." I could sense his brain whirring, trying to grapple with the concept of friendship. "A couple of guys in minor hockey. Will Stasnik, he's had a few stints with the Sharks."

"As a child, who was your best friend?"

"Karl, from grade nine, Karl . . . I can't come up with his last name."

No mention of girls, and I expected none. "But now, as you say, there's Lyall."

"He's stuck with me through thick and thin. He's the only one who visited me in Riverview."

"What do you and he share?"

"In what sense?"

"I'm interested in what makes your friendship tick." Lyall was beamed on me now, frowning.

"Same interests in sports, movies, that sort of thing. Similar outlooks."

"Like?"

"A belief you can improve yourself, get ahead, return some good to the world."

"What do you say to that, Lyall?"

"I'm easy." When asked to amplify, he said, "I go along with whatever's going on, Doctor."

A hazy response, but maybe he didn't want to commit himself while Grundy was here. Lyall bothered me, his relaxed, confident posture, a manner of dress that seemed fascistic: pressed brown shirt and pants, hair recently shorn – the fastidious sort who tend to be structured, inflexible, and narcissistic. It wasn't much of a reach to discern an authoritarian family background but also, in counterpoint, an inner rebelliousness. Behind the rigid adult who takes pains to preserve cleanliness, one often discerns the defiant child who flings soiled toilet paper.

"And you're with Bob pretty well most of the time."

"Me and my shadow."

"Do you ever see him writing notes, mailing them?"

A pause. "I'm not with you."

"It's a simple question, Lyall."

"I simply have no idea what you're going on about." I found the mocking lilt to his voice irritatingly flip.

"What's all this about, Dr. Dare?" said Grundy.

"I have a question for you, Bob."

"Sure."

"Do you know where I live?"

I watched for the first unstudied reaction but saw only confusion – perhaps affected, for Grundy is a capable performer. Lyall, however, looked away, settling his eyes on the self-portrait by Sally: her mischievous smile, her wide startled eyes – the artist as seen in a mirror, dappled smock, paint brush in hand.

"I have no idea where you live," Grundy said. "Why would I?"

I passed him a photocopy of the second hand-printed note.

After reading it, he said, "No way, that would be a crazy thing for me to do." He dropped it, as if hot to the touch.

"Let me put this as gently as I can. It wouldn't be the first time you did a crazy thing."

"Dr. Dare, I wouldn't dream of threatening you. You'd look for any excuse to . . . I don't mean it that way." He set course upon a sea of bathos: "Whatever feelings you hold about me, I don't return them. I've the greatest respect for you, and if anything, my history, the terrible thing I did, has made me aware of my need for the kind of help you can give me. I'm trying to understand myself, that's why I want to be a psychologist – I want to know how a person's sanity snaps."

Although this glib outpouring only reinforced my mistrust, I knew, as a behavioural scientist, that I must acknowledge my bias and struggle to retain an open mind. After all, why would Grundy risk sending such a note, threatening the man who could return him to Riverview?

I looked at Lyall, who was now examining his manicured fingernails. It occurred to me that Lyall, possibly the owner of a warped sense of humour, might have written the notes, but it seemed unlikely that he'd want his ward to be shipped back to the keep. That would jeopardize his career with the Grundison empire.

I decided not to mention the earlier note, *You are next*, or my still-niggling notion that Grundy had been following me, and instead told him I was giving him the benefit of the doubt. I asked how he was getting on with his in-house anger therapy with Dr. Martha Wade. Grundy said he was learning to pause before reacting, to give his brain a moment to catch up and his body to cool down. He was learning new cognitive skills, self-control methods. What he was reciting was a memorized list.

Had there been any recent episodes of anger? Absolutely not, sir. Even minor? That's pretty well under control, Doctor. Irritation? Ill feelings? He admitted to having shouted at the gardener for running a weed trimmer outside his window while he was studying.

I looked at Lyall. "He's been a pet bunny," he said.

"You're taking your medication, Bob?"

"Absolutely."

Buspirone, when he feels one of his "tensions" coming on. That's what he calls them: his tensions. They occur two or three times a week. I reminded myself to call Dr. Wade, to cross-reference our observations. What were her impressions of Grundy's smart-aleck buddy?

I saw them out, wished them well until the next visit. Dotty came back, grimacing. Grundy's cloying manner had grated on her too, but we agreed he didn't seem to represent an immediate danger. Neither of us could fathom why he'd send anonymous threats: his anger wasn't the slow, calculating kind — it erupted. And, frankly, he wasn't dense enough to compose such notes.

From the window we could see Grundy and Lyall at their vehicle. Grundy was plucking a parking ticket from the windshield, tearing it up. Lyall was laughing.

I recalled Barbara Wiseman's reference to a seething, barely suppressed anger she could not break through. *I sense a terror lurking within him, but its source and character are not clear.* What critical information was in her missing notes of their last session?

CHAPTER FIVE

Date of Interview: Friday, August 15, 2003.

Tim Dare arrived – at the correct time, on the correct day – agitated and wet, having been caught in a heavy downpour while bicycling over Burrard Bridge. It had not been a week "to wish on anyone," he said. I had to urge him to stop pacing, to lie down, to compose himself.

The significant events of his week – which he spoke of morosely but with interludes of rapid, animated speech – included a sudden move to a new office, Sally Pascoe's return to Vancouver, and another, as he put it, "fun-filled" episode with Vivian Lalonde, who has temporarily replaced Bob Grundison as the person he most fears. As well, he was bothered by another bizarre dream.

Again, he spoke of conspiracies being directed at him. When I suggested he might be seeking a means to deny his own responsibility for reordering his life, he seemed resentful, saying, "I don't buy it. Someone, somewhere, is trying to drive me insane. Let's mail him an anonymous note, something that will fuck his head up."

Dr. Dare is proving to be a most difficult patient. He is bull-headed; he competes with me in the interpretation of his dreams; he closes off the early past; against my advice, he continues to resist using antidepressants. Despite all, he demonstrates qualities that many – particularly women – would be drawn to: he's vulnerable, unthreatening, and – when he wants – engaging. He elicits a maternal instinct: one wants to straighten his tie or tell him that his shirt is improperly buttoned.

But I think we both realize that deeper problems are at the nexus of his various fears and phobias. His life has been much defined by a need to find closure regarding his father, but he continues to pull away from the subject. We spend too much time in the present, too little in the past where the roots of his discomfort lie, the forces that shaped him in childhood.

When I asked him about significant childhood memories, he pondered, then told me his most traumatic memory was being separated from his mother during Christmas rush at a department store.

How old were you?

Three. My ochlophobia got fixed into place that day, on the third floor of the Bay. I was afraid I was going to be crushed. As a child, I was very impressionable, bedevilled by fantastical worries – Victoria used to tell me terrifying ghost stories.

For instance?

He refused to be diverted.

But so what? I still panic in groups of more than a dozen. I can't go to a crowded bar without breaking out in a sweat. I can't look two storeys down without swooning. I can't stand the sight of blood – I regularly fell sick during anatomy classes until I learned some coping skills.

Slow down.

I'm sorry.

Can we get back to your mother, Victoria?

Okay, she conceived me when she was seventeen, and somehow managed to nurture me while supporting herself through college on student loans and odd jobs. She spent every spare dime she had on my education, until the scholarships finally began to flow. She's superwoman.

How did she meet your father?

What's there to say? My father, Peter, the medical student. He used Victoria for his practicum in female anatomy by the banks of Kootenay Lake on September 2, 1967. He blew her off in the morning. She never saw him again. I have no real image of him, just what may be a fantasized description – tall, dark, spare, and, to use Victoria's embroidery, gorgeous. I've no idea who or what he's become.

What do you feel when you think about him?

A pause here.

I'm sorry, I can't seem to focus on that right now. I want to talk about what's driving me mad.

Note his tendency to control when he feels under pressure. Sally Pascoe must have felt it too.

Do you want to hear about the nude photos? I had an imbroglio with my landlord. I lost my keys. I've had to move my office.

Childhood traumas must wait their turn. His avoidance tactics test one's patience, but I have learned he needs to vent, to settle immediate concerns, before settling into a rapport with me.

Yes, let's hear about it, Tim.

⚭

I could hear your resigned tone, Allis. This was yet another instance of the patient sneaking out a side door to escape the past. The early years are critical, I agree, but however misshapen with neuroses, the man who grew out of childhood proved capable. He went to school, amassed degrees, set up shop. He led an imperfectly normal life.

Until the prankish Fates chose me for their sport. Why? Did they consider me weak and susceptible? Maybe they've selected me as a kind of lab rat, a stress experiment. How much voltage can the poor fucker take? I imagine them sitting around Zeus' throne, bored. *Just for fun, let's see if we can break this fellow's tenuous grip on reality.*

As an example, they conspired – using the services of a crafty terrestrial agent – to plant evidence on me of a salacious nature. They arranged to drive me from my place of business.

I'd been restless through the weekend, pent up in anticipation of Sally's return, but I kept a busy schedule: a long bike ride to Riverview to interview an alleged arsonist, an afternoon sail, dinner at my mother's on Saturday, at the Pondicherry the next night.

Nataraja's advice to his moping customer was "to get your ashes hauled." Take advantage, he urged, of the generous offer of that "knockout who barged in here a few weeks ago, hot after your body – *I* should be so lucky." The concept of getting my ashes hauled actually had some crude appeal – long abstinence from sex was causing me some physical unease.

On leaving the Pondicherry, I remained so preoccupied by thoughts of Sally that I began walking in a drizzling rain to the wrong home: to *her* home, on Creelman Street. I was almost at Kitsilano Beach when I remembered I'd come by bike to the Pondicherry, and had left Vesuvio there.

During my return walk, I had the sense I was being followed. It was a frightening feeling, but it was strong, in my gut. I glanced behind once and saw advancing, half a block down a poorly lit street, a hooded figure in a wide, flaring coat who quickly disappeared behind a parked van. I couldn't make out the features of this funereal creature – it was as if he'd emerged from my dreams,

Death's messenger. A few minutes later, I snapped a quick look back and he was gone.

While biking to Granville Island, I was followed briefly by a dark minivan. I couldn't shake that gut feeling . . .

When I entered the office on Monday with my takeout coffee and toasted bagel, James was already at his desk. He remains the bright spot in my life – my office looks every day less like a junk store – and I now wait eagerly for the next session of the discipline committee, at which I'll produce this prince as witness to the orderliness of my practice.

After passing a few pleasantries with James, I went into my consulting room to prepare for the day's patients. Soon, I felt the slightest nudging that something was amiss, and it was only as the coffee began to stir my neural cells that I realized that for the last several moments I'd been staring, in growing confusion, at Sally's portrait.

It had been hung upside down. By whom? Why? The building remains locked all weekend, the cleaners come only on Tuesday nights.

James was equally astonished and, fearing I might suspect him of negligence, assured me that on Friday, as the last to leave, he'd locked both the office and the downstairs door. Neither of us had been back since.

James directed a severe look at me, as if I were the culprit, and, producing his set of keys, asked if he might see mine. A search through my pockets generated a wallet, several coins, various crumpled reminder notes, and keys to the *Ego* and my bicycle lock. The office keys, on a ring with a nametag, were missing.

I can't remember when I last used those keys – not for a few days, because James had regularly been first to arrive at the office, last to leave. If some felon had come upon them and deduced from the nametag they were my office keys, why would he have been content just to fiddle with Sally's painting? Nothing of value seemed to have been stolen; our filing cabinets were unlocked. James checked the current files and they appeared undisturbed.

Now locks would have to be changed, and I'd be forced to endure the landlord's ire – this has happened once too often, Ivan Kolosky will say. He is seeking any excuse to get rid of me and the accountants who share my floor – the lease has a year to run and the ground-floor graphics firm is impatient to expand.

What message was I supposed to read in Sally's upside-down portrait? A threat to her? Grundy was, of course, in my mind, but I knew another who had the spite and brass to do this, Vivian Lalonde – but how would she have got my keys?

Ivan Kolosky arrived brandishing a copy of the lease, directing my attention to boilerplate requiring tenants to ensure building security. (There has been one similar incident, plus one false alarm when Sally found the keys in the laundry basket.) He was horrified to learn that a nametag was fixed to the keys.

He phoned a locksmith, then said, "I will pay you three thousand to go now, immediately."

My suspicion fastened on Kolosky – had he engineered this incident to send me scurrying from the premises? He has been known to prowl the building at night: I caught him once at ten p.m. testing my door: "Checking security, Doctor." I dismissed the notion as bizarre.

I explained to him I had too much on my mind to be seeking new quarters, then ushered him out.

I had lunch later with Dotty Chung, and we conjectured about Grundy being the office sneak-artist. I remembered the dark figure following me: Grundy's height. And what about Lyall DeWitt? He had stared, bland, expressionless, at Sally's portrait. Had I left my keys in the open where they could be swiped? I'm too loose with them, James has warned.

It didn't make sense that Lyall or Gundy would chance arrest for unlawful entry, but my mind was aflame with anxiety. I felt at risk. Sally was at risk. They know where I live. They know where I used to live.

Then I reminded myself – as I'm doing continually these days – that I might be devising paranoid scenarios. I sometimes wonder if I'm approaching a true illness, a DM-V 301.1 delusional disorder.

Dotty has taken an almost sisterly liking to me, finding much satisfaction in my male helplessness, and as we were going through my files, compiling a list of those with kleptomaniac tendencies, she offered a solution to my landlord-tenant problems. There is a vacant office below hers in Pier 32. I'd already tied up the *Altered Ego* nearby. Why not move my practice, as well, to Granville Island, with its bustling market, its galleries and live theatres, its relaxed ambience?

"And I could use the company," Dotty said.

I've noticed that she often seems lonely. With her heavy build, her rather flat, pugnose face, she isn't one to attract many male admirers; on her rare dates, she disconcerts her companions with her laconic manner – she eschews small talk. A failed marriage to a womanizing telephone installer has added to her distrust of men. Because of my general inability to fit the macho stereotype, I'm on her short list of exceptions.

"Anyway, you need someone to watch over you." She reddened, as if embarrassed by the borrowed lyrics, and turned gruff. "I want to be around if Grundy decides to have another psychotic attack."

I hugged her.

She took me on a tour of the space: it was bright, bare-walled, needed renovations. No elevator required: the rental space was just above ground level, with a balcony suspended over the water and affording a view of salt inlet and mountains and sky. Nearby are the Emily Carr Institute of Art and Design and the metallic glitter of Granville Island Hotel, with its micro-brewery.

I told James to negotiate the lease and to advise Kolosky I'd accept his three thousand dollars.

I spent much of that evening and the next day in a futile search for the keys – they hadn't been left at Riverview or on the *Altered Ego*. Then I discovered that my windbreaker was missing too. I'd worn it on the weekend, but where?

I could swear I had on a sweater when I visited my mother on Saturday, but still I went to her house that evening for a quick rummage. The keys weren't behind the cushions of the stuffed chair on which I'd sprawled, or in any closet.

Victoria put her writing on hold and watched – she prefers to work at night, through the witching hour. "I can't concentrate with someone prowling like a thief around the house. You should have your damn keys sewn into your pants pockets."

Over one of her herbal tea concoctions, I was treated to a discourse on Clinton Huff. Her adversary had risen wounded from the trenches, regained strength for the battle, and filed a motion to continue the trial.

The court jester, Victoria called him: "He ought to be laughed *out* of court." But benevolent, bend-over-backwards Judge Lafferty had agreed to hear his petition, and the hearing was set for the next day, Wednesday. I told Victoria I'd pop in. I've developed an interest in the case, in the bumptious mayor of Jackson Cove. I have some admiration for him, in fact – he isn't without nobility and resolve.

Distracted by my worries, I reacted like a stammering fool when Sally called that night from Rome, greeting me with a lilting "Hi, sweetie." I managed a garbled greeting, asked about her holiday. She was pleased with it but exhausted, was soaking her feet, blistered by her new Italian shoes. She and Celestine would be flying home the day after tomorrow, arriving in the evening.

I took a breath and began pouring out my woes: I'd received threatening notes, my office had been invaded, I was concerned not only for my safety but hers. I begged her to taxi non-stop to Celestine's and bunk there. I would meet her there and explain everything, she wasn't to worry. I'd received her postcard, had a laugh over the shepherd and his elk horn, the guy looks like some-one I met, it's a message, I'm being summoned to the mountains.

"Are you feeling all right?" she asked. I lied reassuringly, wished her a boringly safe flight.

As I cycled that night to the Pondicherry, continuing my quest for the keys, my mind was heavy with Sally, with an anxiety pro-voked by what she'd not said on the phone: that she wanted our life back as it was, that she'd been wrong to exile me from her bed.

At the restaurant, I explained my mission to Nataraja, who lis-tened, nodded sagely, then said God had given him the key to understanding. I admire his way of making the meaningless seem profound – in headier days, he had a hundred saffron-wearing followers.

"Please speak plainly."

"You left your jacket here."

"And where the hell is it?"

No other customers were within hearing, but he lowered his voice. "That looker with the long legs? She came in just after you left, winked at me, took the jacket from the chair."

Vivian Lalonde. "And you *let* her?"

"She said, 'Tim left his jacket.' I figured, okay, she'll give it to you. I thought you were waiting in her car, like you took my advice, made a date to penetrate the gates of divine paradise . . ." Nataraja began to look less confident in this theory as he saw the dismay in my face.

I sat down. I ordered soup. I berated myself. Vivian hadn't been concentrating on her studies, had failed the simple test I gave her. She'd stalked me to the Pondicherry. Seeing me leave without my jacket she'd filched it, found my keys in a pocket, entered my office in stealth that night to leave a jealous message: she isn't the one for you, Timothy, she is upside down, I'm right-side up, accept the fact she's gone from your life.

At the same time, I felt relief, for I'd been twitchy at the thought of the pet bunny and his keeper grubbing about with the portrait of the woman I love. I was beginning to wonder, too, if Vivian, not Grundy, excited my fears of being followed. I'd underestimated Vivian's obsession with me, it was deep, not some sudden fancy.

The next morning, I asked James to tell Vivian I was withdrawing my services and recommending she see Dr. Allison Epstein instead. (It seems to me she needs a good Freudian cleaning-out. You have the advantage of already knowing something of the file. Disinter *her* memories.)

I asked James to bring me the Lalonde file, and he produced a three-inch-thick folder bulked up by psychological tests and interpretive comments, some Rorschach and other test material, and my own scrawled, barely readable notes. When I riffled through them, I spotted an unsealed manila envelope, postcard size.

"What is this?"

"Those would be the *photos dénudé*, sir."

My jaw fell open. "Nude . . . how did they get here?"

"I assumed you put them there." James put his hand to his mouth. "Oh, dear . . ."

I fumbled the envelope open: half a dozen glossies of Vivian artfully baring all, stretched across a chaise longue as if modelling for Ingres. I hurriedly replaced them. I'd underestimated Vivian's capacity for mischief. What game was she up to? An attempt, obviously, to embarrass me in some way, possibly to embroil me in accusations of misconduct.

Unsure what to do about the photos, I told James to stash the file in his desk, then I raced out to catch the next act of Victoria's drama. I slipped quietly to the back of the courtroom, hiding behind a woman with big hair, not wanting Clint Huff to see me – I was reluctant to exercise my supposed powers over him; it would feel like bullying.

Huff had the floor and was speaking well from a prepared text, seeking forgiveness for having walked out when we last assembled. He had been taken ill, had found his way to a medical clinic. His proof was a note from a general practitioner: hyperventilation, high blood pressure. Bed rest had been ordered. If the trial were allowed to proceed he was prepared to produce many witnesses who would attest to the fact he isn't a serial killer.

John Brovak and the publisher's Q.C. described themselves as, respectively, blown away and incredulous at the plaintiff's effrontery in demanding such pampering. Brovak growled, "Why don't we give him a teddy bear, too, and tuck him into bed?"

But Betty Lafferty acceded to the request of our brave bantam rooster, warning him he may ultimately have to pay the defendants' costs.

"I shall take that chance, my Lady. I remain persuaded of the rightness of my cause."

Day books and palm computers were consulted. The lawyers' calendars were crowded, and it was agreed the trial should recommence in October.

After court recessed, I came upon Huff again staring at Queen Elizabeth and Prince Philip on the mezzanine wall. He spotted me as I was passing by and, instead of faltering under my fearsome analytical gaze, denounced me.

"What do you know? Nothing! They betrayed the one great shining light of this world."

Presumably by "they" he meant his defamers, and he was the shining light. Though perhaps he was speaking of the royal couple.

I take some pride in my ability to unveil hidden personas, and realized that in his case I had merely done a surface scan. I felt challenged by him, by some mystery deeply hidden. What *did* I know?

I wanted to ask him who in Jackson Cove resembled me, but he hissed at me like a snake. "Fetish? You're a fraud. I intend to expose you."

I was startled by his vehemence. He rushed away. This threat – added to some events I'm about to share with you – continues to persuade me that my life is beset by some vast, complex Shakespearean plot. What are the odds that one person can have so many problems dumped on him simultaneously? Clearly if there is no logical explanation, the answer lies in the realm of the arcane. Or are there solutions hidden in the clues that float through my dreams?

Consider the one that came to me that night. I was in a Roman city, following Sally. She'd flit in and out of view, running from one colonnade to another, stopping to peer at me, hurrying off again. Then I heard someone behind me saying, "Open him up," and I realized I was also being stalked – by not one but a throng of ill-wishers: Vivian Lalonde and Grundy and Lyall and the entire disciplinary board, all wearing togas, with Clint Huff trundling behind, a distant threat. But others were after me too, their faces hidden in their togas.

And there was someone else chasing me – someone who for the moment I feared more than the others. It was you, Allis, and you were the only one armed – you were brandishing a scalpel, ready to do business upon me.

(Upon coolheaded review, I'm unable to fathom why I so resist being opened up. I think it's just that there's too much of the present to dig through, too much going on, rattling me, blocking distant memories.)

As my dream continued, I found myself on a bicycle, gaining distance from my pursuers. The setting morphed into a country lane leading to a cluster of wooden buildings, a church, a store, a one-room school. I heard a banjo, lively music that seemed to lure me there. But as I approached, my way was barred by Irving Kolosky, who was locking the village gates. "You can't come here," he said, "without the key to understanding."

Then Huff materialized beside me, in his lederhosen. "He luffs you," he said. To luff is to sail close to the wind, so likely the phrase, deciphered from German-accented English, becomes "He loves you." Not *she* but *he* loves me. The words seem swollen with meaning, cryptic, ominous.

Freud has said that in our dreams, our *dialogues intérieur*, we keep a blind date with an unknown self. But what am I saying, so often, so confusingly, to my other self? I accept your theory that the village is my notion of Jackson Cove, that the dream reflects a repressed need to connect with my father. But why is the gate locked?

Or does the locked gate represent frustration? I've expended hours, weeks, months trying to trace my father's whereabouts. There are few clues – first name Peter, in his early twenties, a second-year medical student (but where?). I've tracked down every Peter enrolled in every medical school in 1967, made contact, made awkward explanation, and earned only regrets and sympathy.

A sudden insight: I fear the key to understanding; I lock that gate because I can't face the truth it hides. Peter is a failure. He never made it through medical school. He's a quack, he's in a mental institution, maintaining his frayed sanity through weekly electroshock. He is the village idiot of Jackson Cove. But Victoria claims she loved him . . .

James greeted me in the office Thursday with the news that he'd upped the ante from Kolosky to eight thousand dollars on guarantee of immediate departure. I decided, yes, let us make a quick break – a new start in a new space might help me escape my ghosts. I cancelled my appointments and we attended to the various tasks of departure – change of telephone listing, notices to friends and clients, hiring a crew of student movers.

Files were boxed, my five-hundred-volume library packed. By late afternoon all was gone but some of the heavier furniture, to be saved for tomorrow: two desks, filing cabinets, refrigerator, couch, armchair.

Alone now – James had gone off to organize my new space – I stood by my desk amid the dust and scraps of seven years of professional labour. I swept the desktop contents into a drawer: pads and pens, a loose shirt button, bicycling gloves. I'm too embarrassed to ask James to enter any of these drawers. I'll clear them out myself.

I brought out Vivian's file from James's desk, found myself perusing those nude photographs more closely. They're tastefully erotic, as one should expect from a design student: one assumes she herself was the photographer, that she used a timing device.

Shamefacedly, I admit my body heat rose as I studied her in repose, lying on her side, lips parted, beckoning with an arm outstretched. I felt dismayed that I was reacting physiologically, and quickly put the photos down and went to the window.

The lowering sun filtered in wan and yellow; outside, the going-home traffic hummed. Into the emptiness came Sally, flooding me. In two hours I would be meeting her at Celestine Post's Gastown loft. I wouldn't be comfortable enduring Celestine's sardonic manner or dealing with the trauma of reunion. I didn't allow myself to hope Sally has abandoned her experiment in singleness.

I snapped open a beer, drank, paced, wandered down the hall for a piss in the washroom that I share with the accounting firm. They hadn't yet quit for the day, so I dropped in to say my goodbyes, had a whisky with one of the partners. I learned that Kolosky had offered them only twenty-five hundred dollars to quit their lease. I had the dubious honour of being worth more.

When I returned to my office, the door was ajar. As I entered, I smelled a familiar perfume wafting from my consulting room. I looked in: Vivian Lalonde was lying on her stomach on the couch, reading a book. As usual, she was wearing the barest slip of a dress, backless, held up by only a shoestring knot behind her neck. The dress was blood red, the same shade as the toenails on her raised, wiggling feet. Her skirt had ridden up, and between her parted thighs I could make out a furry pudendal shadow.

I pulled myself together and marched in, and gave her an arms-folded show of body language as I stood over her. "How did you get in here?"

"The door was open, Timothy."

"Why were you buggering about with Sally's painting?"

"I thought if you saw her in a different way, you might come to your senses. But I see she's disappeared from your wall. That's ironic, isn't it? Psychologically speaking." She looked around, at the dust shadow left by the painting, at the skeletal remains of my office. "You moving out, Timothy? Have I scared you away?"

I was irked by her casual attitude. "This appointment has been cancelled. Wasn't my message blunt enough?"

She turned on her side and put a page marker in the book. It was my own work: *Shrinking Expectations.*

"Relax, Timothy. I'm not going to bite you." She sat up. "I just came to return your jacket. Your keys are in it. You're really delight-ful, you're so absent-*minded.*"

There was my jacket draped over my swivel chair, along with her own coat: ankle-length, with a hood.

"I thought I'd request, as a last favour, that you sign this for me. Is that too much to ask?" A pout, as she extended the book. "'To Vivian, with love' would be nice."

Did she think me such a fool? "You've been stalking me, you filched my keys, snuck in here, and tampered with my files. *Your* file!"

I walked out to James's desk, swept up her glossies, strode back, flung them at her. Vivian watched with amusement as they flapped through the air and spun across the floor.

"What do you think you were trying to prove?"

"That I was worth a second look? They're from a class in photography, Timothy. They dared me to pose." She laughed. "They were shocked when I did. But they produced some interesting work, don't you agree?"

I must say I was rattled by her sang-froid. I fought for composure, said in a level voice, "I want you out of here, Vivian. Out of my life."

She sighed. "Still in denial. What a pity." Again she extended the book. "Just sign it then and I'll be gone. That's it, Timothy, then I'm out of your life, your muddled life."

I felt it unwise to continue berating her, scrawled a signature on the book, nothing more. I was desperate to believe she'd come to her senses, was seeking a final gesture, a polite closure. As she stood, tugging at her dress, there came to her face a look of melancholy, of acceptance. Seeing that, my anger died, and I felt a little sorry for her.

I urged her to continue her therapy elsewhere. (I gave her your card, Allis, and forgive me for that. You won't want to touch her after you hear what comes next.) I pompously told her I was sorry our relationship had taken an awkward turn, that I expected her to be a celebrated success in the field of design arts.

She walked to the uncurtained window, looked out on busy Fourth Avenue. "I hope you're not moving from here just to run away from me."

"The landlord is buying me out."

She turned to see me holding out her coat. Her eyes were wet. "And you're setting up shop on Granville Island." There was a slight hoarseness in her voice that I've learned is a harbinger of emotional display.

"Vivian, you must promise to stop following me."

"Do you think you can hide?" She continued to reject the coat, seemed in no rush to go anywhere, in fact perched on my desk – I sensed I'd lost the moment. "I've been doing a little research. Some newspaper clippings, your interview in *Psychology Today*. You don't like to travel. You hate crowds. You've had only one female relationship. That's what's amazing. It sounds so restricting. I'll bet sometimes you just want to explode inside with the need to break loose, to dare your heart to go where it wants."

"Please leave now."

"You don't know who your father is. It's wonderful you can admit that. You're so open . . . I can't talk to my father, I never could. But why do you lie to yourself about the important things?" She slid onto her feet, began advancing on me. I turned, made for the door, but she beat me there, blocked my path. "I'll never lie to you, Timothy. You once told me to stop playing, to be real. Okay, this is real. I'm real, look at me."

She reached behind her neck and loosened the tie. I found myself dumbly staring at her bared taut breasts as her dress floated down. She skinned it from her hips, kicked it free, then stood before me, calmly offering.

"My God! Vivian, get dressed and get out of here before I have the cops drag you out."

"Don't fight it, Timothy. Recognize the inner being, know yourself, your moods, your desires. It will make you whole again."

Where had she got that – out of some pop psychology paperback? In growing panic, I looked about for the telephone, but it had been unplugged and removed. As I checked my pockets for my cellphone – where had I left it this time? – I noticed, with dismay and humiliation, that I was starting to get an erection.

Should I have to explain this? There had been a long sexual hiatus. Vivian, need I remind the world, is superbly attractive.

—

"Don't lie to yourself," she repeated, aware now of the protrusion in my pants. "I can be everything she's not. I can be anything you want."

She reached for me and I fell backwards onto my desk, and she on top of me. Her hips were pressed against mine, grinding against them. "Damn it!" I yelled. "Stop this!" As I turned to avoid her mouth, I felt her lips slide along my cheek, a wet, red smear.

The events are distorted in memory, such was my turbulent state, but I know that her hands were tugging at my belt and that I resisted, pushing at her body, finally rolling free.

I managed to gain a standing position, discovering then that she'd loosened the belt, and that my trousers were slipping. "Vivian, don't be a whore. Where's your self-respect?"

She seemed astonished at my rejection; suddenly her face clouded. "You bastard," she hissed.

I picked her dress up and tossed it to her, and, pulling up my pants, escaped to the outer office, where, as the fates would have it (but not unexpectedly, given their caprices), I almost collided with Irving Kolosky. He'd just come in from the hallway, on silent creeping feet.

"I heard voices," he stammered. "Your door was open. I was just checking to see if the movers . . ."

His words trailed off into silence as he saw the longitudinal red smudge on my face, my belt and shirttails hanging loose. Then he peered through the doorway into the consulting room. I turned to see Vivian stepping into her frock, swearing, "You complete and utter total bastard."

I strode past the gaping landlord down the hall to the toilet, and after washing the lipstick from my face, returned to find Vivian gone, and Kolosky too. Likely he was wasting no time finding ears for his tale of debauchery in the shrink's consulting room.

You can imagine the scenarios that raced through my mind. My fear, of course, was that some garbled version of the facts would come to the attention of our wardens of correctness, and I would be faced with some prurient questioning into my conduct.

So the first thing I did when I gained the street was to find the nearest pay phone and call Irwin Connelly for some quick and desperately needed advice. I reached only his answering machine, but at least made sure I related the facts.

Then I went down to the Kits Pub, recuperating there until my hands stopped shaking, downing two double whiskys. My hormones were still racing through me, and I developed a headache. It was only when my bleary eyes made out the wall clock that I realized Sally must have arrived at Celestine's loft at least an hour ago.

It took an agonizing ten minutes to flag a taxi to drive me to the heritage building in Gastown where Celestine Post maintains home and gallery. I stumbled into the ground-floor vestibule, hesitated by the elevator, then attacked the stairs, five storeys up. I was breathless as I lurched into the loft, Celestine Post holding the door, looking at me as if at a sick cat come home to die.

"My God, it's Captain Phobia, drenched in sweat. He smells like swamp gas, Sally."

I panted, caught my bearings. Though only with one bedroom, the suite is spacious, with half-sized windows but many skylights, a spiral staircase to the roof, where Celestine likes to smoke pot. She's a competent artist, and her walls are covered in stark abstractions – slashes of brilliant colour. She's also non-representational in appearance, cerise hair, rings in her multi-pierced ears, green tights over her thin legs.

Sally rose from a chair, tanned and healthy. More beautiful, somehow, maybe after a visit to an Italian salon, her hair different, fluffier. She studied me for a moment, dared a subtle kiss upon the lips, then drew back. "What's this?"

I had washed the lipstick from my face, but she spotted a splotch on my collar, and her smile became a frown.

"You've been drinking. What's going on, Tim?"

"Everything. The world has gone mad. Maybe not, maybe I have. A patient just tried to rape me. They know where I live. I'm moving offices."

"Whoa."

"Have a hit of this." Celestine handed me a glass containing a liquid whose fumes caused me to gasp. Grappa, from a long-necked duty-free bottle. I knocked it back, excused myself, went to the washroom, washed the sweat from my face, stared at the baggy-eyed wretch in the mirror. I'd forgotten to shave that morning, my hair was tousled, matted.

It took me about an hour to summarize my Dadaist life through the last fortnight, and I finally achieved some sympathetic response. "You've every right to be the total mess you are," Celestine said. Sally expressed concern as I related my near-defilement at the hands of . . . I'm afraid I used the term *nymphomaniac*, now banned in the colleges.

My main worry, I emphasized, had to do with the notes. *You are next. I know where you live.* I didn't want Sally to be alone.

"Sally will stay right here. We're used to sleeping with each other now."

And who else? I wanted to ask. Sally, as if atoning for some guilt-inducing episode, took my hand, caressed my cheek.

We talked for hours, debating and conjecturing our way through the grappa, through the quality Bardolino Sally had brought me as a gift. Celestine claimed to find artistic inspiration from my dreams. Sally was locked onto the Huffian melodrama, to the hints of consanguinity. It is her view that the key to my happiness (to ours?) lies in the unearthing of my roots, my male inheritance.

I listened anxiously to their tales of travel for hints of moral lapses, becoming suspicious when not a single encounter with a man was mentioned, even in passing. Celestine enjoys her romantic adventures too much for such history to be blank. My concern for Sally (not jealousy, I'm over that) was as to her health; infectious diseases abound.

Finally, I asked, "Meet anyone interesting?"

"We only had eyes for each other, darling," said Celestine.

I turned, expecting to see her winking at Sally, but she was deadpan.

The women had begun to stifle yawns, so I made ungainly to my feet. Sally shepherded me to the door, Celestine finally granting us a minute alone. I had a hard time summoning courage to make a case for our reunion.

"How long will you stay here?"

"Not long. I love her, but she's too nuts. I'm not going to be denied my own home. I have to go back. You should think of going away for a while."

I shook my head. Escape would be cowardly; like Sally, I couldn't let fear rule my life. Again, I wondered if I was making too much of this. Maybe I wasn't being threatened, merely teased, however maliciously.

I plunged: "I could move back home, sleep downstairs. Just a housemate, of course, I'd just be there for your protection, nothing expected."

"Tim, I'm just not ready. I want you to understand."

"Okay, I do." But I didn't, and I felt the pain of renewed rejection.

As I stepped out into the gloomy hallway, she turned me about, came into my arms, holding me. "We'll talk, okay?"

"What went wrong, Sally?"

"I don't know. Maybe it was the time that you . . . You know."

I know.

CHAPTER SIX

Date of Interview: Friday, August 22, 2003.

Tim arrived wearing a baseball cap, T-shirt, and floppy shorts: loose, he said, so he doesn't sweat as much. He doesn't wear "that spandex shit." He has accelerated his training for his charity rally in October, *le prix de Okanagan,* as he calls it. He concurs with me that this is a healthy sublimation, a converting of his array of worries not only into an athletic effort but a worthy cause: all funds go to Médecins Sans Frontières.[1]

I've noted how his body, always lean, has become more sinewy with strenuous exercise. And he was in a sanguine mood, having come to a view that Sally "hasn't completely garbaged" him. There was, indeed, a brief coming together during the week, and it has given him hope.

I feel we are finally making progress with the difficulties that

---

[1] This event is to be run concurrently with the convention of the B.C. Medical Association in Kelowna.

caused their separation. I'm surprised that he was so slow to tell me about an interaction that occurred a few years ago, but the incident explains much.

As to my attempts to bring buried feelings and memories to the surface, he remains recalcitrant, though I have at least drawn from him more specifics about events surrounding his conception.

Almost miraculously, given recent history, no untoward incidents have occurred to mar his week – no threats, no letters, no awkward episodes with sexually assertive patients. All told, he presented as more emotionally stable than at previous sessions. His improved mood has had a salubrious effect on his appearance. A new face shows.

I suspect he has an unclear self-image, and doesn't realize he can be quite attractive when he smiles. His long hair was tidily knotted at the back, and he had remembered to shave.

I have to do another thirty kilometres before the sun goes down, hit the hills – there are a few stiff climbs in the Okanagan. Care to join in sponsoring me? I'm getting a hundred here, a hundred there. I'm soliciting the rich law firms I work with.

I'll put in a hundred. And five times that if you win.

That's clever. Encouraging my healthy mania. We're up to about fifty registrations already, looking to double it. We have categories for men and women, so there'll be two first prizes. I'm probably taking it too seriously, it's supposed to be a fun affair, pancake breakfasts, a barbecue at the finish. That's on Halloween – appropriate, because I've a sense my demons and goblins will decide to back off if I make a good showing.

Excellent, your spirits are up. Before we get under way, Richard and I are inviting a few friends over for dinner next weekend – on the patio if it's nice – and I was wondering if you'd care to join us. Seven or eight people – you won't find it oppressive.

Very kind of you.

We're at 55 Ridge Crescent, rather high up in West Van, I'm afraid.

May I ask Sally to come? I'm no longer banned from her life.

Of course.

We had a couple of evenings together. Working out a kink, something that happened a few years ago.

Have I heard about this?

I guess I've been containing it . . . I'll be honest . . .

Please do.

I feel ashamed, afraid of what you'll think. I hypnotized her. It was intended as a playful thing. We had come back from a restaurant, were relaxing by the fireplace – this was in the winter – and we got on the topic of the powers of suggestion. I offered to demonstrate.

He winced . . .

⌥

I accept full responsibility: it was at my urging. Sally was unsure at first – uncomfortable with the idea of not being in control of her thoughts and actions. But the more she hesitated, the more I tried to convince her that the exercise would be benign. I was her lover, her partner, her best friend: she could trust me above all others.

Coincidentally, at around this time, she'd briefly abandoned her children's illustrations in favour of the large canvas (landscapes, moody winter scenes), because she'd been having difficulty conceptualizing Miriam's trip to a country fair, and the carrot I held out was that I might help Sally pull out memories of a similar event she'd attended as a child.

Ultimately, she put down her glass of wine, took a deep breath, lay back on the rug, and said, "Okay, take me there."

I had always suspected that Sally was a good candidate for hypnosis. During a playful demonstration a decade earlier – no deep or even light sleep – she'd been shocked by her faithful obedience to a suggestion that she scratch her nose.

In a thrice, she was out – at the count not of ten but of three. Before taking her to the rural fair, I resolved to rid her of her artistic block (perhaps I shouldn't have taken that second glass of wine). You will be able to visualize, I promised, you will be pumped up with creative energy.

"Yes," she said. "I can feel it."

We dallied for a while at the fair, took in the judging of livestock, bought a candied apple, witnessed a pie-eating contest – we were having a fine old-fashioned country time. I wasn't expecting anything untoward. But then she remembered – relived – an incident. She was with her parents, John and Gwen, and was being a brat, pestering them to be allowed to compete for a fluffy teddy bear: one of those ring-toss games.

Perhaps it was the heat and dust, or there was a pathological determinant, but her mother fainted, collapsed on the sawdust. Unfortunately, her frantic father – I know John well, a loving man, and it isn't his style – blurted out a few harsh words at Sally, blaming her, as they knelt to Gwen. Medics quickly arrived. Gwen lay reviving for an hour in a first-aid tent, Sally standing by in guilt and shock.

Sally wouldn't have suffered the kind of overpowering trauma one banishes from memory had not Gwen been found to have a ventricular fistula – a hole in the heart. Two years later she died.

Sally didn't emerge from her hypnotic trance, but lay weeping on the rug. I suffered a loss of professional poise, began to flounder. I wanted to bring her back, but I hadn't told her what the release signal would be – I usually rely on a clap of the hands. Still, I thought, surely she'd awake if urged to do – but it was as if she couldn't hear my words. I tried, foolishly, clapping my hands. No response but a suddenly calm exterior. I gently shook her, and she opened her eyes – but they didn't seem to observe me.

She rose. She walked upstairs to her studio. She stood before her array of brushes and oils and other painterly devices. She began to sketch and dab. I watched from behind her, anxious and fascinated, urging her to speak to me, to become aware of her surroundings: this is the winter of 1999, my darling, you're in a hypnotic state. She ignored me, shook off my hand.

She remained for ten straight hours at a stretched piece of canvas on her drawing board. I waited her out, watching, pacing, my mind churning through published histories of when-hypnosis-goes-wrong, learned articles I had too carelessly perused. I knew that one ought not to shock the subject into coming back too quickly and brutally.

It was about six o'clock in the morning when she laid down her brushes. She'd created a vast, complex country fair, crammed with activity, and eight-year-old Mildred was standing alone and lost in the midst of it.

Sally returned to this world, began to weep. I held her in my arms, but she was rigid, angry, rejecting me.

"It's all right," I kept repeating. "You're home again."

"I'm not all right," she said.

Altered, I suspect now. Forever altered, divided from me . . .

Flash-forward to last Sunday night, to a quiet table in a fine French restaurant. The promised date. Sally was in a serious mood, rebuking me, but gently.

"I don't think I ever fully trusted you after that. You'd promised . . ."

"I'm sorry, honey."

"You made me afraid of you. I've never really got over it . . ."

She had *believed* in me, in my mind, my ability to intuit, my skills, but the episode caused her to question my careless use of them. It scared her that I was able to exercise this awful power over her. That wasn't the only problem.

"I felt I couldn't own my emotions. And you seemed to be reading my mind. Simple things such as, 'You look contrite, like you spent too much shopping.' Or, 'I really don't want to go to that gallery,' when I hadn't even mentioned the opening. I began feeling like a plaything, an experiment."

I was uncomfortable that she was using the past tense, but at least she was opening up.

I said, "You might have concluded I was merely well tuned in to you," then explained, as I've done many times, that the so-called ability to read minds rests on a firm foundation: an insight based on clues that may only be subliminal. I became pedantic, citing Freud, his theory that telepathy is a subsensuous phenomenon; clues are conveyed by ancient senses that, like smell, still exist but which humans have allowed to atrophy from lack of use.

She listened patiently, smiling. I was boring her, I thought, or her mind was elsewhere. "There were never any romantic surprises," she said softly. "I wouldn't have minded a few."

Ever buy her flowers? I hear you, Allis. I felt blind-sided by her gentle complaint, shocked that I'd been so neglectful in matters of the heart.

"I love you, Tim. But love alters." Her eyes were damp. "Sometimes the passion isn't there."

I was deeply hurt and didn't know how to respond, and I was some time recovering.

We concluded with an excellent almond flan, and I felt partly released from my funk when she said, "I wish you'd learn how to cook." Future conditional tense. Was there hope yet?

The rewooing of Sally Pascoe has continued – that was only the first of two dates during a week in which I was able to patch my tattered soul. My spectres began to recede and my dreams didn't seem as fearful – but just as pulling, intense, and eccentrically coded.

Remarkably, one powerful dream was a seamless continuation of the standoff at the village wall – you will recall how we tried to pick it apart: the gates to the town swinging closed to me, the gates to my history, my reality. I was willing those gates shut, but was an opposite and equal force, symbolized by the merry sound of the banjo, pulling me there?

No doubt my incessant puzzling over that dream encouraged me to produce this sequel. I was again at the gate, but this time its keeper (now Clinton Huff, wearing the chains and robe of chief magistrate) asked me if I played an instrument. He seemed shocked when I told him of my familiarity with the clarinet. Clearly this was the key. He opened the gate.

As I followed him into the mountain village – a few wooden structures, of Bavarian design – the sprightly banjo music was supplemented by other instruments: guitar, accordion, brass, perhaps a washboard. I arrived at the town square, at the centre of which were a bandstand and a group playing what one might call hillbilly music. I was seized with the discomfiting sense that *they all resembled me.*

Huff asked me to produce my clarinet, and I was unable to. "He is a fraud," he yelled, "an impostor."

An angry mob seemed to be assembling, so I ran. Huff followed, and suddenly, confusingly, I was standing with him in the foyer of the courthouse, under the portrait of the Queen and her consort. Huff was sobbing. "She died for our sins," he said.

The message is too obtuse.

I spent some time during the week studying cooking shows on

the Food Channel, and was otherwise occupied by setting up shop in my new Granville Island quarters. Sally, though under pressure of a deadline, announced she'd come by mid-week and check out my new digs, and I boldly invited her for dinner on the *Ego*: Scallops Florentino, a project suggested by a book titled *Anyone Can Cook*.

I received no further word or contact from Vivian Lalonde. I remain hopeful she'll recover her senses. I did consult with Irwin Connelly as to whether to call the paymaster, Dr. Lalonde, to tell him why I've withdrawn my services. Let sleeping dogs lie, Irwin said.

On Wednesday, however, came a different undesired visitor: Bob Grundison. James had notified him of my address change, but his regular appointment was for the following day. At the time, my protector, Dotty, was in Seattle trailing an adulterous husband, but since I was consulting with an interior designer, and burly carpenters were installing a door, I wasn't perturbed that he arrived unannounced.

I was behind a partition but could hear him greet James. "Yo, sweet buns. Guess the good doctor isn't in."

"I'm here." I showed myself. A normal person might have blushed when caught being snidely familiar to the boss's secretary, but Grundy merely grinned in his cocky, college-boy manner. I asked, "Where's Lyall?"

"In the car, we're double-parked, we couldn't find a parking spot. I know you're expecting me tomorrow, but Lyall and me, we have a chance to do some extreme rafting on the Skeena if we drive up there in the a.m. Any chance that could happen?"

"This come out of the blue?"

"Yeah, Dad wanted to give me a graduation gift. Camping by the river, great whitewater, it's going to be a real rush."

Grundy had completed his summer-school course in social psychology: presumably, he's learned something of how normal

humans interact. The rafting trip was to be no brief excursion —
they'd be four days on the Skeena, in northwest B.C. I told him he
had my permission if he also had the consent of Dr. Wade, his anger
counsellor, whose regime of therapy was to conclude in two weeks.

"That's all been arranged."

So we could talk privately, I drew him outside to the balcony,
then asked how he'd been getting on. Great, no problems, he
hadn't had an anger episode, not even one of his "tensions." During
this, he was looking inside, at the comely interior designer, his
thumbs hooked in his belt, a sexually suggestive stance.

"Great pad," he said. "Feels like you're right on top of the water.
Sign says there's a detective agency upstairs."

"Dotty Chung. You remember her."

"I do. I like her. A bulldog. Who does that beauty belong to?"
He was looking at the *Altered Ego*.

"She is mine."

"Real pretty. Well, okay, thanks, I'll be going."

He took his time doing so, admiring the designer's backside as
she leaned over her colour charts. I reminded myself to meet with
his anger counsellor, Dr. Wade, with whom I'd only chatted on the
phone. She feels her efforts have been sufficiently rewarded in that
Grundy has kept the lid on his tensions — at least as far as she's
aware. Martha doesn't share my concerns about the enigmatic Lyall
DeWitt — she believes he exerts a beneficial influence upon
Grundy, helps him stay on the straight path.

She's picked up Grundy's misogyny, though, a mixed lust for and
hatred of women. I sense there's something else, more twisted.

But am I able to trust my senses any more, my instincts, my pre-
monitions, the mixed signals of my dreams? I reject the erotic but
perverse message from this one: I was sharing a bed with Sally,
making clumsy efforts at coitus, while my efforts were critiqued by
a sneering Celestine Post: "That's not how you do it."

Likely, this imagery found inspiration as a result of Sally showing up – for my planned intimate dinner – with Celestine in tow, like a protective aunt. I assured them I had scallops to go around, and Celestine, after a not very credible show of reluctance (Intrude? Hell, no. I just wanted a quick peek at your joint), said she'd just have a few on a plate.

I made martinis, and we sipped them as we toured Dotty's houseboat – she was still in Seattle – then up the gangplank to Pier 32 and my new offices: reception area, small lamp-lit study, and consulting room prominently adorned with Sally's self-portrait.

From the balcony, we scanned the vista: a sunset sky that coloured the mountains green and gold; Grouse and Seymour, the Lions – and beneath, Vancouver's spiky downtown panorama. A man puffed by in a scull. A woman in a wetsuit grappled with a dis-obedient wind surfer. A harbour seal poked its head from the water, grinned at us, then sank from sight. The evening would have been exceptionally romantic had the balcony been less crowded.

"Sort of reminds you of Venice," said Celestine.

"Ah, Venice," said Sally.

They had memories I couldn't share. I felt like an outsider, a witness to the happiness of others.

Celestine asked me if I'd like to smoke a joint, and I declined. I'm leery of pot, have been since I was eighteen, an episode at a college dance when I was too stoned to move or speak except in garbled phrases.

Sally took a quick puff – she was in an ebullient mood. She'd just been chosen in a competition to illustrate a collection of children's stories by an award-winning writer.

Celestine summoned the good grace to leave after her few scal-lops on a plate – and a slice of garlic toast and three glasses of Chardonnay – and later Sally and I lay near the bowsprit, fending off the early chill of night with hot toddies.

I wanted her opinion of dinner – hadn't my scallops come out of the pan tender and tasty? (Celestine had offered a backhanded compliment: "You can teach them to cook, but you can't teach them to fuck.")

"Not bad. I'll give you an A-minus and a bonus for trying so hard." She kissed me on the cheek.

And what did we talk about? You, my dear Allis, my doctor, my mender. It seems that Sally feels I've gained some insight, as a result of your counselling, into my former unmindful behaviour. She wanted to know all about you. ("Is she attractive?" she asked. I told her the truth.)

"Is she tackling your lost daddy syndrome?" That's the crude term Sally uses. Like you, she's made insistent efforts to engage me on the topic. ("Millions of people don't know their father, and they're normal – why can't you be one of them?")

She can remember – I've known her since the age of six – my boasts: my father was a renowned surgeon, a Nobel-winning scientist, he was teaching in Boston, he was teaching in London, he'd written important books. One day he'd come for me . . .

Ah, the past is so cluttered with maudlin yearning. Perhaps I'm merely embarrassed to go there. But I give you credit, Allis – your tireless rummaging through the forces that shaped little Timmy must be penetrating the sunless depths. Your digging stirs up the worms, and they're busy within, itchy, wiggling, chewing at me.

I remember deciding my father was on a secret mission to save the world, that's why he couldn't come home. Or he was in danger – government assassins were trying to eliminate him, along with the dire secrets he held. I used to play pretend with him, pretend he was with me, pretend he was beside me on a bicycle.

But I don't know where the journeys of life and career have taken Peter; I have only Victoria's picaresque tale of a chance meeting, a fairy-tale romance, aborted with the dawn (as ultimately

I might have been, were she not – as she dreamily insists – so tragically in love with him).

Victoria was seventeen, a college frosh. They both had itinerant summer jobs in the Okanagan, picking peaches. Their evenings were spent in bunkhouses with other pickers, so they were unable to consummate their growing affection. Oddly, she never asked his last name. Nor did he offer much of his background.

"He was tall and handsome, just like you, and brilliant," she told me. "We played backgammon and he beat me easily. He was transferring to another medical school, somewhere in the East, and I was so sad, because it would take him out of the country."

At the end of season, they hitchhiked to the Kootenays, and on arrival there, they camped over a lake, under a moon, loons calling distantly. Early in the morning, he gently awakened her, kissed her, and said he had to catch his bus.

"He had a girlfriend. I understood. I loved him, and for what he gave me upon that one beautiful night, I still do."

This is, however, Victoria's most recent and possibly final version. Earlier accounts had him as a prince who'd met her at a ball and who wasn't allowed to marry a commoner (this when I was four), a brave soldier (age of six), then he became a sailor, then an athlete who'd won Olympic bicycling gold (I'd just been presented, on my eighth birthday, with my first two-wheeler).

But I was coming to realize that Victoria was a storyteller, and as I entered adolescence I began to demand less varnish, more fact. Her retellings became more specific, less fanciful, and for that, the more romantic, a touching tale of how I became the windfall of a peach-picking romance. They'd swum naked in the lake in the glistening moonlight. They'd made love until they were taken by exhaustion.

Victoria has never found love since, though there've been intimate relationships, usually unsatisfactory: abusive in one case, other candidates uncaring or immature. Currently, she's being squired by an arts bureaucrat, but I don't think much will happen there.

For some reason, when I graduated from adolescence, Peter became a closed subject, and I've never understood why Victoria showed so little interest in my efforts to track him down. He's history, she would sigh. But he's *my* history, damn it.

Sally feels I should go to Jackson Cove, scout the territory, root around for my roots in the land of Huff. But will I have the courage to confront the unknown, to face some shattering truth?

From the bow of the *Ego*, Sally and I watched the moon rise and shimmer on the saltchuck, as it had on the lake for Victoria and Peter thirty-six years ago. Sally had lost a mother, I'd never known a father – and we were banded together by shared emptiness.

Finally, she came into my arms, kissing me once, gently, and I fought not to be hopeful or aroused. She was merely seeking comfort, and her closeness was enough. I didn't dare ask her to stay the night – she didn't want to be pressed, and I feared rejection.

"I have to go now. Celestine said she'd wait up for me."

She was kind to let me down even with such a paltry excuse. I suggested another date, on the weekend, and she seemed to contemplate saying yes but remembered an "engagement." With whom? My anxiety was assuaged by her apparent lack of enthusiasm over it.

"The weekend after," she said. "We'll do something fun."

When next I talk to her, I'll tell her we have an invitation to dinner on the patio of Richard Spencer and Allis Epstein. You will like her, Allis. I will like Richard.

I walked Sally to her Saab, some distance away because cars aren't allowed thereabout, and after she kissed me once more lightly upon the lips, she said, "You know what, I think I'm doing this for you – you're too dependent on me – and you're too damned smart for me, and maybe you don't find me challenging enough. Hang out, make some friends. Open up your world a bit. That's what I'm trying to do."

Abruptly she pulled away from me, and I couldn't divine the source of the sadness in her eyes.

CHAPTER SEVEN

Date of Interview: Friday, August 29, 2003.

Timothy presented today as unusually restrained, yet this has been another unsettling week, much complicated by the added stressor of Vivian Lalonde's complaint to the College. Also weighing on him is a recent senseless murder. He has had a role in its aftermath.

Tim took to the couch right away, but from the beginning of the session I had the sense he was holding himself in. Indeed, his body was clenched, and his affability seemed forced.

Ultimately, I had to challenge him to free himself, to let his anger loose. The result was more than I anticipated.

Excerpt One:

> I suspect you're not thrilled at having to deal with my depressive personality – you'd rather be home preparing for your party tomorrow.
> Sally's coming?

Yes, she's curious to meet you. She's good at parties. I either mope – I can't handle the banalities of cocktail conversations – or I trap some victim into listening to a long-winded soliloquy. I hope I haven't met your other guests. If so, they'll be the ones avoiding me.

Do you think you're boring?

Only to myself. I make people nervous.

Why do you suggest that?

Doesn't that happen with you? People think we're always dissecting them, seeking out repressed fantasies.

I don't think anyone in this crowd will harbour any fantasies worth repressing. I'm sure you know Evelyn Mendel from the UBC psychiatry department.

You and I would never have met without her.

Oh, of course, she sent you to me. And Werner Mundt.

Mundt?

You obviously know him too. The sexologist.

And lackey to the drug industry. Hell, he's on my discipline committee, Schulter's henchman. He's . . . well, I won't say.

Oh, yes, you will.

A pill-pushing arrogant womanizing prick with an agenda against me.

Yet another fan of *Shrinking Expectations*?

Don't worry, I'll steer clear of him.

I'm not keen on him, either, Tim, but he's acting head of psychiatry at UBC. I should have mentioned – I'll be teaching a course there this semester.

Good, maybe you can present me as a case study.

Otherwise, they're Richard's friends, two from the office, one of his partners, Patricia Lang, plus a few clients. Not all will have spouses, but I'm afraid the group has expanded to fifteen.

I promise not to freak out.

So how are you doing?

Okay.

He was supine, clenching his bicycle helmet over his stomach.

How are you *really* feeling?

Been worse. Looking forward to the party.

You seem a little tense, Tim.

Do I?

Excerpt two – about thirty minutes on:

I think you're having trouble letting go.

I guess I don't want to let go.

Are you afraid you're going to spoil my party? If you maintain this mask of composure, you'll only further unsettle yourself.

What would you have me do?

Get it out! Rant!

But he went silent, looking around, at the ceiling, then the prints on the walls.

Those are Batemans, aren't they? I like that one – the osprey taking flight. Soon to sink its talons in a fish . . .

His face began to work.

That mendacious *bitch*!

He hurled the helmet, which struck my dieffenbachia and broke it.

I'll sue that lying harridan! That . . . that fucking . . . The C-word, I'm going to say it.

Let it all go, Tim.

You had me dead to rights – I *was* suppressing anger, striving to maintain high spirits. But it is better that I exploded in your office than on your patio tomorrow evening.

So I'm sorry about the plant. And the rant. Maybe you were unaware of the breadth of my street vocabulary. Is this better? – narcissistic obsessive hyperactive sexual disorder. I suppose Vivian told this fairy tale to her father, in an effort to reach him, jab him, draw attention to her needy self. Dr. Lalonde, in turn, would have engineered the complaint to the College. He found an eager ear in Herman Schulter.

Yes, the author of this week's letter puts all other threateners to shame. Dr. Schulter has added professional misconduct to my list of sins. I'm accused of having sexual relations (Vivian was thoughtful enough to describe them as consensual) with a patient suffering from a recent marriage breakdown.

The hearing is set for next week, and Irwin Connelly is urging me to hire a lawyer. But no, I won't legitimize such a burlesque by treating it so seriously. Vivian will have no choice but shamefacedly to withdraw the complaint. Though the hearing is to be in camera, the profession will be deluged with rumour. The damage to my reputation may be such that I'll have to sue her, even at the risk of putting the matter in the public domain.

I am trying self-hypnosis. I won't let thoughts of Vivian bother me. I won't bring the matter up tomorrow as a subject of dinner conversation. I'm freed of it. Free. (I must stop denying like this. I'll end up taking out my ire at some innocent guest at your party.)

I picked up the slightest note of doubt in Sally's voice when I railed on to her about this counterfeit allegation. (One merely has to whisper scandal and one's closest ally begins to speculate. In my growing condition of emotional zombie-ism, I may soon be questioning myself.) "Of course I believe you," she said with what seemed forced enthusiasm.

That conversation was by phone. Sally has returned to the house on Creelman, but I haven't seen her this week – I'd only depress her in my beleaguered state; I'm determined to show her only a happy face. I'm following your advice to give her space, the sense of independence she's striving for. I've reduced my number of phone calls to only a couple a day. We have a date on your patio tomorrow, that is enough for now.

Creelman Street is, however, on my training route, and I continue to take pleasure in seeing her daubing away behind the wide windows of her studio. (On Saturday night she went to a gallery opening, driven there by Celestine Post in her beat-up campervan. I did suffer a twinge – Wednesday night, I believe it was – when I saw Ellery Cousineau's car parked behind her Saab in her driveway, but as her editor he must regularly collaborate. His car was gone when I next wheeled by, well before eleven.)

I was on my bicycle most of the weekend, out of touch, and only became aware Monday morning that a murder had occurred Friday night in Stanley Park. The newscast reported that the police couldn't explain the motive for the attack on a popular character actor. Chauncey Wilmott was strangled by an unknown assailant during his nightly stroll in Stanley Park.

I remembered Wilmott from the local stage: he had a sharp comedic sense, played butlers and foppish uncles with panache. He taught theatre arts at Douglas College until retiring a few years ago, at seventy, but continued to perform bit parts on stage until slowed by a stroke last year.

Vancouver, like all metropolises, sees its share of murders, but this one was particularly contemptible. Wilmott was a frail man who walked with a cane. Police have released few details other than that he was "asphyxiated" – media have speculated about the use of a rope or a cord. His body wasn't found until the early Saturday joggers were out.

In the office, I found James in high tension. I feared he'd forgotten his medication, but he explained he was in a "horrible state" because of the murder. Chauncey Wilmott was prominent in the gay community, and James had been proud to know him socially. Indeed, he'd been with him and other friends earlier on Friday night, in a wine bistro, and they'd even walked with him to the park entrance at English Bay.

James spent some time with the police on the weekend but hadn't called me, hadn't wanted to disturb me. I stopped myself from reproaching him for that.

Whenever I hear about a murder, it never takes much prodding for me to flash on Bob Grundison, and it didn't take a leap of imagination to picture him as the killer of Chauncey Wilmott. I remembered Grundy nudging DeWitt, whispering "fag." The more unsettling thought was that James himself could have been the original target: a message more bloodily graphic than a threatening note.

I wasn't due in court for two hours, so I suggested he sit down, relax, and get his feelings out. He remonstrated, apologized, he didn't want to burden me. James is a shy, decorous man (however reserved, he's forever attending upon me, brushing lint from my shirt or straightening my tie), and it was only after continued prodding that he allowed himself to grieve.

He spoke of his admiration for Wilmott: "Such an open person, never afraid of strangers, always engaging them. To a fault. A deadly fault, I'm afraid." He related a few of their "delightful" conversations, remembered him as effusive, with an "*esprit sel*," a salty wit. Finally he attempted a smile. "I assume flamingly gay is the concept that would come to the mind of some."

"I have the picture."

"Certain aspects of the case are disturbing. There has been a great deal of talk about it in the West End. We're concerned that the police don't share our views."

The West End and its forest of highrises has a substantial gay population, elects only politicians who are out of the closet. I could see the point James was making: Stanley Park adjoins the West End, many would be afraid to take their regular nighttime strolls.

"He had no enemies?"

"Goodness, no."

I didn't mention Grundy, didn't want to frighten him by suggesting that he himself might have been the intended quarry. "You believe it's a hate killing. That's the view the police don't share."

"*Exactement*, sir."

"James, would you mind not calling me sir? It makes me feel awkward. Tim. Timothy if you like. Dr. Dare."

I told James I was not without influence in the homicide detachment. I phoned their office, arranged to see the case officer the following morning

I had to run off to court but counselled James to take a day or two from work. "*C'est impossible*," he said. There was much to do setting up the new office. He insisted to be allowed to work, and I gave him his way – then called Dotty Chung, upstairs, to ask her to keep an eye on him.

I spent the day in the witness box in fractious argument with a lawyer defending an alcohol-addled arsonist – whom I deigned to be sane, despite some delusional, persecutory thinking, not uncommon in cases of chronic alcoholism. The jury took forty minutes to agree with me, and by the end of the afternoon I was back at Pier 32, exhausted from combat.

I went up to Dotty's office, met her at the door as she was seeing out a distressed client, who strode by muttering, "That fucking creep." (It had just been revealed to her that her husband maintained a mistress in Seattle.) We chatted about the Wilmott murder, about my meeting tomorrow with the inspector running the case:

Jack Churko, a veteran plodder. He isn't the brightest light on the Vancouver force, but regards me highly.

Dotty groaned. She and Churko are professional foes from the days when the air in the department was thick with gender bias. "Wrong guy for this case," she said.

Thoughts of Grundison and DeWitt were working through my mind. Grundy couldn't have done such a deed alone; he's never alone. *Me and my shadow.*

Dotty reminded me that at the time they would have been on a rafting expedition on the Skeena River, seven hundred kilometres north. I'd forgotten that Grundison cancelled his Thursday appointment to drive up there. Of course his expedition could have been a lie, an excuse to hang about, celebrate the end of summer school with a homophobic assault.

But this did not seem the case; Dotty said they were not only on the Skeena but in the news. She showed me a printout from the *Vancouver Sun* on-line. The headline: "WOMAN TRAPPED IN FRIGID RAPIDS, PLUCKED TO SAFETY."

The episode occurred Sunday. The heroes were Bob Grundison ("controversial heir to the Grundison corporate holdings, recently released from Riverview," and so on) and Lyall DeWitt. The woman fell from the raft as it shot a waterfall. Grundy and Lyall jumped in after her. Grundy reached her first and bore her to shore. "I owe my life to him," said the woman, an Edmonton hairdresser. There was a photograph of her saviour, wide smile, cold eyes. I had to give him credit – acts of heroism aren't out of nature for the psychopathic personality. Bob would savour the moment, the grandeur of it – and the attention.

The next morning, over my garlic-pill-and-toast breakfast, I read details of the murder in the morning paper. Wilmott's body had been thrown into a clump of salmonberries not far from Lost

Lagoon. A wallet containing nearly three hundred dollars was in the pocket of the victim's white linen jacket, a Rolex on his wrist. To complete the sad picture, a boutonnière was in the lapel.

I pedalled off to the Public Safety Building, better known as 312 Main Street. It is in the very gut of the Downtown East Side, Vancouver's high-crime zone, where, despite its prime location, hustlers of dope and sex rule the streets, where spent syringes and empty wine cartons litter the alleys.

On the second floor, in the homicide squad room, a couple of detectives were working the phones, calling acquaintances of Chauncey Wilmott. I could see Inspector Jack Churko through a glass partition, butting a cigarette, waving at me. He is about sixty, a jaded endomorphic old-school cop, with the face of an aging boxer dog.

Churko came out to escort me in, an arm around my shoulder. He has a lot of patience for me, ever since I laid waste a temporary insanity defence argued on behalf of a man who shot his wife and her lover.

"I hope you ain't here as part of the homosexual lobby, that's all I got to say, Doc." That wasn't all he had to say, he began a harangue. He'd received a delegation from the local gay pride group. He had been called by a gay city councillor. By a United Church minister. "A homosexual preacher – families go to his church, that's what this world is coming to."

He showed me the report of the pathologist, who concluded Wilmott's throat had been looped from behind, probably with a wire. It had lacerated the skin: "a circular lesion anterior to the vocal cord, compressing the upper trachea."

I told Churko that if it was a hate murder, I'd be keen to draw up a homophobic profile.

"We ain't there yet. Look for the motive, Doc, that's the first rule. We can't assume we got a crazy on our hands."

"He might not be crazy. What kind of motives are you talking about?"

"He could have stiffed someone with a bad loan, simple as that. Maybe he was blackmailing someone, maybe it was a lover's quarrel, we're going to check out every lead."

"Do you *have* any leads?"

"We're working on it." He tapped a cigarette from his pack, ignoring the no-smoking regulations. "No fucking prints, no hair sample, no DNA, we got shit, frankly. A year from pension, and this lands on me. It could have been a robbery gone bad, simple as that. Just some punk."

"Mr. Wilmott had three hundred dollars on him. A pricey watch. Whoever did this didn't lack for money. What kind of punk wanders around Stanley Park with a coil of wire?"

Churko knew I was making sense but resisted the obvious premise. "All I'm saying, Doc, is we have to keep all options open. Maybe the old guy began hitting on some weirdo who was fucked up about queers. Or maybe you're right, it was a random gay-bashing. We had a couple of incidents this summer, no one got hurt bad, but that sort of shit goes on."

"Okay, so let's bring out the files on these incidents, and go over them. Let's draw up a list of known homophobes with records."

"I ain't got tons of manpower on this. We're beefing up our patrols in the park, in the West End. But if you're able to help, I can squeeze some money out for you."

"Done. Draw up a list and bring them in, I'll sit in on the interviews."

I considered mentioning Bob Grundison's name – he'd likely fit neatly within any homophobic profile, and three hundred dollars would be pocket change to him. But I refrained from fear of sounding foolish. He and Lyall had left for the Skeena River two days before Wilmott was attacked.

But did they actually drive all that way? Five hundred miles of mostly single-lane highway, it would have taken them a day and a half. Could they have dallied in Vancouver for two days, then flown up there Saturday morning? The rafting trip was a gift from Grundy's father: wouldn't he have sent them first class? Two main airports served the area, at Prince Rupert and Terrace.

Upon returning to Pier 32, I dropped in on Dotty, who despite all her grumbles and doubts agreed to make discreet inquiries with the airlines, the area hotels, and the whitewater outfitters.

I was pleased to tell James that I'd nudged the police in a more productive direction. To allay his anxious state, he'd been vigorously cleaning up and organizing the mess in my desk drawers.

He directed my attention to an array of detritus from those drawers. Disregarded invitations; papers that should have been filed long ago; preposterous gifts: a mobile composed of Jungian symbols; a pencil sharpener set in the mouth of a bronze bust of Sigmund Freud. Old photos, torn clippings.

A childhood snapshot had been stuck in a niche at the back of a bottom drawer. I'd meant to frame it, give it to Sally for her birthday, a reminder of The Way We Were. She and I are standing by a birthday cake. She's just turned ten. She's wearing a set of false, waxy red lips (these enjoyed a brief vogue among our set), I have a Jimmy Durante nose tied about my head, and I'm grinning at her, already in love, spiritually, pre-carnally.

I took it to a framing shop.

Predictably, that scene popped up in this dream: I'm standing in a crush of people, wearing a false nose, my crowd phobia in full, flagrant bloom. As I fight my way toward open space, someone hands me a martini, and it dawns on me that I'm actually at a crowded cocktail party. Some of the faces seem familiar – and, in that self-referential way of dreams, they're talking about me, about my affair with Vivian, my forthcoming trial.

Among the guests (at what has become your patio party) is Ellery Cousineau, the Don Juan of the children's book industry. Ellery, I regret to say, is a notably handsome man, silver-haired and tall and fit and glib, and he easily draws women into his orbit. One of them, on this tossing, turning nightmared night, is Sally, clinging to him, but dressed as a little girl and wearing those sumptuous false lips. Miriam Goes to a Cocktail Party.

Standing at the border of all this coziness, I feel dejected. Then, as Ellery whispers a sweet nothing into Sally's ear and the pair of them break into laughter, I feel humiliated – it comes to me that I'm wearing no pants or undergarments. This dream symbol is so trite that I'm embarrassed it has been permitted entry into my unconscious, but its source is obvious and I suppose it speaks to various fears relating to your party (expanded to eighteen!), my bleakness causing dampened spirits among your husband's important clients, my phobias driving at full thrust. Or worse, some cocktail-glass-shattering eruption of anger and despair.

Herman Schulter is in this dream, addressing a cluster of colleagues: "The patient has blocked it from memory." I find this comment disturbing – in dreams one's voice is heard through others, so questions arise: Is it remotely possible that I've repressed some aspect of my encounter with Vivian? By some freak of fate, might I actually be pronounced guilty of the sin charged against me? Did my nakedness represent a fear of public exposure?

But where were you in this dream, Allis? Richard was present (his face was amorphous), but he was occupied with a woman from his office. Patricia Lang, his partner? (Had I picked up a tightness, a sense of distaste when you mentioned her name?)

Meanwhile I was still feeling shame, and I covered my genitals with my false nose. (The symbolism here is unclear.) Then I noticed everyone had donned party masks, and they were running about like children. I've a faint memory of Sally turning to me with her false lips, saying something like, "Even if I'm bad, you'll always be my friend, won't you?"

I rose at dawn, bleary with images from that dream, and I rode Vesuvio high into the wealthy suburbs of the North Shore: twenty-two minutes, thirty-five seconds, from the Seabus terminal to the Grouse Mountain lift. Then I sped downhill unhelmeted, my hair flying, the wind in my face, slapping me back to reality.

I continued my hard training that evening: Point Grey, the familiar neighbourhoods of Kitsilano. Biking down Creelman, I spied Sally and Celestine on the back deck of my former home, drinking wine and gabbing and laughing. I stopped behind the cover of Celestine's van and tiptoed closer, to the fence, but made out their conversation poorly.

The only words I heard were Celestine's, "I *dare* you."

I couldn't hear Sally's response and skulked silently away, back to Granville Island, to the *Altered Ego*, to bed. But those three imperative words were with me through the night, continually jangling me awake.

I slept in as a result, until ten, and I started when I made out James leaning over my bunk. "Are you all right, sir?" He apologized, but because of the lateness, he thought he should check on me. Some legal documents had just arrived by registered mail from Jackson Cove.

I groaned, donned some clothes, followed him to my office, downed a mug of coffee, and tried to make sense of Clinton W. Huff's "Petition to this Honourable Court in the Matter of Huff versus Dare." The mayor of Jackson Cove was seeking to have me declared "a hostile witness" and banned from giving evidence at his continuation. I was "biased by blood relationship" and therefore "incompetent in law."

He needn't worry. I've no intention of again sharing a courtroom with this bristling leprechaun.

I recalled John Brovak mentioning that Huff had a Web site, promoting a creed called "FreedomFirstForever," and I asked my Web-wise secretary to track it down. James quickly located it, and suddenly Mr. Huff was on the screen frowning at me, beside a banner proclaiming LIBERTY OR DEATH.

FreedomFirstForever contained various screeds he'd written; the first was an essay replete with pumped-up cries for liberty from that great oppressor, Government (they want to know all about you).

There was a page on "the inalienability of property rights," a weighty, multi-syllabic sermon touting Libertarian philosophy. Another was titled "Clinton Huff and the Court of Revision," this a confusing history of his battle with municipal officials for the right to keep ducks on his half-acre lot. The text of his nomination speech for his failed run for Parliament was here too.

There were biographical notes, but they revealed little of the man. Born in 1953, in the East Kootenays, the fourth and final son of a storekeeper and housewife, head of his high-school debating club, twenty-five years serving the needs of education in Jackson Cove, a history of his many tries for public office.

Huff kept his Web site up to date with references to his libel action, in which I found this: "Also present as a hireling of the defendants was a doctor with a reputation for prying into the private affairs of individuals. A newspaper review of his recent book exposes him as a charlatan." The word *review* was hyperlinked to a savage critique of *Shrinking Expectations* by a prominent Los Angeles analyst whose name won't go mentioned here.

There was no further reference to me, but questions abounded. Why was he in such a lather about me? What secret sinful activity was he concerned that I might pry into? Was he a threat to my physical as well as my emotional well-being? Or was he just a harmless nuisance – a grumpy pedagogue emotionally deformed by harsh toilet training? I can't deny being tantalized by his mystery, but I'm determined to ignore him, to dampen his irrational response to me. There's danger in riling him – the acutely obsessive personality is unrelenting and easily spurred to excesses.

On the following day the notice arrived from the discipline committee, over Herman Schulter's signature, that an ugly charge had been added to my indictment. (The letter was, of course, couched in the hypocritical cant of reassurance: they were "merely seeking clarification with respect to this unfortunate allegation.")

Dr. Schulter, no less than Clinton Huff, is fixated on me. At least he's animated by a recognizable motive. Professional jealousy may not be the noblest of emotions, but neither is it out of the range of common feeling. But Huff is a nuisance, a flea bite compared to Schulter, who's prepared to put my career and reputation to the torch. I've been told that a lack of diplomacy is one of my failings, so I resisted the urge to notify him he's a vindictive son of a bitch.

Vivian, Schulter, Huff, Grundy . . . How has a simple seeker of truth managed to inspire such a throng of ill-wishers? I founder for answers; a conspiracy of prankish unseen forces remains the most likely possibility. Though, as a scientist, I mustn't reject the possibility that I suffer from a massive system of delusional ideation. A convincing body of literature (see Kendler and Gruenberg, 1984) suggests that a predisposition for schizophrenia is transmitted genetically, and I've started to seriously wonder if my father, Peter, was a paranoid psychotic.

CHAPTER EIGHT

Date of Interview: Monday, September 1, 2003.

Tim called by phone to ask that I squeeze him in for a few minutes today, and I told him that if he wanted to apologize, he could wait till Friday. But he insisted, so I offered an alternative – an end-of-day drink in a wine bar near my office.

He was there when I arrived, looking penitent. I assured him that everyone thought it had been a lovely party, and no one was seriously upset over the incident.

Tim felt he had to explain. He'd had too much to drink, had been upset that Sally was being herself, vivacious, a social butterfly. He'd lost his temper, but had been provoked. He was thankful only that the party was almost over, that he hadn't entirely ruined the evening.

I told him Richard and I later shared a chuckle over it, and others might have quietly applauded. Finally, he, too, was able to find humour, and soon we were both laughing.

Date of Interview: Friday, September 5, 2003.

Tim was favouring his right leg as he hobbled in, having suffered a bicycling accident on Wednesday. He greeted me with a smile that seemed so resigned and stoical that I gave him a hug, which he returned. Then he stretched out on the couch with a sigh but also with a fixed expression. He was fiercely determined that his injury, a sprained ankle, would not keep him out of the Okanagan Rally.

He knows Sally Pascoe was here two days ago, for an hour's friendly discussion, but held back from asking about it. He understands, of course, that all matters between Sally and me were expressed in confidence.[1]

Tim and I again discussed my weekend party, in a more serious vein than when we met on Monday, and I had an impression that he was holding himself back from remarking on the other guests.

He was able to work with me today, even to offer the gift of being more open about his childhood. A powerful dream had brought it spilling out. An exchange about the significance of the Labour Day weekend, as recorded below in transcript, bears following up.

It's the one holiday that truly unnerves me.
    Why?

---

[1] Sally was friendly, gregarious, and much concerned about Tim's welfare. There is no doubt she deeply cares for him, but she was quick to agree that the relationship involves a dependency – perhaps unhealthy – in that she serves as an anchor, a cord connecting him to old comforts. We discussed our shared desire for children and the metaphorical "clock" that both of us hear ticking. Childlessness is clearly central to her difficulties with Tim. She is conflicted about the future of the relationship and about whether to take up other invitations. I felt it not my place to ask about such romantic possibilities or offer advice. Apparently however, her friend, Celestine Post, has been doing so.

The Saturday of a Labour Day weekend was when the seed was planted from which ultimately grew the nut that is Timothy Dare. Though I actually should have celebrated a few days ago. I call it Insemination Day. Saturday, September 2, 1967. Victoria guesses about ten p.m.

She was able to be that specific?

She kept a journal of some sort. She says it's full of puerile poetry, and she won't show it to me. Very stubborn about that.

Well, a teenage diary . . .

Sure, but . . . Is she hiding something?

Here, lie down. Rest that foot. I hope it's not the ligaments.

Just muscle strain. It'll be a few weeks before I can put my full weight on it. I should be okay for the rally, I won't let my sponsors down.

How are you doing otherwise?

Well, as you've personally observed, I've found myself being somewhat quick-triggered lately. I don't know what's wrong with me . . .

ᏇᏊᎾ

What *is* the cause of my sudden brittle temper? Maybe it was in concealment all along, waiting to emerge, to take its turn after fear and despair were exhausted. Anger at someone who kills out of blind hate, anger at Schulter too, and Mundt and Vivian Lalonde. Even at Sally, for her agonizing wait-and-see attitude. At myself, for my panicky flight, my twisted ankle. At the gods.

In part, I blame my behaviour at the party on my frustration over the Chauncey Wilmott case. A promising lead had evaporated that morning. The computers had pulled out the name of a forestry worker with a history of three attacks against gay men, one this summer. But it turned out he'd been in a logging camp for the last month.

Another factor: I was weary. I'd worked all day drawing up a homophobic profile for the police: high incidence of sociopathy; aggressors come from all economic levels; as well – and it's all balled up with fear – they usually hate women too.

How well Grundy fits the bill. I really *want* him to be the murderer, want to hear him explain to a judge how he'd suffered another psychotic episode: Chauncey Wilmott playing his final dramatic role, the devil in disguise – à la Dr. Barbara Loews Wiseman. I hadn't considered, till now, that her homosexuality might have been a factor in her death.

But the evidence continues to point away from Grundy. Dotty Chung reported that he and Lyall weren't on passenger rosters of any scheduled flights to the Skeena area on the day after Wilmott's murder, nor on any return flights. They'd spent only one night in a hotel – in Terrace, after the rafting trip. The other rafters, a dozen of them, had been put up there as well, before heading homeward.

The couple running the whitewater tours have closed the operation for the season and have left for a holiday in Cuba. The woman Grundy pulled from the river, the Edmonton hairdresser, hasn't returned Dotty's calls. We found that odd, and Dotty intends to persevere.

I still can't accept that they drove all that distance. A day and a night on the road: it doesn't make sense. Had they paid cash for airline tickets, flown up on false names? A charter flight? But I mustn't let my repugnance for Grundy exaggerate the hints that grumble in my gut.

I've gone off track. Let me clear the air over my poor behaviour at your party. Sally had picked me up in her Saab, and was perky in a way that seemed unrelated to the fact we were a couple for the evening. She warned me not to mope in a corner – this was a chance to make new acquaintances, broaden my friendships.

She wasn't in the mood for tales of murder, didn't want to hear about the Wilmott case, didn't want me to raise it in company. "Don't dampen the party," she commanded. Little did I know that I'd ultimately do so more than figuratively.

You were gracious to leave your other guests in order to show us through your home. Sally was delighted with your taste in art and architecture, and I enjoyed – with just a gentle squeamishness – the panorama of city and sea from your swimming-pool patio.

Richard was all I expected him to be: charming, attractive in a hefty masculine way, and with a robust wit. I laughed too brightly at one of his risqué stories, and I later found myself being chastised for that by Evelyn Mendel. She may be your closest friend, so you must forgive me if I find her political correctness wearying. She was carrying on about the fickleness of men, and I was concerned at first she'd heard rumours (I wouldn't dream of accusing you) of my supposed fling with a patient.

But I soon understood that Evelyn's censure was directed elsewhere – she was drawing my attention toward a tête-à-tête involving your husband. Let me think about how to state my impressions . . .

Later.

Anyway, as Evelyn and I chatted, we engaged, as shrinks like to do, in the game of analyzing those present – the insecure, name-dropping PR consultant; the political pollster with his suspect candour (be suspicious when you hear the mantras of "frankly," "honestly," "to tell the truth"); Patricia Lang, your husband's partner, showing off her bare midriff and silver-ringed belly button. And Werner Mundt, who in his mid-fifties can't accept that he's no longer young, but retains enough charm to intrigue his way into the beds of many women.

Sally seemed to be enjoying herself in her breezy way, sizing you up as she chatted with you, flitting off, basking in the praise of a parent who had all the Miriam books, and finally finding herself in

Mundt's orbit – he'd been slowly, relentlessly, sidling up to her. He'd never met her before and must have assumed she was available.

"God's gift," Evelyn muttered.

Mundt dominated the conversation – as Sally told me later – and it moved from the impersonal (dazzling sunset, excellent Merlot, and, when he learned she was an illustrator, trends in painting) to the suggestive (all art represents an unfolding and a flowering of the sexual drive). He seemed pompous to her, expounding upon his narrow range of expertise: sex and the unconscious.

Mundt talks in a soft voice that forces his listeners to come close: a tool of the arrogant, a power play – you'll have to listen carefully if you're to hear the gems that drop from my lips. He'd trapped her against a railing, and she was able to stall his advance only by explaining she'd arrived with me, her long-time partner. Unfortunately, he must have gathered we were no longer together, and he pressed her enough to determine that as a fact. (Sally can be fearsomely guileless.)

Jealousy distorts perception, and though rationally I should have expected Sally to dismiss Werner as a bore, I didn't read her signals well: she seemed interested, was nodding, smiling brightly.

I'm afraid that's when I found myself drinking to excess of the excellent Merlot, and feeling discomfort from the closeness of those crowded around the barbecue. All the time, my eyes were on Sally, who finally gave Mundt an escape line and skipped away, then joined me – while the roué looked on.

But we were unable to exchange any confidences because I was half-listening to a political party hireling who was carrying on about how elections are won or lost not on policy but scandal. In a lowered voice, she added, "Is one about to erupt, Dr. Dare?"

I had the sense that she'd learned – from whatever secret sources – that the item in *Frank* magazine about the high-ranking member of the B.C. cabinet related to a patient lately in my care. Whose file I'd mislaid.

I was in enough of a bind over that – especially with one of my overseers hovering not far away – that I mumbled only a vague response and quickly changed the subject to the Stanley Park murder, causing the conversation to peter out.

Sally allowed herself to be drawn away by another Miriam fan. I was having that congested feeling I get when surrounded by smokers, so I drifted to the sidelines again, strolled around the pool with affected nonchalance. Twilight had set in, lights twinkling through the gloom of Burrard Inlet.

From the far side of your oval pool, I watched the byplay within a clot of people, a hydra-headed organism in fluid movement with drinks and plates of lamb kebabs. I felt like an alien, fretful, disoriented, and lonely. Was an anxiety attack coming or was I merely feeling a massing of irritation – at myself, at my weaknesses, my poorly integrated being?

It was then I saw you alone, perhaps taking a break, a reward, the party sufficiently ignited, and you were craning this way and that. I realized you were looking for your husband, because you seemed relieved when he came from the house bearing two bottles of cognac. But two minutes later, you tightened – as Patricia Lang exited the house.

It isn't for me to say . . .

Yes, it is. Don't I owe it you as a friend? The fact is that Evelyn and I saw – earlier, as we stood unnoticed in the background – Ms. Lang's hand lightly caress your husband's rump. Evelyn said nothing, just glanced at me with an acknowledgement that required no words.

Ah, Allis, what can I say? I won't insult you with reassuring lies, but my sense from their various touches and glances is that the affair is a mere novelty, that it lacks substance and, as these things do, will deteriorate into predictability and guilt. Have strength, my dear Allison. Don't feel diminished. You're an attractive woman of warmth and sensitivity – and strength.

But before I become maudlin, let me escape back to your patio, to Werner Mundt, who sauntered lazily toward me, snifters of cognac in either hand, and extended me one, perhaps as a token of apology for having tried to mousetrap my wife. I seemed pensive, he said, adding that he had some inkling of what might be bothering me. I merely nodded.

"Sordid business. Ugly accusation. Don't quote me, Tim – I can't say this strongly enough: deny, deny, deny. The Lalonde woman's a stunner, I hear. One could hardly be blamed, but it's your word against hers, and you have a clear advantage – if she was a well-balanced person, she wouldn't have engaged your services. And for God's sake, hire a lawyer."

"She's an obsessive stalker. That should be apparent to someone with your experience."

"You *are* in a state, Tim. I gather there've been marital problems."

I barely touched him, just a nudge of my hand to push him away, but he must have expected worse because he took a step back, lost his balance, fell flailing into the pool. Fortunately, it was the deep end. Unfortunately, he was a capable swimmer. I helped him out with an ill-intended apology. While towelling off, he made light of the incident, hinting I'd misunderstood his sense of humour.

If Richard, as you say, was able to laugh over it, he's worth salvaging, and I hope you both can accept my invitation to take another plunge: risk my table. Next weekend? You will call to let me know. I'll also invite Sally.

There were other misadventures this week. For instance, this episode at the Hastings MediCentre, on a stormy mid-afternoon Tuesday. Dripping wet, I stood before the elevator, gaining courage before, finally, entering it. My destination was the office of Martha

Wade, anger counsellor to the hero of the Skeena River. Martha wanted to discuss what she described as a puzzling tidbit with him during her last weekend session – he'd been typically insincere and (never before seen) upset, even hostile.

The building was old, the elevator slow, and I stood flat against a mirrored wall, taking deep breaths. As the elevator crept past the seventh floor, I had (I swear) a premonition. I was going to suffocate in here.

Almost immediately the elevator shuddered to a stop between floors, and the lights went out. A battery-powered auxiliary came on presently, but I was on the verge of a panic attack. I began punching all the buttons. I shouted, banged my fists on the door. There was no response, and I turned in despair and saw my wet, haggard reflection in the dim light, the fear in my eyes, and I had a flash of memory, from childhood, of another, more dreadful prison, a locked box of horrors . . .

The vision vanished as the lights came back on and the elevator lurched, rose several feet, stopped, and opened at the eighth floor. I staggered out on legs that had turned to jelly.

In Martha Wade's waiting room, a harried mother and her two squabbling boys went silent as the dripping ghoul with scarecrow hair announced himself to the receptionist. Martha Wade, a gentle greying woman, came out to claim me. As I followed her in, I heard a trembling voice behind me, "Mommy, is that him?"

"Quiet, Walter," was the sharp response.

Martha explained, as she brought me a towel, that this censorious mother's preferred tool of discipline was to raise the spectre of the bogeyman.

I found the boy's question pertinent. Was that me? The neurotic mess in Martha Wade's office – was that all there was of Timothy Dare? Was there another saner, centred Timothy, buried under an avalanche of early trauma?

Martha made me tea and nursed me back to a relatively level plane before telling me about her abbreviated one-on-one with Grundy Grundison at their final session – her service contract was over at the end of August.

"He was just back from the Skeena River, and still puffed up." She showed me a note transcribed from the tape of that session: *That rafting trip was like a major catharsis for me, I feel I've changed big time. I really feel different.* Martha refused to play to his need for applause.

This has been a sexually active summer for Grundy. During Martha's weekends at The Tides she has seen various young women around the pool with him and Lyall. Grundy couldn't hold himself back from confiding that the woman he'd rescued later "gave herself" to him in a hotel room in Terrace.

Martha winced. She had lately adopted a more confrontational approach with Grundy, trying to get him to verbalize his feelings, to vent them harmlessly. She says he is mastering that art, has learned to make non-confrontational responses to scenarios suggested by the texts. (You're behind the wheel of a car in heavy traffic. A motorist cuts in front of you, raises his middle finger . . .)

When Grundy stumbled trying to remember the Edmonton hairdresser's name ("Betty something. Janzen, Jensen? We weren't exactly on a last-name basis"), Martha decided to focus on this supposedly romantic episode, to get him talking about the woman, about sex, about love. This is from the tape she played for me:

"What are your feelings about Betty?"

"I like her. Of course. Who wouldn't?"

"What do you mean, who wouldn't?"

"She was bright and she was okay to look at. Nice body. You must have seen her picture in the paper, or on TV. Of course I liked her – I saved her."

"And are you going to follow this up?"

"I don't think so. It was just a date. I've got someone regular who lives closer to home."

Martha paused the tape to tell me this was likely Jossie Markevich, blonde, tattooed, street smart, his most frequent visitor of late. Martha has a sense, which I don't share, that Grundy is capable of settling down with a woman.

Grundy's tone, when his voice came on again, was one of disappointment in his anger counsellor. Since his return from the north, he's obviously been dining out on the saga of the rescue, but she wasn't handing out the complimentary desserts.

"With this girl it was like, okay, I bought her dinner, wine, we ended up in my room. Well, Lyall's, too, but he did a quick evacuation when he saw the scenario, and . . . well, it happened, the natural thing between two people."

"You said earlier: she *gave* herself to you?"

"She got into it."

Grundy spoke defensively, as if he'd been accused of forcing himself on her. I wondered if the evening had turned ugly, as many others had before Grundy was sent to Riverview. If so, that might explain the Edmonton woman's reluctance to return Dotty's calls.

"I'm confused, Bob. *How* did she get into it?"

After a silence: "I don't get what you're asking, Dr. Wade. If you're asking, did I have to push her into it, no. She was totally into it after a while, totally. I don't know how many times we did it, I stopped counting. I don't come on heavy like some guys, I've got too much respect for women."

"Bullshit."

That rare instance of bluntness from Martha caused a loss of composure, and an unravelling that accelerated. "Are you . . . Hey, Dr. Wade, if you're suggesting . . . Hey, now just a minute, you talk to her, I got her phone number somewhere, and if she says something different, then someone got to her . . ." A pause. "I *like* women." Another pause, heavy breathing. "I get it. This is one of those games where you try to piss me off. You know what? I don't care!" He shouted. "Too many people are on my case. And *you're* on my fucking case! I don't get credit! I'm tired of this shit! I have a headache!"

He stood, fists clenched, body taut, and seemed about to advance on Martha. She was momentarily in fear, but Lyall had heard the yelling – he was always posted outside the door – and rushed into the room. It took him a while to settle Grundy down, and Martha's only subsequent dealing with him was, as she was departing, to accept an apology, the insincerity of which was as obvious as neon.

Again, I pondered: Had Dr. Wiseman led Bob through some *real* catharsis during her own final session? Had a truth been revealed to him so hideous that he made sure it would be forever interred in her grave? Psychopaths don't feel guilt, but in their narcissistic aspect they can be stressed by fear of shame.

Does he dream of being naked? I did that night (the anniversary of Insemination Day), finding myself nude in that storybook Alpine village. Staring down at me, from the bandstand, was the Bavarian hillbilly combo: a trumpet player in a Kaiser Wilhelm helmet, an accordionist smoking a Meerschaum bent (I smelled marijuana), a red-suspendered rustic at the washboard. And again, beneath their motley wear, their faces were all familiar from my morning shaves.

These men, I presume, represent facets of the Dare personality: one was fidgety, another scowling, a third looked wild-eyed and haggard. Their music was discordant, and one player seemed missing – a chair at the front was empty, as if set out for an absent leader: the non-conflicted, integrated ego that they lacked?

The band was urging me to join them, and I wasn't sure why until I suddenly realized the phallus hidden behind my hands had taken the form of a clarinet. I wanted to join them, but I'd regressed to childhood, to naked toddlerhood, in fact.

"He can't play," said someone behind me, a child's voice.

I turned to face several young boys and girls. "You can't play!" they shouted in turn.

I was no longer in the Bavarian hamlet but in a bedroom of a student housing unit where Victoria and I lived when I was only four years old. I remembered the setting vividly in my dream, though my conscious mind has long forgotten it. We were in my mother's bedroom (the dream and reality – an episode in 1972 that has now come back to me – run on parallel lines), and the children were examining items inside an open trunk, surreal and frightening costumes, a skeleton of plastic bones, death masks – Victoria's collection, inspiration for the mystery stories she'd begun to write. My only toy was a wooden flute; I was trying in vain to make sound with it.

"You can't play!" The children taunting me were all bigger, including a couple of girls who tugged my shorts off and threw them into the trunk. Bare-bottomed and red with shame, I climbed in to get them, and they closed the lid on me. A fastener clicked. I heard little feet running away, giggling.

In my nightmare, that echo of the distant past, I was plunged into a horror of ghouls and monsters and clutching plastic fingers that was so terrifying that I woke on my cot on the *Ego* thinking I'd suffered a stroke: I was immobilized, smothered by thirty-year-old memories.

Victoria had been in another room, banging on a typewriter, hadn't heard my muted howls. She'd assumed I was playing with our neighbours' normally benign children, that they were old enough to be responsible, and she wasn't aware they'd fled the house. Maybe they hadn't heard the trunk lock shut. Maybe they were just being children, unthinking, forgetful, even cruel.

For little Timmy, it seemed a century had passed, but it was only two hours before my mother came down in search of me. She freed me, clutched me in her arms, gave love, but by then the damage was done. She never talked about it later, even when soothing my nightmares, probably because of the guilt she felt, or because, in her innocence, she thought cure could come from forgetting. But now I remember, now I know – my two hours in that black pit of torment has scarred me forever.

How excited you were when I told you about the nightmare, this recovered memory. Let's go to work, you said, now we have a starting point. Your weeks of hectoring me to unblock repressed memories needed only a lever, a climactic event, a stalled elevator, to spring open the lock of that trunk.

I'm sorry I felt too debilitated to do more work with you – scars remain after psychoanalysis just as after a successful operation, and they ache in stormy weather. Let me sit on it a week, process it, gather myself. But already I feel a healing – time and reflection are beginning their cure and I hear the demons snorting and fuming as they make their travel reservations.

In turn, however, I'm less healthy of limb, though I'm lucky to be alive.

It happened Wednesday. I'd invited Dotty Chung for dinner at the Pondicherry, to review the Grundy file. She'd been working tirelessly, prying what information she could from charter firms, visiting their offices if they were reluctant to help, telling them she was investigating a phony insurance claim. Three charters had flown to northwestern B.C. on Saturday, August 23, but none bore two well-built young men, and all were paid on credit cards by regular customers.

Dotty finally connected with the Edmonton hairdresser, but learned little we didn't know. The woman had no idea whether

Grundy and Lyall had driven or flown to the Skeena, or how and when they returned to Vancouver. She refused to say anything about spending the night with Grundy, admitted only that he bought her dinner and wine.

"Was he drinking too?" Dotty asked

"I have nothing more to say." And she hung up.

It was as Nataraja was treating us to his daily homily that matters turned hectic. "Do not fight the river, let the river take you . . ." He stalled, looking past me. "Oh, shit – that traffic stopper, she's at the door."

Vivian Lalonde had just entered, was peering about. I ducked but too late, and she wove her way toward me, between the tables, with hip-swinging grace and voracious parted lips. She was, as usual, dressed for the eyes of others, a blouse open almost to midriff. I said to Dotty, "Let me handle this." She looked embarrassed, but went on the alert – how disturbed was this woman, did she have a handgun in her bag?

"This is important," said Vivian, leaning over me, like a threat.

"Vivian, I suggest you back off. Take a few deep breaths to calm yourself."

"Timothy, it's about the hearing. They want me to testify. Can we talk alone?"

"I'm very busy, Vivian. This is Dotty Chung, a private detective with twelve years' experience in the Vancouver police."

"I know who she is."

I scraped my chair back and signalled Nataraja. "Please show this woman the door."

The other tables fell silent.

"No, just listen. I'm only trying to *help* you." Vivian's voice lowered. "I'm not going to let them crucify you. I'll lie if I have to, if you want me to – I'll say nothing happened between us."

When she drew up a chair, Nataraja summoned courage to intervene, taking her elbow. "Mademoiselle, you are a very beautiful woman, but I got to ask you to go."

Vivian looked at him for a moment, smiled in acknowledgment of the compliment, then shrugged free of his hand. "I'm prepared to lie for you under oath, Timothy. Is that what you want, you want me to perjure myself?"

"I want you to tell the truth!"

Nataraja seemed unable to cope with her. I had enough, and I hurriedly rose, knocking over a chair on my way out.

Vivian legged it after me as I made for the door. I jumped on Vesuvio and bumped over the curb onto Fourth Avenue. If I hadn't been so upset I might not have ridden into the path of a Toyota sedan. It braked, burning rubber, but by then I was braking myself, and, miraculously, I vaulted onto the hood, slid over it, and onto my feet, though it was then I twisted my ankle.

I heard Vivian crying, and looked up to see her in Nataraja's arms on the sidewalk. Dotty grabbed the business card of the woman in the dented Toyota, assisted me to her own car, and we sped away. At VGH emergency, I was X-rayed, fit with a splint, and given a crutch.

Vesuvio didn't survive.

CHAPTER NINE

Date of Interview: Friday, September 12, 2003.

Tim was in a dark mood today, for good reason – there had been a "grotesque" session of Dr. Herman Schulter's committee. But I noted a continuing improvement overall, compared to several weeks ago, a determination to seek strength. He continues to back away from the edge.

He seems more philosophical about his separation from Sally, despite suspicions she's being "unfaithful" – in a way that puzzles more than threatens him. His dreams continue, as he puts it, "to prophecy, to confirm hidden aspects of reality."[1] While I'm reluctant to take that leap with him, I'm surprised by their prescience.

His limp is less pronounced. He has been undergoing physical therapy to ready himself for the Okanagan rally, and has bought a replacement bicycle.

---

[1] For example, the powerful lesbian sexual images from Monday night.

After a brief encapsulation of his week, he demonstrated a quality that was more playful than flirtatious, but which caused me to lose my rhythm for a moment.

. . . Just when everything seemed to be settling down.

I think you're bearing up extremely well.

I hope you and Richard are still able to make it tomorrow. Wild sockeye – it won't be pumped up with fish-farm antibiotics. There'll only be the three of us – Sally and Celestine are off to some arts festival in Victoria.

Oh. Then we should reschedule. Richard is in Ottawa giving image advice to the Leader of the Opposition.

I hope your husband can help the guy. I read about the last outburst. Lunatic fringe, Clinton Huff would do a better job. So. The two of us. More intimate that way.

Intimate . . .

An awkward adjective. Cozy.

I'm sorry, I don't know where my head . . . Yes, of course I'll come. I'd like that.

He raised himself on an elbow to look at me. My unconsidered reaction was to tug my skirt down over my knees.

Let's go back to work, Tim.

Tomorrow evening, rather than talk about me, let's talk about you.

Tell me about your dream.

Tell me about yours, Allis. In your flights of nighttime fancy, I doubt you preside at a formal tea party. A different picture is coming into focus. For example, didn't I observe a shorter hemline today, a naked knee? Quickly censored by a tug of a ringless left hand.

I shouldn't have teased you – your blush spoke with the voice of a trumpet. But that was likely prompted by the myriad influences that come into play when marriages are in stress. I don't flatter myself. The so-called rebound effect, when one is compensating for lost love, operates more powerfully through revenge than desire.

But we are experts, you and I. We aren't your normal vulnerable losers, we know how to deny temptation, we understand how the injured can behave irrationally. We acknowledge our feelings – but we accept the boundaries. Still, just in case, and because I know you're eager to meet her, I'll invite Dotty Chung tomorrow evening.

I've no good news to report on the quest for Chauncey Wilmott's killer. I've spent some time at 312 Main, watching through a one-way mirror as detectives interviewed skinheads and homophobes, names culled from police records. Most had alibis. Many had records for theft and weren't likely to have left behind a wallet with three hundred dollars.

Jack Churko spends almost less time working on the case than bemoaning the pressure he's under from the frightened gay community, most of whom are staying off the streets at night. "An isolated case," he says. Let us hope.

The dream. I was wandering alone in the streets of an Italian city – Bologna? – and from a museum or gallery I heard the unmistakable voice of Celestine Post, her challenge: "I dare you." I knew, with that oppressive sense of certainty that dreams often generate, that Sally was with her, and that they were up to mischief.

I hobbled inside, my right leg dragging, and stumbled into a room strewn with abstract art – it was Celestine's loft. Equally expressionist was the montage being played out on a mattress, where Celestine and Sally were assuming Karma Sutric positions. Yet they seemed to take no carnal joy in doing so.

I was overcome with a sense I'd been here before, that I'd witnessed this scene many times. I felt ambivalent, felt I should be disturbed, jealous, but instead I was resigned – but also aroused. In fact, I thought to join them, but I was unsure of the protocol: I was an outsider.

I awoke in an erotic sweat and limped to my coffeemaker.

Let us put aside the obvious: I haven't had a sexual partner for two months, so my night erections are becoming more frequent.

Given that my dreams have become a research tool at least as reliable as the *Farmer's Almanac*, I'm tempted to subscribe to their latest divination: Sally is involved in a lesbian affair with Celestine Post (who, according to rumour, has enjoyed the occasional same-sex frolic). I'm not sure, however, whether Sally is merely a dilettante, an experimenter. I may not have lost her completely – in my dream she seemed to be more curious than passionate. I'm remarkably sanguine about the matter – maybe there's a greater sense of diminishment when one's wife is stolen by a man.

The dream may have drawn from events on Sunday, Celestine's thirty-second birthday. My gift was a day's sailing with Celestine and Sally and several of their friends: artists with a propensity for illegal substance intake. Both weather and winds were fair, and we crossed Howe Sound to rustic Gambier Island, where we had a pub lunch.

I suspect Celestine was treated to a snort or two of Freud's drug of choice, because she became hyperactive on the return leg. She insisted on perching on my lap while I was at the tiller, teasing, whispering, "Getting laid much, honey?" "Or did you forget how?" Her lips tickled my ear. "Sally says you're not exactly a stuntman in the sack – is it a medical problem?" With that, she slipped her hand between my legs, causing the inevitable reaction despite my efforts to pry her hand free. "Hmm, feels like there's still some life down here."

"Damn it, Celestine!" I looked quickly at Sally, who was sitting amidships, her eyes closed, enjoying the sun.

"It's my *birthday*. Maybe I can teach you some new moves. I might save your fucking marriage."

I'd let go of the tiller, and the jib was flapping. "Christ, Celestine! I have to put her back into the wind."

She laughed and jumped up. "Coming about!" I yelled in a strangled voice.

After returning to home port, sour and tense, I let the others go their way, cleaned up the party mess, and, to burn away the testosterone, went for a ride on Vesuvio II, brother of the deceased (eighteen hundred dollars on my stretched Visa limit, but they agreed to swallow the GST). At midnight, racing down Creelman Street, I saw Celestine's old Volkswagen van in the driveway; the house lights had been turned out.

I dare you.

Let me describe the obscenity that took place Tuesday in the hearing room of the Broadway Medical Centre. I'd hoped Vivian had found the sense to drop the charge, but I found her in the hallway, dressed as if for a job interview, in subdued makeup and long skirt.

I limped past her into the room, and found Schulter, Mundt, and Rawlings with their heads together. The scrum quickly broke apart. A slight pinking of jowls told me they hadn't been talking about the latest theories in rational-emotive behaviour therapy.

"Good morning, Tim," Schulter boomed. "Bit of a bum leg? You seem to be favouring it."

"I'm fine." I would explain to him in due course how this happened, how my stalker went off the rails at the Pondicherry. There would be some embarrassed faces around here when the truth came out.

"We were just discussing a few matters of process that maybe you could help us with. We gather you and Werner had a little tiff."

Mundt took on a penitent look. "I want it put formally on the record that it was all my fault, Tim."

147

I may not have mentioned that Mundt phoned me a couple of days after his involuntary swim. An excess of the fine Merlot had influenced him to speak foolishly, out of turn. He abundantly deserved the reaction he got. Can we put it behind us?

"I'll understand if you want me to remove myself," Mundt said. "Herman and Fred can carry on – two is a quorum." A chuckle. "I have to lighten my case load anyway, the fall semester is in full swing."

He seemed unduly eager to withdraw – but now I wanted him to stay. It struck me that the new allegations were too close to home; Werner had enjoyed unprofessional liaisons when in practice, so condemning me would be condemning himself. Without him I'd be left with Herman and his lapdog, Fred Rawlings, who at seventy-seven has long eased into the comfort of retirement and senility.

"Not to worry, Werner. Happy to have you stick around."

Werner's smile was strained. "Good. All's forgotten."

However oppressive, these stop-and-go hearings were beginning to entertain me, and I was curious as to how the next episode would play out. Vivian would quickly fall apart when confronted with the episodes of stalking and her public pronouncements that she was prepared to lie to this tribunal. They'd see her for what she was and feel compelled to apologize.

Irwin Connelly, my mentor, strolled in to a round of greetings and sat, leaning to my ear.

"Christ, Tim, you still don't have a lawyer?"

"This is my favourite entertainment," I whispered. "A lawyer would only derail it."

"Do you know who they're bringing as a witness?"

"An utterly confused woman by the name of Vivian Lalonde."

"Yes, but first a certain Mr. Ivan Kolosky."

My intrusive former landlord. Either out of stupidity or a need to blot out the fact of his existence, I hadn't given thought to the damage he could cause. I was expecting to confront my accuser first, and through her to expose this sham. My mind raced back to the episode in my consulting room – what had Kolosky seen and heard?

"Very well." Schulter was beaming. "Let's hear from Mr. Kolosky. Fred, do you think you might fetch him?"

Rawlings looked blankly at him. "Sorry?" To boot, he was hard of hearing.

Louder: "We need Ivan Kolosky – he's in the next-door waiting room."

Rawlings rose.

"Hold on here," I said. "What happened to the complaint about the state of my office?"

"Yes, of course. A marked improvement, according to Dr. Connelly. You're to be commended, Tim. So there's just this last little item of business. Ah, here we are."

Kolosky was wearing a checkered suit and mismatched tie. He was told to be comfortable. He took a chair. He wouldn't look at me. Vivian had turned this witness over to the authorities, Vivian Lalonde, who promised to lie for me.

Relaxing under Schulter's avuncular manner of putting his questions, Kolosky left no detail unturned. He described going to the building late on August 14 to determine whether I'd evacuated my office and to ensure it was locked. He found my outer door open and upon entering heard raised voices from the consulting room.

"The lady seemed to be protesting." The defendant then emerged, pulling up his pants, a longitudinal scar of lipstick on his face. He saw "the lady" half-naked, hiking up her dress, and heard her describe me as an utter, total bastard.

And add this: While I was in the washroom, he asked her, "Are you all right, miss?" Vivian replied, "I feel totally used," and strode out. It was then that he observed, scattered on the floor, Vivian's nude photographs.

"Sir, you've been most kind in volunteering to come," said Schulter. "Tim, I don't doubt that you have some questions."

Werner Mundt seemed to be straining not to smile. He'd never been so careless as to be caught with his pants down. Or with photographs of a naked patient strewn about his office.

Kolosky had made nothing up, and had painted a credible picture of seduction. I hadn't fully considered the perils of circumstantial evidence.

I stood. "I will be hiring counsel. I'd like an adjournment." My words rang hollowly, like guilt. I felt defeated and ashamed.

"Of course. I think that's best, don't you, Tim?" Schulter was all sympathy.

We adjourned until the call of the chair. I no sooner made my spineless way from the hearing room than Vivian pounced. "Timothy, what have I done? They won't let me withdraw the complaint."

In fury and exasperation, I roared at her — she was a sick, manipulative witch from darkest dungeons of hell. She backed away ashen-faced. I fled down the stairs.

I spent the rest of my day fuming at my desk, drafting a presentence assessment of a small-budget filmmaker who'd kicked a yapping dog at an outdoor shoot. I identified with him, felt a kinship.

James entered tentatively. "Ms. Lalonde is on the line again, sir."

"For Christ's sake, stop calling me sir."

"My, we're being quite crotchety. She says to tell you she's done a terrible thing, and it's okay if you call her names, she deserves it. She'd like to express these sentiments to you directly."

"Tell her to choke on it."

"I will do that, sir."

She'd called three times that day, theatrical, remorseful, demanding forgiveness. All of which feeds my suspicion she doesn't want a lawyer coming between us.

I asked James to call the firm of Pomeroy, Macarthur, Brovak, and Sage, and make an appointment. John Brovak had grown in my estimation as a result of his show of blunt skill at Victoria's libel trial – hire a brawler, she said.

Brovak was able to see me the following day. His firm is in Gastown, in a heritage building overlooking Gassy Jack Square, named for the rowdy saloonkeeper whose statue can be seen from Brovak's cluttered office. The room smelled of stale cigar smoke and whisky fumes, the latter from an open bottle of malt and a half-filled tumbler.

He poured me a drink, and though it was mid-afternoon, I didn't protest. Brovak was disappointed that I'd rejected a chance to further discombobulate Clinton Huff at the upcoming trial. His petition to the court to bar me from attending "ain't worth asswipe"; it showed he was running scared.

"What's with his fixation about you?"

I explained my theory: Huff senses I hold some mysterious power over him, that I might expose a fetish or some shameful event in his past. But another, more dangerous person was fixated on me, fastened to my skin like a leech. As I recounted my ordeals with Vivian Lalonde, Brovak listened quietly, except for the occasional grunt of sympathy. At the end he poured another whisky.

"Any chance this dame is wigged out enough to think you actually fucked her?"

I thought about that. Clearly, Vivian suffers a form of erotomania, a belief that I'm in love with her. Could she have persuaded herself that we connected sexually? Delusions can cement themselves into the psyche. (On the other hand, have I persuaded myself the act didn't happen? Was it possible that in the frenzy of the moment I lost my head? No. That is inconceivable.)

"She's definitely manufacturing. She's obsessed, but she's not close to being psychotic. Hell, she'd flunk a lie detector test."

Brovak made a note. "She said she'd lie for you?"

"Her lies would be my truth."

"You got witnesses to this conversation?"

"Dotty Chung and the owner of the Pondicherry Restaurant."

"Well, shit, we're laughing. Frankly, I can't see how it got this far."

"Vivian Lalonde's father is a prominent surgeon and Schulter is as obsessed as she is."

"Stuff Schulter. It's a walk in the park, pal." I found his confidence stimulating.

Retaining John Brovak, even at his princely hourly rate, provided quick-acting relief, at least for the next couple of days. But I had to monitor my calls. Vivian had somehow obtained my cellphone number. At home, in the evening, I would listen transfixed to her recorded voice. "Honestly, Timothy, I tried to withdraw the charge, but Dr. Schulter thinks you pressured me. He thinks I'm under your sway."

I'd listen for a while, then blip the rest: "That terrible kangaroo court. Oh, Timothy, I know you're hurting . . ." "Timothy, if I could only apologize to you face to face . . ." "I'm going to keep calling . . ."

On Thursday, yesterday, Bob Grundison showed up for his biweekly checkup after classes – he's now registered for the fall semester in psychology at SFU. He was in the company of Lyall, as usual, but also with a tall woman in tight cutoff jeans, a snake tattooed on her arm – Jossie Markevich. Martha Wade had mentioned her, Grundy's favoured female companion. Though the day was cloudy, she was wearing sunglasses. I thought that odd.

I sent her and Lyall to the balcony, feeling secure enough to sequester myself with Grundy. Still, I was leery of showing my limp, and remained seated at my desk. Predators sense such weaknesses.

"Not bad, eh?" he said. The reference was to Jossie. "She's nuts about me. It's a happening thing, Doctor. I never felt this way about a girl before."

"What way?"

"You know – totally out there."

"*Out* there. I'm not sure what you mean."

He wasn't sure either, because he stalled, seeking words for feelings not felt, not comprehended. Love of another being? How might a full-blown psychopath cope with that concept? In the manner of one born sightless who seeks to grasp the qualities of vision?

"I feel like I've been . . . zapped. Hit with a charge of electricity. She's something special."

This effort to convince me of his normalcy would have been amusing if it hadn't been so cloying; it was obviously devised to reassure me, following his outburst in front of Martha Wade, that he was capable of normal affection toward women. He tried on a moonstruck look, his eyes not meeting mine.

"How did you meet?"

"Lyall and I picked her up hitchhiking a few weeks ago." She'd been on her way to a job interview, he explained, but is still unemployed.

"What about the woman you rescued from the river? I understood you were interested in her. Dr. Wade said you spent a night together."

"I really liked her. She wasn't my scene, really. This is different." He gestured toward the balcony: his scene. Again, I wondered about her dark glasses: hiding a black eye?

Grundy confided, "I never mentioned to Jossie about making out with the other girl. You know how women are."

"You erupted in front of Dr. Wade a couple of weekends ago. Tell me about that."

The quick shift put him in a stall before he found his prepared script. "I'll be truthful, she was egging me on, trying to get me upset, kind of testing my limits, and, ah, well, she made her point. I kind of blew my top a little. You, know, I *vented*. I had a headache, one of my tensions, it just chose a lousy time to come on. Everything's okay. I apologized. She's been great, she's really helped me." He handed me an envelope. "Anyway, back to the Skeena River, here's some clippings for your file. Hey, it was nothing, I just reacted on instinct. They're talking about a life-saving medal."

Afterwards, I showered long. That evening, I biked up Little Mountain, Queen Elizabeth Park, and watched the setting of the sun, watched the city light up like a many-candled cake – but I was unable to shake his aura, the immoral stink of him.

But this is a sour note upon which to start the weekend . . .

Bring something warm tomorrow, Allis, I'm cooking outside and an early autumn chill is in the air.

CHAPTER TEN

Date of Interview: Friday, September 19, 2003.

Tim arrived in a sombre mood. He has been much affected by what appears to be a second hate murder, and feels frustrated by his inability to aid the police forensically. That having been said, he showed no signs of unwarranted anxiety this day. I continue to sense a mending, a healing of the wound of marital separation.

He is now convinced that Celestine Post is playing a dubious role, exacerbating the situation, the "gremlin in the gears" who is sabotaging his effort to reunite with Sally. To this purpose, Tim says, Celestine's strategy includes "vamping" him – though I found his reasoning obscure, given his suspicions that she and Sally are romantically involved.

His recovered memory of being in the locked trunk has helped him come to grips with his claustrophobia. He has been feeling less discomfort in such situations, and is taking elevators more frequently. His fear of crowds has lessened as well, and he has expressed eagerness – and I believe he's ready – to deal with his problem with heights, with flying.[1]

Despite what he calls his "highly unprofessional loathing" of Robert Grundison II, he finds himself wavering about whether the man poses a physical threat to him or can realistically be considered a suspect in the recent murders. Tim's other major concerns have paled significantly, the burden of addressing them having been shifted to his lawyer, John Brovak, who has assured him he'll be fully exonerated by the discipline board.

The appearance of Tim's mother in a dream is a hopeful signal that he's preparing himself to deal with major causative factors in his neurotic behaviour pattern: the issues surrounding his provenance. But he feels threatened by this dream and is reluctant to discuss it with his mother.[2]

You're walking better.

Two-thirds of the way to full recovery. James's partner recommended a first-rate therapist. She works with the ski patrol.

How do you feel otherwise?

I'm in my usual state of transcendental bliss. How do you feel?

Okay. A little tired. Relieved, though.

After the letting go? That's good. You made a decision about your marriage, it frees up a lot of emotional and mental energy for better use.

You were very kind on Saturday. Anyway, let's shelve my own stress factors.

Yeah, let's get the bad stuff out of the way. There's been

---

[1] He indicated this while entertaining me at his home Saturday night. That event, solely a social occasion, need not otherwise be remarked upon.

[2] Victoria Dare called to say she's "willing" to meet with me. Tim has been pressing her to do so, and I'm curious as to her earlier reluctance.

another hate murder. It looks like we might have a serial killer out there.

I heard about it, some poor homeless man . . .

Homeless and homosexual. What hasn't come out in the news yet is that Moe Morgan has a brief court history, an indecent act in public. The police have dismissed him as a reprobate – it makes their lack of success easier to bear. We're trying our best, could have been worse had the guy been a deserving citizen.

How is this impacting on you?

I'm discouraged. Anyway, enough – murder seems to make my other concerns seem picayune.

Can you expand on that?

Well, violent death does tend to add a certain perspective, doesn't it, when one has been a self-obsessed, whining bore.

Don't put yourself down.

You're too forgiving.

How are things with Sally?

I sent her flowers finally, even though she broke a date and sent a proxy. I've survived yet another assault on my innocence. I feel besieged – it's the new sexual age, I'm not prepared psychologically for it.

Forgive me if this seems blunt – have you ever had sexual relations with other women than Sally?

There were some early débâcles, mostly during my teens. Nothing since we started living together.

How important is that to you – being sexually faithful?

I'm not sure any more.

You've indicated your lovemaking with Sally had begun to wane in intensity. Would you like to talk about that?

Relative to other long-term couples, I'd say we were on the normal curve . . .

I sensed discomfort. He abruptly changed the subject.

You're okay about Saturday night? I thought you might need a
follow-up, because you were a little . . .

Out of character? Not the Allison Epstein you thought you
knew.

Fourteen years of ballet training . . .

Where were we?

⌒ᴖᴖᴖᴖᴖᴖ⌒

The following case study is based on behavioural observation and
may require test-retest reliability correlation. Subject is mid-thirties,
five-foot-ten, but of slender build – indeed, willowy. Of her many
attractive features, the most notable are large, percipient eyes that are
capable of expressing sympathy and scorn with equal intensity.

Subject arrived ten minutes late, initially presenting as tentative
and polite in manner. There was no clouding of consciousness,
and she seemed alert and aware of her surroundings, to the point
that she described them as "delightful and cozy," though she found
preposterous the Sigmund Freud pencil sharpener retrieved from
the office.

I observed that her hair had recently been cut and styled, and she
was stylishly dressed in silk blouse and scarf, long skirt, all in muted
shades of Titian brown in complement to her hair. Subject's
concern with grooming and appearance might suggest, in others,
insecurity and a longing to gain social acceptance, but in Dr.
Epstein's case, it stems from her innate sense of aesthetics.

At one point, as I led her aboard, she stumbled into a coil of rope
and may well have pitched into the sea if I hadn't grasped her waist.
There seemed little reason to suspect that a subconscious suicidal
motivation was a factor – Dr. Epstein, though mildly depressed
by the infidelity of her partner in marriage, is in vigorous health,
is engaged in a challenging vocation, and is on the threshold of
achieving a miraculous cure for one of her most difficult patients.

As I held her by the rail, she turned and gripped me by my arms, and we embraced briefly. After a moment of awkward laughter, we parted, and I led her below to safety. She accepted with alacrity a glass of chardonnay. Her anxiety was contagious, causing me to babble on about my vintage cutter, the hard work and joy and peace of sailing, the wind in the face clearing the mind, bringing answers, solutions . . .

I hope, Allis, I was able to bore you enough to put you at ease. I'm as sorry as you that Dotty was able only to drop in for drinks before running off with a custody order. I'm sure your impression was a positive one: tough, blunt, and as protective as a tiger to her cub.

I was outside, at the propane unit on the dock, unaware you were contracting her services, and when Dotty, as she left, thanked me for the referral I realized why you had wanted to meet her. (By the way, she thinks you shouldn't have challenged Richard with your suspicions, however valid, because he may try to cover up. On the other hand, he's an image-maker, and will dread the prospect of messy court proceedings.)

Later, you watched admiringly as, with flourishes aped from *The Shiftless Chef* (Channel 52, eight p.m. Tuesdays), I brush-stroked my sauce orléans over two red fillets with the tenderness normally reserved for a lover.

I waited. It was your turn, your chance to take out the garbage. You were staring at the sky, but then shook your head and turned to me with a smile and announced your plans for a divorce. And suddenly you released, you let go. (Was it embarrassment at those tears that triggered your nervousness today in your office? It was beautiful to watch. Allison Epstein, unguarded. Impassioned! Angry!)

I found your childhood, the life you bared to me, fascinating. I've been pondering it since, working up this case study:

During your early college years, you were lonely, living at home, yearning to break free. And suddenly along comes Richard

Spencer. Mom wails and rages. Her only child is barely eighteen, immature, not ready. She has plans for her ballerina: graduate school, a profession. But Dad, the corporate merger consultant, takes your side. He likes hard-driving Richard, that boy is on his way.

You were at the idealistic age when one rebels against parental authority. Your mutiny was a fair reaction to overzealous parenting, particularly by a mother who drove you mercilessly. (Fourteen years of ballet training from the age of five: I find that mind-boggling. But it explains something of your grace, as much as your unhappy feelings toward your mother.)

When you entered into your marriage, theirs broke down, and you've taken on the burden of their divorce, blaming yourself for it. You loved your father too much, were racked with guilt for feeling less affection for your mother. (No wonder you aspired to be a psychiatrist. I suppose I had reasons just as deep. Doctor, heal thyself.)

Richard had a year to go on his M.B.A., and already the offers were pouring in. You were in love with him, he was handsome, outgoing, generous, witty. He still is.

He supported you through your medical studies, financially and emotionally. You were happy with him. You told me you blamed yourself for your childlessness, but that was blurted without reflection, your training deserting you for the moment. If Richard, as a result, doesn't feel like a man, why is that your problem? That he no longer puts much effort into trying confirms his lack of devotion. Your love for him has also waned. You should be thankful: it cushions the fall.

Love alters. That is a lesson we all must learn, I suppose . . .

The above is, I hope, a less garbled version of what I tried to say over our decaffeinated coffees, but something of my instant analysis must have worked because I saw the trace of a smile. After we moved to the couch, so I could raise my leg to ease the ache, I sensed you loosen.

You suggested that Richard's lover is everything you're not. I agree wholeheartedly. Ms. Lang is as effusive and giddy as you are regal and poised, as aggressive and flashy as you are subtle and elegant. She wears a silver belly-button ring.

My act of taking you in my arms was natural, instinctive, human. To do otherwise would have constituted aberrant behaviour. You leaned your head upon my shoulder and pressed my hand. We were close, yes, but in no intimate sense. Good friends.

I continued to bore you with my spiel about my recent conquests of tall pinnacles by elevator, my new staying power among crowds. It was then I asked, with an intended lightness, "When are you going to teach me to fly?"

I only vaguely heard your whispered reply.

"Right now, if you want," is what I thought I heard.

For the remainder of our evening together, I was stinging with desire for you, and held myself from touching you with all the power I could summon. It wasn't until we stood by your waiting taxi that we embraced again, fiercely.

I walked for an hour, then took a shower and stumbled into bed. Soon you and I were alone at what seemed the edge of the planet, a mountain ledge beyond which the lights of the city melded with the stars. You were dressed in white gossamer, like an angel, or like some creature out of *Swan Lake*, and you were urging me to soar with you wingless over that sparkling, terrifying void. "Fly with me," you said.

I declined. You floated effortlessly into the air, still beckoning me, white and ghostly. I was pleading with you not to leave before giving me the key to understanding. You shook your head sadly, as if to say that I alone had the answers, and as you glided off there came from me a wail of loneliness.

I called Sally the next morning (feeling preposterously guilty about having enjoyed even the innocent comforts of another woman), and she answered in a voice muffled with sleep – she'd arrived home late from Vancouver Island. Was she available for dinner this evening or next? I thought we might try the Pondicherry for old times' sake. (I was determined to remember flowers. I would ask Nataraja to order two dozen roses.)

Her only off night was Tuesday – otherwise she was on deadline to do late touch-ups for the next Miriam book – but she'd committed herself to dinner with Celestine. She'd love it if I'd join them. I stifled a groan. Once more, I was being the assigned the role of odd man out, an awkward extra appendage to a gender-bending love affair.

"Celestine really likes you, by the way. Don't be fooled by her manner."

Did I detect a plot? Maybe, but it wasn't confirmed until two evenings later, when Celestine glided to my table at the Pondicherry, unaccompanied, made up like a courtesan, a cherry-red dress slit to the hip, a gallon of makeup. All eyes were upon her – Celestine is a striking woman at the worst of times.

Nataraja planted a kiss on her hand, seated her, and recommended the special of the day, a fish curry, complete with aphorism: "Though you swim upstream, sooner or later the river will take you. What'll you have to drink?"

"We'll start with the Châteauneuf," said Celestine.

"As the lady desires."

She took my hand. "It's just you and me tonight, darling."

Nataraja trundled off, with a frown of confusion. Was this painted woman the new romantic interest in my life?

"Sally can't make it," Celestine purred. "Something has arisen."

Celestine has a facility for making the simplest phrase sound suggestive or even lewd – the inflection in her voice, the lift of eyebrow. I asked her what, exactly, had arisen. It appeared Sally had been summoned for a last-minute revision: her art editor had detected a subtle hint of bestiality in the manner in which a jolly shepherd was positioned behind a ewe. Mildred Goes to Switzerland.

This explanation seemed fanciful: Celestine loves an elaborate fib. I suggested we clear the air over her sexual assault last week on the *Ego*.

"I had a sudden feeling of affection. You got a phobia about human sexuality too? I mean it, I can teach you a few tricks. What's with your attitude about me, anyway? I may be skinny, but I'm sexy. Maybe I have warped taste, but I've always thought you were a Zen guy. Cute, to boot. But mainly, it's kind of endearing how your socks never seem to match."

I felt a fuzzy discomfort. *Celestine really likes you.* Was I being set up for a fall? Was Sally complicit?

We managed to survive dinner with a minimum of stress. Celestine skilfully diverted the topic of Sally whenever I raised it, and I let her ramble on about her career, her future, her horoscope, a recent palm reading: she diddles about with such nonsense. Metapsychology, Freud called it.

Celestine shows almost enough schizotypal tendencies to be classified as such – bizarre in dress and manner, wacky ideas, promiscuous, histrionic, an attention-devouring, centre-of-the-stage persona. In others, such gaudiness might suggest a need to be noticed, an insecurity: not Celestine. Let's call it artistic temperament. I can't deny she's entertaining.

Her palm reading had foretold a dinner with a strange man. "And here I am, dining with a really strange man."

Drinking more than her share of the Châteauneuf, she meandered through the occult practices, finally arriving at hypnosis, a subject she likely classified with reading bumps on the head. Celestine was a virgin to the art: "I'm at the level of hypnotism for dummies." She wanted me to "do" her.

"Right here and now, Celestine?"

"Later, when you come up to my place."

"You are joking."

Her offer included coffee and brandy and this: "I don't want you to put me to sleep – give me just enough of a hit to loosen me up. There's a couple of items I want to get off my chest."

Like what? The truth about her sexual games with Sally? Something worse? *I dare you.* No, I decided, this was only an attempt to compromise me. Afterwards, Sally will be told I had the audacity to screw her best friend.

"Hypnotism isn't a game of pretend."

"I'll be totally in your hands."

I told her I would pass up the invitation.

Afterwards, while she was in the washroom, Nataraja offered some clinical advice: "After a night with that dame, I'd want a medical checkup. Jeez, I forgot." He'd bought two dozen roses but, misunderstanding the situation, he slipped them to me as Celestine returned, obliging me to present them to her as we were leaving.

Outside, she kissed me on the lips. "The flowers that bloom in the spring, tra-la, how fucking sweet. Sally is wrong – you *do* have a romantic bone in your body."

She offered to drive me home. I explained I'd come by bicycle. No problem, she said, just stick it inside her VW camper. I was foolish to agree, and I fully realized that when she detoured to Locarno Beach and pulled in to the parking area.

"I'm not through with you. I've got to release some inner feelings. Concentrate. You're supposed to be good at this. Read my mind."

"It's saying, 'I wonder if I can seduce him.' No chance. I don't go to bed with devotees of horoscopy."

"You're not seeing me, you dork, you're seeing what you want to see. Here's a fucking insight for you. I like you. I've always dug you. I never let on when you were with Sally, but you aren't any longer, and what this evening boils down to is we have two single, mature, horny adults in a Volkswagen camper with a bed. Yeah, I want to lay you. For some ungodly reason, I'm attracted to you."

"Celestine, you are a masterful liar."

She glared. "I ought to slap you, I'm pouring my fucking heart out." Before I could react she was on my lap, her arms circling me, her tongue in my ear. "It took three seconds to get you hard last time, don't pretend you're not interested. Come on, if you're human, you've had fantasies of doing it in a Volkswagen." She reached behind and began to unzip her dress. "Let's not tell Sally."

The id, the caveman within, was in grunting combat with the superego, that moralizing preacher. My will to resist was flagging, but I found the strength, lifted her away, saying hoarsely, "It isn't going to happen, Celestine."

She looked coolly at me, small breasts bared proudly. "My God, you are the gallant knight. You can't love her that much."

"What have you and she been up to?"

"Girl stuff."

"Where is she tonight?"

She pulled up her dress. "I'll take you home, you nerd."

Not a category recognized by the DSM of the American Psychiatric Association, and the more painful for not being a disorder that might attract sympathy. As old phobias recede, obsessive guilt invades, guilt about cheating.

On the following day I sent Sally not roses but a brilliant display of heliconia. She called to thank me, but added, "Was it out of guilt?"

"What lies did Celestine tell you? Nothing happened except that I had to peel the bloody woman off. Where were you last night, anyway?"

"A work thing. I'm sorry, it came out of the blue."

Could I believe her? She promised there'd be a makeup occasion. I insisted upon a clearer agenda, became pushy: what was she doing tonight?

"Tonight . . . Okay, sure. Late, okay? I have a meeting."

I was dismayed by the hesitation in her voice. But more by the fact I'd just displayed the behaviour that had driven us apart: the possessiveness, the control. I kicked myself. I'd absorbed little from two months of therapy.

The gods played one of their tricks that evening, Wednesday. As I was pedalling to meet Sally at one of our better Italian restaurants, my cellphone rang. I was required at police headquarters. Another murder, another looping.

I locked Vesuvio II to a post and brought a taxi screeching to a stop. On the way to police headquarters, I called the restaurant. Sally wasn't there yet, so I left a message.

Jack Churko greeted me with a complaint about how this death has added to his burden, the gay lobby was going to be howling, he resented the fact "the fag file" had been dumped on him. "Anyway, again we got no motive, so it's looking like you're right, Doc. Name is Moe Morgan, a known person, he's as queer as Liberace. He's what in polite talk is called an itinerant. He's a bum. It's not as if the cream of society is under attack, is it?"

He ushered me into the squad room, where he showed me photographs of the body that were still wet from the darkroom, the face a ghastly blue. Again the likely cause of death was strangulation by a wire loop that had cut into the victim's throat.

Brighton, in the East End, is one of the less fashionable of Vancouver's hundred neighbourhood parks, near the train tracks, a haunt of the homeless. The assault had happened behind a clump of firs. Morgan had set up camp there: a few blankets, discarded tins of tuna and Spam. It was surmised his murderer had followed him to this lair.

A woman walking a dog had heard a muffled cry, the sound of flight, someone whacking his way through the bushes. She raced to the nearest phone, then led the response team back up the path. The body was quickly found.

Again, no fingerprints, no footprints, not a stray hair from which to take a DNA sample. No wire was found either. Churko has imposed an information ban to avoid compromising the investigation; he intends to say no more than that Moe Morgan was strangled.

He looked at me as if expecting some magical formula to identify the killer.

"Killer or killers?"

I couldn't hold back my suspicions about Grundy and Lyall. Despite my efforts to convince myself I was creating phantoms, I continually heard these names like a warning whisper. I gave Churko a synopsis of my dealings with them, and suggested they fit the profile.

"What you call homophobic."

"Yes."

"What proof have you got against these guys?"

I had to admit Dotty Chung's inquiries (he snorted at the mention of her name) pointed to their being on their way to the Skeena River when Wilmott was attacked. "At least, let's find out what they were up to tonight. As for their rafting trip, we don't know when they actually left. I'm working on a theory they hung around town, flew up Saturday after doing in Mr. Wilmott."

They might have bought air tickets with cash, using false names. Churko said he'd look into it, but he didn't seem to relish the prospect; unspoken was the fact that Robert Grundison Sr. was a generous contributor to police charities.

Sally never got my message at the restaurant, and waited, then left without ordering more than a drink. I was contrite on the phone the next morning, but she understood, and we rescheduled for the weekend.

James was badly shaken by the murder. This time he agreed to take the morning off – but only to help organize a downtown demonstration at lunch hour. Anger has emboldened him. A placard was leaning against his desk: TAKE BACK THE NIGHT.

The brutal slaying led to a turbulent dream last night, in which I was banished from my little Alpine village. A man prodded me at the gate with an electric guitar, called me a nerd, told me to go find my mother. Other band members were among the eviction party, but they were no longer hillbillies but rock musicians.

As I stood outside the town walls, I felt a sense of estrangement, of being denied my birthright, my heritage. The band struck up a familiar song from the sixties, a blues tune. But I felt frightened – killers were about, and night was coming. I slipped into the cover of a grove of fruit trees, down a darkened path, my heart in my throat. I wanted my mommy. I *was* a little nerd.

The band played on. From a rise, I saw that the village had morphed into a rock concert, distant and merry. Suddenly, from the shadows, a cloven-hoofed creature jumped onto the path, and I shrank away. But the expression was good-natured. He was Pan-like, a satyr. Before he bounded away, he said, "He loves you."

"Who loves me?" I cried.

I raced after him, finally coming upon a tent beside a lake upon which the moon glistened. On approaching closer, I heard the rustling and groans of intercourse. Then came a howl of male release as I was conceived.

He loves me. My father loves me.

When I woke I groggily assumed the dream was revelatory, a grant of insight. But as my mind cleared, I realized I had been played the fool. The dream represented only the longing, the fatherless longing.

CHAPTER ELEVEN

Date of Interview: Friday, September 26, 2003.

I was tense in anticipation of this session, expecting Tim to be in a highly emotive state, perhaps accusatory. He rang me earlier in the week anguished over a difficult turn in his relationship with Sally, and called again this morning demanding to know the essence of my discussion with his mother. I had to tell him Victoria had broken her appointment yesterday.

All this has come on the heels of a third murder, of another man of little means, and, as I learned today, Tim has been feuding with police investigators.

His ankle sprain is now largely healed, but he was in a state: laces undone, unshaven, his hair a mess, a scrape on his arm from a bicycle fall. He kicked off his running shoes and fell back on the couch, saying, "We need to talk." Though exhibiting anxiety symptoms, he was more subdued than I expected, and subsequently I learned he'd prescribed himself Xanax, a mood elevator. It may have enhanced his absent-mindedness, for he left initially without his shoes, and was not aware of that until he was out the door.

Central to his distress was "an ironclad case" that Sally Pascoe has been having an affair: "a real one, with a person not of her gender." He accused Celestine Post of covering up for Sally – and intimated that I was in league, that Sally had confided to me about adulterous acts, and that I was withholding this from him.

Plunging his mood lower is a new hypothesis about his genesis. He was conceived, to use his euphemism, "in a socially unacceptable manner."

Did Victoria say why she was cancelling?

I gather she had an upsetting talk with you.

I blew it. I was a zombie, I was in a state of shock. I'd just found out! Cousineau, how could she . . . that fop! This fucking drug makes me feel too detached, I can't rage.

I don't think it's slowed your mental processes.

Yeah, but I went off the road, I could have broken my arm. Hell with it. Maybe I'll try Benzedrine, shoot up before the race. A month to go, I'm falling apart. Why did she have to skulk behind my back? We're separated, she's free to screw whomever she wants, even a sleaze like Cousineau. Is it the thrill of cheating, or is sex more enjoyable when illicit?

Maybe she didn't want to hurt you.

Sure, and maybe she intended to tell me in her own good time.

And maybe you're continuing to make demands on her. Is she so free as you claim?

He made an effort to control his anger.

Okay she's free, but does she have to be so ridiculous? Ellery Cousineau, he's as shallow as a rain puddle, he's . . . there's something abnormal about him, too. You can see it in his eyes, the way he's constantly studying women, but it's as if he's seeing them only on the surface.

This is a man she works with . . .

A writer, shmoozed his way to senior editor at Chipmunk Press. He's been trying to get into Miriam's pants . . . Sally's, I mean . . . for years.

Let's explore that slip of the tongue.

Miriam . . . Okay, maybe that's the message I'm getting from Cousineau. A Humbert Humbert, he preys on little girls in dirndls.

Seek another direction. How deeply do you associate Sally and Miriam?

That's obvious. Miriam is Sally at the age of eight, there's even a resemblance in her old photos.

Go deeper.

He reflected for a minute.

Okay, you're right. I've been treating her as a child.

What are some of examples of that?

I make all the decisions. The plays and restaurants. The rented movies. The choice of Oscar Peterson over Diana Krall. The hour we go to bed.

Another silence.

I wonder why it took her so long to bolt.

ᘓᙡᖚᕯ

I was more a mess leaving your office than coming in. Walking off without my shoes . . . Was it the wounding insight? The Xanax? Had my struggle to maintain sanity taken too great a toll?

Murder, betrayal, a crippling truth revealed: the past seven days were designed by the devil in hell himself . . .

Yet it all began so innocently: Sunday, my backup dinner date with Sally. She'd picked me up, was subdued during the ride.

Though bothered by *l'affair Celestine*, the incident in the VW van, she preferred not to talk about it. "I don't want it to dominate the evening. I intend to have some words with her."

What she wanted to talk about was you. I took some small pleasure in confessing – in the broadest outline – to our cookout at the *Ego*. I found it odd that her initial reaction was pique, but presumed she was castigating herself for her haste in dumping a master chef.

She wanted to know what level of intimacy had been reached that night. ("Did she stay over?" "Please, darling, Allis is my therapist." "What kind of therapy was she offering?") I remained vague, didn't even mention you've sent Richard packing – though others seem to know. Evelyn Mendel phoned me. I gather she's being a pillar of support.

Left to her speculations, Sally treated me with silence for most of our date – this was upon a moonlit setting by the Fraser River: the Floating Lotus (my choice, okay, but only after she suggested Chinese). We sat by candlelight, studied menus, drank wine, listened to the river. I'd vowed to stop probing, to let her fill conversational gaps with her own words. I sensed she was rehearsing them: her lips were softly working, and there was that telltale tilt of her head.

The silence was so tense that I jumped when my cellphone rang. Once again, it was Jack Churko. Once again, he had ugly news: another body had been discovered, mouldering in an East End basement suite, multiple stab wounds with a pair of scissors.

I pleaded for an hour's grace. Churko reminded me I'd been placed on a retainer. He needed me at the scene of the crime. I might be able to help connect this with the other attacks, he didn't know yet if this victim, too, was gay. "And this time we're talking killers, plural, at least two." I put him on hold and turned to Sally, who sighed and offered to drive me.

Our wonton soup, crab-in-the-shell, and shrimp with baby asparagus were already coming from the kitchen, so management provided takeout boxes. We ate as we drove, a slapdash, shirt-soiling ride. Soon we saw flashing lights ahead and stopped by the crime-scene tape. I told her I'd call her later.

"It's all right. We'll talk tomorrow when you're fresh."

We kissed, tenderly enough, but in no lingering fashion. "I love you," I said.

"We'll talk tomorrow."

I nodded. She looked away, and as I stepped from the Saab onto a dreary street of wood-framed one-storeys I felt a hint of nausea (we'll talk about what, tomorrow?). After watching the tail lights disappear, I turned wearily toward a shabby cottage, the scene of the crime, and I put my worries aside, grasped at the lifeline of cold reality. A savage murder had been committed here.

I identified myself to a uniformed woman, and as I ducked under the yellow tape I felt as if I were passing between zones of the psyche – it was as if the tape marked the boundary of two personalities, the neurotic nerd and the forensic investigator, the two faces of Tim Dare. I've told you, Allis, how I'm morbidly allured by the murderous mind – and I think this helped me concentrate that Sunday night.

The roof of the cottage was sagging, patched with tar shingles, and the yard was overgrown with weeds. Churko was near a side door leading to a half-basement, and he motioned me over to meet the homeowner, Mr. McLaird, in his eighties, a squint-eyed fellow with unwashed ears.

"This is Dr. Dare," Churko said. "He's going to want to talk to you."

He excused McLaird for the moment to put me in the picture: the late tenant of the downstairs suite, José Pierrera, was an immigrant from Portugal, a laid-off bricklayer subsisting on employment benefits. A loner, according to McLaird, with no close friends. His only occasional visitor was a married older sister, but on Wednesday evening last he'd entertained two or three men, presumably the assailants.

McLaird hadn't seen him for several days, and tonight, noticing a gamy aroma, entered the suite to check. He found Pierrera's naked body lying in the kitchenette, the blood that had poured from multiple wounds pooled around it. He had died several days ago – the pathologist would give a more exact estimation later.

Churko suggested I might apply my forensic expertise to the motive behind a macabre joke; a pair of bloody shears had been in the corpse's stiffened right hand – as if, impossibly, the victim had stabbed himself. I told Churko it seemed a very Grundyesque gesture. He snorted and lit a cigarette.

Inside I could see a worn couch, a table and chair, a bed behind a partition, its sheets rumpled, clothing strewn over it. The ID team was still probing into crannies, bagging hairs, food crumbs, beer-bottle caps. Fingerprint dust mottled the many beer empties strewn about.

I stood aside as the morgue crew removed the sheeted body: a short man, a pot belly. I looked into the tiny kitchenette at its stained wallboard, loose ceiling tiles, and worn linoleum. The silhouette of the former José Pierrera showed on the floor in a wash of red. I felt sickened, struggled with an urge to vomit.

When I returned outside, Churko drew me into a huddle with the landlord. "I want you to tell Dr. Dare what woke you up Wednesday night."

"Like I said about José, I never known him to have friends, but he was having a party, and that's what waked me up – they was laughing, making a racket. Couldn't tell how many. Two, three fellers. No girls. They didn't have girls. I wouldn't of allowed it."

"Could you make out their words?" Churko asked.

"Can't say I did."

"Even when you put your ear to the floor?" I asked.

McLaird looked uncomfortable, as if exposed as one who per-
forms unseemly acts.

"To be honest, I didn't hear nothing. No screams, nothing."

"You might have felt something," I said. He looked blank.
"Vibrations. Thumps."

"Well, now, the fridge makes that kind of noise, so I wouldn't of
noticed."

He hadn't been able to identify Pierrera's voice. "Never spoke
much, anyway, and you couldn't understand him for his accent."
He had no idea whether his visitors came by foot, taxi, or private
car. He was asleep before they left.

"Any reason to think he was homosexual?" Churko asked.

McLaird couldn't say, but hadn't considered him "of that fashion."

Churko led me back inside, where we looked through a box of
personal papers. Correspondence, letters from Portugal, bills, a
passport. Nothing to hint he was gay.

The only reading material – it was folded under the phone – was
a page of classifieds from the *Georgia Straight*, the giveaway weekly.
Not employment listings but personals, pleas from the lonely for
companionship. On a margin, someone, presumably Pierrera, had
inscribed in pencil, in laborious, crude letters, the name *Jimmy*.

The phone had a redial function. Churko isn't dull, and after he
checked with identification to make sure they were finished with
it, he put it on speaker and pressed the redial button. An unctuous
voice answered. "You have reached the Adonis Hot Line. Do you
want to speak with Philip or Conrad or Jimmy?"

Churko hung up, preferring not to give notice that he'd be
dropping by to talk to Jimmy and seize any records or tapes. "Guess
we're going to have to put some effort into this one."

This murder happened Wednesday, September 17, the same night
the homeless man was killed in Brighton Park, and I asked Churko
if he'd learned the whereabouts of Grundy and Lyall that night.

"Relax about it, Doc. To make you happy, we checked. They were home. We got two employees confirm that."

A night watchman and a live-in maid at The Tides insisted Grundy and Lyall had been there all evening. They had been interviewed at a "neutral" location.

"We had to tell them to keep their mouths shut about this. We don't want to get in a hassle with prominents. I'm a year shy of retirement with full pension."

What about August 22, the night of Chauncey Wilmott's death – had he asked about when Grundy and Lyall actually showed up for their rafting trip?

"For Christ's sake, Doc, why are you beating this dead horse? They were up there, it was in all the newspapers, Grundy saved some girl's life. Okay, he has a bad report card from the past, and I know you got a hard-on for him, but cut him some slack, he's a hero. We can't allocate all our resources to one wild theory."

I shut up. Keep things safe and simple: that is Churko's attitude, don't get caught up in something messy on the eve of retirement.

I followed Churko outside, where reporters had gathered. He took on a grave look for the cameras, responded to a few questions. Yes, there has been a murder, a stabbing, that's all we're going to say right now. Don't know if it's tied to any previous incidents. All avenues will be explored. Now let us do our work.

I lingered for a while, then found my way by foot to Kingsway, the yellow scar that runs across Vancouver's right cheek: fast food, fast gas, fast in-and-out motels. A teenaged boy on the corner, obviously a prostitute, living dangerously in these ugly times. Down the street, a woman plying a similar trade. I was lonely, in need of companionship that was healthy and real and proven. I felt incomplete after my aborted evening with Sally, in need of answers: had she intended to announce it was all over or to hold out a carrot of hope?

I was desperate to know, to be with her. I flagged a taxi, and soon was standing in front of the house on Creelman. Only a porch lamp was on, Sally's upstairs bedroom was darkened. But something was missing: there was no Saab in the driveway or carport. No Saab on the street.

I rang the doorbell three times, insistently. She'd told me she was going home . . . I was concerned, then frightened. I dialled Celestine on my cellphone, and after several rings a sullen, sleepy voice replied.

"It's fucking after midnight."

"Just tell me if Sally's there."

"Why would I tell you?"

"Because she has disappeared. I'm at her house."

After a moment, she spoke with lowered voice: "She's here, asleep on the futon in the other room, and I'm not going to wake her. Go home to bed." She hung up.

This was an alibi more likely prepared than off the cuff. Celestine's role was to bear false witness for an under-the-counter affair.

Pause to let me catch my breath. Pause for an academic aside: Reik speaks of a sense-perception that seeps unrecognized into the unconscious, a telepathy still available to the life forms from which we evolved but largely lost to us. It can still communicate beneath awareness, can even emerge within our dreams. I'd seen Sally dressed as a little girl, as Miriam, I had dreamed of Ellery Cousineau by her side, whispering words of seduction.

He is a pedophile.

Cousineau lives in a West End condominium: I have been there once for drinks. I took a taxi there, a spindly tower near Stanley Park. Cousineau's condo was on the ninth floor – was that it, the one with the light glowing?

I walked toward his building, thinking I'd buzz his suite, but then I saw the ghastly proof of my fears: a blue Saab was parked out front – the grinning Miriam doll hanging from the rear-view was distinctive, the cold truth of perfidy.

I waited under a chestnut tree in a mindless fog. I felt again that sense I was outside my body, lost in a world without reality. But ultimately I was no longer able to shut out Sally and betrayal and jealousy, and when mind joined body I found myself still under the chestnut tree, still a hundred feet from Cousineau's building.

I waited through the night, shivering in the autumn cold. At a quarter to six, she emerged, wearing her dress of the evening before, and started her car and drove away.

You can't begin to comprehend the crushing loss I felt. There was no dealing with this feeling, no way to placate it. I could only bury it, like the dead, bury it deep beneath anger. So despite my exhaustion I carried on savagely into the day, gulping bitter coffee at an all-nighter, arriving at the office at eight a.m. to find James already there. I barked at him: Cancel my patients for the day, I'm feeling too foul to deal with the lesser problems of others. He withdrew from me and silently set about his tasks.

I lay down and tried to nap – to no avail. I stood, I paced. I went out to the balcony, clenching my fists, wanting to scream, to be heard across the inlet. I slammed on my helmet and strode off to unleash Vesuvio II onto the streets of Vancouver.

I was gearing into high on the Burrard Bridge when a four-wheel sports pickup swerved at me so suddenly that I skidded, fell, scraped my arm. It sped away before I could read the plate or see the driver, but I didn't assume the act was intentional. All my thoughts were directed to exposing Ellery Cousineau for what he was: Category 302.2, exclusive type, sexually attracted to female children, extremely high recidivism rate, typically justifies his acts by claiming the child was sexually provocative. I pictured myself confronting Sally with the truth, watching the revulsion play on her face.

I worked my way through the West End, through the checkerboard maze of one-way streets, then to Denman Street. There, looming ominously, was your building, and I stalled. Was this my destination? Had unconscious impulses urged me to seek the safety of Allison Epstein's couch? Will she recommend a straightjacket when I run out of fuel, when my rage deserts me?

But you, too, I've learned, are capable of anger. You were correct in dumping all over me today. I apologize for accusing you of withholding information. My irrational suspicions had Sally uttering a dark confidence to you, an admission of adultery.

Obviously, you weren't implicit in the scheme – for that is what it is – or aware of its extent, or that Celestine Post is pulling the strings. Oh, yes, she's the hatcher of this plot, the author of my misfortune. It all comes clear, her Iago-like urgings in Sally's ear: *If you think Cousineau's such a hunk, go to bed with him. I dare you.*

So I'll direct my anger at where it belongs. It is the witch, not the pedophile, not the children's artist, who deserves my outrage. What impels Celestine? Lesbian possessiveness no longer seems likely. She dared Sally, challenged her to enter Cousineau's bed. But why? To clear the way for an even more bizarre romance? Behind the acerbity, the sharp, digging elbows of her repartee, was there an attraction to me? Had Celestine actually been honest in saying she was pouring out her fucking heart to me?

If so, how long had she felt this way about me? And why hadn't my antennae picked up the signs? I was always too focused on Sally, unable to make out Celestine in the background. She might have planted the seeds of marital rupture many months ago, pressing on Sally the notion that she should have a life of her own, that she should undo the shackles. Find freedom, oh, my sister: challenge the nerd, insist on Bologna, if he really loves you, he'll let you go.

A blacker thought: Had Sally been having affairs all along? Had I blocked the clues, refused to read them? Is this the way it ends? With ugly irony? Sally will have Ellery. Celestine will have Timothy. We will live happily ever after.

I'd stopped by a lamppost while embroiled in these thoughts and was staring at your office window, imagining you at work with Mrs. Pianissimo, who complains strange men are following her, when suddenly Tim Dare, M.D., comes bursting through the door. I visualized the resulting scene: Dr. Epstein can't take it any more, she's off the case, go find another shrink, someone with infinite patience and forgiveness.

Still in a fuming gloom, I cycled off to 312 Main for another session with Jack Churko's task force. I practised anger management en route, but my temper, like a volcano seeking fault lines, spewed over once I got there. I stepped on toes, badgered Churko with irksome advice as to how to run his case.

Circulate José Pierrera's photograph, I urged – someone might have seen him with the killers. Check the liquor stores in his home area, where they may have bought that case of beer.

"I know my job, Doc."

"He could have been picked up in a gay bar."

"We're doing the gay bars. There's no end of them. I ain't got an army working for me, it's taking time, this town is as bad as San Francisco. Anyway, you already told me you don't see Pierrera in bars, you figure him as a loner, a homebody, a guy who gets off on phone sex."

"I've been wrong before."

"That's real encouraging."

Jimmy, the voice at the other end of the Adonis Hot Line, had been of scant help. He told Churko he did this job just to earn a buck; he wasn't even gay. He could barely remember Pierrera, had no idea of his habits or haunts. Jimmy did most of the talking – purred sensuously from scripts.

I went on about Grundy and Lyall, implying – without a scintilla of evidence – there was a conspiracy to shelter them.

"I'm listening," Churko would say. (I'm not listening.) "I hear what you say." (I ain't interested.)

I demanded to know why Grundison and DeWitt weren't being watched each hour of day and night; insisted that I be allowed to talk to the two lying staff at The Tides, the watchman, the maid; there was a coverup; the authorities were cowed by the power of the Grundison family, afraid of their cunning lawyers, of multi-million-dollar suits for false arrest.

Churko diagnosed me as obsessive.

What's worse, he'd retained a charlatan without a minuscule of professional training. A psychic! A clairvoyant! A matronly woman who, it was alleged, had led police to other murderers by dint of her ability to visualize the scenes of crime after absorbing them through her supernatural pores. She'd been taken to Brighton Park, to the East End basement suite, and now was sitting in a darkened room, her eyes closed, while Churko waited with a few other gullible detectives.

Finally, she waved us in. "I see two young men," she said, still seeming in a trance. "One is very husky, the other lighter but also strong. He has short hair, I think. His head seems shaved. While he looks on, the bigger of the men raises a weapon. I see it now, a pair of scissors, long scissors, shears . . . dear God, I see a hand come down . . ." She opened her eyes suddenly. "I'm sorry, but my mind rejected the image as too painful."

I followed Churko to his office in a fury. "'I see it now, a pair of scissors' – what a pile of baloney. A shaved head – she read the papers, the speculation about skinheads. All it proves is you don't have to spend ten years in university to conjure up the obvious. What did this amateur guessologist tell us we didn't know?"

"That there were two assailants and they looked like Grundison and DeWitt. She supports your theory." Churko squinted at me through the smoke of his cigarette, took in the wan, sleepless eyes, the embittered expression. "Are you having a problem, Doc?"

"Yes, I'm having a problem."

"Maybe I don't read people as good as you — I never got a college degree either — but you're not acting normal."

"When am I going to be allowed to question The Tides staff?"

"On my good time. Go home. Take a break."

For how long, I wanted to know. He would call me. I told him I expected to see Grundy this Thursday, his regular visit, I could confront him, try to debunk his alibi, break the case wide open.

"Postpone it," Churko said. "Go for a ride on your bike."

I protested, they'd need my advice when it came time to take down Grundy, he had to be handled like delicate china.

"We're not taking Grundy down until we got evidence."

It was only during my glum journey home, cycling into a head-clearing wind, that my *idée fixe* about Grundy and Lyall lost its grip. Where was the proof, what right had I to convict them, in my own mind, without evidence? Churko was right: I must postpone that session with Grundy, I was acting irrationally.

When I got home, I was hailed by the young couple in the next-door houseboat. They were organizing a party tonight, they'd be pleased if I'd come, they were planning some music, I could bring my clarinet. I declined, but thanked them.

Sally was on my machine. "How did it go last night?" *How did it go?* "I'll be home after seven."

Vivian Lalonde came on after that. "We have to meet, Timothy, we have to talk about what I'm going to say. You do want me to lie for you on Monday, don't you? Call me, this is urgent." A second call was to similar effect. A third was her invitation to go fuck myself.

I fell into bed at a quarter to five, dinner not taken. I twisted in my sheets, fending off my demons, then floated into a vague, enervated wakefulness before blackness came.

This is my dream: I'm in a carnival tent where Celestine, in gypsy dress, is laying out tarot cards, telling me she can teach me a few tricks. She flashes a card at me, but it's a photo that I faintly remember: Victoria at seventeen, a mischievous smile. "You don't want to know the truth," says Celestine, dismissing me.

There are many others in this tent, people I recognize from my dreams of the Alpine village, all in elaborate costume. I'm the only person not wearing some strange outfit, and again I feel that sense of not belonging. Among them is a man looking out vacantly from many eyes dispersed about his torso, and I am horrified.

As I make my way toward an exit, I come upon Sally and Cousineau. He's tossing garments out of a trunk – girls' dresses, stockings, underpants, ribbons – and he seems displeased with the available choices. "Wear this one, my dear," Cousineau says, handing her a Mary-had-a-little-lamb dress. Next he extends a tall, rounded shepherd's staff, and the sight of this phallic insinuation causes me to stumble out, blinded by tears.

Now I'm at the shore of a lake, from which loons call; goats rut by the shore. But one of them is half-human, the satyr again. The sounds of a banjo come from the lakeside tent where I was conceived. I see a light flicker within it, and I hear Victoria moaning in distress. I'm overcome by the thick, pungent fumes of cannabis . . .

The smell woke me, and my first thought was that Celestine Post was smoking pot on the *Altered Ego*. But the smell, along with the sounds of a party, was coming from next door. Someone was playing a guitar. It was midnight.

I was only dimly aware of the party, I was concentrating on the dream, pulling it back, and as I worked at it, I was nagged by a sense that Victoria had lied – yet again – about Peter.

I wasn't prepared to come to grips with that, to act on it, not immediately. I stumbled through the next few days, not returning calls, half-listening to the woes of the patients I couldn't cancel, clashing with a judge in court, offering him harsh advice on what to do with a pederast, taking shots at a defence lawyer. James nursed me patiently through my crisis, arranged to reschedule Grundy and Lyall, advised Churko of the alternative date.

I didn't phone Sally back. When she made no effort to call me either, my sense of bereavement worsened. Maybe she was ashamed for kissing me Sunday night before going to the bed of another. (He owns a small airplane. Sally loves flying. That's what this is about. But I'm flailing, refusing to see reality. I may have to free myself from Sally just to save my sanity.)

My mood wasn't lightened by a visit from Celestine Post the other day. I was in my consulting room, in a bleary state of angst, when she slipped past security. James had lied poorly, and she saw when she peeked in that I was not, in truth, occupied with a distraught patient. She entered uninvited.

"What do you do in here, jerk off all day?"

"This is my quiet time."

"I want to say I'm sorry."

I studied her, expecting irony, the raised eyebrow, but what I saw was the flaccid facial tone of the mendicant, of one who has been on the run too long and has decided to turn herself in.

"I accept that I am a nerd," I said.

"I'm not sorry for insulting you. Or for having the hots for you. I'm sorry about Sally. I'm sorry that you're hurting." She sat on the arm of the stuffed chair, stiffly, like a bird. "I felt like shit after I checked my horoscope today. It was like, 'Confess your sins to a friend who is in pain.'"

I felt a bleak satisfaction in learning I was right. Sally had been titillated at the prospect of a sexual adventure, Celestine had taunted her to bend to Cousineau's importuning, then covered for her. When I spurned Celestine's advances, she realized she'd made "a horrible mistake."

I felt a dull pain when Celestine added, "I didn't think it would lead to this. It's gotten serious. He's been taking her out on his Cessna, and maybe she likes flying more than she likes fucking, but he's head over heels, and she's flattered. She's going off to some pokey Gulf Island to think things over."

I said I was too depressed to talk further.

Images from my dreams continued to plague me: the lurking satyr, the rock music, the sounds of the banjo from the tent, a woman's moans. These weren't products of a mysterious power that permits me to crystal-gaze upon past events – they came from a lifetime of receiving Victoria's signals. Unspoken truths she'd struggled with over the years had been absorbed by me, in the deepest part of me, and were now seeping from my unconscious.

Finally, on Wednesday evening, I stopped procrastinating and invited myself to Victoria's home for an encounter session over a bottle of wine.

She was welcoming but seemed harried – she's been trying to catch up on her obituaries, which she's been neglecting while she concentrates on her second novel, *Desirée*. Is Desirée, with her witchlike powers, to be burned by the vengeful townsfolk of Chickadee, B.C., or is she innocent? Horror grips yet another small town.

Her publisher was pestering her to complete it. *When Comes the Darkness* is selling well as a result of publicity over her libel trial, and *Desirée*, if finished in time, would grace New Millennium's spring catalogue.

We sat at her dining-room table, where she prefers to work – it was laden with manuscript and notepads and reference books, the computer humming. On the screen: *Recently honoured with the title*

of life member of the Teamster's Union, Mr. Kozak came peacefully to the
end of the road on the day of the Autumn Solstice, after a brief illness.

"What do you think?"

"How about, 'Completed his last journey'?"

"I used it last week for a train brakeman."

In a vase on the table was a huge bouquet. Sending flowers seems all the rage these days, and in this case the sender turned out, on brief cross-examination, to be a TV producer Victoria has been seeing, a new suitor. She'd already had one date with this bearded, sensitive yet rugged designer of a cable arts show. Fifty, divorced (twice, two teenagers), climbs in the high Rockies when on holiday.

Before I could say anything, Victoria began a lecture about how I, predictably, would not approve of this liaison, how I could always be counted on to discover some wart of character.

I assured her I wanted her to enjoy close male friendship, intimate even – or better: a life partner. But I also wanted her to be loved. She has a history of choosing unwisely. Maybe this Edmund Hillary was the right person – she should check him out but take her time doing so. He may be a paragon, but she should be aware of the statistics regarding twice-divorced men.

"I'm not planning to marry him. I'm just going out with him. Open the wine, dear."

She needed a drink, she said: tomorrow she had an appointment with my psychiatrist. "I'm not keen on it, but from the look of you, I can see I'd better talk to her. You look like the ghoul that emerged from the cesspool. For God's sake, tell me what happened."

I filled our glasses, then told her of my cold night outside Cousineau's love nest. As my tale unfolded, Victoria softened, tut-tutting, shaking her head, squeezing my hand across the dining table, offering words of solace.

"Why don't you just let her have her affair? Maybe she won't feel complete without her romantic adventure. Is she being dishonest with you? I don't think so. Sally dealt with you squarely, she had the grace and courtesy to ask for a trial separation, for the space and freedom and moral right to do this. Wait her out, honey. This isn't the end of the universe."

I was hearing but wasn't listening. Victoria's words didn't bite in until today, as I recounted them to you, when you made me realize that I'd been deaf to her counsel. Sally isn't my bond slave. This is the age of sexual freedom, I mustn't adhere to an obsolete Christian ethos. Artists, say the texts, are characterized by a willingness to recognize their irrational impulses. I can accept that. How might going to bed with Ellery Cousineau be anything but an irrational impulse?

Hadn't I been anticipating this? Hadn't I settled my mind that I could endure Sally having a trial affair? Not with Ellery Cousineau, that still sits thickly in the stomach. On the other hand, our relationship will be made stronger by her realization of this gross error in taste.

But at the time, I was mired in self-pity, unable to drown it in Cabernet Sauvignon. Only with great effort did I hold back from telling Victoria about my speculation as to Cousineau's forbidden tastes. And I was hesitant, after Victoria's kindness, to raise a topic pregnant, as it were, with possible friction, so I let her hold forth about Clinton Huff, about the trial that was set to resume in October. With the uptick in sales of *When Comes the Darkness*, her publisher, confident of victory, is happy to let the trial spin out. Victoria wants a quick end to it, though, and Brovak has come up with a strategy (foolish, I feel, and risky) to abort proceedings by having Huff declared mentally incompetent. Which is why, Victoria said, I should testify. I had the goods on Huff, only I could testify to his obsessiveness, his paranoia. And wouldn't I feel more comfortable if my bête noir were made a ward of the health system?

I disagreed. If I were dragged into a courtroom, Huff would accuse me of whatever evil practices he thinks I indulge in — I don't know what delusions he holds, what slanders he's capable of. (A sudden sneaking thought: What if it is Huff who was writing threatening notes and skulking after me?) My presence could cause a deterioration in his condition, and I didn't want to be responsible for that. When he recovers, he might be forever on my backside, a life of unremitting hassle.

That led to a tiff, I'm afraid. To put it bluntly, Victoria blew up at me, accused me of disloyalty, of putting self-concern ahead of feelings for her, of not caring, not loving, of abandoning her.

I bolted the last of the wine, attacked the cognac in her liquor cabinet. It fuelled my stubbornness – I was falling apart, I'd only blow it in court, I had a charity bicycle race in October, I'd be in hard training.

This trial was her goddamn *life*, she shouted. Writing had been her abiding dream, as long as she could remember, and she had a chance to launch a *real* career in it, escape from the ignominy of Literary Consolation Services. If she were to lose this trial, she'd be a one-novel flareout, a laughing-stock, condemned to everlasting literary failure.

I hate myself for this, but I'd drunk enough courage to pursue my mission, and I non-sequitured right into the subject of how I came to be. "I need to ask for the truth about Peter."

A startled response from Victoria. She set down her glass unsteadily.

"Well?" I said.

She seemed lost, my change of tack took the wind from her sails. When she spoke, it was with subdued voice. "I'm sorry, I'm really behind with my body count. We'll talk about it when you're sober."

Why was she withholding, why was my mother, despite a history of so much love and closeness, afraid to talk about Peter with me? I was hurt, and spoke harshly. "When you see Dr. Epstein tomorrow, I hope you'll have the courage to tell her what you can't tell me."

I could see her face working. I was suddenly awash with remorse. Victoria has always resisted displays of grief, even or especially in front of me, so I just held her, kissed her, told her I loved her. I promised I'd be there to support her at her trial. She clutched my hand, then released me, and I could see tears coming, so I left.

I blew it, Allis, it exploded in my face. I was thoughtless, consumed by my own needs. This is a woman who survived on grants and loans, who raised me in student housing, working as waitress and housecleaner while she slugged it out for a university degree.

That's when I decided to do the Xanax.

Maybe she'll get a more sympathetic hearing from you. Maybe she'll find it easier to talk to you.

I know the truth anyway; it has resounded in my ears like a thunderclap. It is shame that causes Victoria to shun the subject. Not the shame of having told me fairy-tale accounts, not the shame of having allowed herself to be a pushover, easily seduced. No, an act of enormity occurred by the shore of that lake. That is what she doesn't dare tell me, that is what she fears I cannot face.

I am a child of rape . . .

CHAPTER TWELVE

Date of Interview: Friday, October 3, 2003.

I was put on alert today by Tim's agitation, sweating, and general dysphoria. I thought he might be suffering sedative withdrawal, and I asked if that was the case. He confessed to having experimented, during the week, with a cocktail mix of serotonin reuptake inhibitors,[1] "seeking the right blend for my state of despair."

An unhappy consequence is that he lost his zeal for the Okanagan bicycle rally, and he has been off his training. This has been such a healthy interest, one that has kept him focused and driving, that I spoke sternly to him about his excessive use of antidepressants. He assured me he has now stopped these experiments.

Somehow, in this state, he managed to drift through the week, seeing few patients and suffering through another session with the discipline committee.

---

[1] Non-prescribed medication, received in promotional mailings from pharmaceutical companies.

Frustrated at being "out of the loop" of the murder investigations, he went on a tangent, visiting The Tides on a whim. There, while dealing with Bob Grundison and Lyall DeWitt, he felt a "jolt" that came to him, "like a missile disappearing into the ocean of the unconscious." He became aware only the next day of the catalyst for this profound inner event, and it has launched the police investigation in an unexpected direction.

Meanwhile, he hasn't seen or spoken to Sally Pascoe, who in any event has been unavailable, instructing at a weeklong artists' retreat on Cortes Island.[2] He has been immersing himself in studies of the creative impulse, seeking answers to "her mystery." I'm tempted to the view that envy of her gift is an unrecognized element of his feelings for her.

Another unwelcome side effect of his drug misusage was an inability to remember dreams. Though this is in one sense benign, he would rather be aware of disturbing dreams than have them caged within, "gnawing away like rats at my unconscious." I agreed: there were important messages in these dreams.

However, he erected few of his usual defences when I broached his unresolved feelings about his origins. I was able to tell him that Victoria and I had finally met and she's now ready to be forthcoming: she is very concerned about his emotional state and feels her reticence has created an unnecessary barrier between them.

One hopes he'll hear Victoria openly. She's been such a dynamic figure in his life that he feels his vision of her is impaired "by an emotional force field." I've noted that his percipience in picking up various cues often fails him when he contends with significant others such as Victoria and Sally; in other words, his

---

[2] She did telephone me, and to state the point simply, she is in a state of turmoil. She felt unable to "deal with" Tim, and begged me to put matters to him gently.

ability to read the signals of those for whom he deeply cares may be distorted by his deep responses to them.

Are you hearing me?

I'll be okay, I'm getting back to normal, whatever that is. How can I discuss mood-altering substances with my patients if I don't try them? I can appreciate how people get hooked, though. Nice buzz from fluoxetine, it was like the gentle fog that comes off the ocean in the morning. When I was lying on the grass doing a Rorschach with the cloud formations, I saw God's profile, if that's of therapeutic significance. How are things working out for you, Allis?

It hasn't been great. Richard phoned – he wants to patch it up.

And?

And I don't think so.

I wish I could . . . never mind. You saw Victoria.

This morning.

And what came of it?

You need to hear it from her.

What's her concern – that I'd love her the less because she was raped on the shore of Kootenay Lake?

Tim, please return to the couch.

Sorry, I'm restless. I had a revelation, Allis, as I was seeing God in the clouds. A confirmation of the terrible truth of my conception. Victoria has never explained why she wrote a horror book, and suddenly the answer came – it's because she was raped that her novel features a sadist, a guy who's sexually perverse. We both missed it, Allis, the signal from my dreams – the satyr, for God's sake, Pan, god of forests and fertility. He gave us the word *panic* – did you know that? From the ancients' fear of the lustful, lurking goat-man . . .

Tim, that's very interesting, but aren't you making quite a jump . . . ?

She couldn't bring herself to say my father raped and abandoned her, but the information kept seeping through her psychic pores and I caught it like a contagion, a disease. It's why so many of my hinges are loose. It's the whole answer.

I think Victoria would like you to visit. Why don't phone her and say you'll make dinner for her this weekend?

⁂

I remember little of what passed between us after that because my mind was on a recipe for bouillabaisse I wanted to try. It calls for a dollop of Pernod and an array of shellfish, herbs, and vegetables, and I was trying to recall the ingredients, planning my trip to the market tomorrow.

You must have asked about my week, for I remember taking you on a wandering path through it. Another ordeal with Vivian, Schulter, and his two lickspittles. The Tides, Grundy and his ménage à trois, his protective staff. A psychic jolt that caused a brief power outage and disabled me, followed later by another jolt, of remembrance.

I am steadily losing patients. They're fleeing like rats from my sinking ship, and poor James has been making alarming noises about my bank balance. I'm on the whole unconcerned about such trivia, they are a mouse squeak as against the roar of wifely betrayal and violent conception and murderers prowling the night.

I'm sure my garbled accounts have only added to your diagnosis of sedative withdrawal, but I've stopped being my own lab rat – my experiments validated my addictive tendencies. Now at this late-night hour there's a barbed edge around my shrinking comfort zone, an inner scratching that announces worse is yet to come.

I know I've disappointed you, Allis. You've invested a hundred dollars in *le prix de Okanagan*. I swear now, by all that is sacred, that I will return to harness, that I'll sweep past that finish line, arms raised in triumph whether I be first or last.

The meds, however, did help me get through another session of the Schulter hearing. Despite the theatrics of Vivian Lalonde, I felt detached, more a bemused spectator than a participant, at least until my rambunctious lawyer pulled a boner.

I'd forgot that the hearing was to resume on Wednesday (chalk it up to extreme avoidance). When the summons came I was in my dressing gown, absorbed in treatises on the artistic impulse. I'm no artist; diddling on the clarinet doesn't make me one. I have no instinctive sense of the creative itch that Sally feels. (It's like a living thing, says Jung, implanted in the human psyche. The nature of artistic achievement is inaccessible to us, says Freud.)

At about half past ten, John Brovak interrupted with a gruff telephone inquiry as to whether I might want to show up for my character assassination, already in progress. He'd asked Ivan Kolosky only a few questions, Vivian Lalonde was waiting to testify, and Schulter's patience was wearing thin at my casual attitude. I told Brovak I had confidence in him to carry on without me; I would call a cab after I showered and shaved.

The Prozac was making me feel almost relaxed about the affair, though I was curious to know what fanciful version Vivian had finally settled on. Her blunt "Go fuck yourself" on my answering machine hinted she might not be a friendly witness.

When I walked into the hearing room, she was still testifying. These were the chilling words that greeted me: "Afterwards, he seemed a little embarrassed — we both were, it happened so suddenly."

My three judges were in rapt attention, Schulter hiding his glee, Mundt leering, Rawlings craning to hear. Vivian was sitting cross-legged on an armchair, dressed for a show of cleavage and thigh.

She cast me a look that I had no trouble reading: *I gave you a chance, you turned me down.*

Schulter held back from commenting on my lateness and allowed me a moment to confer with Brovak. He was uncharacteristically subdued. "She's good." My faith in my counsel began to slip – had he, too, been gulled by this dissembler? "She either believes this shit or she should be on the professional stage, they're drooling all over her."

"I warned you. She's a skilled liar. Who allegedly made the first move?"

"You did. There was a moment of silence, you were staring intently at each other, then you seized her and kissed her passionately. She couldn't resist. You seemed lonely and in pain, you had just broken up with your wife."

I muttered an oath. How credible that might sound, with its clever mix of truth and lie. Anxiety began to work like a worm through the protective armour of my Prozac. Could I actually be found *guilty*?

On resuming, Schulter asked, "Just to clarify, Ms. Lalonde, you say this was the second time Dr. Dare made physical advances?"

"Yes, some weeks earlier he drew me into his arms, and . . . it was quite silly, actually, we fell over a footstool and I ended up on top of him. You should ask his secretary about that, he saw us embracing on the floor."

"Yeah," said Brovak, "that was the first time she took a run at him."

Mundt eagerly picked up on that. "And that incident didn't prompt him to end your relationship? He didn't cancel further appointments?"

"Oh, no, he wanted to see me again."

Mundt carried on in eager pursuit: "On the latter occasion, when you say, 'We made love,' you're referring to what act?"

"Sexual intercourse."

"There was full penetration?"

"Yes." She didn't blush at this rude inquiry, or drop her eyes.

"And was there a discharge of semen?"

"There was."

Mundt wasn't satisfied with that. "Can you be sure?"

"A woman is always sure, Doctor." She smiled at him. He reddened. The sex expert.

"And for how long did intercourse take place?"

"Not long enough." She sighed. "I don't deny being caught up in the passion of the moment, but . . ."

Mundt urged her along. "But what, Ms. Lalonde?"

"But the moment was very short. He had an orgasm very quickly. I wasn't ready. And . . . and he withdrew abruptly. As I say, he seemed surprised at himself, embarrassed that he had succumbed to his desires. He became brusque, and I . . . I felt he'd simply dismissed me after satisfying his sexual appetite, and I'm afraid I became quite angry."

"That's when Mr. Kolosky came in," Schulter said.

"Can we just let her tell her own story?" Brovak was piqued. I think he'd expected Vivian to be more zany and scattered, less credible.

"He walked in just as we were dressing. I'm afraid he heard some rude words from me."

"Such as?"

"Well, I told Dr. Dare I felt used, I called him an utter bastard."

"Thank you." Schulter looked woeful, as if he found the fall from grace of his lustful colleague too much to bear. "I'm afraid I must ask you to stay put, Ms. Lalonde, because counsel may have some questions."

Brovak eyed her for several seconds before commencing. "Let's get some background here. When you came to see Dr. Dare you were suffering a deep depression, right?"

"Yes."

"You were having marital problems. You left your husband only after half a year of marriage."

"Our relationship didn't work out."

"And basically what happened is you became infatuated with my client."

"There was an attraction. It was hardly one-sided. He told me he loved me."

"That's pure crap." Brovak ignored Schulter's reproachful look. "You were living in a dream world, you were having fantasies about making love to him."

"I'm sure everyone in this room has had sexual fantasies."

Mundt nodded wisely.

"Ms. Lalonde, let's not play games here. You were the aggressor, he was the victim of an unprovoked attack. You jumped him, got your lipstick all over his face, tried to pull his clothes off."

She shouted. "I am telling the truth!" She levelled an accusatory finger at me. "Just as you told me to, Timothy Dare!"

Schulter called for order. "Just a minute. Ms. Lalonde, do I understand you *met* with Dr. Dare?

Vivian took a while to recover, a tissue at the corner of her eye. "Occasionally, yes, in different restaurants."

Brovak barked: "Because you were chasing him all over the goddamn town." He turned to the committee: "She burglarized his damn office, left a bunch of naked pictures. My client almost got himself run over trying to escape from her. We have witnesses up the yin-yang. They'll say this woman announced she was going to perjure herself at this hearing, and that's what she's damn well done."

Schulter looked at him unblinkingly. "Do you have any further questions?"

"Yeah, why don't we just shut this whole thing down?" Brovak had finally got his lather up.

Schulter looked at Mundt, then Rawlings. They looked at Vivian, doubt showing on their faces.

"I'm in total agreement," Vivian said. "He's in enough pain. I've forgiven him."

Their heads came together. Was this the end of my ordeal?

The huddle broke up. "Under the circumstances," said Schulter, "there remains a possible element of undue influence. We will continue."

Brovak sighed with exasperation and returned to Vivian. "Okay, let's put this to a test. You're damn sure you're telling the truth?"

"Yes, I am."

"So I guess you're willing to take a lie detector?"

"Absolutely."

My throat went dry.

"You're positive that's what you want her to do, Mr. Brovak?" Schulter asked.

"Yeah. I think it's time we brought this to a head."

"Let's look at our calendars and see when we can reconvene."

I sat in a state of dulled helplessness as they debated dates, and a few moments later found myself with Brovak in a nearby bar, gulping from a tankard of beer.

"For Christ's sake, John – a polygraph! They're totally unreliable."

"Maybe you got me confused. You said she'd definitely flunk a lie detector."

"I was being *rhetorical*." I felt hollow. It was well within possibility that Vivian's responses would show little electrodermal activity. She'd been so self-assured in testifying.

Brovak was unconcerned. "It's a cakewalk." He was more interested in Victoria's trial. "Huff is nuttier than a granola bar, and you can prove it."

"He's eccentric. He's not certifiable."

"Yeah, and you don't think he's dangerous? You're working on these serial murders, right? Speaking of loopiness, don't you find it coincidental that two of the victims got choked that way?"

I wasn't following. Brovak explained he'd heard scuttlebutt in the courts that Wilmott and Morgan had been looped by a wire. I still wasn't following.

"Same pattern as the book we're hassling over, except the victims were women."

I nearly dropped my pint, but managed to set it down with a shaking hand. I remembered the opening day of the libel trial, the mayor of Jackson Cove reciting that appalling passage, a rape victim, looped by a wire . . .

Yes, the fictional Huff, jolly, suspender-slapping Clint, had killed his first hostage that way, maybe also his second. I admitted to Brovak I'd never read beyond the first few chapters, then went silent, tried to work through the implications, my mind sluggish.

Brovak drew a copy of *When Comes the Darkness* from his brief-case, handed to me. "You ought to read it, pal."

"How were the others murdered?"

"We got a couple of loopings, we got an axe, we got a hanging, and a drawing and quartering. Not counting Clint, who gets his head chewed off by a grizzly."

I stared at the cover: a moonlit town hall, a skulking Rigoletto with a sack on his back. Was this the key to understanding? But little was making sense right now. I pushed my pint away.

"Maybe I'd better switch to coffee."

I spent the rest of the day struggling through *When Comes the Darkness* with a jumpy, queasy stomach. Imprisoned female hostages, orgasms begot by violent acts of homicide. I got through the axe murder and the hanging but didn't make it past the drawing and quartering.

And you don't think he's dangerous? The antipathy Huff holds for me caused me to wonder again: Had *he* been following me? Had *he* been writing the anonymous letters? *I know where you live* – that note had been mailed from Vancouver just after his stressful experience in court.

I indulged in fanciful leaps, assembling the case against Clinton Huff, three counts of murder one. Had he been in Vancouver when Chauncey Wilmott breathed his last? Yes, his application for a change of venue was around that time. And on September 17, another grisly visit? He couldn't find an axe in Pierrera's suite, used scissors instead . . .

No, there were two men. Huff with an accomplice? Doubtful.

The voice of sanity intruded. Come back to earth. There's another answer. I heard my psychiatrist telling me to look deeper . . .

I took a double dose of Xanax the next morning for a headache – a punishment for my addled speculations of the day before – and moments later Bob Grundison called. As far as I was capable, I went on alert. He wanted to know if we could "do a rain check on our get-together today." He was struggling with an essay due Friday: theories of unconscious human motivation.

I asked where he was calling from. He was at home. I told him I was sorry, but I'd set the time aside. He pleaded, he needed to finish this project for his passing grade. I told him I'd think about it, call him back.

Jack Churko and a technician were supposed to come by at noon to set up monitoring devices for this interview. Thanks to the soothsayer and her preposterously lucky guesses, Churko was no longer so dismissive of my theories. But I wasn't much in his plans. The Attorney General had beefed up his crew, now a task force of twenty, but it was mired in futility.

Meanwhile, Vancouver was almost in a state of siege, demonstrations were continuing. Gay rights activists were camped on the doorstep of the Attorney General's office in Victoria.

According to the best estimate of the city pathologist, José

Pierrera had died Wednesday, September 17, four nights before his body was discovered. It seemed beyond coincidence that the vagrant in New Brighton Park was murdered earlier that evening by the same men.

As with dogs gone wild, one slaughter only excited the killers' thirst for blood – I believed the murder of Pierrera reflected a growing appetite for death, a need that might be building anew: thrill killing offers the sufficiently depraved a gratification more addictive than heroin.

Yes, Allis, I was drugged and depressed and dysfunctional, and I was working on little more than a hunch from deep within that Grundy was involved, but a makeshift plan took form. It didn't involve Jack Churko, who would only try to waylay me. In fact I asked James to call Churko, to tell him he didn't need to come by, because Grundy had cancelled his appointment.

It was early afternoon of a balmy fall day as I taxied down the abdomen of Vancouver, south across the flatness of Lulu Island, under the Deas Tunnel to the Delta farmlands, through Ladner to River Road. Protected by a dike where the river makes a wide curl was the Grundison estate, the imposingly Edwardian house visible from a distance.

The property is walled, but the gate was open and the guard-house empty. No one tends the gate during daylight hours, but from seven p.m. to seven a.m. a watchman is stationed there: on weekdays this is Greg Stairs, twenty years old and "a bit slow," according to the report I read. He'd told detectives that while at the gate or patrolling the grounds he saw all comings and goings. These he recorded in a log: the traffic for September 17, when Moe Morgan and José Pierrera were killed, didn't include Grundy or Lyall.

The taxi wove through a pitch-and-putt course, sparkling wet from the sprinklers, and stopped in an oval driveway where a late-model compact was parked. The turreted mansion was as grey as a prison. Some distance beyond, close to the dike and secluded within trees, were several cottages. Some of the staff lived in these, others commuted by car. I recalled mention of a dock beyond the dike, but it was out of view.

The first clue that my investigative tools might be chemically dulled came when I made to pay my fare – I'd left my wallet behind. The driver, one of my regulars, had no problem with it. He agreed to park in the driveway and wait.

I introduced myself as Dr. Dare to the bronze-skinned young woman who greeted me at the door, and asked if she could announce me to Mrs. Grundison. She told me the lady of the house was indisposed and urged me, pleasantly enough, to return in the morning.

I said I was really here to see Robert, but that I also wanted to talk to the staff, her included. She hesitated, then asked to see identification. I felt foolish having to explain about my missing wallet, wished I hadn't taken those last pills. I also regretted not bringing a tape recorder.

I assured her Grundy would be prepared to see me, and she became flustered. She was sorry, but Bob was busy with "something," and she wasn't even sure she was allowed to talk with me.

By now I'd managed to wedge my way into the house. An interior designer had been given carte blanche – finely chosen antiques, an A.Y. Jackson, a Lismer, but there was an eerie sense about the place, a heavy silence penetrated by what seemed the groaning of ghosts in the oak panelling. The Xanax was really starting to kick in.

I presumed that this plumply attractive woman, with her slight Spanish accent, was the live-in maid whom detectives had quietly interviewed: Louisa Ramirez, twenty-three, Honduran by birth.

I was set on interviewing her, but my way was barred unless I took a chance. Was she under police orders not to talk? Then maybe we should give Inspector Churko a phone call. She went into a nervous stall, then escorted me to a small parlour with a phone. On the wall were photos of the Grundison family, framed certificates, awards from charities acknowledging their gifts. Golf trophies behind a glass case. Shelves of leather-bound great masters.

Sounding of a mouth full of doughnut, Jack Churko sputtered as I explained: Grundy had asked me to delay his appointment, so I advanced it – and in the meantime Louisa Ramirez was here and would he kindly lift the gag order.

"You want to tangle with the Grundisons? Be my guest, I'm going to maintain deniability. Aw, shit. Put her on the line."

She listened, nodded, voiced a weak, "Yes, thank you."

I congratulated myself for having walked a tightrope. I told her to relax as best she could: nothing would be repeated to her employers. I had a mandate to supervise Grundy's progress, and to fulfill it I must speak to those who see him daily. I assured her Bob would understand that.

I found a pen and paper. She sat stiffly as I asked about Grundy's routines, his interaction with Lyall and other staff. I gave her openings to express her feelings about him, but she was careful not to say anything negative, though distaste showed in an occasional flaring of nostrils. There had been no temper displays; he had been steadfastly sober, hadn't consumed so much as a beer.

When I asked about Grundy's escapes to the city, she showed unease yet said she was certain that he'd been home on the evening of September 17. Thelma Grundison had hosted friends that afternoon for a regular Whist Wednesday, a busy day for the maid because trays had to be prepared and drinks served. Ramirez recalled Grundy having words with his mother over her heavy drinking, then locking himself in his study at around six p.m. His radio was on, tuned to his favourite music station.

Thelma Grundison had "retired early." She regularly did that, and Ramirez would usually take a dinner tray up to her. This was prepared by the cook, who leaves the house by eight p.m. and spends her nights in one of the cottages. Only Ramirez and DeWitt among the staff were resident in the house.

Lyall was in his room most of that day, playing computer games or surfing the Internet: interests he'd never mentioned to me. He was a "joker," Ramirez said, enjoyed doing imitations, Hispanics, East Indians, gays, and he could go on like that for an hour or more, Grundy laughing, easily entertained.

Did she remember them leaving for a whitewater rafting trip in August? "Oh, yes, they took the pickup truck – it was packed with camping gear." A high-riding four-wheeler, one of several vehicles the family keeps.

I asked her if Greg Stairs, the night watchman, was available, and at the mention of his name she flushed slightly and broke eye contact. I wasn't too mentally dulled to infer that some hanky-panky might have prompted them to lie.

As I was asking Ramirez to fetch Stairs, a voice called: "Louisa, where's that pack of Lo we bought."

She blanched as Grundy yanked open the door. He was in bare feet, wearing only sweats. He froze as he set eyes on me.

Flustered, the maid quickly stood, straightened her dress. "They're in the back of the fridge, Robert."

He was having trouble pulling himself together, but he worked up a smile. "Hey, Dr. Dare, this is unexpected. What are you doing in this neck of the woods?"

I told him I wouldn't take up much of his essay-writing time: a short session, then I would continue inquiring after the staff about his progress. Louisa Ramirez had given him an A on his report card, but what, I asked, did he mean by a pack of Lo?

"I was getting a Löewenbräu for Lyall. He likes his kraut beer. Hey, how about you, Doctor – care for a cold one?" I had never seen Grundy quite this unsettled: he had the look of a distressed rat eyeing a lab scientist.

I declined the beer. I was functioning on too fuzzy a plane to take an incisive reading of him, but his discomposure told me I'd arrived at an awkward moment. He seemed overheated, like a horse after a race.

I advised Ramirez I would be back in half an hour, then followed Grundy down a hall and past a doorway leading to an exercise room. He'd been taking a break there, he said, working out, getting up his energy to attack that darned essay.

The kitchen was a wide, tiled, sterile space presided over by Bernice, Beatrice, something like that, who was preparing dinner. We chatted about nothing I can remember while Grundy pulled a bottle of Löewenbräu from the fridge, uncapped it.

He told the cook that I would be interviewing her, "so be as helpful as you can."

It's in my notes that Bernice then asked if "Miss Markevich" would be staying for dinner, and Grundy replied, "Negative, I think she's already gone."

He wanted to show me his study, "where I'm busting my brain." The oak-panelled room did give proof of his labours: textbooks open on the desk, a foolscap pad crammed with his writings, a screen-saver drawing whorls on his computer monitor.

"I'll run up and deliver this beer. Make yourself comfortable." Grundy seemed too anxious to deposit me here. He handed me a couple of sheets of paper. "Hey, maybe you can give me some help with this essay."

A laugh died in his throat when I proposed another plan: we would see Lyall together; I needed to talk to him anyway.

"Right now?"

I nodded. I tried to jot down some of my observations, but my mind drifted as I read a line from his essay: "Man is motivated by two basic drives, aggression and sex."

Grundy was aware of the conditions of his release, but his long silence hinted he was thinking of not cooperating. I looked up and saw twitching in his upper cheek. "I don't know what he's doing, I'll just check."

He left abruptly. I followed. Upstairs, I found him with his head wedged through a partly open doorway. He turned and said, "Looks like Jossie's still here."

Lyall showed himself at the crack in the door. "What's up, Doc? Be with you in a split second." The door closed.

Nothing was meshing, I was being buffeted by too many impressions. Jossie Markevich was Grundy's girlfriend – what was she doing in a room with Lyall?

Watching me warily as I tried to scribble notes, Grundy continued with his staccato explanations: Jossie's between jobs, hangs around here a lot. You never know what she gets up to. She's a free spirit. But I just can't get mad at her.

When Lyall opened the door a few minutes later he appeared freshly dressed and combed. The bed looked hastily made, sheet edges hanging out, coverings loose. A closed door presumably led to an en suite, where it seemed Markevich had fled.

"Yeah, the doctor's doing his rounds," Grundy said. He shouted, "What are you up to in there, honey, come out and say hello."

Lyall was scanning the room as if for evidence still unhidden. His laptop was open, an Internet search engine loading. I was being treated to a charade but having the devil's time processing it.

Jossie emerged, her lipstick gleaming, fully dressed but for footwear. One sandal was missing, the other was in her hand.

As she greeted me, Lyall reached under the bed and withdrew the other sandal. I glimpsed a pair of high-top running shoes there as well, about Grundy's size.

Jossie made departure noises, shouldering a small backpack, while I casually prowled the room, looking for other tidbits. A bookcase – I'll say this much for Lyall, he's a reader – hardcover thrillers, military biographies.

"You got what you were looking for on the Internet?" Lyall asked Jossie.

"Yes, thank you very much."

"Okay, I'll turn it off."

How stagy this conversation sounded, especially since the computer had obviously just been turned on. I was standing before it, looking at Lyall's list of bookmarked Web sites, and when he reached in front of me to shut it off, one item caught my eye: White American Christian Brotherhood.

The tranks, the stilted theatrical atmosphere, the sense of decadent carryings-on, and now this little whiff of fascism, made me feel queasy. I had to sit down.

Grundy left with Jossie, promised to be just a minute. Lyall was too preoccupied to be aware of my physical unease. Stiffly grinning, he began speaking rapidly, one of those trips into the fast lane that suggests one is lying, in this case a progress report on Grundy: he's been cracking the books, Doc, he's a grind, it's been real boring around here.

He looked out the window, at Grundy and Jossie standing by the compact car. They saw him and waved. I caught Lyall blowing them a kiss, a gesture that seemed inappropriate, out of character. "You plan to hang around much longer, Doc?"

I was leaning against the bookcase just then, and suddenly I felt a jar, it was as if I was going through some kind of warp. I had a macabre feeling that something had just imbedded itself deeply within the unconscious.

"I think I need some fresh air," I said, gasping for lack of it.

"Hey, you don't look good."

I rose unsteadily. "I'll take a little walk."

I declined Lyall's offer of help, held myself close to the hallway wall, letting it guide me, tightly grasped the banister down the stairs.

I felt I'd suffered a major head trauma, and I had to steady myself by one of the veranda pillars. Something had entered my mind, a subliminal truth. What had prompted it – that mock effeminate gesture, the blown kiss? Something I saw? Something Lyall had said to me? I was engulfed by a deep intuitive knowledge that Lyall DeWitt and Grundy Grundison were steeped in blood; they'd murdered Wilmott, Morgan, and Pierrera.

It took me a few minutes to focus on what was happening around me. I remember Jossie Markevich at the wheel of the compact, Grundy leaning to her, talking low. My driver, standing by his taxi. Louisa Ramirez on the grass of the oval, talking to a young man – Greg Stairs, I guessed.

I willed myself to walk across the driveway, waving at Grundy with an effort at nonchalance as Markevich drove off, indicating I was taking this opportunity to continue my interviews.

"Beautiful day," I said as I joined the maid and the watchman. Both looked oddly at me; I was shaking. What had DeWitt said just before I suffered that jolt? *You plan to hang around much longer, Doc?* Why would that trip something in my brain?

At my request, Greg Stairs sat on the lawn beside me, and I asked him some questions about Grundy's behaviour, not recording much. It gave me time to recover.

I asked Stairs about the Wednesday evening of two weeks ago.

"They was definitely here," he said, not looking at me, glancing up at Ramirez as if for confirmation.

He'd gone on duty sharp at seven p.m. He'd entered the guardhouse a few times, where he kept his log of comings and goings, otherwise he had been outside.

By now, Grundy had disappeared, doubtless to huddle with Lyall. I was too weak to endure more, too scattered, so I asked Ramirez to tell my host I'd spare him further inconvenience. I followed Stairs to the guardhouse to look at his log, a loose-leaf binder.

His notes for September 17, which I copied, were few but to the minute: at 7:07 p.m. head groundskeeper leaves for home, at 7:12 Mrs. Baumgarten leaves with party of five women, at 7:35 process server leaves summons re Chrysler Town & Country minivan. The latter was for a string of long-ignored parking tickets – Grundy, as I recalled, rips them up. That was the entire night's traffic.

How did he know the vehicle was in the garage all night? Stairs said he was "supposed to" check the garage nightly. Was there another route out of The Tides? "There's only the one way out of here." Does Grundy ever go boating from the dock? "Sometimes he goes fishing, but that ain't his cup of tea, he don't like the slow life."

Could they have taken another vehicle, the pickup? It was "usually" in the garage too. But it wasn't today – I could now see it parked beside the house: ochre, high off the ground, wide tires. It was familiar somehow. In fact, it resembled the truck that swerved at me on Burrard Bridge, sending me spilling. I went into another stall, the import slow to hit, that it might not have been a mere accident. When was it? After the sleepless night in front of Cousineau's building, I'd been in a frenzy. I was close to one now, ready to flee.

Be smart, I told myself, they only kill at night, without witnesses.

I returned to the binder, flipped a few pages back. Grundy and Lyall had checked out occasionally in the evenings, but Stairs hadn't always diarized their returns. Few entries after eleven p.m. Stairs may not have been a zealous employee: the guardhouse accommodated a small cot.

What was the date they returned from their Skeena trip? Why couldn't I remember? They left Terrace on a Thursday in late August . . . Yes, August 28, here was an entry. "Bob and Lyall in at 9:14." I asked Stairs if he remembered that night.

He scratched his head. "That must have been . . . yeah, they'd gone up north to run some rapids. Bob saved some girl from drowning, it was in the news."

I puzzled over the entry, the arithmetic seemed wrong: they returned at 9:14? They'd have had to travel a hundred miles an hour, non-stop . . .

"Are you telling me they drove all the way there and back?"

"Well, as I recall, it was his dad's treat. I imagine Mr. Grundison sent them up there in the Lear."

"From where?"

"Local airport. Boundary."

"Did you mention this to the police?"

"They never asked."

I went to my taxi, reeling.

My plan was to go directly to police headquarters but that wasn't necessary. As we turned past a dilapidated former cannery, a patrol car pulled in behind us, turned on its wigwags. My driver stopped, flustered, unsure what law he'd violated, he could have been driving his own mother, he'd been five miles under the limit.

Jack Churko slid into the back seat with me, told me he'd like a nice long chat. I suggested my office, so I could pay the driver. We carried on to the city in utter silence. I wanted Dotty to be present, and as soon as I got to my office I called her to join us.

I'll give Churko credit, he's a good listener – he inquired only about the bottle of pills I was playing with, fighting the need. Dotty explained they were for an erectile disorder, and asked whether Churko was interested in trying one. The inspector glowered and went silent. The scenario I laid out seemed to depress him

– it pointed him in a direction he hadn't wanted to go, toward the good family Grundison.

At the end, I summarized: "The mother's a lush, she's in her room every night by five or six. The only employee who sleeps over is the maid, and after eleven o'clock she's too busy screwing the night watchman to notice what goes on. They get together in the house, probably in her chamber. They'll get fired if the Grundison family finds out, so they're scared to say anything. Greg Stairs probably sleeps through the last of his shift. Essentially, his log can't be relied on for the late hours."

Churko paled.

"When our two heroes aren't prowling the streets of Vancouver looking for people to kill, they're surfing Nazi Web sites and going two-on-one with Jossie Markevich – by the way, you'll want to check *her* out. They didn't drive to the Skeena River, they flew there and back on Daddy's jet. They left their truck at Boundary Bay airport Saturday morning after strangling Chauncey Wilmott."

I added that Churko might want to cross-reference the dates of Grundy's parking tickets with his homophobic excursions into the city. I didn't mention my baffling psychic experience. Churko might start wondering what was really in those pills.

"And here's something else – I think he tried to run me over, tried to kill me." Churko was interested now, even nodding as I told him about the sports pickup, my scrape with death. He phoned headquarters, told his underlings he wanted eyes on Grundy and Lyall, and a twenty-four hour discreet watch of The Tides and the Simon Fraser campus.

A sense of foreboding plagued me through the rest of the day. I spent a couple of hours conferring with detectives, puzzling through my notes, some of which were indecipherable, and trying to remember the gaps, but I remained unable to bring back . . . what? Something that had registered at the far periphery of awareness.

Another day has passed. Twelve hours ago (it is about midnight now), Grundy delivered his essay to an associate professor of psychology. He and Lyall stopped to watch a football practice, then left the campus to pick up Jossie Markevich at her apartment before carrying on to The Tides. There are a couple of minor entries on her sheet, by the way, one for shoplifting, one for prostitution.

Tonight I'm still edgy, raw-nerved, but determined to stay off the tranks. I'm hoping to stay awake all night to avoid the nightmares that drugs denied me. Tomorrow, I will prowl the market for clams and mussels and savory and Spanish onions. Tomorrow, I'll hear Victoria's truth.

And that reminds me of the task I've been avoiding. *When Comes the Darkness* is on the shelf, waiting, a bookmark at the drawing-and-quartering chapter.

The book refuses to vanish, haunts at the edge of my left visual field . . .

Remembrance comes with a thud, and I feel faint.

That is what I'd seen in Lyall's room, at that same edge of my left vision – sitting on his bookshelves between other hardcovers: a title on a spine, the author's name: Victoria Dare.

The light comes flooding. The deaths in the novel, the two loopings, the stabbing. Grundy and Lyall are copycat killers.

CHAPTER THIRTEEN

Date of Interview: Friday, October 10, 2003.

Tim showed up today only to cancel. He was sweating profusely, having sped here by bicycle with a heavy backpack. He announced he had a train to catch – he was travelling to the Okanagan for the Thanksgiving weekend "to learn the course."

I urged him to spend a few minutes with me, and he reluctantly sat down. He tried to divert me when I asked about his discussion with Victoria.

I'm concerned about how you reacted to what she said. I tried to call you early in the week . . .

I got the message. Allis, I'm sorting through my thoughts, I'm not ready to talk about it.

When does your train go?

In two hours.

That's plenty of time.

I'm a worrier, I like to be early.

If that's so, why do you tend to be late?

Okay, I'm lying. I have too many things on my mind . . . confusing nightmares. I can't get my head around the repeated motif of masquerade balls. What lies beneath all the gaudy costumes – the alter egos I've tried to disown? It's too complex for my overtaxed mind.

Why must you always seek complexity? The answer may be simple.

How so?

Think about it.

I'm lost.

Okay, this bicycle rally that you're so totally absorbed in – it ends on what day?

October thirty-first. I get it. Halloween. I unconsciously associate the rally with people dressing up. You really have a knack of . . . Never mind. Anyway, there's some stuff I can't talk about to anyone, to do with the police investigation. So I thought . . . maybe we can do two hours next week. Maybe we could spend the afternoon together.

Let's try for that. You're still off inhibitors?

It was ugly.

Sure. You go ride your bike in the Okanagan hills. That's the best thing you can do.

ommo

As twilight falls, my train snakes through the Fraser Canyon, the rhythm of the rails soothing me, their gentle jump and bump. Darkness comes suddenly as we pass into a tunnel, then evening light returns. From a few seats down comes a tune from a banjo, musical enough but sardonic to my ears, another jest of merry Zeus.

I nod off. I awake and return to Jung. ("Do not expect psychology to offer a valid explanation for the secret of creativity.

Nobody can penetrate to the heart of nature.") I try not to listen to that banjo. My dreams haven't lied. They've always led me to truth. Peter, with his banjo.

I should have undergone my weekly head adjustment today, Allis, but I need to sort things out. I'll be more clearheaded when we meet next. You'll seek to reassure me that Peter and Victoria didn't conceive a mutant. You'll tell me I'm not missing vital chromosomes.

We have emerged from the funnel of the Fraser River and are snaking uphill. The banjoist has, thank God, packed it away for now. A night prowl up the aisle reveals, snoring, an unkempt middle-ager. On his lap, not a banjo but a lute. Only a scattered few are in this coach, dozing or with books or crossword puzzles.

It will be two a.m. when I get off. I have a hotel room booked in Kamloops, and in the morning I plan to bike to the starting point of the rally, in Vernon. I'll do the most punishing leg first, the run to Arrow Lake, then down the Okanagan Valley, my trial run finishing on Thanksgiving Day.

Huff versus Dare is set to lumber back into action in two weeks – God knows for how long. I held off telling Victoria that *When Comes the Darkness* inspired murder, though I will after I'm released from silence – Churko has put a clamp on the investigation. (He doesn't know I tell you everything.)

So this is classified information, Allis. I've unravelled the subterranean message that rang like a gong in my head. Grundy and Lyall are mimicking Clint Huff, the fictional mayor invented by my mother.

I didn't sleep last Friday night, not a wink, as I worked at the implications, though I woke Churko to demand assurance Grundy and Lyall were still under surveillance. He agreed to meet me for breakfast with Dotty at a nearby café.

Though Dotty had read *When Comes the Darkness*, Churko hadn't, and he had difficulty with my hypothesis, kept demanding to know why I'd "forgot" seeing the book on Lyall's shelf. Unconscious observation is a concept I had difficulty explaining.

This was my pitch: Lyall's interest in the book was whetted by the publicity over the libel case, by the fact that Grundy's overseer was the author's son. He had shared the novel with Grundy. They were fascinated by the concept, orgasmic murder, and decided to experiment. What had Huff said in court? *He obtains sexual release through murdering . . .* With the first killing, they had found that release, and they sought it again, two more deaths in their pursuit of a climax they could find no other way.

Dotty sought holes. The third fictional murder was by axe. My answer: It was still a form of butchery; they used what was handy. Grundy and Lyall targeted gay men, she reminded me, not women. However misogynous, I argued, the two men were impelled more strongly by their homophobia. This departure from the text seemed significant, though. I couldn't grasp why.

I pointed out that the recipe in *When Comes the Darkness* calls for a hanging next. "Well, they ain't going to get that opportunity," Churko vowed. No longer dismissive of my theory, he went off to buy a copy of the book.

The investigation made significant progress over the next few days. My parking-ticket theory panned out. On the date of the Wilmott murder, the Town & Country had been ticketed near Stanley Park at 7:15 p.m.

The pact of silence between Stairs and Sanchez has been broken. They wilted after being threatened with public mischief, with aiding and abetting by their silence. The watchman and the maid confessed to having been in her room, between the sheets, on the night of the double murder. Regularly, late in the evening, Sanchez lets Stairs in through a back door.

But Stairs has betrayed me to DeWitt, telling him I was asking about specific dates. He hadn't thought there was anything wrong in that – they'd been chatting one evening, and Lyall had asked a few questions. An awareness that the boss's son is of interest to the police has finally penetrated the thickness of Stairs's skull, but too late.

It was Dotty who urged me to take this extended holiday – these guys were capable of anything, she said, they might evade detection, commit bloody piracy on the *Altered Ego*. It hadn't escaped me that another factor had influenced Grundy to copy the script of Victoria's novel – it was a means of taunting the author's son, his nemesis, his trustee, his prospective jailer.

I hadn't intended to call Sally – we haven't talked since I spotted her leaving Cousineau's apartment – but since I'd prevailed upon Churko to cover my former home around the clock, I had to let her know.

I was official and grave, biting back my despair. I gave her a resumé of recent events. I told her there'd be an unmarked police vehicle outside her house. I urged her to keep her antennae tuned for danger. I'd be spending a few days on this training run. When I ran out of pronouncements, there was a momentary silence.

"You know," she said.

"I know."

"I'm sorry."

"Sure. Take care."

I had to hang up for fear I would disassemble. A dream of her came back, her words: *Even if I'm bad, you'll always be my friend, won't you?* Once again, I found myself struggling for the courage to admit I'd lost her, that she's better off without me. To accept is to heal. To forgive is to heal. But can I really do that? Cousineau! How insulting, how demeaning.

When the phone rang a few minutes later, I thought, hoped, it was Sally with more to say. It was Vivian.

"Timothy? Oh, thank God. Don't hang up, *please*. If I take that polygraph, it will only get you in deeper, so I have an idea. We tell them we're seeing each other socially. If we're having a romance, that puts the whole thing in a different light . . ."

I hung up and went for sushi.

A moon is out, weaving ghostly patterns. The lights of a village flash by. A glimpse of a boy at a second-storey window, waving at whoever will wave back. I think of Lyall blowing the kiss. Now comes an illuminated billboard advising the wages of sin is death – it brings back the worst of my nightmares. It came after that night's dinner of slightly tainted tuna in the sushi, complicated by withdrawal pangs.

I'm standing in a meadow. A fortress fills the horizon, a mental hospital – I can hear the cries of the distressed from within. (No . . . now as I reflect, that was no meadow but a pitch-and-putt course, and the forbidding structure represented the manse of The Tides.)

I'm frightened when I see, rising from the gloom, men in white robes smeared with blood. They're coming toward me. I run for the nearby trees, but my flight is sluggish, and I realize my feet are tangled in rope; there are ropes everywhere, around my ankles, my wrists, my neck, and I become horribly aware that they're meant for me, for my hanging . . .

I exploded from sleep to find my sheet tangled about my neck. I stilled the tremors and took my bearings. I was in my bunk in the *Altered Ego*, the boat rocking silently in the wake of a passing boat.

It was easy enough to connect the dream to the hanging death in *When Comes the Darkness*. But my mind was racing beyond that: I was buffeted by a deep sense that a hanging had actually occurred.

I thought back, a week ago, to my encounter with Grundy and Lyall at The Tides. I'd picked up something from them, from the very smell of them – the hint of a fresh kill? I couldn't get rid of the notion; it was itching at me, flitting like a bat in the dark caves of forgotten nightmares.

I played with words from this nightmare: rope, hang, tree. Hadn't Grundy and Lyall said something similar? Seemingly innocuous words maybe, but used because they'd been rattling about in their minds following a significant event. Then it came to me, a word association that might win the applause of Freud himself. When I surprised Grundy at The Tides, his response had been this: *What are you doing in this neck of the woods?* And later, Lyall DeWitt's offhand remark: *You plan to hang around much longer, Doc?* Neck, hang, woods . . . They had committed another murder, by hanging, probably in a wooded area.

The heat I'd sensed emanating from them came not from sexual lust but the lust of murder. That was the reason Grundy begged off seeing me that day: they'd just returned from the kill, and planned to celebrate with Löewenbräus and Jossie Markevich.

Why had no body been found?

I imagined Churko trying to follow my thought processes, grappling with psychoanalytic deduction, free association, the concept of sense-perception. Maybe he'd buy into it, though. He hires soothsayers.

I told him anyway, the next morning in his office. I'd been proved right before, so he wasn't prepared to scoff.

"Read my mind, Doc. It's asking, Where's the body? Where's the opportunity? Grundy was in school that day."

Investigators had already established that on that Thursday, the second day of October, he attended two hour-long classes at SFU, an eight-thirty and a ten-thirty. Lyall DeWitt was likely on campus too. He's been allowed to audit a physical education course to fill time while he waits for Grundy. Otherwise, he usually stays in the van or drives aimlessly about.

Churko said if I turned out to be right he'd back me to the tune of two hundred dollars in *le prix de Okanagan*. But I couldn't persuade him to send search parties into the forest that surrounds the university.

It is midnight, and our train has just pulled out of Ashcroft after taking on a young woman, now seated across the aisle, piercings and tattoos, a small pack. She has pulled out a fat novel, a romance saga. Maybe she's off to pick fruit in the Okanagan orchards.

Victoria hadn't lied about that part . . .

I'm sure, Allis, you've concluded I begged off talking about Peter because I wasn't able to grapple with Victoria's many versions of him — I could never be sure if she'd embroidered a rhapsodic version of her lakeside romance, but I was satisfied with that, wasn't interested in hearing a less palatable version.

Let's get into it then. Let us go to the Victoria's little house in Grandview. Saturday evening.

I bundled my groceries into the kitchen, where Victoria was perched on a stool beside a nearly overflowing ashtray, a wreath of smoke around her. She was fidgeting, seemed anxious. (As was I: this was my second day of abstinence.)

I had no intention of raising the issue of the copycat killings or her novel's unintended role in them. That would put her even more on edge. Instead, I opened by asking how her romance with the mountain climber was faring.

"We've gotten beyond base camp."

Victoria said they were planning to spend the long weekend in a mountain chalet. I wanted to meet this arts producer, to size him up. I'm trying not to judge: he may be the right man for her. If so, I don't intend to be the pebble in the shoe of this romance.

I found a large pot, arranged my working space.

"I hope you know what you're doing. I didn't raise my son to be a cook."

"I think you'll find this very interesting. What gives it uniqueness is the Pernod."

I fussed about, washing my hands, finding pots and utensils. Victoria chain-lit a cigarette.

"You've got two packs worth of butts in that ashtray."

"Please don't lecture."

There was no point in stalling. "Victoria, it's time I was taught the facts of life."

"So says your shrink. Very attractive woman. I suspect her interest in you goes beyond the professional, by the way. She dropped a bomb on me – it seems I've been lying to protect myself, not you. I'm sorry, Tim, I haven't rehearsed this very well."

"Like a drink?"

"No, I'll just get soused."

I opened a beer for myself. While I cooked she talked, staring at her hands, fiddling with her cigarettes, occasionally glancing at me for my reaction.

"I thought my stories about Peter would help you feel good about yourself. I suffered so much mothering guilt, Dr. Epstein says, guilt about having brought you into the world fatherless, guilt that I wasn't there for you a lot, guilt at working, studying, writing, when I should have been with you. There was love, there was always that, but I felt I hadn't been a great mother. Once, some kids locked you in a trunk when I was upstairs writing. You don't remember that, you were very little, but I was a long time finding you, and you were extremely upset. I lived with that, and I hated myself . . ."

"I remember it, Victoria. It wasn't your fault."

Her shoulder bag was sitting beside her, and she reached into it and produced her old diary.

"I went back into that old trunk the other day."

"I thought you lost the key."

"I hid it from you. Some notes about my night with Peter are in here. I'm afraid that what I told you . . . well, I embellished the truth a little, Tim."

"Okay, I can handle it." Was *I* being honest?

"I was in the Okanagan, picking peaches, trying to earn enough for school – your grandparents were helping with money too. But basically, I was playing a fairly stock part for the times, hippie chick, peace and vibes, sex and drugs, rock and roll. I was discovering life, gorging on it – I was free, I was cool, I was seventeen."

Her work in the orchards done, money in her pocket, Victoria hitchhiked to Nelson to attend a rock concert in a baseball park. That's where she met Peter.

"I was attracted to him. He was tall and sinewy and handsome, if you can forgive the scraggly beard. He'd been hanging around third base, surrounded by girls, and I thought, Who is this guy – some kind of movie star? When I got closer, I realized he was hawking grams of hashish."

When he was finally alone, she came up behind him and said in a low voice, "You're busted." He froze, started running, glanced behind, then stopped abruptly when he saw Victoria laughing. They talked, connected. He said she was the most beautiful creature he'd met since escaping prison. At first, she thought the prison reference was a joke.

"I don't know how old he was, early twenties. He was American, from Portland. A deserter, he went AWOL. His story's all in here, I wrote it down. Don't read the poems."

For God's sake, I thought, a dope dealer, an army deserter, and, if his initial reaction of running from Victoria meant anything, a coward.

"Pete, he called himself, though I preferred Peter. I don't think he wanted me to know his last name – he was, to put it bluntly, wanted by the law, at least in the States. He lived in the Kootenay Valley. Just hanging around and moving about, he said. Currently, he was following a band called Brain Damage from town to town."

"Brain Damage?"

"A local version of the Grateful Dead."

A smarmy entrepreneur, a rock-and-roll tent-follower setting up shop at every stop. My recurring dream came back. The town square, the longhairs playing music on the bandstand, their scraggly beards hiding the different faces of Timothy Dare. The smell of marijuana.

"Did he play a banjo?"

Victoria almost jumped. "Yes. My God, where did *that* come from?"

"Primal knowledge."

She looked puzzled, shook it off, continued: "We got on like a damn volcano. We went for a walk by the lake, and we . . . Well, we got stoned on his hash, and I invited him into my sleeping bag."

Proof that the product of their union was damaged – high-THC spermatozoid cell meets high-THC egg, creating an unstable life form.

"And we tripped." She waited for me to respond.

"Over what?"

"Tripped, darling. On LSD."

"How much LSD?"

"Four hundred micrograms a hit." While Brain Damage played on.

I stopped stirring the bouillabaisse. "Victoria, can I ask you another question?"

"Go ahead."

"Was this before or after I was conceived?"

"In between."

"What do you mean?"

"Do you want the clinical details? I can't remember the number of times we made love."

"Willingly?"

"I beg your pardon?"

"Willingly, on your part?"

"Of course. My God, *yes.*" She seemed astounded by the question.

I'm relieved that Victoria wasn't raped, but the truth was harsh enough. I was conceived during a hallucinogenic high, my two fusing cells ripped on eight hundred micrograms of acid. It is a miracle that I'm not a drooling ghoul with five eyes.

"He was bright, Tim. He had his B.Sc. He wasn't a medical student, but he hoped to be one. I had a backgammon set in my pack, and we played it, and he beat me – I thought I was a bit of an expert. He was politically committed. He got fairly garrulous, and began telling me his history. He'd joined the U.S. Marines, and he was politicized in Vietnam. After he made the run to Canada, he helped organize an underground group helping draft dodgers cross the border. He was selling pot to finance it."

As I doled out the bouillabaisse, I found myself softening to Peter – he was anything but a coward, held ideals that I didn't find unworthy. Victoria had told her story cleverly, the bad news first, the psychedelic impregnation that she'd gone to such pains to withhold. I understood now why she shied from the subject while I was in my teens.

Victoria and Peter parted the next day. She had to return to Vancouver, to register at UBC. Peter was heading off to the bush, the undefended border, to smuggle in a couple of Californians. He offered no forwarding address, though Victoria gave him hers.

"Peace," he said as he left.

She was still coming down from the lysergic acid and went into a deep depression.

There was no thought of an abortion. I would be her only memory of him. Though love may not have completely cemented after a single night, Victoria's feelings for him were strong, and she was slow to abandon hope he'd reappear. But he hasn't communicated since.

So I'm still left with that troubling question: Where is he now? Has he returned to the States, and does he sit rotting in a military prison? Or has he become the hermit of Jackson Cove, spotted occasionally by Clinton Huff selling beads at the weekend market?

I left it at that, gave words of love, embraced her, thanked her for telling me the truth. We talked about other matters through dinner, then I settled into an armchair with her diary.

"Please don't read the icky poems," she said and retreated to her room, a little flushed. But she had unwound, and it showed in her expression, her carriage. No medicine could have been as effective as your advice that she'd been protecting herself – out of fear of rebuke, of filial censure from a drug-born sleeping-bag baby sired by a fan of Brain Damage.

I confess that I read her post-pubescent poetic maunderings. I shall put it kindly: Victoria wisely chose a less hazardous literary direction. Some of her prose, however, was riveting: the account of her one-night fling with ex-Private First Class Peter Without a Surname (perused with a flush of embarrassment) and the history he had related to her.

When he was twenty, seduced by thoughts of adventure in far-off places, he quit college to join the Marines. His naïveté was stripped away in the rice paddies of Vietnam: it was an unwinnable war, futile. When Peter witnessed his best friend die in a booby-trapped barn, he became a dissenter in uniform. He returned to the U.S. on leave, deserted, found his way across the border. Soon, he was smuggling others to Canada. There were perilous border crossings, harrowing escapes, once from the military police.

And that's all she wrote. But the news isn't so bad. I may be a scrambled egg, chemically unbalanced, thanks to Peter, but there's also a genetic inheritance of bravery that I find encouraging.

North Kamloops Station. I heist my pack and disembark. The air is sharp, a cool cloudless night, and I can only hope the weather holds for my trial run. I must try to record which curves are dangerous, which can be taken at full speed.

As Vesuvio II is released to me, I notice that the man with the lute has also got off here. He is sauntering toward an old farm truck, and I chase after him.

"Wait, what's your name?"

He frowns, looking me over with hooded eyes. "Harry Baker."

"It's not Pete."

"No. Harry."

We shake hands. "I enjoyed the music."

CHAPTER FOURTEEN

Date of Interview: Friday, October 17, 2003.

Earlier this week, Tim telephoned me from Kelowna, inviting me for a sail, which he hoped would serve as an apology for his abruptness of last week, and I accepted. On the phone, he'd reported himself as in good spirits, but when I joined him today he appeared troubled and angry. A fourth murder has occurred, though it hasn't been labelled as such or been in the news. He was frustrated at the lack of evidence implicating the two prime suspects.

As well, he has found himself "nonplussed" by an unexpected turn of fortune in his mother's libel trial.

He did his best to present a more tranquil face during our sail, and seemed pleased that I knew some boat craft. I picked up a sense of determination from him, and he may be correct when he says anger has fortified his strength. He has refused to move to a secure location, as advised by the police, who are concerned he may have compromised his safety by his blunt inquiries at The Tides.

When I urged him not to dismiss this advice, he said he would not hide from phantoms any more, "whether real or fantastical." However reckless, his more resolute attitude must be seen as a sign of further healing. During his training run, while camping in a provincial park, he had a dream that spoke to his growing boldness.

During our sail, he entertained me on his clarinet with a few jazz standards but otherwise was silent for long periods. I was reluctant to break into his thoughts, given that he regards sailing as a meditative exercise.

We did chat briefly about Sally Pascoe – he claims to have come to grips with his "fading hopes for reunion." I've some doubts about this, because of his past wavering, but I feel I should encourage this more resigned attitude, as the relationship may not be repairable.[1]

Victoria's diary discloses a rather robust history of his father, but Tim won't reject the medically improbable chance that his genes were damaged during conception. This gives him another tool to avoid dealing with his identity crisis as it relates to his father. I went to pains to convince him there are no easy outs, even bolstering my case with the medical literature.[2]

⌇⌇⌇

Okay, Allis, but I'm not sure if Mazurky and Hall controlled all the variables. They weren't able to provide many examples of conception *during* an LSD experience. Nor did they take into account

---

[1] Sally called me before flying to Japan on Thursday. She was concerned about Tim's emotional state vis-à-vis her affair with her editor. I reassured her that he was well. Though the matter was not spoken of, her interest in Ellery Cousineau seems not to have abated. He is travelling overseas with her.

[2] Mazurky and Hall (1979), *Personality Trends among the Post-LSD Generation*.

those raised by single parents, particularly male subjects who never knew their father. So it seems a reach to say there is behavioural correlation.

Look instead at the proof that stares you in the face. Why are you so insistent that I'm within the normal curve, or at least fluttering about the margins? "It's okay to be imperfect," you said. "It's an attainable goal and ultimately more fun."

Maybe you're right, maybe I enjoy not being content with myself. Maybe I should take pride in being, as you put it, a unique medley of internal contradictions. And maybe I should stop seeking excuses for what I am, stop blaming Victoria and Peter for their hippie drug experience.

I was surprised to learn that the ballerina knows how to reef a sail. You kept the *Ego* in the wind nicely, I must say. You looked radiant with the wind and sun playing on your face. Clearly, you like periods of thoughtful quiet, and were grateful that I didn't present as my usual yammering bundle of neuroses. I didn't want to cast gloom with another tale of murder, and gave you the merest outline, but I need to vent about it, get it out of the way.

You haven't heard about this latest death because it's been hushed up. Two weeks ago Thursday, probably only hours before my visit to The Tides, young Sylvester Frummell was hanged from a tree on Burnaby Mountain.

Churko might have found the body faster had he followed my advice to send dogs into the deep woods near Simon Fraser University. But there hadn't been any reports of missing persons, and he joshed me: my mysterious powers must be failing me.

Then, two days ago, he phoned me. Hikers had noticed the furious activity of ravens in a wooded ravine on Burnaby Mountain. They'd been attacking a body hanging from a maple tree.

A ninety-minute, heart-pumping ride on Vesuvio II brought me to the Simon Fraser campus, where I met Churko and members of his team. Churko wouldn't look me in the eye; under the tragic circumstances, I couldn't feel any vindication. I was led on a fifteen-minute scramble down the gully to the maple tree; there I saw a nylon rope dangling from a branch. (In *When Comes the Darkness*: a chestnut tree, a cord from a bathrobe.) The remains had been removed.

Sylvester Frummell was seventeen, a freshman from Fort St. John. Nobody noticed he'd disappeared. I find it outrageous that a young student could be so lacking in friends and caring relatives that no one would report him missing for two weeks. His landlady had been interviewed: Frummell had his own key, his own entrance, she wasn't monitoring his comings and goings, he was a very private person. Acted a little strange, mumbled to himself.

The RCMP in Fort St. John have talked to his parents and a few acquaintances. His divorced mother claimed he rarely phoned. His father hadn't talked to him in thirteen years. Neighbours recalled him as strange, a loner. So did the SFU students whom the detectives interviewed.

"Everyone says he was straight, not a homo," Churko said. "Doesn't fit the pattern. I don't know about murder, he could have climbed the tree and jumped."

Churko can't seem to stifle his eagerness for solutions that don't involve work. However, he came around, reluctantly accepted my hypothesis: Frummell wasn't gay, but Grundy isn't discerning and may have chosen to believe so. Frummell was different, that's all that mattered. Grundy hadn't shared any classes with Frummell, but obviously he and Lyall had taken note of him on the campus. They had chosen this friendless soul, enticed him into the thick woods of Burnaby Mountain.

So as not to warn the suspects, the official verdict has been announced as suicide. Churko is confident they don't know they're being watched, but I'm not so sure. They've been lying low since my visit, sticking to their routines, only once going out for an evening, to a hockey game.

This death has impacted deeply on me. Frummell had entered college on a generous scholarship. He had hoped to be a mathematician. His habit had been to wander along the mountain trails working out equations in a scribbler.

Grundy had a sufficient window within which to act: an hour-long gap between classes. Professor Walton (Biology 200) remembers Grundy at his eight-thirty – he made a point of looking for him each day. Professor Sewell (Statistical Analysis) recalls Grundy hurrying into his ten-thirty: he seemed distracted, tense, and when called upon wasn't able to define the coefficient of correlation.

Both these teachers know Bob Grundison's background, as does the entire faculty, but were unaware till now that their student was a suspected serial killer. They were sworn to secrecy, of course, until the police could buttress their circumstantial case.

It's a political hot potato now that the Grundison family is linked. Churko was summoned to the Attorney General's office, and by the time he finished his report, the A.G. had subsided several inches in his thronelike chair. Churko was warned to make no mistakes. He is to operate by the letter of the law; the government can't afford any fallout. Churko has developed a slight facial tic.

The investigation plods on. Of the four victims, only José Pierrera may be a source of leads, but former workmates shrugged when asked what they knew of the man, his hangouts. His only relative, a sister, rarely visited him. Uniformed beat constables have been checking out the gay bars, showing his photograph, but so far no one has recognized him. How could someone, even a recent immigrant, be so invisible? I worry that slipshod work is being done by inexperienced constables, but Churko claims he doesn't have enough detectives to put on the street. "These ain't the only unsolved murders on my dance card, Doc."

James took umbrage when I asked if he knew of some hangout where Pierrera might have sought male company. "I don't frequent such establishments." But while I was in my consulting room, toiling over some new referrals from the criminal bar (business is picking up, by the way), he must have been logging on to some manner of gay newsgroup or chat room, because he bustled in and handed me a printout.

"These three bars are within a radius of approximately one kilometre from where the victim lived." I was impressed: James had seen the logic of starting close to home – Pierrera had no car. And Churko's foot soldiers might not have concentrated much effort in the working-class East End.

I could have asked Churko to recheck these three addresses – if they'd been visited at all – but he was chafing at what he claimed was my assumption of command. Dotty wasn't trusting his uninspired approach either: she worried that some "male aggressive" would make a botch of things. She will spend an evening cruising these bars.

Though Dr. Martha Wade hadn't seen Grundy since his anger therapy ended in August, I thought I should confer with her. (I took the elevator to her office, no sweat.) She was alarmed by the indications her former patient was a murderer, and upset over her misconceived regard for Lyall DeWitt.

Martha had met Jossie Markevich, whom she found rather coarse and self-centred. Like me, she felt Grundy's avowals of affection for Markevich were feigned – she shares my doubt about his ability to love others. Still, she'd encouraged Grundy to pursue the relationship – he needed the stability of a female partner and wasn't likely to make a better fit.

But my account of walking into the aftermath of a *scène ménage à trois* at The Tides took her aback. "That doesn't make sense, he's too possessive, it challenges all his self-perceptions of being manly, a stud."

Given Churko's overly cautious line of attack, I'm going to try to bring matters to a boil. I have an appointment with Grundy next week, a session in my office that will be secretly monitored by Churko and Dotty. I must find a way to get behind his cool façade.

You can see how absorbed I am in this case, Allis, and it is well that I am: the occupied mind has no room for sadness and loss. I don't dwell much on Sally any more, don't phone her, don't go bicycling down Creelman Street. So I hope you don't mind my detailed accounts of these murders: I'm pouring out what fills me, as I must, as you've counselled me to do.

Anyway, these investigative musings filled my own silences on this truant afternoon as we beat our way off the Point Grey shores. You smiled softly at me, as if in conspiracy, as you brushed back wayward strands of salt-wet hair. You seem to be surviving your bad patch with far more grace than I.

In a way, you're luckier – you're no longer in love with your former partner, the worst is over for you. Dotty caught Richard in a compromising position, so he must consent to the divorce. Let him wed the business partner, as he threatened in that hostile message he left. When forbidden fruit becomes legal – especially in around-the-clock relationships – lovers face boredom and disillusionment.

Of course, the same must go for Sally and Cousineau – since they regularly work together, they may not go unscathed. An unworthy thought, but jealousy is unhealthy only when obsessive, so let me enjoy my malice toward Ellery Cousineau: that is how I purge myself.

He and Sally have taken off to Japan for a promotion, along with a few other representatives of Chipmunk Press – the entire Miriam series is being brought out in translation. After a week of hotel-room tag, she may have her fill of Cousineau in more than a physical sense. I'll be a tower of strength when she needs me. (The patient, despite his claims, is still conflicted, shuttling between hope and hopelessness.)

By the way, my practice run in the Okanagan Hills went well, and my times were pretty good, given that I was encumbered with a backpack and saddlebags. I may not win the gold, but I won't shame my sponsors. The only glitch came when I had to resist taking the ferry across Arrow Lake, to Jackson Cove, only fifteen kilometres away. The town was pulling like a magnet.

One night, I camped by a waterfall in a provincial park, where my dreams literally took flight. Indeed, my bicycle sprouted wings – an old-fashioned flying machine with pedals – but I couldn't urge it into the air, I was a flightless bird, a mechanical dodo on a mountain highway.

Suddenly I'm lost, I don't recognize the terrain. There are rice paddies on either side of me, and fires are burning, and I hear the distant thunder of war. I know I have to escape, and I swing north, toward the Canadian border. Night falls as I flounder through the forest, the sound of barking dogs behind me. I can hear the river, the waterfall, and I know I'm close to the border, but I have to pee. I stop, go behind a tree, and there, close by my ear, I hear a voice: "What's up, Doc?" I whirl and I confront Lyall DeWitt with a roar of anger. When he sees what I'm holding in my hand, he looks at me with confusion and fear. He turns and flees.

At which point my full bladder woke me.

I was heartened that in this dream (you hardly remarked on it, except to make mock applause) I had no fear of Lyall; I challenged him, flourished a weapon at him. Maybe my anger has become a shield, my loathing for Grundy and Lyall has filled all my emotional space. Or maybe I've simply confronted fear, dug deep, found strength.

But why does Lyall run away at the sight of a penis? An aversion disorder?

In the morning, I sat with my tin-cup coffee watching the ferry chug across the lake toward the village of my many dreams. Eventually, I headed back to Vernon, where I bought a bus ticket to Vancouver.

My mother's libel trial was to reconvene on Wednesday in New Westminster, but was slow to get underway, the court lists backed up. I waited outside with Brovak, while he puffed on one of his Cuban cigars. The trial was in the bag, he insisted, my expertise might not even be needed.

He was no less upbeat about the hearing into Vivian Lalonde's complaint. He has retained a polygraph examiner, Charles Lougheed, a retired RCMP officer with psychology training. Given the limits of his art, he's more than capable. A psychopath like Grundy can beat the polygraph. But can Vivian, who does not lack moral sense? I wish I could think of some way to derail this risky test.

Fleeing the cigar smoke, I joined Victoria, asked how her weekend went, the tryst with the mountain-climbing producer.

"We made it to the peak."

A Mona Lisa smile. I followed her into court.

I settled myself in the back row, hoping to make myself small. Presently, I was soon joined by a beefy man with a farmer's tan. For some reason, he gave me a nudge and said, "What the heck are you doing here?" I shrugged and smiled – I couldn't remember having met him.

Clint Huff was looking more dapper than usual, in a tweed suit, and also more composed, almost confident. How would he react on hearing Victoria's novel triggered the imagination of murderers?

Probably less with horror than scornful vindication. The copycat aspect was a secret well kept hidden.

Huff turned to scan the room, spotted me, made me the first order of business, demanding that Judge Lafferty declare me a hostile witness. She explained his motion was premature.

As this was going on, the man beside me whispered, "When did they let you out?"

Don't try even to imagine my reaction to this tricky question. How was I to respond? I'm on a day pass. I'm allowed to be free as long as I take my medication. I escaped. I'm still in. It seemed too simplistic to suggest he'd mistaken me for another.

I settled for, "They never put me in."

He frowned. "But I heard you got two years."

I indicated we would talk later. Huff was back on his feet.

"Very well, my Lady. I now turn to some crucial proof – dare I call it incriminating? – volunteered by one of the good citizens of Jackson Cove. I now have confirmation that the defendant horror writer not only knew of me but has bandied my name about in a newspaper. I call on Victoria Dare to be cross-examined."

This was so unexpected that Brovak was at a loss for words. Judge Lafferty allowed him to sputter a bit, then said, "Plaintiff has that right under the rules, Mr. Brovak."

"Okay, I'm asking for an adjournment. Ms. Dare wasn't expecting to take the stand."

"That's *your* problem." Lafferty was stern. "This trial has gone on long enough."

Victoria went to the witness box, flustered and unready.

"Before I commence," said Huff, "I wish to put on record certain statistics compiled from the Registry of North American Municipalities, which records that among 21,738 towns of a population of two thousand or more there are only two Mayor Huffs, none of them bearing my given name. That is in response to the defendant's argument of innocent coincidence."

"Get on with your cross-examination, Mr. Huff."

"Thank you. Do you continue to maintain you never heard of me, madam?"

"Of course I do."

"I see. Well, have you heard of Joe Beauregard?"

Victoria hesitated. "Joe . . . I don't think so."

"I warn you, he's in this courtroom."

"If he is, I'm afraid I don't know him."

My neighbour leaned to my ear: "We never actually met. I talked to her on the phone."

This, then, must be that same Joe Beauregard. It would seem that, like Huff, he'd mistaken me for one of his townspeople. You will now understand, Allis, why I felt trapped in another waking dream. It gets more bizarre.

Huff carried on: "How about his father, Michael Beauregard? Affectionately known to his wide circle of friends as Mike."

"I'm sorry, Mr. Huff, but you're losing me."

"It is not I, madam, who is losing." With that sortie, he drew out a newspaper clipping, and as he read from it, I sank lower in my seat. "'Prior to his retirement, Mr. Beauregard served twenty-eight years in the Canadian Army, rising to the rank of Master Sergeant. Sadly, on December 12, in his eighty-ninth year, he passed on to a higher service.' Did you write that, madam?"

Victoria hesitated, glanced at Brovak, receiving no comfort. "I imagine I did."

Huff passed out copies to lawyers and judge. He was impressive, drawing from Victoria that she runs an obituary service, that she'd been retained by Joe Beauregard to prepare this notice, and that it had appeared in a newspaper serving the area, the *Nelson News*.

"I have no specific memory of it," Victoria said. "I've done as many as twenty obituaries a week, they're full of names."

Huff quoted further from the obit. Bad enough that the town of Jackson Cove was twice mentioned. Worse, the item ended thus: "'Among the distinguished friends planning to attend the service will be Mayor Clinton Huff of Jackson Cove.'"

Huff might have hoped for more reaction than the dead silence that greeted this bombshell. Victoria's mouth opened, but no words formed.

"For the record, my Lady, this piece of doggerel was written two years before *When Comes the Darkness* was published in a hardcover edition by New Millennium Press. Mr. Joe Beauregard from Jackson Cove is here and can testify that I've never been known to torture or murder anyone."

"I find as a fact that you haven't, Mr. Huff," Lafferty said.

"A joke." He chuckled and sat, amiable now.

Joe Beauregard whispered, "The mayor is gonna owe me big time for this."

I whispered back, "Do you remember my name?"

"What kind of question is that? You're Dub, you're the Dooberman."

"The *Dooberman*? How long have we known each other?"

He looked at me with consternation. "Since you was ten years old and I caught you stealing fifteen bucks from my fruit stand. You gone off your rocker? Look at me, I'm Joe, I live half a mile down Chicory Road." He was frowning at me now, maybe not so certain.

"When did I get busted?"

"The last time?"

Lafferty broke into this. "Would the parties who are in debate in the back row kindly take their business outside?" We fell silent.

Brovak and the Q.C. were making convoluted points of law.

They wore such strained looks that I suspected terminal damage had been done to their case.

When the morning break came, Joe Beauregard rose and squeezed past me. "I got to get back to Jack Cove, I got a family to feed. Catch you later." He walked quickly out.

I thought to pursue him and engage him further, but Brovak pulled me aside. "We've got to figure a way to deal with this schmozzle, Tim."

I had no answers, but insisted he abandon the idea of my testifying about Huff's mental state. He had proved himself more than competent, had outshone the crack lawyers for the defence. Moreover, I might have to concede the obvious: that the name of the mayor of Jackson Cove had become embedded in Victoria's mind, in the unconscious murk.

Was that sufficient to make her liable? Brovak wasn't sure.

Victoria's testimony, when court resumed, was too apologetic. She had only a vague memory of preparing an obituary on information received from a Mr. Beauregard. She'd meant Clinton Huff no disrespect or harm, and neither his name nor his hometown had registered.

The day ended with an articulate summation by Huff and a response by the defending lawyers that was muted enough to betray doubt. Innocent mistake, they pleaded. Thievery of a man's good name, said Huff.

Judge Lafferty didn't find the issue simple. She adjourned to give a written judgment. Huff seemed displeased at being denied the immediate victory warranted by his stunning new evidence. As he left, he gave me a peremptory nod, as if to say "Got you."

Victoria and I joined the lawyers at a nearby bar to rehash the day – it felt like a wake. I tried to lighten matters by recounting how I'd been confused with a reprobate named the Dooberman, but no one seemed much interested. The publisher's Q.C. was wishing he hadn't withdrawn the settlement offer. Brovak was moping, Victoria in despair. "I'm ruined. My literary career is in shambles. I may as well write my own obituary." I tried to buck her up, to no avail.

A sad note to end on, but that fleshes out my week for you, Allis, fills the silence of our sail.

As we returned to False Creek, I stifled an urge to ask what thoughts were behind your distant smile. Mine, I'll admit, had to do with this pleasant time with you continuing to the evening, into the unpredictable night.

I warned myself that we were too comfortable with each other, susceptible. You're my therapist, I'm in danger of displacing, making you a surrogate for lost love. But, as we tied up at Sea Village, your eyes were on mine like a silent question, and I stammered this awkward invitation: "You wouldn't be interested in joining me for dinner?"

"That seems rather negatively put," you said, then hesitated. "I would be interested, except . . ."

I waited.

"I think I should go home and water my flowers."

Cheeks were kissed. We went our separate ways.

CHAPTER FIFTEEN

Date of Interview: Friday, October 24, 2003.

This has been an extraordinary week for Tim, highlighted by a confrontation that put him in peril. I phoned twice to express my concern for his well-being but was able to reach only his secretary. When he failed to call back, I assumed he intended to cancel. He surprised me by showing up on schedule.

He was so highly energized that I was allowed little chance to speak.[1] Much of his eloquence was devoted to the "sub-average intellectual functioning" of a senior police officer responsible for a "Keystone cock-up."

I noted a recurring manic tendency, but otherwise my observations are positive: he grows in self-assurance, and exhibits a

---

[1] As time has passed, and as I see increasing signs of health, I sense myself becoming less a therapist than an audience being entertained. I must remind myself not to become lax.

toughness that in the first weeks of therapy was hard to locate. Indeed, he is well recovered from the traumas that led him to treatment.

There is still pain related to Sally, but he seems able to follow my advice to feel it, understand it, and release it. He was saddened by the sudden resolution of his problems with the disciplinary board, particularly by "the bittersweet agony of the moment."

He is fascinated by the picture he now has of his father, and feels an even more powerful urge to find him, to make a link that would finally "integrate" him. The fact that a Mr. Dooberman from Jackson Cove bears a close likeness – a man who apparently has been in trouble with the law – has fortified this mission.

Following the session, he accepted my offer of dinner at his favourite restaurant.

Sorry I didn't call back, but your messages got to me late . . .

I understand absolutely . . .

. . . But you'll have to put me on hold next week, I leave Wednesday for the Okanagan, the race starts at dawn Thursday, ends Friday afternoon, in time for the BCMA convention. We have about sixty signed up, and at least that many volunteers. We'll have one overnight in Penticton, then it's on to Arrow Lake and a barbecue that evening.

Sounds like fun. Are you going to the convention too?

Avoiding it like the plague.

Same plague that keeps you from visiting Jackson Cove?

I'll stop by there when my head is screwed on tight. After all the shit settles. Who the hell is Dub Dooberman? I checked the police records. Nothing. I can't find the name in any phone listing, or the directory for Jackson Cove.

Where do you want to start today?

There's so much. The fiasco at my disciplinary hearing . . .
I'm not sure . . .

I'll start with you, Dr. Epstein, in an effort to unravel my confusion. A change has come over you, a softness in your eyes, where before was the steely intensity of the analyst. You're not working me as hard. Today, you were unusually quiet, in your consulting room and at the Pondicherry. What's with this constant distant smile? Maybe you're just pleased with yourself: the patient is on his feet. They said he'd never walk again.

I am going to assume (against contrary, troubling evidence) that you're merely displaying the sweet sadness of the therapist whose work is almost done. I've felt it many times – a closeness develops, a kind of love, but it must end: the patient must leave, must hope his new coping skills will help him tough it out alone.

Nataraja approved of you, though typically he mistook the nature of our relationship. ("You been horizontal with her yet?") He has an avid interest in sex, and fondly recalls those halcyon days when many women of his New Age tribe sought enlightenment in his bed.

After you dropped me off, I carried your gentle kiss to bed with me, and you featured in a dream . . .

I'm going off track. Okay, I'll start with Monday evening – that was when Dotty Chung summoned me to the Sapphire Lounge, when I met the gracious Lolita L'Amour, when the web tightened on Grundy and Lyall.

I was on a training run, racing over the Second Narrows bridge, when Dotty lit up my cellphone. She'd been prospecting the gay bars recommended by James's search, and had just struck gold. Lolita L'Amour, a bartender, recognized José Pierrera from a photograph, remembered serving him – and "two lovely young things he was with" – several weeks ago.

I sped to the Sapphire Lounge, which is in a small hotel on Hastings Street, in Burnaby, not more than half an hour's walk from Pierrera's home. The decor is vaguely Levantine, with faded murals of ocean and olive groves, and many of its clientele could be described as working-class transvestite. Thirty people would pack it, but on this night there were only a dozen present.

Dotty had also summoned Churko, and he was already there, on a bar stool looking massively uncomfortable. Dotty was beside him, chatting to the person I took to be Lolita. The several customers in drag looked dowdy in comparison to Madame L'Amour: striking in a slinky green gown and hot lipstick. Her given name is Lawrence Green; one can't easily tell her age – maybe early forties.

Churko greeted me with a grunt, glancing past me at a table where a couple was holding hands. He then watched with open distaste as Lolita offered her hand, and I kissed it.

"My dear, you have to be utterly the *last* gentleman standing," she said.

"Let me go back over this," Churko said. "You remember this José Pierrera guy?"

"I never knew the poor thing's name. She spoke about two words of English. I think she'd been here a few times, but one really doesn't *notice* José. The word *nondescript* comes to mind."

"How come you never called in? We ran his picture on the fucking TV."

"I don't do TV, darling."

"You don't do newspapers either?"

"Too depressing. This is all so maudlin. I hope I'm not going to be dragged into some horrendous courtroom situation."

"If we find you've been withholding . . ."

I gently interrupted, my hand on his elbow. "Hey, Jack, this party

244

came forward, let's . . . let's have a beer." Dotty, who was also dismayed at his brusqueness, had been nursing a lager, and I ordered a couple more. Churko declined a glass, wiped the mouth of his bottle with his sleeve before taking a pull from it.

Lolita excused herself to attend to other customers, and I grabbed the opportunity to urge Churko to change tack. What I really wanted him to do was relax. He is more than slightly homophobic, and his lack of judgment was showing.

"I want to ask you, Doc, how is this party, as you put it, going to look in the witness box? She . . . he better be able to give us faces." Churko was clutching a photo album, shots of two dozen young men, Grundy and Lyall among them.

"Hey, Jack, get into the spirit," Dotty said. "You may get lucky. That brunette over there has eyes for you."

"I got three daughters. This is the world they're growing up in."

When Lolita rejoined us, Churko pressed on resignedly. "I'd like you to describe the scene — José came in with those guys, or met them here, or what?"

Lolita explained she'd been working alone that night. She remembered Pierrera wandering in, taking a back booth, ordering a beer. She was struck by how lonely he looked.

At about ten p.m., two young men came in, strangers to her. "Brutes, if you know what I mean. A muscle shirt, for goodness' sake, and the muscles to go with it. The other one wasn't as hefty. Utterly adorable in their quiet, strained way."

She thought they were straight at first, until they started chatting up Pierrera, flirting with him, the slighter man talking in a falsetto. "I mean, really," Lolita said, "she was coming on like a little tramp." Soon they joined Pierrera in his booth.

"You didn't figure that was strange?" Churko asked. "These two studs coming on to this lonely . . . this nondescript who could hardly talk English?"

"I don't ask, darling. That isn't part of my job description. One is *discreet*."

However, she thought they were hustlers, or maybe drug dealers. They seemed high on speed or cocaine. They had another round of drinks during the next half-hour, and since the bar was becoming busier, Lolita lost track of them. The booth was deserted when she next looked, a fifty-dollar bill tucked under a shot glass. She had no idea if they left together.

"Okay, I want you to look at some pictures here. You'll see they got numbers, and I want you to tell me if you recognize anyone from that night."

She didn't study them for long. "Number eight," she said. "Number twenty." Grundy and Lyall.

Churko told Lolita to keep her silence, thanked her, and motioned for Dotty and me to join him outside.

"That joint gave me the creeps," he said, pulling deeply on a cigarette. "Looks like we got our guys, but they'll hire a ten-thousand-a-day lawyer who's gonna rant about how it's highly circumstantial. I got to talk to some higher-ups. Be close to a phone."

I was picked up by a squad car Tuesday morning to join the task force in a conclave with a special prosecutor – Foster Cobb, a former Crown counsel now in private practice.

Churko's office was crowded, so I stayed by the door, exchanging greetings with Cobb. I've worked several murder cases with him, found him able and quick of mind, and he seemed on top of this file already. "We are having a debate, Tim. We have two schools of thought. The first school is represented by my old friend Jack Churko."

The inspector took his cue. "We give them a chance to explain themselves. We offer the normal courtesy of inviting them for a lineup, and if Lolita fingers them again, we got some friendly questions we want to ask them. We go by the book. We got a prominent family here."

Cobb nodded, contemplative. "You'll want to give them the standard warning, I suppose, Jack. The one about how they have a right to a lawyer."

"We cross all our t's, that's my attitude."

Cobb rested a hand on Churko's shoulder. "Now, Jack has been around the block a few times, I've got a lot of respect for him, and he believes we should go into The Tides with warrants, toss their rooms, bring these bad boys downtown, separate them, and grill them till they're well done on both sides. Some of these other gentlemen feel we need something harder. What do you think, Tim?"

"I don't like the first scenario. You'll be lucky to get a squeak out of these guys. If they exercise their rights, what have we got?"

"A few lies. Association. Opportunity. Sick motive. Your copycat theory: interesting, not compelling."

"How about giving me one last shot at Grundy? If I get lucky, you can go in with handcuffs." Grundy can't refuse to talk to me, I explained, the terms of his release require him to submit to my monitoring, to close cross-examination.

Cobb was interested, and we worked out this plan: my consulting room would be wired for my regular Thursday appointment with Grundy. Police would listen from Dotty's quarters above.

Afterwards, I sped off to the Broadway Medical Centre. My disciplinary hearing was to reconvene this day, as soon as the results of Vivian's polygraph test were in. That had been set for ten a.m. – it had been delayed twice at her request, and Brovak felt she was trying to squirm out of it.

When I showed up, the hearing wasn't yet in session, and an unusually subdued Vivian Lalonde was leaning against the boardroom door. "It's over, Timothy," she said in an oddly thick voice. "It's all over." She was dressed in the black of penitence, a clinging dress. I was heartened by her words, her slouch, the posture of defeat.

Brovak was closeted in a nearby office with the polygraph examiner, Charles Lougheed, leaning over the graphs. Brovak grinned at me. "Don't start feeling sorry for her. We should sue her sweet ass off."

Lougheed nodded. "She did not perform well."

He showed me several jumps on the graph. The kymograph pens had been active when she claimed I'd made romantic overtures, my alleged declaration of love. Her versions of the stalking incidents ("Mostly, we would just casually bump into each other") caused a sweaty skin response and a skip of the heart.

As to the alleged romp on my couch, their exchange had gone like this:

"I'm not under oath, am I?"

"No, you're not."

"So if I lie, I'm not perjuring myself."

"This doesn't work, Ms. Lalonde, if you don't agree to tell the truth."

"I don't know any more . . . I don't remember exactly. I don't want to destroy his career."

"What is the answer?"

"We didn't make love on the couch."

"Is that the truth?"

"Well, we were on his desk."

"You had intercourse?"

"Of a fashion. I . . . I didn't resist. It's confusing. I know he wanted me. I know it."

A chilling footnote: I'd proposed that she be questioned about the notes *You are next* and *I know where you live*. Lougheed found these useful as control questions. Her answers were unhesitant and honest: she knew nothing of them.

The sender had to be Grundy.

I was absorbed in the implications of that, and almost walked into Vivian as I entered the hearing room. She staggered, and when I put out a hand to steady her, she started crying and walked unevenly to a chair. I was concerned – her lack of balance seemed unnatural, as if induced chemically as much as emotionally.

For a few moments, the only sound to disturb a tomblike silence was her sobbing. That was proof enough that Vivian's edifice of lies had collapsed. Neither Schulter, Mundt, nor Rawlings could look me in the eye.

Brovak laid Lougheed's written report in front of them, along with the graphs, then slouched in his chair. "She flunked, gentlemen."

As they perused the material, another silence set in, punctuated by the shuffling of paper and clearing of throats and, finally, as Mundt looked up, his lugubrious sigh. Schulter offered me a rigid smile intended to mask clenched teeth. "Thank goodness. Just as I hoped and expected."

Vivian was weeping audibly. Mundt cast a regretful look at her, disappointed at her show of frailty. "Let's put this thing to rest."

Rawlings was staring at Vivian. I don't know if he'd followed much of this. He came to with a nudge from Schulter, and said, "Yes, of course, not guilty."

"Very well," said Schulter, "I am gratified to make it unanimous."

Vivian was saying something through choking sobs, her words incoherent.

"I'm sorry, Miss Lalonde," said Schulter, "we didn't quite catch . . ."

She was on her feet, steadying herself with a hand against the wall. "I told the truth . . . about one thing . . ."

"What's that?"

She was looking at me, trembling. "That I love you, Timothy. It's the only truth that matters."

With that, she pitched forward, over a chair. "Get a doctor," someone yelled, Schulter, I think.

I was the first to reach her, raising her limp body in my arms, carrying her to the door, Mundt scurrying ahead of me.

"Sleeping pills?" he said.

"I expect so."

We found an internist down the hall and left Vivian to his mercies and his stomach pump. *It's all over.* Her life, she meant. I rebuked myself for not having picked up her signals – she'll need intensive, long-term care, the help of a worthier psychiatrist than I.

At last report she's recovered from all but her despair; her father has taken her in and hired an around-the-clock home-care nurse and a therapist recommended by the Suicide Prevention Centre. Dr. Lalonde, however, hasn't called to express regret, nor has he paid my last bill.

I told Brovak to drop any thoughts of an action against Vivian – I actually grieve for her. There was reward enough in the hypocrisy of Schulter's formal letter exonerating me and paying tribute to "a fighter, a caring physician, and one of the keenest minds of our difficult profession." But I intend to send a hefty final bill to her father.

On the day following the hearing, I rode Vesuvio II like the devil's horseman, up the Squamish Highway, in heavy traffic, trying to erase my sadness at having failed Vivian. In counterpoint to my melancholy, it was one of those perfect days of autumn, a blue sky that showed no hint of the coming sullen months of grey.

We have to hope the weather continues to hold, particularly in the Interior – it's a tricky time of year, mists lingering through the morning, nighttime freezes, always the possibility of sudden fronts, of storms.

My main challenge will come from an orthopaedist who in his student days tried out for Canada's Olympic team in the thousand-metre sprints. But does he have the lasting power? The entrants include other amateur athletes, but (aside from stair-climbers and trained ballet dancers) most of our colleagues are overworked, overstressed, and overfed. None can have trained as hard as me.

Now let's move on to yesterday, October 23, a date forever enshrined in the honour roll of law enforcement fuckups.

James had called Grundy earlier in the week to remind him of his two p.m. appointment, his regular time on his regular day: everything must seem normal. "How's the good doctor?" Bob had asked. "He was under the weather last time I saw him." Polite, relaxed.

Jack Churko and a dozen of his crew – three in SWAT gear, just in case – packed themselves upstairs in Dotty's office – my own offers no hidden alcoves. James, however, had bravely volunteered to be at his desk.

He'd phoned Grundy to tell him: "The doctor requests he see you alone" – without his soulmate and brother in crime. Was I exposing myself to a supposedly psychotic attack? *You are next.*

Grundy was late, and I assumed he couldn't find a niche on Granville Island to park – the Vancouver International Writers Festival was in full swing. More time passed, and we began to wonder if he was even planning to show up. As of half past two it seemed not: surveillance officers, parked near the gates to The Tides, reported no sighting of Grundy, or Lyall, or any vehicle leaving the estate.

Churko had missed his lunch. "How long are we going to wait? You better call him. He leaves now, it'll take him an hour, so some of us are grabbing some chow." I watched as he, Dotty, and several others strolled off to the Granville Island Hotel, leaving a skeleton crew upstairs.

James was just about to dial The Tides when I glanced outside and saw to my consternation that Bob Grundison was coming up by a stairway from the pier. As he entered, he was smiling as if at some private joke. James quickly hung up.

"Real sorry, Dr. Dare, I didn't think we'd take so long by boat. Lyall and I had plans, but . . . it's okay, we can be late."

Lyall was trespassing on the *Altered Ego*, lashing a line from a sleek inboard launch, hitching fenders between the boats, balloon floats.

I called from the balcony: "Careful of my boat, Lyall, it's freshly varnished." That would alert the officers above, in case they hadn't noticed this back-door arrival. As I later learned, they saw Grundy coming up the staircase, took up their headphones, eavesdropping while keeping an eye on Lyall.

I led Grundy into the consulting room, so our conversation could be picked up by the hidden microphones. The dialogue that follows is as recorded:

"You said you had plans?"

He shrugged. "We were going for a little harbour tour with a friend."

"Who?"

"Jossie."

"Ah, yes, Ms. Markevich. Exactly *whose* friend is she, Bob?"

"What do you mean?"

"Three's not a crowd in Lyall's bed, is it?"

He went stiffly into the stuffed chair, took a moment to answer. "I think you got the wrong impression, we weren't . . . All I did was let Lyall have a piece of the action. He asked if I minded, it was all very open. She . . . okay, she kind of went for him. I wasn't going to get in their way. Like I told you, she's a free spirit."

"I thought she was the love of your life."

"I guess it wasn't meant to be. You win some, you lose some. Isn't that the way?" He was looking unblinkingly at me. *I know where you live.* I know you can't keep a wife, either.

"You don't like women, do you, Bob? Use them, toss them, pass them down the line." Dr. Wade's confrontational approach had reaped interesting rewards, and I was intent on turning up the volume.

"You're making a big leap. There's a lot of females I admire. Just because I . . . Okay, maybe I had some bad experiences. I'm trying to learn about girls, I'm adjusting." I waited for more. "You're the psychiatrist. You going to tell me it's related to my mother?"

"No, I think it's something more disordered."

He tensed. "That isn't very charitable. You mad at me? I break a rule or something?"

"These feelings aren't just related to women, though, are they? Gay men – do they bother you too?"

"Nothing personal, but I don't think God intended that kind of union." Grundy's expression hardened, and spots of anger showed on his cheeks. "Okay, let's get it out on the table. I know why you're bugged about me, you've been asking people a lot of questions, you want to connect me with these murders of homosexuals. You'd love it if I was the guy who did this, wouldn't you? Send me back to the funny farm. Forget it, I got Lyall as my witness, I got an army of witnesses. I really feel insulted, Dr. Dare. You've had it in for me ever since that jury threw out your evidence against me."

I let the reverberations die down. He was panting slightly, like a dog after a run.

"Okay, so tell me how you feel about homosexuals."

"I'll be honest, I've got moral objections. They got a choice, God didn't make them that way."

"We have a right to choose who we are?"

"And to choose what we do, how we live."

"Dr. Barbara Wiseman – did she have that choice?"

"Nobody forced her to be a lesbian . . ." He checked himself. "If that's what you meant."

It wasn't what I meant, but I followed it up. "You were aware she was a lesbian?"

"She made no bones about it."

"You were resentful at being placed under her care — was her sexual orientation a factor?"

"I didn't know I needed help then."

"You recall meeting any of these men who were murdered?"

"I don't hang around with the gay crowd."

"How do you feel about these deaths? They bother you at all?"

"I feel bad, same as anyone, it was lucky they didn't have families."

"How do you know they didn't have families?"

"It was in the news, all of them were loners. Maybe not the older guy, the others."

"The other three."

"Yeah, the . . . I only heard about two others."

He'd nearly slipped on the ice of his lies. A shadow crossed his face, a suspicion that I knew too much.

"Do you read books, Bob? Fiction? Novels?"

"Occasionally, if I got nothing else. Lyall's the reader."

"Ever discuss books with him?"

"Yeah, he put me onto a couple of good ones."

I pulled a copy of *When Comes the Darkness* from my desk drawer. "How about this one?"

He screwed his face up, concentrating on the title. "*When Comes* . . . No, can't say I ever heard of it."

"Remember Lyall talking about it? Serial murderer. Gets a sexual high when he kills. Can't get it any other way. Ring a bell?"

"No way."

"My mother wrote it. It's been in the news."

"Really? That's something."

I wasn't getting far with this, though he was clearly uncomfortable. I left the book in plain view, opted to stop circling and to move in. "Where were you the night Mr. Wilmott was murdered? You weren't on the Skeena River."

Again, he rallied. "Okay, you want to make a big thing about it. Lyall and me were going to drive up there, but then my dad made his plane available. So we took a little extra R and R, buzzed down to Seattle, picked up a couple of girls, shacked up for a couple of nights. Ask Lyall."

Grundy hadn't prepared well: this alibi failed to account for the parking ticket, but I held that in reserve. I don't think he expected this session to be so inquisitorial, and he was becoming rattled.

"You want proof, we'll go down there and locate those girls, we know where they live."

I amended the phrase. "I know where you live."

It took him a moment to react. "You think I made a Freudian slip or something? I already told you, I didn't write that note." He tried to work up a smile, quickly lost it. His hands were in his jacket pockets, balled-up fists.

"Where were you and Lyall the night the other two men were killed?"

"I was at home. Lyall will tell you that, Mom too, everybody." Sweat beaded on his lips, and he sounded frantic. "You think I'm some kind of freak? I don't do those things, I got to live with myself. Is this all we're going to do? I sit here and you bait me, is that it? I had some other plans." He began to rise. "I've got a headache."

"Sit down!"

He subsided, tight-lipped. "It's hot in here. I think I'm getting one of my tensions."

At room temperature, he was sweating. "I'll open a window."

When I did so, I saw Churko strolling from the Granville Island Hotel. I had an inkling of the muddle to come from his casual manner.

"Let's talk about these tensions. The medication doesn't always do the trick, does it?"

"Helps a bit."

"Did you find another way to beat them?"

"Sorry, Doc, I'm not following."

"It builds up, doesn't it?"

"What does?"

"The drive, the need. Is it a kind of sexual urge, Bob? Like the guy in this book? Sometimes do you feel like you just can't control it?"

This produced a galvanic response, he was sweating profusely. He went deep into his chair, fighting the impulse to fly at me, knowing I was daring him to do it. I decided to tone things down. I wasn't prepared to risk goading him into violence, wasn't sure if the SWAT team had returned from lunch.

"Okay, Bob, try to relax. Obviously, we're going to have to get you some help. Maybe we should be looking at more efficient drugs, a stronger regime of therapy. There are some excellent clinics that offer intensive care. Frankly, these recurring tensions bother me."

"I'm dealing with them, okay?"

"I've never properly understood them. I want you to help me with that. It's not as if you can stop yourself when the tensions come, is it? They're out of your control. Maybe we don't have free choice in some things, Bob."

"It's . . . you mean like an irresistible impulse? That's a defence in court, right?"

He was reaching for a lifeline. I played it out. "That's why you killed Dr. Barbara Wiseman, isn't it? You had one of your tensions."

"Yeah, it was out of my control."

"She found out something you didn't want her to know, didn't she? That's why the tension came on. What did she tell you, Bob?"

"I'm not feeling very good. I've got to go to the bathroom."

"Try to hold it a little longer. Let's grapple with this." The moment seemed right. Regardless of consequences, I decided to let fly: "That's when you get the urge to kill, isn't it, Bob — when the tensions come. That's why you had to murder those men."

He rose slightly, a cat taking position to spring. I could see the venom in his eyes . . .

It was at this vastly inopportune moment that Jack Churko chose to stride into the consulting room. He failed to notice Grundy and said, "Got any more bright ideas, Doc?"

I later found out that while tucking into his hamburger platter, Churko had checked again with his surveillance team at The Tides: still no sign of Grundy. Instead of consulting with his remaining crew upstairs, he barged past James to tell me my plot had flopped.

When he saw Grundy, he at least managed not to show shock or dismay. "Oh, sorry, I didn't realize you had a patient."

"Still can't sleep, Mr. Wilson?" I said.

"Ah, yeah, that's the problem."

I grabbed a pad, scribbled on it, called to James, who was standing in the doorway, wringing his hands. "Will you send Mr. Wilson to the pharmacy? I'm doubling the dosage."

Grundy stayed fixed on Churko until I gave James the fake prescription, showed the patient out, and closed the door. But I had little faith our play-acting was fooling Grundy. Churko had got his face in front of a camera outside José Pierrera's basement suite, and Grundy must have seen the coverage.

I was still by the door when Grundy sprang. For a fleeting second I thought he was leaping at me, in an orgasm of rage, but he ran instead to the balcony door, threw it open, knocking over a potted geranium as he vaulted onto the railing.

He went airborne with a lunge, diving into the cold salt water just aft of the *Altered Ego*.

I raced to the balcony, watched Lyall frantically slipping the moorings free, starting the engine, Grundy swimming hard, grabbing a float, clinging to it, being pulled along as the boat began accelerating to the opposite shore.

Cops were streaming from the quarters above, guns out, bulling their way through a knot of sightseers. Churko was yelling into his phone, calling all cars. Dotty bolted for her runabout, a couple of SWAT members on her heels.

Lyall briefly let the launch take its own course as he hauled Grundy aboard, then hastened back to the controls as Dotty's slower boat began its pursuit. I saw Grundy stripping, rummaging through a packsack for dry clothes. A glint of steel that might be a firearm. Within a minute Lyall found the nearest beachhead, a rocky shore, the launch hitting with a thud. They leaped ashore, hit the ground running as startled onlookers backed away.

My last view of them was as they scrambled to the street and up an alley, between the towers of Vancouver's West End, toward its bustling downtown.

This much we have learned since: they raced to the main branch of the Toronto-Dominion Bank, arriving just before closing time. Grundy, a valued customer, told the assistant manager he was anxious to close a cash deal on a two-year-old Ferrari. He withdrew sixty thousand dollars.

That was yesterday. Last night, Churko had to handle some awkward questions at a press conference. Today, airports are being watched and border officials have been put on alert, as well as ferries, bus, train, and taxi companies. Photos of the two men are on the front pages of the dailies under screaming headlines. But they have vanished within the anonymous sprawl of the city.

CHAPTER SIXTEEN

Date of Interview: Wednesday, October 29, 2003.

These remarks are being dictated into my microcassette as I return to Vancouver along the Coquihalla Highway. I have just deposited Tim in Vernon, the starting point of his race. My decision to free up my day was prompted, as I explained by telephone last night, by his earlier kindness in taking me sailing.

When I picked him up with his bicycle and gear, he seemed exhausted: he'd been "squeezing a week's work into two days," with every spare moment allotted to help the police in their unavailing search for the two suspects.

He told me he was enduring a "spasm" of self-doubt regarding the rally and was no longer confident of his chances. "I'll be lucky to get close to that orthopaedist. If I end up halfway through the pack, I'll be in mortal shame." I tried to persuade him that he shouldn't let the significance of the race overwhelm him, nor should he see losing as a calamity.

Despite his tiredness, he was emotionally stable, though he's still worried about the outcome of his mother's trial and remains unresolved about Sally.[1] In that regard, he continues to seesaw. This is a wound that will not heal.

Tim dozed off a few times en route. At one point, I heard him mumbling, "Don't call the police." He was reclining almost to the horizontal – eyes closed, mouth working, and waving his right arm, as if in warning.

As we approached Vernon, he roused himself, and I asked if he remembered a dream in which he used those words. He went silent, as if reassembling it, but changed the subject, and I had the impression he didn't want to speak of it.

I helped him carry his bicycle to his hotel room, wished him luck, and departed.

. . . I'll be in mortal shame.

Of course you won't. Actually, I'm pleased you're finally doubting your sterling qualities as a racer. Much healthier than constantly pumping yourself up.

Is that was I was doing?

You've been at least marginally obsessive about this race. You don't have to win, and you don't have to doubt yourself. You have to have fun. It reduces the impact of possible letdown. Given your tendency to go to spectacular extremes emotionally, I think I'd be some time cleaning up the mess.

He turned to inspect his bicycle and equipment.

Hand pump, spare chain links, spare tires. Remembered my helmet, there is a God. I brought a pair of wider tires, just in case it snows. I'm going to try to draft off the leaders for the first few klicks. Don't want the orthopaedist to get distance on me

---

[1] At one point, he rather jarringly used her name in addressing me.

though. Jib Faile, he was a college champion. He'll tire on the inclines, I think, he's more of a straightaway racer. What kind of car is this?

Volvo station wagon. Safe vehicle, safe driver.

This seat go all the way down?

Yes.

A few moments passed.

Don't get me wrong, Tim, I do hope you'll win . . . Tim?

Silence.

Sleep tight.

⟨༄⟩

In this dream of winter, Vesuvio II and I are puffing along a mountain road. The ground is carpeted with snow, and the going is slippery. I'm confused – where are the others? Why am I alone in this race? Can it be I am running ahead of the pack?

I sense a familiarity with the area, as if I've been here many times, it's somewhere near Jackson Cove. I shouldn't be here, though, I've screwed up, taken a wrong turn.

Smoke rises from the many skinny chimneys of the village. In place of the wall is a yellow banner proclaiming FINISH LINE, DO NOT CROSS. I become aware of gaiety in the town square, the hillbilly band playing, the townspeople in costume, dancing around a barbecue fire. I wonder why so many of them are dressed as doctors.

Then I see the bicycles. There are hundreds of them, the race is over. I am last, I don't even want to finish.

Dejected and exhausted, I stumble into a roadside inn. Other losers are here, sitting in the bar with tankards of German beer. Over there is Clinton Huff, on a stool. Here is Jossie Markevich, here Jack Churko. She's telling him, "That's the way they like it."

"Where's Grundy?" I ask Jossie.

"You don't understand. He loves you."

"I know where he is," Lolita L'Amour whispers. "He's waiting for you."

I wonder if she means not Grundy but Peter, my father. I sense he is again in trouble with the law. "Don't call the police," I urge her.

She points to a cabin at the top of a hill. I hope it is Peter who's waiting. Then I see a two-headed monster up there, Grundy on one neck, DeWitt on the other.

The rest of the dream is lost in the gloom; I can't bring it back. Since dreams often turn words around as children do, we have to be aware of reversals. The recurring refrains – *He loves you, he's waiting for you* – may mean, *He hates me, he wants to see me dead.* What is the mystery of these scraps of speech? I may soon find out. Dreams are but echoes of reality . . .

But tonight no dreams come. At the witching hour, my sheets are tangled from my contortions. I worry that unless I get enough sleep, I'll be slow and groggy on the road. I know: I'm taking this race too seriously. (Though I felt affronted when you warned me of the perils of letdown. It was as if you felt I had little hope of placing.)

Your abrupt leave-taking is the cause of this, my sleeplessness. I'm unsure whether I should feel ashamed or merely confused by how you vanished into the night, but the awkwardness remains.

Was it on the spur of the moment that you offered to drive me here? I suspect so. Thank you for saving me from a bus full of chattering M.D.s and their backup teams of spouses, partners, and assorted helpers. Thank you for escorting me past the cocktail lounge to the sober safety of my room.

In the close confines of that room, you gave off a slight, delicious scent of anxiety. I felt nervous too. That queen-sized bed was staring at us, and neither dared return its gaze.

"We could order up something to eat," I said. "Some wine."

"You're very tired, and I have a long drive."

"You could get an early start tomorrow."

You took a moment to consider, then said, "That's very tempting . . . I'm not sure."

Your voice trailed off. The moment seemed charged with unpredictable risk and promise. I don't know who first broke from the starting blocks, maybe we jointly came together. I'd teased my mind many times with thoughts about how your lips would feel opened to mine, of our bodies pressed close, but hadn't prepared myself to be so overwhelmed.

I shouldn't have allowed the flame that has been flickering between us (and let's stop pretending) to ignite into passion. But ethics, morality, prudence – all those useless imperatives – vanished. My hands went to your body, and yours to mine, fumbling for clasps and buttons, and . . . well, then I blew it.

How flustered you were as you tugged at your bra strap and tucked in your blouse. My attempts to make light of the moment clanged like a stale joke.

"Godspeed, Tim." And you left without a look back.

I'm utterly mortified at having made the one-time, totally mindless, softly whispered Freudian slip of calling you Sally. How humiliating for you.

All I can say in defence is maybe it was for the best. Had we gone tumbling into that bed, how would we have dealt with it afterwards? Therapy misfires when passion intrudes, and risks a tragic end when colleagues are involved. You and I know that what happened – and what *almost* happened – can't be ignored away. We must talk.

I can expand little on what I told you about the murder investigation, but these are the essentials: Grundy and Lyall are now equipped for the wilderness – shortly after leaving the bank they stocked up with hiking and camping gear and PowerBars. A salesperson in a sporting goods store came forward after recognizing their photographs in the weekend papers.

I've been trying to figure out where they might be holed up. They may have pitched a tent in the mountains – Vancouver is surrounded by wilderness, and the two men are fit. But they can't hibernate all winter like bears. These are men who like their comforts, and they may not stray far from civilization. The Lower Mainland abounds with summer homes, on lakes, by rivers, in the forest, and it's my hunch that Grundy and Lyall are hiding out in one.

Teams were all weekend at The Tides, combing through their rooms. As expected, Lyall's Internet visits had included several racist sites. The men hadn't kept any incriminating papers or photos, but the copy of *When Comes the Darkness* was still on Lyall's shelf. A small quantity of cocaine powder was found in a desk drawer. Why am I not surprised that is their drug of choice?

We have delved more deeply into Lyall's past; investigators who talked to his parents found few signs of the kind of upbringing that turns boys incorrigible, though his father was a believer in strict discipline. Lyall had been conditioned toward authoritarian attitudes, and his ambition to be a police officer had been encouraged. He was close to his mother and fond of his three sisters, and, as the oldest sibling, was protective – he'd delivered a beating to a young man who'd made improper overtures to one of them.

His parents maintained they were ignorant of his racist proclivities, but one of the interviewers, a Sikh, picked up their discomfort, their manner of deferring to his white partner. Their daughters told them Lyall had "hung" with a skinhead crowd in his teens, enjoyed acting out versions of effeminate gays, camping it up.

Lyall was not likely an instigator of murder but was probably the pit bull his pal kept on a leash, so what kind of power did Grundy exercise over him? Was it a kind of psychopathic *folie à deux*, the sharing of the delusion of the master race, each inflating the other's bigotry?

That they're armed seems certain. A .38 revolver has disappeared from a safe at The Tides, according to Grundy's father. Bob had pried the lock of a desk drawer, found the combination written in a directory.

Robert Grundison Sr. is remaining out of view of the cameras waiting by the gate. The family spokesperson, Reverend Ephriam Wright, says everyone is praying for "a just resolution of this sad, shocking affair."

Jossie Markevich hadn't anything much useful to say to detectives, who sensed she was holding back and turned her over to me. She claimed she had indulged in only the one threesome – fuelled by cocaine, which Grundy supplied in liberal amounts.

"He bought you a car too, right? Expensive drugs, expensive jewellery." I pointed to the gold watch on her wrist.

She pulled her sleeve over it. "Okay, sure, and he paid my rent."

I asked her if Grundy had ever assaulted her. Just once, when he struck her in the eye. "We made up."

I verified, to my satisfaction, that she had no inkling that Grundy and Lyall had been on a homophobic rampage. "I'm disgusted, they just snuffed that poor kid, and they come onto me like racehorses."

I asked her to amplify, but she was guarded.

"It was your average orgy. I don't want to even think about it. It's too fucking weird that they got hot by killing someone." She shuddered.

Police also interviewed the Edmonton hairdresser whom Grundy plucked from the Skeena River. Despite Grundy's claim they'd made love through the night, she insisted he was so drunk he could barely hold an erection, and passed out after half an hour of trying. When asked if he was rough with her, she said, "He hardly touched me."

She admitted Grundy asked her to lie if anyone inquired about his drinking that night. Given that, and given Grundy's boasts to Martha Wade about his sexual stamina, I didn't know what to believe.

Now it is half past five on Friday, the last day of October. The sun is setting over the Monashee Mountains, glinting from waves on choppy Upper Arrow Lake. The race has been run.

You'll have heard the results by the time I get back, so I won't be able to spin out the suspense as I usually do. I'll fill your ears when we meet.

A few entrants chickened out or went to the convention instead, in Kelowna, and as of yesterday morning we had sixty-one left. Nearly a third were women, and in age we spanned several decades: there were a couple of fit seniors, one I know to be seventy, a cardiologist.

Festivities began Thursday with a pancake breakfast on the lawn of City Hall. Jib Faile was there, standing off to the side, looking around, sizing up the competition. He was focusing on a woman doing warm-ups, exhibiting her long, muscular legs. She in turn was giving me the once-over. I was to meet her later: Dr. Josephine Guild.

Almost everyone but me seemed relaxed about the trials ahead, joking about their chances, vying for last place (for which there was actually a consolation prize), and treating this rally in the manner advised by my therapist. *You have to have fun.*

We headed off behind a farm truck (tricked out with a banner to warn oncoming traffic that *le prix de Okanagan* would be puffing along behind). Our shoreline route would be the busy Okanagan Highway, south to Skaha Lake, then back. There'd be another overnight in Vernon (gathering in the Sasquatch Lounge as our lapsed times are tabulated), then (after another outdoor breakfast) a final gruelling climb over the Highlands to a town called Needles on Lower Arrow Lake. A lamb barbecue at the lakeside farm of a retired pediatrician. Back to our Vernon hotels by chartered bus.

The sun was bright as we set out for the first leg, the few clouds seeking shelter by the hills above the peach and apple orchards. I stayed comfortably in the pack. On our return jog, a few doctors began to clump up in front. I joined them, drafting off them. When I glanced behind, I saw Faile drafting off me. And Josephine Guild close behind him.

I had opportunity that evening, in the Vernon pub, to compare a few notes with Faile. He, too, had been training hard – I recognized him, a sinewy fellow whom I'd occasionally spotted pumping down the False Creek bicycle paths. "Watch out for her," he said, indicating Dr. Guild: darkly attractive, a confident bearing, a teasing smile. "She's a ringer. Bronze in the Canada Games three years ago."

But that event, he told me, was mountain biking. Road racing requires different skills, different training. She might easily win the women's competition, but overall . . . ? Not to be sexist, but God has endowed the male body with the speed and endurance of the hunter . . . I don't think I'll develop that notion.

I didn't have to wait long for a chance to meet her. Indeed, she made the move, joining me at the bar as I was ordering another grapefruit juice. She asked for a single malt.

"I've been watching you," she said.

"You haven't escaped my attention either." I hoped that sounded more gallant than flirtatious.

"You've been training. That's a cyclist's tan." The white of my forehead where the face is shadowed by a helmet.

As we continued this light exchange, she moved closer, thigh to thigh. We traded resumés, she expressing keen concern in the forensic arts, I learning she was a G.P. who runs fitness clinics. It turns out we both were recently separated.

Intending to hint I must soon retire, I mentioned I hadn't slept well the previous night. She may have taken that as an invitation. She had special training in relaxing the body through massage. "Would you like me to do some work on you?"

I thanked her with the lame (and, on reflection, tactless) excuse that I might fall asleep in the process. She immediately clicked off. With a sardonic, "Yes, you'll probably need to save all your energy," she ordered another Glenfiddich and turned to the long-haired intern on the stool beside her.

I fled to my room, to the shower, to bed, entertaining ignoble hopes that Dr. Guild might not only tire herself out with someone else tonight, but she might be hungover tomorrow, as well.

I watched her the next morning over my bowl of granola as she wolfed down a plate of scrambled eggs and toast. This was an indication she might be out of training, though she showed no signs of weariness.

Yesterday's leaders started first in order of elapsed time, and it wasn't long before only four of us were up front, taking turns against the wind. Then, as we began to climb, one dropped back, then another, and there were only Faile and me. Dr. Guild was slipping back.

I was tiring too, calling for resources from deep within, seeking my second wind. I sensed Faile was struggling mightily, weary from the unforgiving uphill. I had already scouted the point at which I'd make my break, fourteen minutes from the summit of the Okanagan Highlands. There, I passed Faile on the inside, at a curve.

The road dipped, and I bolted down, then up, the last ascent. I surprised the driver of our lead truck, coming almost abreast of him. He flashed me a victory sign and sped up.

I glanced behind. Faile was fading, thirty metres behind. But there, around a bend, came Dr. Guild, head down, arms stiff, legs pumping. I didn't let up. The summit approached, a first sight of the Arrow Lakes in the hazy distance, the road spiralling downward now, a rushing creek beside it.

One has to brake for some of the sharper curves, and the art involves knowing the exact pressure to apply. Too strong and prolonged, and you lose vital seconds. Too light, and you go off the road into the pine trees. My advantage was knowing this road, knowing which curves were dangerous. Guild was drafting off Faile now, saving energy for a final push.

Finally, I could see the unpretentious burg of Needles, and just beyond it, our host's lakeside farm, a bus, some SUVs, lambs on spits over wood fires. The ferry to the Kootenays had docked, and cars were disembarking. The finish line was in the town itself, a community where apparently not much happens because the locals were out in force, gathered about a tape stretched across the road.

Suddenly, as I swept around a final curve, I sensed I wasn't alone. There she was, only fifteen metres behind, and our route was bottoming out into a valley, the town only minutes away.

I was working my heart out, Allis, fire was in my lungs. And this female Mercury was gaining, and soon we were almost wheel to wheel. This couldn't be happening. But it was. All my training, my local knowledge, my clever tactics, my whole uncontrollable obsession over this stupid race – all were for nought.

Josephine Guild was a length ahead of me when she broke the tape (a roll of pink toilet paper).

The applause of bystanders came mockingly to my ears. Several young women were jumping and screaming. Those of my sex, the side I'd let down, were laughing self-consciously, and one – presumably the village redneck – whistled at me with contempt.

Halfway down the block, almost to the waterfront, I caught up to the gliding Dr. Guild. I congratulated her, and she was magnanimous in response. I was about to turn back but noticed that the last cars were loading on the ferry.

I don't eat lamb. I've less fondness for humble pie. I had just enough time to catch that ferry, and did so unthinkingly, without stopping to retrieve my warm gear – left behind in our chartered bus.

Now, as I stand at the railing pondering my impetuous act, I choose to be stubborn. There will be no going back. I have my wallet, and can buy a coat or jacket along the way.

The declining sun dapples the lake with flecks of gold. The eastern shore approaches, drivers are heading to their vehicles, and I to Vesuvio II. Twenty kilometres to the north lies my destination, and it is taunting me.

It is now several hours later, close to midnight – a guess only, because they've taken my watch. I am staring out of a barred window, at the cold black lake, at the lights by the shore, illuminating the pools of the Warm Springs Hotel. I can hear the distant thump of guitars and bass, bearded men playing rock and roll. Goblins and ghouls dance in the hall. An explosion of fireworks . . .

I'm still slashing through the undergrowth in my head, slowly emerging from a fog of Kootenay Brainfuck. Images from the night mock me, then evaporate like the mists from the springs. *Willkommen!* Snoopy the Bear. Princess Di and Dodi.

I've made my one phone call – to John Brovak's voice mail. Likely he's at some Halloween function, cellphone turned off. I shouldn't have tried to call a known drug lawyer, that only made the Mounties smirk in confirmation that they had their man. I was denied a second call, to Jack Churko. "He's an *inspector*," I yelled. "VPD *homicide*." They laughed, thinking I was a kidder.

Finally, I can start to piece it together. I was on the Arrow Lake ferry, about to disembark, when a young man in a toque, an unlit cigarette dangling from his lips, beckoned me from the cab of his dilapidated pickup. "Dubbin, that you? Hey, Dub, it's me, Louie. Fucking A, welcome back." I stood there, bemused. What shall we call this episode? The Return of the Dooberman. He's broken out, he's back, he's unstoppable.

He told me to sling my bike in the back. My first mistake was to accept this offer, but it was growing dark. In the cab, he thrust out his hand, squeezed mine hard – clearly, he regarded Dub as no small hero. I intended to set him straight, explain I was actually a wandering psychiatrist, but that seemed as absurd as the rendition he preferred.

Once underway, he asked if I was coming to the dance. I hedged, asked where it was. The conversation went something like this:

"At the hall, man."

"I might just crash."

"That don't sound like the Dooberman. The joint's gonna be jumping. Speaking of, got any of that good stuff?"

Dooberman had to be a nickname. I was the doobie-man, the local dealer. They say there is for everyone, somewhere on this crowded planet, a person who goes about wearing the mask of another, his duplicate. But why did Dubbin Dooberman's counterpart have to be an addle-headed shrink with relationship problems who'd just lost the race of his life?

I should have told him I was in the business of dispensing only prescribed drugs, but made my second regrettable decision – to play him along. Otherwise, my theory went, he might succumb to silence and suspicion, like Joe Beauregard. I told him I was clean, man, on parole and going straight.

This caused him to snicker. Louie was his name, nineteen or twenty, a skinny kid with a scrawny beard. I, Dub Dooberman, was almost twice his age. How long had we known each other? How long had I been gone, why had I been serving time?

Louie asked what was with the bicycle, the weird getup, the number eighteen. A charity gig, I explained, my mouthpiece had got me off with community service. (I was still reasonably clear-headed, and must have thought I was being clever.)

"I got a half a number in the ashtray, want to light it up?"

I felt the Dooberman was being tested, asked to prove himself, his unalterable Doobness. I was obviously someone incapable of turning down a toke. I was in the Kootenays, where it is considered discourteous to do so, where cannabis is an important export industry.

I lit, took a draw, made a show of holding it in, passed the joint to Louie.

"Good bud, man," said the Dooberman.

"Just the regular Brainfuck," said Louie.

It was a potent strain, and as the cab filled with perfumed cloud, I achieved an almost instant high. My voice cracked with alarm: "Where'd you score this?"

"Imagine it's off one of your old man's clones."

"My old man?"

"Right on."

He plugged in a tape, early Led Zeppelin, turned up the volume to one level below ear-shattering screeching.

I shouted, "Is he still, uh, hanging around?"

"Yeah, of course. I'll take you to his joint after I drop off some shit at the hall."

You can't possibly comprehend how depressed I was by this time. Peter was the local godfather, his son (my half-brother?) had a record as long as the *Oxford Dictionary*. Did I want to visit him? No, I preferred to check into the Warm Springs Hotel, take a walk, clear my head.

I wanted to shout more questions at Louie but was too befuddled, and he was lost in his music. Twilight had set in. The highway clung to the lake on the left, offered misty valley views. I was scarcely able to appreciate them, too stoned, too anxious.

Small farms appeared, with fruit trees and chicken coops. SKI BIG JACKSON, said a sign. Another advertised the Warm Springs

Hotel, and yet another announced our arrival at the town limits (WILLKOMMEN! ENJOY YOUR STAY!)

We turned up a side road to a sturdy wooden building, the community hall. The front door was wide open. "Check," boomed an amplified voice. "Check. Check." A band was setting up inside. I jumped as a man dripping blood staggered out, half his face torn away. I looked at Louie, expecting shock, but he was laughing.

"That you, Roscoe?" he yelled. "Fucking A, man."

What was fucking A about Roscoe? Then I flinched again as a stout woman emerged, a grand moustache, whiskers. "The bearded lady," Louie shouted, getting out of the truck. "Guess who I brung?"

Awareness came to me with a rush of relief: it was Halloween, for God's sake. I laughed, but with an edge of desperation. I stayed in the truck, stuck my bike helmet on my head, hoping I might seem disguised too.

The man in the ghoulish mask came closer, peered at me. "Fuck me," he said.

"The Dooberman is back," Louie said.

"Man, this is going to be some party."

"Supposed to be a surprise," I mumbled.

The bearded lady frowned at me. "What are you supposed to be, Dubbin, some kind of athlete? I got it, running from the law. Shit, the cops are gonna recognize you in that." He went to the trunk of a car, rummaged through a box.

Others came out. There was a lot of, "Hey, Dub, what's up, what's happening, man?" and other questions that didn't seem to require answers, as they unloaded the pickup – hall decorations, cases of beer, fireworks. I stood about in a daze.

The bearded lady returned with a furry outfit with paws. "I was gonna give this to Clyde, but he already passed out." He handed me a mask, as well: Snoopy with a Snidely Whiplash moustache and in leather headgear.

Another joint was produced, lit, passed around. I couldn't simply pretend to inhale, and felt obliged to take a puff. Then I stepped out of the truck, zipped myself into the costume. It smelled of long-dead bear, but at least I was warm.

Louis then drove me a ways up a rural road. I thought I might be hallucinating when the name "Clinton W. Huff" flashed by. An illuminated mailbox, his house lit up too, behind some trees. Was the mayor receiving tiny guests, handing out FreedomFirstForever pamphlets to their parents?

Louie made a loop up a rise, and I was deposited by a wooden gate, where a jack-o'-lantern beckoned with a crooked smile. I had to be reminded to retrieve my bicycle. "See you at the dance, Dub."

The mailbox was designed as an imitation birdhouse, a roof that opens to receive mail, a name carved into the wood: *Walker*.

As Louie drove off, a couple of small ghosts flitted into view, hastening up the walkway to the Walker house. I stood there awhile, recording my impressions: a hand-built look, cedar logs and shingles, a turret with stained glass.

A woman's voice behind me: "Don't run!"

The two children slowed, gained the porch, knocked on the door. Their mother waited by the gate, and I wheeled my bike to her. She found my costume a source of humour. "What are you, Snoopy the bear?"

"It'll have to do. I just rode into town." She was as confused as I about that, and I wasn't able to assemble an explanation. "Do you know Mr. Walker?"

"Oh, yes. Very nice man. They say his son, Dubbin, is a rotten egg." Her hand went to her mouth. "Oh, I'm sorry, are you related?"

"Maybe."

Now comes my first glimpse of Walker. But his face is in the dark, the light behind him. A tall man, but hunched over. He shuffles forward, and the children shy away nervously: now I see why – he's a two-headed monster . . . no, not quite, there's a human form over his shoulder, a head hidden by falling hair, gloved hands dangling: a stuffed corpse.

"Trick or treat," a little voice pipes.

"What do you want first, the trick or the treat?" A gruff voice.

"Really, Mr. Walker," the mother loudly chides.

The children back off farther. "Now, now, boys, it's just me." Walker stands to his full height, extends bags of sweets, but the boys seem unwilling to come closer.

Their mother walks into the yard to offer courage. "Todd, It's just Mr. Walker getting all dressed up. See, Freddy, that's a big pillow with arms sewn on it."

I followed her, and was now able to make him out more clearly: a white bathing cap over his head to simulate baldness, tufts of beard glued to chin and jowls – he resembled someone I know too well. The dummy over his shoulder was a replica of a woman with long hair. An imitation chain of office around his neck completed the picture.

"Who *are* you?" said the woman. "The hunchback of Notre Dame?"

"He's the mayor of Jackson Cove," I explained.

"Exactly right." He seemed startled. "And who the hell are *you*?"

Walker was a few inches over six feet, a big handsome man, probably in his late fifties – I felt I could see the family resemblance behind the Huff-like disguise. Brown eyes, not blue like mine.

The boys had accepted his offerings by now and scampered off, their mother in tow. From behind the house came a loud quacking, as if from a duck in its death throes.

"Must have got one of them," Walker said. "I let some weasels loose." I could make no sense of this. He peered at me, trying to penetrate the Snoopy mask. "I say – do I know you?"

This was the moment of truth, the moment to which my yearning-scrambled life had been dedicated. I took off the mask. My voice quavered. "Hello, Peter. I'm your son."

"I'll be buggered, Dubbin, is that you?"

"Your other son."

"I don't have another son, thank God for that."

"The one you conceived in 1967. In a sleeping bag in the outfield of a ballpark in Nelson. During a rock concert." I can't remember everything I said, words were pouring from me, a disjointed history that provoked only a frown. "Am I bringing it back, Peter? Her name is Victoria. She gave birth to your other son on June 7, 1968."

I waited for the shocked face of revelation. But he said, "Peter? I'm not a Peter, though I've been called worse. It's Alexander. In 1967, I was in bloody England. Looks like you could use a drink, old fellow."

I don't know why I hadn't picked up the English accent right from the start. As he led me in, I took in a rear view of the dummy on his back, a long dress, nylons, beat-up runners. The house was cluttered, a cedar table bearing the tools of recent efforts – cloth, scissors, swatches of fur, foam padding. A bottle, half-full, of vodka.

"Came over in seventy-five with my wife and son. She left me, and I raised my son to be a bit of an asshole." He examined me under a naked light bulb. "Well, if you aren't a carbon copy of Dubbin. But no, the ears are wrong, no scar. Good thing too, or I'd have run you out."

I was in a stew of incredulity, embarrassment, and relief. As I piece together this jigsaw night, I realize that I ended up in the slammer because I began foolishly celebrating my unDoobieness.

Walker seemed eager to prove we weren't kin. His full name was Alexander Myerscough Walker – old passports were produced in proof of that, along with a marriage notice in an Uxbridge weekly, a diploma from an agricultural college, June, 1968, the month of my birth. For my part, I could only offer a confusing explanation of who I was, my bastard state, the clues that led me here.

Our chat was oiled by vodka tonics, and soon we were deep into his bottle, laughing at my gaffe. There was much to like about the man, he was hale and forthright, even confiding he kept a grow op in the basement, the remnants of a thriving business. His worthless son had been stealing the buds, selling them, attracting heat. But Clint Huff had caused even greater damage to his trade.

The aim of Walker's costume was to get the mayor's goat. There had been similar taunts over the years — it was Walker who'd stencilled *Wanted* on Huff's campaign posters. They are the Hatfield and McCoy of Jackson Cove.

I think it was earlier — I haven't got this account in order — that I explained Huff is suing my mother for libel. He snorted. "What a bloody fool." (Our shared nemesis brought about a bonding, and now I'm unable to ask the Mounties to drop by to verify my identity: Walker's house reeks of pot.)

He led me up a narrow wooden staircase to the turret, where a telescope was set on a tripod. "This here is my watchtower, so I can see the horsemen coming. That's where the little nuisance lives." I could see the back of Huff's tidy frame house, the second floor still lit.

"I used to have an outdoor grow, a wholesale business, respectable customers. Then he got ducks." They'd torn up his plants. Walker had to move his grow indoors, hasn't had a decent year since.

I looked through his scope: a second-floor window partly curtained, the headboard of a bed, and above it a smiling portrait of Princess Diana.

"He's got her plastered all over his walls. I swear he's got a life-sized blow-up rubber Diana. Likes to pretend he's Dodi al Fayed."

I was transported back to the mezzanine of the New Westminster Courthouse. *They betrayed the one great shining light of this world. She died for our sins.*

Huff sauntered into view, dressed for Halloween in what appeared to be ancient Egyptian dress. I watched a while longer, but Huff vanished, and the lights went out.

Walker led me back downstairs, poured more drinks, produced snapshots taken with a telephoto lens. They showed the Diana doll, though no intimate moments were captured.

"Should I report the twit to the Board of Education?"

"Not unless you want to spend the rest of your life in a courtroom."

I was given several prints, though I was unsure what use to put to them. (The photos – plus my watch and wallet – are in the custody of my jailers, in an envelope that I pray they haven't opened. Why haven't they received confirmation that the Dooberman is behind bars? Maybe he *has* escaped jail.)

The vodka bottle emptied, Walker urged me to join him at the dance. He had a few chores first, so I donned my Snoopy mask, zipped up my bear suit, mounted Vesuvio II, and rode back to the Community Hall. Through the open doorway, I could see the musicians (remnants of the Brain Damage of 1967?), bearded, greying, with middle-aged paunches.

Suddenly I halted. The man and woman leaving the hall were dressed in the boots, jackets, and stripes of the Royal Mounted. The Dooberman heard a quiet voice of warning, pedalled his way back across the uneven lawn to the road.

I lost control momentarily and nearly slid into the RCMP van, had to grab the side mirror to steady myself. I looked back – the two officers were on alert. I bolted, swept downhill to the village. Stupidly, I'd aroused suspicions with my clownish flight.

But they didn't follow me, and I was soon on the main street of Jackson Cove with its charmingly hokey Bavarian façade, the town hall a high-steepled image from my dreams. By the lake was the Warm Springs Hotel, steam curling from its pools. I intended to check in, but first made my way to the general store. The pot and alcohol made its choices bewildering and the transactions complex. When I doffed my Snoopy mask, the saleswomen examined my credit card suspiciously, picking up the phone as I walked out with clothes and swim trunks.

She alerted the local RCMP, of course: the Dooberman was back in town with a credit card stolen from a doctor. That, at least, is what Corporal Netty Krepusch theorized as her underling handcuffed me at the check-in counter of the hotel. My explanations were seen as preposterous, and I worsened matters with my lurid flow of loud complaint.

But now comes Netty herself, jangling keys, looking frazzled and contrite. "I'm *so* sorry, Dr. Dare."

The next day, nursing a hangover, I phoned Jack Churko from the Warm Springs Hotel. The search for Grundy and Lyall continues to frustrate him, but he had a great gloating laugh over my arrest – it is all through the VPD – and he claimed to have had thoughts, when Corporal Krepusch phoned him, of telling her I was wanted on a nationwide warrant. Dubbin Dooberman, by the way, was in the pokey all the time.

Netty Krepusch bought me dinner Sunday, an effort at amends, and was relieved I wasn't contemplating a suit for false arrest. When I sounded her out about local characters, I learned, to my lack of surprise, the mayor is a "fucking headache" with his constant advice and interference. His sworn enemy is thus widely tolerated: it's known Alexander Walker keeps a small grow, but the law is selectively enforced.

On Monday, I took a spin to Nelson, an old and pretty town snuggled into the valley by Kootenay Lake. I strolled about the ballpark, seeking an impossibly distant memory of being. Here was third base, where Peter told Victoria she was the most beautiful creature he'd met since escaping prison. Here in the outfield, they made psychedelic love, and the supposed miracle of me began.

The skies had been darkening all day, and as I was standing lost in left field, the weather turned brusque, a cold front from the north, flurries. The grounds quickly went white, a clean sheet covering the sins of 1967 – so virginal that I didn't want to disturb the cold peace of it all. By the next morning, as I began my bus journey home, several inches of snow had fallen. I was experiencing ennui, an old familiar sense, fatherless again, the weary search continues.

Chapter Seventeen

Notes for Wednesday, November 5.

I telephoned Tim this morning, to welcome him home but also to let him know I might not be fit to see him at his regular time because I've come down with the flu. He insisted on coming to my home to make mushroom soup.

Though stricken with an unseemly nasal drip, I found some comfort in his droll exposition of Halloween night in Jackson Cove and his "close encounter with consanguinity."[1]

As for his showing in the bicycle rally, he dismissed it as being of relatively trivial concern – though I doubt those are his true feelings – and shrugged off my compliments at his trophy for the men's section. He is setting his sights now on the United Appeal's race in Vancouver, in the spring.

---

[1] There is such a gap in his life that I almost wish he had made the connection he was seeking, even if he was forced to modify his high aspirations for his father.

He has rejoined the search for Grundison and DeWitt, who are believed to have fled into the North Shore mountains and are equipped for a long seige.

Celestine Post has been scheming again, and her efforts have, conversely and perhaps unfortunately, rekindled his hope of regaining Sally's affections. I continue to wonder at his stubbornness in that regard.

Otherwise, Tim has achieved a level of emotional stability that further intervention may not significantly enhance. Yet another side of him showed during this visit. He is a thoughtful caregiver with an easygoing manner, generous with his advice on non-traditional medicine.

Before he left, I raised the issue of discontinuing my services to him, given that he has gained as much emotional balance as one could expect. He was unsure whether he was ready "to leave the nest and fly."

☙

I'm glad we were able to air out that hotel-room happening without being hobbled by a tape recorder – no need to tuck it away in the file with the rest of my psychobiography. Freud put it well: in therapeutic relationships, one owes discretion even to oneself.

"Do you think it's best if I refer you elsewhere, under the circumstances?" A ridiculous question. I won't have you throwing me to the wolves because of an unguarded moment. Relax, Allis, there were no consequences other than some awkwardness. All regrets will pass with time. Soon we will be laughing at ourselves.

Disease fattens on stress, so it was good that you were able to unload your marital concerns (my prescription: take his offer of the house, mortgage free, forget the squabbles over money). Your temperature actually went down after the unburdening; the virus seems to be retreating to the nose for a last-ditch stand.

And don't worry about me – I never catch colds or flus. To summarize: You should be getting out more, exercising. Vitamin C, Vitamin E, echinacea, don't be afraid of garlic on your breath: it's the smell of health.

But I'm afraid much of my advice was lost on you – it came with a false note of bravado from one who seems incapable of freeing himself from the web of love and need and hurt. Sally is back from Japan. I found her message on my machine when I returned from Jackson Cove, congratulating me for being the second-fastest doctor in the West. Did I hear a tremor of misgiving, a hint of disappointment about the Japan trip? About Cousineau?

Victoria was not amused by my adventures in Jackson Cove, my false encounter with consanguinity, my arrest. She scolded me for my foolishness. I described Huff's paraphiliac obsession in the hope it might cheer her up as she waits, pessimistically, for Judge Lafferty to render her decision, but she found the whole matter disgusting.

John Brovak, however, was keenly interested in Huff's pretend love life, and whisked over to Granville Island, persuading James to slip him in between a Dependant Personality Disorder and a Social Phobic. He goggled at the pictures that Walker gave me, insisted on pocketing them for "safekeeping."

I reminded him he hadn't billed me for the Vivian Lalonde case. He clapped me on the shoulder, demanded instead that I make a donation to my favourite charity. "Professional courtesy," he said. "Maybe I'll get back a little noblesse oblige. I got a real bitch coming up, a junkie so hooked on smack he didn't realize he was firing a gun."

As for Grundy and Lyall, it now seems clear they made their way across one of the bridges to the mountains. A couple of nights ago, a break-in occurred at a small store in Lynn Valley. Only food was taken, frozen steaks, eggs, bread, about thirty kilos of canned goods. Police are going door to door on Grouse and Seymour mountains, checking ski cabins and chalets, quizzing hikers and skiers enjoying the year's first snow.

I've not heard from Vivian. No calls. No visits. No skulking shadows in the night. Doubtless, she's getting over me, though I still can't understand why I deserved her mindless infatuation. On the other hand, Celestine Post and I have become, if not thick as thieves, conspiratorial buddies. I can't deny I'm getting a kick out of her latest amatory scam. She's been insinuating herself into Sally and Cousineau's social scene, turning twosomes into threesomes in restaurants and on country drives.

Last night, knowing Sally was a presenter at an arts ceremony, she inveigled Cousineau to come to the gallery opening of "Virgins No More," erotic works by Celestine and a few of her friends. I couldn't be there last night, but wandered in today – a cramped feminist gallery. A large canvas by Celestine featured wild swipes of exploding colour that drew the eye into a black tunnel thickly edged with red pigment; in case the point was lost, it was titled *Orgasm Number Six*. A price tag for eight hundred dollars, a red dot, proof of sale.

Ellery Cousineau is now the proud owner of this piece of Celestine Post-Modernism. "I made him a deal: half-price plus he goes down on me." She showed me her tongue, a mock, catlike lick. "He's coming by the loft tonight."

I was shocked, though I knew that Celestine, with her bent for hyperbole, had given me a coloured version of the bargain reached. Which is this: Cousineau has promised to bring a cheque tonight and perhaps enjoy a glass of wine, and there's no reason Sally has to know, because he intends the painting as a gift to her. I suggested Celestine wear a dress from Toddlers for the occasion.

I suspect Cousineau will be less resolute than I in resisting Celestine's charms. I picture her in the throes of artistic creation:

Orgasm Number Seven. I feel no guilt: I didn't counsel or encourage her scheme, and I will proclaim my innocence if Sally learns she took on a false lover. *When* Sally learns . . .

It is Thursday. Hope has risen from the ashes of marital loneliness, I must grab it, hug it to my breast, and pray. Ellery Cousineau has met his undoing!

For this, I must give thanks to Celestine, for her schizotypal impudence and her inability to stop rummaging in others' lives. I met with her today over a martini lunch at the Granville Island Hotel, where she jauntily described how Sally had popped into her loft this morning for their regular exchange of gossipy tidbits. Sally found Celestine and Cousineau sitting over coffee, hungover, she in baby-doll pyjamas and he in more modest but incongruous attire: shirt and socks and sweater, but pantless, a green wraparound skirt stretched around his middle.

Ellery tried to explain he'd come by this morning to claim his painting – see his tight smile, hear his cracked, laugh-it-off voice: I intended it as a secret gift for you, my darling! You see, there it is, leaning by the door! And, damn it, he'd ever-so-carelessly jostled his cup, spilled hot coffee on his jeans, soaking them through to his undershorts. As proof: these garments were in Celestine's washer. The skirt was all he could find to wear.

But Celestine couldn't lie to her long-time best friend, and chided Cousineau for assuming Sally was gullible enough to believe him. (The truth, Celestine explained to me, was that a semen spill occurred early in the evening's festivities. "Real impetuous guy, didn't have his pants off, and he went off like a rocket on his first try.")

Cousineau did, in fact, get coffee on him, including grounds, when pot and filter were dumped on him. As well, Sally hit him on the head with Orgasm Number Six, then threw it against the wall, and stomped out.

"I did it for you," Celestine said to me. "No great sacrifice. He was a tiger in bed when he got his motor restarted. And he looked divine in a green skirt. Spent a few minutes in the closet before he chose it."

I played with that image: Cousineau in the closet. Maybe I'd misconceived his proneness to stare at women — was he merely admiring their attire? In my dream, he was searching through a trunk of dresses, stockings, and unmentionables — seeking something that would fit *him*?

Misled by jealousy, I'd defamed Cousineau. Sally had thrown me over not for a pedophile but a prematurely ejaculating cross-dresser.

Ah, but these were merely caprices of the vengeful mind. It is wrong to gloat, I must rise above spite.

I waited for Sally's call, which came mid-afternoon. She was still furious, insisted on blaming Celestine and me jointly, we were in cahoots. I defended myself and offered sympathy but couldn't hide my glee very well, and she hung up on me.

It's late on Friday, when I would usually be in your consulting room, so I hope James reached you in time to cancel me. Briefly, the situation is this: the search for Grundy and Lyall has just turned frantic. A Los Angeles family seems to be missing in the North Shore mountains, a mother and two teen daughters. They'd come up here a few days ago on a post-divorce holiday.

Yesterday, Gladys Moore called L.A. and left a message on her father's answering machine, saying she and the girls had the use of a ski chalet. No location given, presumably the North Shore. Gladys Moore's father tried several times to reach her on her cellphone. No response. Last night, he called the North Vancouver RCMP.

We've since learned, through her friends in California, that Gladys Moore received the keys to the chalet from a friend retired in North Vancouver, a ski enthusiast. It's an architect-designed log building on Grouse Mountain, he told police, and is off any beaten track.

Our fear is that Grundy and Lyall scouted the chalet, found it deserted, and that Gladys Moore and her daughters walked into it blindly and found the two fugitives hiding there.

Churko and a team are on the way, and have asked me to stand by my phone.

CHAPTER EIGHTEEN

At midnight, I'm numbly listening to my pounding heart, reliving the horrors of the night, worse than all my nightmares.

There is no good starting point, Allis, so I'll begin where I left off: the beginning of the November night . . .

I was on the office balcony with James, sipping tea and watching the city light up. The phone rang. "Inspector Churko," said James. "He wants you to haul ass to Grouse Mountain *immediatement*."

Churko's urgent barks over a balky connection made for a distorted picture: "Who's got a flashlight? I'm in snow up to my asshole." Indistinct words, shouts, then he returned to the phone. "They turned the lights out, can't see a fucking thing from down here. I don't know what they done to them, maybe nothing, we hope. You read me?"

Was he talking to me? No – I'd been patched into a call to headquarters. An answering voice: "Okay, Inspector, we read. We have Dr. Dare."

288

I announced myself, asked Churko to back up and slow down. His briefing was peppered with disruptions.

"We got a crisis, Doc . . . Get a light on the house, see if anyone's moving . . . They got hostages, Mrs. Moore, her kids. They got a gun, and they ain't afraid to fire it, a warning shot, when one of the guys tried to go up there . . . Where are those jokers from E-Response? I only got five people up here, it's a trek in . . . What about the chopper?"

"No chance with this weather. We got a mobile unit on its way on a snowcat from the ski lodge. Dr. Dare, there's a driver coming for you – can you meet him outside?"

Seconds later, I was in a squad car, on a light-flashing, siren-sounding dash across Lion's Gate to North Vancouver.

The woman detective who was my escort told me that Churko's squad had arrived at the chalet an hour ago, by commandeered Ski-Doos. No lights were on, but a porch window was broken, and smoke was coming from the chimney. An attempt to approach was deterred by the warning shot and a shouted threat from Grundy: "Back off! Or no one's coming out of here alive!" That's when Churko was patched in to me.

After a long climb up Capilano Road, my driver pulled into the parking area below the gondola. Police were scrambling about, hauling equipment. The glow from lamps on the lift towers traced a route up into the distant gloom. Members of the SWAT team, in their Darth Vader outfits, scrambled onto a car and rose into the darkness.

I hadn't given any thought to the final stages of this journey. The prospect of entering one of those closed cages added more fuel to my anxiety about the three hostages, about the role Churko intended me to play.

My escort pulled me by the elbow. "For Christ's sake, let's *go.*"

I took her arm. "Little nervous about heights."

Soon after we boarded the next carriage, the earth disappeared and we were swallowed in mist and whipping snowflakes. A tower approached, but its light illumined only a dense white blur. Finally, we rose above the fog, and the lodge came into view, lights blazing, figures moving about. I stepped off the platform and gracelessly slid down an embankment. Vancouver was somewhere below us, glowing from beneath the clouds.

Soon, I was grasping my chauffeur about her waist, on a Ski-Doo, racing up the twists of a trail in the conifer forest. We pulled in among other such vehicles, a snowcat, a melee of law enforcers, video cameras, a grunting generator, spotlights shining on a substantial home set precariously on a ledge: wide decks, two storeys and a loft. The lights raking the building didn't penetrate heavy curtains, no persons were in view within.

Churko, smoking furiously, told me that shouted communications had continued with Grundy, who had devised a plan to escape with Lyall by helicopter. The three hostages would accompany them, at gunpoint. They would transfer to a small plane equipped with parachutes. This scheme was "non-negotiable."

While Churko and Grundy were talking, an officer had made his way behind the house, keeping a cautious distance. Equipped with a night-vision scope, he made unobstructed sightings through a tall uncurtained window, saw human shapes on the main floor, two sitting, one standing, two others by the railing of the loft.

Churko had obtained the house plans from the owner, and I asked to see them: the building was an aerie, the only entrance by the deck on the second floor, the living area. From there, one staircase led to the loft, windowless but with an interior balcony, another to bedrooms on the ground level, which sat on a rock dropping fifty metres along a sheer face.

"Got any ideas, Doc?"

"I'm going to try to get in."

I felt nothing else would work: I would have to get close to the two men, close enough to smell their desperation, assess their resolve, use whatever skills hadn't deserted me. I had to get face to face – my last conversation with Grundy had been adjourned too quickly, and I hadn't spent all my ammunition.

"Fat chance of that," Churko said.

"If there's anyone Grundy wants up close and unarmed, it's me." *You're next. I know where you live.* I ventured closer to the house. "Bob, Lyall – can you hear me? This is Timothy Dare."

Grundy called back: "Too late for crisis counselling, Doc. It's gone beyond talk." A pause. "Right?"

This was directed to Lyall, who responded faintly: "That's right." I picked up the clearing of a constricted throat.

"Bob, there's some important stuff we didn't get around to dealing with last time. I have an interesting theory about your tensions, your headaches, I figured out how to cure them."

"I'm not interested in your theories."

That was untruthful. Grundy is too absorbed with himself.

"What do you say I wander up there, Bob? Because it's not something we want to talk about in public." *I sense a terror lurking within him.* He had stilled Dr. Wiseman's tongue, and I had to be prepared to face a similar risk.

A minute passed before he made a response, so likely he'd been conferring with Lyall.

"Hey, Dr. Dare!"

"Yes, Bob."

"This is the picture. I got a sweet little sixteen name of – what's your name again, honey? – name of Ginger, sitting right in front of me. I don't want to harm this girl – really, I like her, the whole family – and all goes well, nobody gets hurt."

"I want to help you out of this, Bob. I'm worried that we're going to have the press here soon. I'd like to talk to you first, before they start asking about you."

Another long period of silence. Then he called, "Okay, but take off your clothes."

There were further shouted instructions: he wanted the police to train a light on me until I reached the house. I urged, without effect, that I be allowed to wear my briefs.

"You got something to hide, Doc? Hey, Lyall, maybe he's ashamed of it. Don't worry, Ginger's seen it before, haven't you, honey?"

A sharper, uglier edge to his voice. I felt a touch of nausea at his obscene insinuations. I realized I could botch this, I wasn't confident I could talk them down or predict their reactions.

Churko was looking at me with amazement. He gripped my hand, wished me luck.

I stripped naked, then braved a chilly slog up a poorly beaten path. The climb was steep, and by the time I reached the deck perspiration had frozen on my skin. The door was locked, and I rapped on it. No immediate response. I'd been played the fool, this was an exercise in humiliation.

I moved nearer the broken porch window, felt heat from within. The curtain moved.

Lyall's voice: "Yeah, he's alone."

"Okay, Churko, now I want that light off!" Grundy called.

When all was plunged into darkness, the door opened. I half-expected to be attacked, thrown to the floor, but I was neither helped nor hindered. "Take three steps and stop," said Grundy, in front of me, not far away. The door clicked shut – Lyall was close behind, I could smell his anxious heat.

As my eyes adjusted to the darkness, human shadows formed, the dim outlines of furniture, dying embers behind the fireglass pane of an air-tight stove. Nearby were the stairways, wide steps descending, narrow slats up to the loft. From its landing came a soft glow – a night light, battery-powered.

"Gladys Moore – can you speak to me?" I said.

"I'm up here," came a soft, frightened voice.

"Your girls?"

"Colette is with me. Ginger is with them."

"Ginger, speak to me."

"I'm here. I'm scared, but I'm okay." Strained, trying to be brave.

"Okay, no more talking," Grundy said. "Stay still where I can see you."

As my eyes grew more accustomed to the dim light, I could make out Grundy leaning back in a reclining chair. Ginger was only a few feet away, upright on a sofa. I could hear Lyall shuffling about behind me.

I might have asked for a towel, to dry and cover myself, but I sensed they'd deny me that, they wanted me vulnerable. The room was warm enough, the air-tight still generating heat, though it had been unattended for a long while. There was also an unlit fireplace opposite, stacks of wood and kindling.

"Lyall, check around his ass to see if he's wired."

"You do it."

A hint of rebellion. Lyall was in far deeper than he'd intended. He'd gone along with the murders, as long as only gay men were targeted. Women were different, girls especially. He'd been fond of his sisters, he wasn't as disordered as Grundy, just enough to put him under his sway. At the nub of his pathology was anger, hatred of his father, even of himself.

Grundy made no motion to rise. "Maybe Ginger would like to do it. How about it, honey?"

"You're sick," said Ginger. She was a brave girl. I'd seen her photograph, pretty, in the bloom of youth.

"Cut it, Bob," Lyall said. "I mean it."

This friction must have been going on for some time, the monster's two heads disjoining. Lyall was no longer behind me, but in dim view, arms folded, defiant.

"As long as you know there's a loaded revolver in my hand, Doc. Okay, Lyall, maybe you can be helpful by stoking up the fire. Dr. Dare is cold. You can see him shivering. Not because he's scared. You're not scared, are you, Doc?"

"Yeah, but I'm more concerned about the women. Let them go, Bob. I'm your insurance. I'll do what I can to help you get away. You can take me with you on the plane."

"I prefer the company of women. I don't think you're going to make the flight, Doc."

"Let's think about it, Bob," said Lyall. He was at the open door of the air-tight, refuelling it with kindling and wood.

"The way I'm thinking is if we make an example of the good doctor, his friends down below will know we're very, very serious. Rid the world of another faggot. You're inclined that way, aren't you, Doc? Use the back door once in a while?"

There was enough strain in Grundy's voice to suggest this was surface swagger. He wanted to spin out this chance to humiliate me.

"Let's talk about you, Bob."

"Yeah, right, you have some theory about me. Don't tell me — you discovered I've an antisocial personality disorder."

"More interesting than that, Bob."

"Well, I don't want to hear about it."

"I do," said Lyall.

The fire had caught but did little to warm my clammy skin. I couldn't believe I was hearing my voice speak with tones so calm and detached. This was a very risky game, but they had to be driven further apart.

"I got a better idea, Lyall. Let's have the doc analyze *you*. Let's figure out why you've turned into a wimp."

"I'd like to know what happened," Lyall said softly. "I'd like to know how everything got screwed up like this."

I could see the log walls now, the beams of unmilled cedar, the loft, Gladys and Colette looking over the railing. All the windows were draped but the tall ones facing the back. Churko must have his sharpshooters out there by now, and I was worried they might not notice Ginger on the couch, her back to them.

"You swore by your blood," Grundy said softly, with menace. "Soldiers of God, together forever." He was in clearer outline now, holding the revolver with two hands, pointing it somewhere between Ginger's head and my navel. Tension rose from him, like heat.

Lyall was still by the stove, his face sober and drawn in the flickering light. "We were just going to make a statement. You said we'd stop. After one. Then after three. The last one wasn't even a fag."

"They want us to think that."

The killing of the student had clearly disturbed Lyall. This bickering was likely the aftermath of a quarrel, maybe several over the last couple of days. Lyall wanted no more killing, but he didn't have the gun.

"Okay," I said, "let's talk about you, Lyall."

"Yeah, let's hear about the wuss. Take the couch, snuggle up with Ginger."

Lyall didn't move. The two men seemed tired, close to exhaustion. They'd have agreed to take turns napping, but both may have stayed awake last night, in mutual distrust.

"You have a sister almost exactly Ginger's age, Lyall. Two other sisters. It's never easy being the only boy in such a family, too much is expected of you. Especially from a hard-driving father. He's a manly guy, isn't he, Lyall?"

"He's a tough dude."

"Likes to drink beer and watch the Canucks. Cracks the occasional joke about queers over the dinner table. Dislikes liberals, called them pansies. But, hell, so what? – millions hold those views. He gave you tough love, but he was proud of you, determined to make you a man. You told him you wanted to be a cop, you knew that would please him. That's the gist of it, right?"

"So far."

"The only son . . . That's hard enough, but in your case it was a burden."

No interruptions from Grundy. He sat forward, interested, this was in his field of study, there'd been truth in his claim to want to understand the warped mind – even if only to disguise his better. I hadn't moved but was keeping spring in my knees in case I had to.

"So much expected of you. So much you couldn't deliver."

Lyall had gone to the side of the tall window, was taking a careful peek outside. He'd begun to fidget, shifting his shoulders, smoothing his hair, a narcissistic compulsiveness. "What's that mean?"

"I want to help you through this, Lyall. I want to make you feel better about yourself. You liked your sisters, but otherwise you didn't care much for the company of girls. They didn't attract you sexually, and you couldn't understand that, you're athletic, a virile guy, not like the others, the limp wrists you were taught to disdain."

A silence set in, broken only by Lyall clearing his throat, until there came another threat from Grundy, in a raspy voice. "Want me to plug him, Lyall? He's calling you a closet queen." A derisory laugh, he was scornful of my analysis, contemptuous at the game I was playing: a crafty scheme to unnerve his partner.

"Lots of famous athletes are gay, Lyall. Artists, entrepreneurs, scientists. Leonardo da Vinci was gay. In the real world, it's no big deal."

I couldn't make out Lyall's eyes, but I sensed he was looking at me intently, rigid musculature, a man poised, on the edge of the unknown. My first clue had come at The Tides, the kiss he blew to Jossie and Grundy from the window. Not to Jossie, just Grundy. It wasn't a woman he desired as they made the beast with three backs.

"We are what nature makes us, Lyall. Or God, if you prefer. There's no shame in that. These are more enlightened times than those your father knew."

He slumped – it was if the air was hissing out of him. Had catharsis come, was this deflation the manifestation of it? No, something else was going on, because, incredibly, he giggled. "Do go on." A different voice, lilting. "He's such a bitch." I was stunned. This wasn't Lyall performing some sexist mimicry. This sounded like a dissociated personality.

Grundy wasn't getting it, was chuckling, relieved now – good old Lyall was giving me the gears.

"It's good to be free of him, isn't it?" I said.

"I mean, he's a *bore* – if you only knew. He doesn't let me come out very often, so thank *you*."

"Nice pickle he's got you in."

"I would just like to forget the whole thing – everything's so *intense*. Bob, darling, do put down that gun."

I couldn't guess what Ginger and her mother and sister were making of this, but Grundy was laughing. "I've seen him do his fruit fly act a hundred times, and I still bust a gut."

Lyall moved toward me with a tight gait, as if in high heels. "You are such a skinny wretch. Let's find something to cover you. Bob, we simply have to come up with another plan. I am not going to live off the land like some *Indian*." He sighed, went to a bedroom nearby, returned with a wool blanket.

"Put that down," Grundy said. "He's fine the way he is."

"Oh, are you enjoying the view? Do you have a hard-on for him, darling? You've been ogling him." He threw the blanket; I caught it but didn't wrap myself in it, merely held it in front of me. Though Lyall was acting the jealous mistress, I was unsure if they'd had sex together – in the absence of a woman to make it seem vaguely acceptable. Grundy was too deep in denial. Lyall, too, had blocked his attraction for other men, buried it deep within, but it had found an aquifer to the surface, was bubbling out as a second personality.

"How do you feel about Bob right now, Lyall – do I call you Lyall?"

"Oh, I've tried other names – they never work. And I don't care what you call Bob, he's my sweetie."

"You like him a lot."

"My pet bunny."

"Okay, cut it out now." Grundy had begun to show confusion. He cradled the revolver in his right hand, wiped his forehead with the other.

"Tell Bob how you much you care for him, Lyall. It'll feel good to get it out."

Lyall found his way to the back of Grundy's recliner, where he ruffled his hair. "I do love you, you big goof."

Grundy jerked away, lowering the gun. "Enough of this shit. It stopped being funny." He struggled from his chair, batted Lyall's wrist with his free hand. "I'm getting one of my tensions."

"Touchy." Lyall moved away with a sham gesture of shock. "But you can see why I adore him." A long, despairing sigh. "I know, I'm a fool. He treats me like a stable boy. Don't you, stallion?"

"Stop it! What's happening, you gone fruity on me?"

"Problem is, does he love me? Or does he just have the hots for me?"

Lyall may have understood that love isn't in Grundy's emotional vocabulary. He may also have guessed, as I know now with sureness, the secret that Dr. Barbara Loews Wiseman took to her death, the diagnosis that Grundy couldn't bear to hear.

"Bob, we're at the end of the road, let's *relate*, okay?" Lyall made a move toward Grundy, who stepped back, averting his eyes. "Tell me it's not just a physical thing. Look at me, Bob." His voice was husky.

"Get away."

"Can't we stop playing the forgetting game? Seven years ago, Bob. After the frat party. Oh, yes, you were too hammered to remember, weren't you? But that's kind of funny, because I drank the same amount, and *I* remember. I was sore for a month, stallion, but that's not what really hurt." He continued to advance.

"Get away from me!"

"You don't have to love me, I don't ask that, but you're such a slut, with all your stupid little whores. Look at me, damn it!"

"No! I got a headache!"

As this macabre dance continued, Lyall advancing, Grundy retreating to the wall, I slipped toward the sofa, grabbed Ginger by the wrist, and pushed her to the floor, toward the landing. "Down the stairs," I whispered, and she began descending. I hoped she could find a room with a lock.

My route took me upwards instead, the narrow stairway to the loft. It was as defensible a position as any.

Lyall's voice had gone low and throaty, the words indecipherable, but the tone taunting.

"I'm not!" Grundy screamed. "I'm not!"

"Won't you kiss me, Bob? Just once."

Grundy let out a ghastly howl of terror. The kiss was a brutal, piercing bark of a bullet, its echo bouncing from timbered walls. Grundy was roaring like a wounded bear, but it was Lyall who was the bloodied prey, staggering back, slowly slipping to his knees, his face a mask of dismay and incredulity.

So stunned was I by this sight – of blood spurting from Lyall's chest, streaming over his cupped hands, his body collapsing to the floor – that I became aware almost too late that Grundy was looking about frantically, for me, for Ginger. I sprinted farther up, I was a step from the top landing as he looked my way, my only protection a blanket.

Without a thought, except to deflect his aim, I spun the blanket toward him as he fired. The bullet went harmlessly aloft, and the blanket wrapped around his head.

I didn't see what happened immediately thereafter – I was diving into the loft, rolling on thick carpet, yelling for Gladys and her daughter to stay down. At the same time, there came a shaft of piercing light, followed by a fusillade of glass-shattering sniper fire, then silence for a second, then another blast, and a splintering of wood, the door flying off its hinges. Then the scuffling of many boots. Shouts. "Freeze! Freeze!"

Grundy was beyond obeying this order. From the railing, I saw his body splayed on the couch, the blanket draped over his head. Death had been relatively kind – it came fast and unseen. While flailing under the blanket, freeing himself from it, he'd staggered into the sites of the rifles outside the tall windows. Only one of five bullets missed him, the others propelling him backwards onto the couch.

I was transfixed by the ghastly scene for a few moments, then I gathered my wits and called downstairs, announcing we were all present and safe. Gladys Moore was frantic about Ginger, but cheering broke out when she emerged up the staircase. Gladys Moore, abashed not a whit by my nudity, put her arms about me, whispering a husky "Thank you."

From a futon in the loft, I took a sheet, a bright coral colour, and wrapped myself in it. I looked like a Buddhist priest. *Do not fight the river, let the river take you.*

Many lives might have been spared had Grundy been emotionally capable of following that advice. His was a case of homosexual dread so severe, so pathological, so morbid, that no narcotic but murder could relieve the pain.

CHAPTER NINETEEN

Date of Interview: Friday, November 14, 2003.

Aside from the occasional sniffle, Tim appeared in good health, substantially recovered from the flu that struck him down on the weekend. I assured him it wasn't intended as my parting gift, and thanked him for his – the two dozen roses he'd couriered to me, along with a potted dieffenbachia.

He was emotionally more stable than I would have expected, given that he had perhaps five hours of sleep in the last two days. His face was lined with exhaustion.

He was so spent that, after telling me about his frightful encounter in the mountains, he fell asleep. I covered him with a blanket and let him rest. When he woke, two hours later, he seemed restored – so much that he was able to speak with enthusiasm about the positive signals Sally has been sending. She has made a significant first step toward their reconciliation.[1]

---

[1] I had a helpful discussion with her on the weekend.

One pressing concern remains unresolved, relating to the father he's never known. There may always remain an emptiness, but I believe he is strong enough to cope with it. In fact, if one of his dreams spoke true, he is ready to rise above his fears, to fly.

He has met his mother's suitor. "I'll let it take its course, see if it really flowers," he said – as if he were the arbiter of that prospect. His qualm that the man has a history of broken marriages led to a dialogue about Tim's antipathy toward divorce in general. The relevant discussion is transcribed below.

They came by on Saturday, Victoria and her guy. I wasn't up for any visitors, but James let them through – he's has been like a bull terrier, especially with the reporters, standing them off at the gate. Victoria's boyfriend is good-looking, tall, fit. A health nut, that's fine. Well-spoken. I don't know, maybe it's his urge to climb mountains that makes me nervous. He's going to try to get Victoria off cigarettes, so credit to him there. But two divorces? He's not a survivor. And he has two kids, *teenagers.*

Why does this bother you so much?

Well, don't you feel . . . All right, I suppose he could have been the wronged party each time, but . . . I have your point: *you're* about to be divorced. That's different, it's not your fault.

Fault?

I'm flailing.

Have you considered it may be the mere *concept* of divorce that causes you discomfort?

A long pause for reflection.

Another syndrome of the fatherless child. Okay, you're right, let me save you the trouble, here's the personality profile: the patient is in need of permanency, of lifelong commitment. He suffers separation anxiety, he's afraid to be alone, he doesn't think fathers should disappear. People should be like geese, mate for life. He grew up jealous of the other kids, even the ones from split families – at least they got to visit their fathers on weekends. On top of all this, he's been abandoned by his wife of many years. He abhors divorce, is frightened of it. Compounding the problem, he's anxious about his mother, fears she'll suffer romantic failure, a pain he, too, will feel, a pain he knows. Throw this into the pot: a desperate hope that his father will miraculously reappear.

Very impressive.

As a corollary, he runs away from other possible relationships, beggared by a similar fear of failure.

Or does he run away because he won't take second best? Because there's no one who can make up for his loss, no one who can compare . . .

Our parting made for some sadness. He claimed to have become "addicted" to our Friday sessions, and wanted them to continue. Our afternoon concluded thus:

Let me put this as flatly as I can. Professionally, you don't need me any more. And I feel that the doctor-patient relationship is interfering with something else.

Another kind of relationship . . .

Well . . . friendship, of course.

We'll always be friends, Allis.

∞∞∞

At the end, Allis, we both seemed at a loss for words, and things that needed to be said remained unsaid. Just before we parted, as we came into each other's arms, I struggled to find a phrase of thanks, some loving words. But you pressed a finger to my lips and said with a smile, "Catch you later, Dr. Dare." And you led me out, and all I could do was wave while blowing into a handkerchief as the elevator doors closed between us.

This is what I might have said:

Thank you for your wisdom, patience, and affection. For your skill, your deep understanding, your fine hearing for unconscious processes, your ability to explore the netherworld of the human soul.

My near-breakdown must have presented, four months ago, a daunting challenge. Here was a blathering, wild-eyed creature in your office, reeking of anxious sweat, playing smart-aleck games: competition, control, avoidance. How well you hid your exasperation.

On our walk in Stanley Park, after you lost a patient to suicide, you let your vulnerability show raw and exposed. I learned from that, learned to trust, learned to give myself up to you. And I gave. And you gave more. And in the process, something happened, an event of the heart that isn't without precedent in this hazardous profession.

This is why therapy must end: you can't allow yourself to do it any more. Parameters have shifted. Ah, Allis, I've fantasized about taking a leap with you. But how could you be happy, even content, with the incompletely parented, self-flagellating Timothy Jason Dare?

Still, there's the unalterable .fact of love. For I do love you (though not in the ways of which the poets sing), and I desire you, so much that I've quaked at the thought of engaging you in that ultimate pas de deux. And maybe such a dance might last a worthwhile time . . . but I ask myself: Why do so many ballets end unhappily? And could you bear to live with one who tends, on inappropriate occasions, to blurt another's name?

Today, again, you struck home – though "second best" isn't my preferred phrase. I can't say Sally's artistic gift is any greater than yours (though I've given up hoping to understand the creative impulse).

The answer is more mundane. I had happiness with Sally, the greatest happiness I've known. Not perfect joy, but enough to deter me from gambling elsewhere – as long as hope hadn't given up its last gasp. On reflection, I probably even felt that hope, unconsciously, when my competition turned out to be Ellery Cousineau.

Sally phoned on Saturday, as I was in bed on the *Altered Ego*, hoarse and clogged. James had described my condition before putting her through, and her words were tender. She didn't want to be the last person on earth to congratulate me for my recent heroics, and she went on about them with the kind of bubbly melody of words that I haven't heard for many months. *Miriam Finds an Unlikely Hero.*

"When you're better, let's do something," she said. (Wherever she wants. Whatever she wants to do. A two-star movie? A Diana Krall concert? I'll convince her I'm capable of abdicating my dictatorship. I'll pick up my socks. If I can find them.)

No mention was made of Cousineau in that conversation. I think I can fairly assume her interest in taking trips in his Cessna has abated. Meanwhile, pouting on the sidelines was a subject of renewed interest, the bad habit who had deprived her of room to grow. Despite all my will and effort to reconcile with Sally, ironically it was a series of violent events, of danger, and my own haphazard heroics that rekindled her interest.

It's odd how I missed the cues from Grundy and Lyall. The threesome with Jossie finally nudged me in the right direction: a rare instance of not one, but two men blinded by the homosexual dread they shared. Lyall protected himself with a subterranean existence that rarely surfaced. Grundy simply buried everything.

Bit by bit, his patterns came together for me. His desperate brief affairs with women. His boasts about his virility – for example, with the Edmonton hairdresser when, in fact, he failed to rise to the occasion. His unwillingness to make male friends when young

– he was afraid of them, of what he felt, he'd grown up in a culture in which homosexuality was an unthinkable concept, a disgrace, an insult to God. What an indescribably powerful denial it was that propelled him to the ultimate extreme of murder. Stop those damned headaches, those tensions. Make it all go away.

Enough. (How odd it is that the events of last Friday have prompted no nightmares. It is as if I have confronted my demons.)

Victoria was in a contemplative mood when she came to see me – a settlement has been reached in Huff versus Dare and New Millennium Press. She has accepted that the spunky English teacher outduelled the lawyer with the oversized testicles. Clint has agreed to accept compensation for his costs, a concession that will save Victoria's budding career. *Desirée* will come out in hardback next year. But Victoria and New Millennium are also required to make florid apology.

I assume that Brovak, in typical fashion, left his scruples parked outside in his car while he delivered a set of prints to the pseudo-Dodi, and promised silence if Huff would let dead dogs lie. The grovelling apology will give Huff enough boasting rights to save face.

Huff has no doubt concluded that I was the agent of his undoing – the word must be all through the cove that I was recently in his neighbourhood. I expect he'll stop harassing me, however, now that he's aware that I know his fetishistic secret. (I pray that neither he nor the public will ever learn that *When Comes the Darkness* was a recipe for murder.)

On Tuesday, when I was finally up and about, Celestine Post came by with her usual bag of mischief. She's gone beyond the bounds of duty, is continuing to see Ellery Cousineau, in whom she has finally met her erotic match. "I like the games." I didn't ask her to elaborate. "He's an artist in his own way."

This reference to his bedroom skills may not have been intended as a thrust, but it hurt. I may not be a stunt flier, but I don't play

Mr. Dressup. Still, the thought of playing second fiddle to this virtuoso galled, as did my concern that Sally, should we ever reconcile, might compare us, remembering him, perhaps regretting . . .

Sally and I settled on Thursday for our dinner date, and I let her choose the locale, of course, and she picked the Pondicherry, a good sign.

Nataraja greeted us with a puzzled look: his valued customer had been playing the field, gorgeous women falling all over him, and here he is with a flame that was supposed to have burned out. (Nataraja, by the way, has got to know Vivian from her visits to the restaurant and has been a faithful visitor at her home; she's healing rapidly under his soothing nostrums. Word has it that Dr. Lalonde is now seeing a shrink.)

"The mind," Nataraja purred, "clouds the eyes with the dust of desire."

Sally and I tried to work that one through, a game we often played. "Maybe desire does confuse your thinking," she said after other possibilities were eliminated. She fell silent, looked sad, but then smiled. "It's okay, Tim, read my mind. I got tired of it. It was like he was performing."

Nothing more was said on the subject, but I was almost giddy with relief and elation. Though it was not yet her birthday, I presented her with the twenty-five-year-old photo that had been sitting in my desk drawer, now framed: Arm in arm, beside a cake with ten candles, are Sally, in false lips, and Timmy, in a false nose. We began to laugh at shared memories: aged seven, getting lost together, ending up at the police station sucking Popsicles, our parents furious with concern; aged twelve, when I defended her for drawing caricatures of the school principal and got suspended too. Aged twenty-one, at a wedding reception, when we discovered my fly was open.

As much as we talked about the past, neither of us mentioned the future. It didn't seem the time do so. Let matters take their course, I decided. I have another date with her tomorrow: on Creelman Street, where I'll prepare stir-fried shrimp and baby peas, my first venture into Chinese cooking.

Meanwhile, I've been talking to a travel agent. Yes, I am summoning the courage to invite Sally on a tropical holiday. Yes, I'm damn nervous about it. (I've joined a fear-of-flying group, alternate Tuesday nights.)

By the way, Sally mentioned that you shared a bottle of wine on the weekend, and I was a little surprised you didn't mention that. I gather you recommended some useful techniques in dealing with my imperfections.

What else? Oh, I've retained Dotty, set her on the trail of my missing begetter. If she can't find him, he doesn't exist. (Freud once wrote that the death of a father is the most important event in a man's life. But can it be more compelling than never having known him?)

I had only one bizarre dream this week. I was on Mount Olympus, standing in snow up to my hips, and in front of me the gods were gathered in the Parthenon. They were leaderless: no bearded Zeus-like figure, just a laughing, raucous group of Ovidian figures in flowing robes. I was demanding my freedom: hadn't they tortured me enough?

The gods debated my future hotly, shouting. A scuffle broke out involving snowballs. "Let's put this thing to rest," one shouted. "He's not guilty." Several of opposing view flounced off, and the meeting disintegrated amid shouted points of order. They were acting in a very clownish way, and I had a sense I was at a Punch and Judy show, perhaps from the way they moved as if pulled by strings.

Suddenly, I was rising, soaring above them, and I realized it was I who was holding the strings.

I awoke laughing.